Who knew that a summer thunderstorm and a lost little boy would conspire to change single dad Cayce D'Amico's life in an instant? With Luke missing, Cayce ventures into the woods near their house to find his son, only to have lightning strike a tree near him, sending a branch down on his head. When he awakens the next day in the hospital, he discovers he has been blessed or cursed—he isn't sure which—with psychic ability. Along with unfathomable glimpses into the lives of those around him, he's getting visions of a missing teenage girl.

When a second girl disappears soon after the first, Cayce realizes his visions are leading him to their grisly fates. Cayce wants to help, but no one believes him. The police are suspicious. The press wants to exploit him. And the girls' parents have mixed feelings about the young man with the "third eye."

Cayce turns to local reporter Dave Newton and, while searching for clues to the string of disappearances and possible murders, a spark ignites between them. Little do they know that nearby, another couple—dark and murderous—are plotting more crimes and wondering how to silence the man who knows too much about them.

THIRD EYE

Rick R. Reed

A NineStar Press Publication

Published by NineStar Press
P.O. Box 91792,
Albuquerque, New Mexico, 87199 USA.
www.ninestarpress.com

Third Eye

Printed in the USA
NineStar Press Edition
April, 2020

Print ISBN: 978-1-951880-94-1

Also available in eBook, ISBN: 978-1-951880-91-0

Warning: This book contains graphic depictions of rape, violence, and murder.

In memory of my mother,
Theresa Annette Comparetto Reed
1928-2007

Prologue

She was only thirteen. It wasn't fair she now lay, bound, waiting for death. Before, there had been struggling: clawing and fighting, scratching their faces, pulling at their hair, batting at whatever part she could reach. Her breath had come in choking spasms, adrenaline pumping, burning, anteing up the hysteria so much she thought her air would be blocked. Then had come the dread that made her lose most of her fight, when her terror-addled brain had begun to accept her fate was to die here, in this tiny, hot room, with the only witness to her demise the sparkling eyes of her killers and the maddening, crooked whirl of a ceiling fan long past its prime and wobbling, doing nothing more than blowing the overheated, moist air around the room. The dread had risen up, a nausea twisting her gut and making her afraid she would vomit. And then had come the numbness, a dull tingling throughout her body that precluded movement, stripping her of coherent thought.

They stood above her. Faces she had trusted, faces she had seen before, around her neighborhood. The man she and her friends had had a crush on. He used to drive by her little house on Ohio Street in his old red Mustang, looking the picture of youth, confidence, masculinity. His hair was dark, cut bristle-brush short, and his face always clean-shaven. Thin lips bordered rows of perfect white teeth, and when he had smiled at her, only hours ago, she had lit up. A tingling had started in her toes and had worked its way up until the color rose to her cheeks. At her young age, the interest of a man in his twenties was inconceivable, although it had been something she had hoped for since the first day she had seen him, back at the onset of summer, when the sun had turned white-hot, burning up the grass and making illusory waves rise from the hot, cracked sidewalks.

He had pulled to the curb and sat there, car idling. She sat in the front yard, sorting through Barbie clothes: ball gowns and swimming suits, miniskirts and stretch pants. He didn't say anything, not right away. She had looked at him once, then looked away, certain his interest could never be in her. Suddenly she felt ridiculous with her metal trunk, her Barbie dolls, and all the outfits she had once been so proud to collect. Swiftly, she returned the clothes to their case and slammed it shut.

She leaned back, resting on her palms, and lifted her face to the sun. Its heat beat down relentlessly, making the skin on her face feel tight.

She felt his eyes on her still. She opened her own eyes a crack and regarded him peripherally. He really was looking at her! The adorable little smile that caused a dimple to rise in his right cheek deepened in the sun's play of shadow and light. She leaned back more, left hand reaching out to surreptitiously move the Barbie trunk farther away. In this posture, here on the withered and brown grass, she felt that her breasts, little more than two tiny bumps an unkind boy at school had once referred to as her anthills, looked larger. She could be eighteen, couldn't she? With the right makeup and her hair pulled up....

But now her long blonde hair was pulled back in a ponytail, clipped with a pink plastic barrette. She wore a pair of cutoff shorts and an oversized *South Park* T-shirt belonging to her older brother. He would have killed her had he known she was wearing it. But he was away at the Y's summer camp and would never know the difference.

The idling of the car was like an animal purring.

And then the sun disappeared, and she sat in darkness. Beneath her closed lids, she sensed someone standing over her.

Why hadn't she heard the slam of the car door? Her eyelids fluttered, but she did not open them. It would be just like her mother to come outside now and stand above her, hands on hips, and ask her what she thought she was doing.

"Lucy?"

Finally, she opened her eyes and blinked at the brightness of the August day. He was smiling. So unlike the other guys in Fawcettville, he was dressed in pressed black slacks and a collarless white shirt, buttoned to his neck.

"How did you know my name?"

"Oh, I make it my business to know the names of all the pretty young ladies around here."

Lucy felt the heat rise to her face once more. She grinned and could not think of a single word to say.

"Playing Barbie?"

She shoved the case farther away, until it was completely out of her grasp. The case lay in the white heat, glinting, looking, she hoped, as if it had nothing to do with her.

"What? Oh...no, no. These are my little sister's. She always makes such a mess of things, and I was just organizing for her."

"What a good sister."

"Yeah, well…"

The two said nothing for a while, and Lucy began to grow uncomfortable under his gaze. She shifted her long, tanned legs in front of her, crossing them at the ankle.

"I was driving by and saw you sitting there, and I had to tell you"—he hunkered down beside her—"what a lovely sight you are. It made me stop just to have a better look."

She laughed and thought she sounded way too much like the thirteen-year-old she was. "Thank you," she whispered, wondering where her voice had gone.

"No, thank you, for being here, for making the heat of this day a little more pleasant."

Oh, stop! she wanted to cry out but whispered again, "Thank you."

He leaned closer, enough for her to feel his breath near her ear. In spite of the day's heat, his nearness caused gooseflesh to rise on her arms, her spine to tingle.

"Listen." He glanced around the empty street with eyes like none she had ever seen: green, ringed with thick black lashes. And in his gaze was a conspiracy that included only the two of them. "My car has air-conditioning. I know this is out of the blue and all, but I wondered if you'd like to go for a ride with me."

Lucy glanced back at her house. She wished suddenly she lived in a bigger house, in a better neighborhood. Here on this modest residential street close to the river, her small white clapboard house was surrounded by other houses very much like it, some of them covered in rusting aluminum siding. She pictured her mother inside, on a vinyl-covered kitchen chair, watching *All My Children* on a thirteen-inch portable TV on the Formica-topped kitchen table. Her mother, she knew, would never approve of what was transpiring here, right in her front yard.

He stood suddenly. "Okay, okay. I get the message."

"Wait." She sat up straighter. A pickup rumbled by and left in its wake a smell of exhaust and a rush of hot air.

He turned. "What? Need to get your mom's permission?"

"Of course not!" Her voice came out higher than she would have liked, the whiny protest of a child. She stood. "I'd like to come with you. But I can't stay out too long." She was about to say "My mom will be worried" but realized how immature that would sound. "I've got some people I have to meet in a little while."

He smiled. And the smile erased any nervousness she had about going with him. After all, she had seen him around the neighborhood dozens of times. He wasn't exactly a stranger, not really.

"That's fine, Lucy. I'll have you back within an hour. I promise. I certainly wouldn't want to get off on the wrong foot with you." He winked, and she followed him to the waiting car.

Lucy tripped getting into the car. Her head bumped against the chrome surrounding the upper doorframe, and her hand slid across the black vinyl seat. The laugh that followed came out high and flighty, a little bird. Lucy reddened once more, embarrassed by her klutziness.

He was grinning, already behind the steering wheel. "Don't worry about it. We are all prey to tiny lapses in coordination."

He drummed his fingers on the steering wheel while Lucy settled beside him, doing her best to recover her composure. With elaborate care, she positioned herself on the seat and crossed her legs. She admired her legs and hoped he did too: long and tan, smooth, the legs of a woman.

It was then she felt, more than noticed, the presence of someone else in the car. Lucy turned and saw her for the first time. In the back sat a young woman. Her hair, like Lucy's, was blonde, but more of a brassy platinum shade. She wore a pair of dark glasses with cat-eye frames, bright-red lipstick, and a silk scarf tied around her neck. Her simple white shift contrasted sharply with her peach-colored skin. Lucy thought she was about the most glamorous thing she had ever seen in Fawcettville.

He noticed her looking. "This is my girlfriend, Myra. Sweetheart, say hello to Lucy."

"Hello, Lucy."

Did Lucy detect a very slight British accent in the gravelly voice? Whatever it was, this woman seemed so self-possessed and confident, Lucy's dismay that this man had a girlfriend was almost overridden. Lucy was fascinated.

Lucy turned back to the man. "I don't think you told me your name."

He laughed, and Lucy forgot about Myra. His laugh was musical, setting her heart to thumping. She wondered what it would be like to slide closer, to rest her head on his shoulder.

"It's Ian." He slid a pair of Ray-Bans over his green eyes and shifted the car into drive. They sped away from the curb.

Lucy watched as her little white house grew smaller in the side-view mirror.

It wasn't long before they were pulling up in front of a trailer on the outskirts of town. Lucy was disappointed;

the dwelling didn't seem to fit Ian's character at all. She had expected something more romantic: a houseboat moored on the Ohio River, a high-rise apartment in nearby Pittsburgh, a mansion, a log cabin, anything but a trailer.

And it wasn't even a nice one. Set up on cinder blocks, the trailer was a big box wrapped in harvest gold and dingy white aluminum. A piece of the skirting had torn loose at one end, and there was rust around the corners.

Ian shut the car off and draped his arm across the back of Lucy's seat. "It isn't much, love, but it's all I've got. Care to come inside, or should we take you home?"

"Oh, just take her home, Ian. She'll be late for supper," Myra said from the backseat, where she hid behind a cloud of cigarette smoke.

"I'd love to come inside. This is where you live, right?"

Ian laughed. "Yes, for now. Are you sure you have time?"

Lucy glanced down at her watch, embarrassed suddenly by the pink vinyl strap and the Hello Kitty face on the dial. She would have to get a new watch soon, no matter what. Mom would probably be wondering, right about now, where she had gone off to. "I have a little time. Let's go in. I want to see."

Lucy followed the two of them toward the trailer. Ahead of her there was a copse of maple trees on a bluff. The Ohio River, looking brown and stagnant in the milky white light, curved as it made its way south.

Inside, the sudden change from the day's withering brightness to the dark interior blinded Lucy, and she felt her first moment of panic. Neither of them said anything, and she suddenly felt helpless. For the first time that day, she questioned their interest in her and thought herself foolish for not having wondered why a young couple in their twenties would want to bring her home.

But she did look older, didn't she?

Of course she did. Ian confirmed it. "We're going to have a glass of wine, Lucy. Would you care for one?"

A flush of pleasure rushed through her. They did think she was older, a peer. Perhaps they were just trying to make friends. Before the onset of the summer, she couldn't recall having seen either of them before. But what would Mom say if she came home with liquor on her breath? She groped in her pocket, thankful for the piece of Bazooka there.

"Well, maybe I could have just a small one."

"Excellent!" Ian clapped his hands together and went toward the wall behind him, where a portable kitchen waited. He took a jug of white wine from the refrigerator and poured three glasses.

After they were settled in the living room and Lucy's eyes had adjusted to the dim lighting, she said, "This is much nicer than I thought."

The couple exchanged glances, laughing, and Lucy wondered why. The place was run-down. The carpeting, a beige-and-brown tweed, was threadbare, and the furniture was a hodgepodge of mismatched pieces, all of it looking secondhand. The scarred coffee table contained an odd assortment of items: a book called *Crime and Punishment*, a ceramic skull, and two black votive candles set on tin jar lids.

But the dimness and stale air bothered her more than anything else. Why were all the curtains drawn? "It's kind of dark in here, isn't it?"

That remark they found amusing as well; their laughter began to make her uncomfortable. She scratched her arm.

Ian said, "Lucy, haven't you noticed? It's hot outside. It keeps things a little cooler if I keep the drapes drawn."

Of course.

After they had finished their wine—well, after Ian and Myra had finished theirs; Lucy thought it tasted horrible—Ian disappeared for a moment. When he came back, he was carrying a video camera. It was one of those tiny ones you could almost palm in your hand, and the red light on it was blinking.

What was going on?

"Smile for the camera, Lucy."

Lucy tried to smile, but things were getting too strange. She managed to turn up the corners of her lips in a grin. Suddenly, Myra was on the couch next to her, too close, really. Lucy smelled her perfume. It was too sweet, with a bitter undertone. It smelled like she had rubbed incense on herself. The scent of the perfume combined with cigarettes and wine caused Lucy to lean back, away from Myra. Suddenly, the woman didn't seem as glamorous as she had in the car.

She put her arm around Lucy and mugged for the camera. "Come on, Lucy, smile!"

Lucy bit her lip, thinking of the Barbie trunk she had left on her front lawn. Kelsey Timmons, just down the street, wouldn't be above taking the whole trunk home, especially with the golden opportunity Lucy was giving her. Kelsey had coveted Lucy's Barbie collection since she had moved in down the street four years ago. "I think I'd like to go home now." Lucy tried to look anywhere but into the lens of the camera. She wished he would turn it off.

"Nonsense!" Ian exclaimed.

"You just got here, dear," Myra whispered to her. Her lips were too red, and Lucy suddenly felt sick.

"Please, I need to go home now."

"Just a few more minutes." Ian hunkered down in front of the two of them, moving the camera slowly up and down their bodies.

Lucy lifted the wine to her lips, just to have something to quell her mouth's terrible dryness. She began to perspire, dampening at her armpits, her hairline. She whimpered, "You said no more than an hour."

"Such a pretty girl," Myra whispered, lifting Lucy's ponytail and turning it in her hand. "Oh, to have such tresses. What I wouldn't give to have hair this color." She giggled. "Naturally, I mean."

"Jealous?" Ian stood and aimed the camera down at the two of them.

Lucy shot up, heat and fear coalescing to make her sick. The walls of the trailer closed in. "I don't feel so good. Can we go now?"

Ian set the camera down for a moment and gave her his most winning smile. "The answer to that question, my sweet, is no."

Part One

Chapter One

Cayce D'Amico felt the hairs on the back of his neck stand up. The gathering clouds were angry, bruised, hulking blue-gray shapes pressing down on the hills.

"Oh, there's one hell of a storm coming. That's for sure." He watched the darkening sky through the kitchen window, pausing from his work of chopping burdock stalks into sticks for the Sicilian fritters called cardoons. The wind kicked up, audible, becoming icy, the leaves turning to display their pale undersides. The last few days had been the opposite: punishing temperatures in the upper nineties and humidity so thick you could drown in it. Miserable. Cayce had lain in front of a fan in his boxers at night as it whirred and blew the hot air around, offering no relief.

It was like lying inside a convection oven.

He beat eggs, added some grated Romano and salt and pepper, and set the batter next to the burdock stalks. He wiped his hands on a dishtowel.

Worse, though, than the brewing storm outside was the fact he couldn't see his son, Luke. Luke, at seven, was prone to wandering away. Usually such distraction wasn't of much concern, because Fawcettville wasn't like Pittsburgh, about an hour east, with its crime and traffic. Fawcettville perched on the banks of the Ohio River, overlooking the hills of the northern panhandle of West Virginia. It was mostly known as a town where nothing ever happened. Sometimes the inactivity seemed like a drawback, dull. Other times it was a blessing—especially for a single dad bringing up a little boy. Then you appreciated blessings like living in a dull backwater town, where the worst crime you could remember was some kids breaking into Bricker's drug store last summer.

Peace of mind.

So why did Cayce suddenly feel something wasn't quite right? Why did the fact that Luke was no longer in the backyard make him queasy?

Cayce and Luke didn't live in some sort of exclusive area. Their little house was surrounded by others much the same: older houses covered in peeling paint, rusting aluminum siding, or asphalt tile that was supposed to look like brick but never did. Cayce had grown up in this little hollow down by the Ohio River and knew most of his neighbors. Just as they had watched Cayce playing from their porch swings and gliders, many of the same people watched Luke, even though their hair had turned gray and their children had grown up and moved away, especially when the steel mill in a neighboring town had closed down, taking any hope of prosperity with it.

"Maybe it's just the wind making me so cold." Cayce rubbed at the dark hair on his forearms, making the coarse black fur stand on end. He was sure the temperature had dropped at least fifteen degrees in the past half hour. This drop, coupled with the slate-blue clouds perched on the southern horizon, did much to raise the gooseflesh on his forearms. The chill might have been welcome if Luke was at the kitchen table, playing with his Hot Wheels.

But he was not. And Cayce, on the younger side of thirty, knew that at least a portion of the goose bumps on his beefy arms was from a distinct yet inexplicable dread and not the cold breeze, the dark clouds, and the imminent storm making its way into Fawcettville.

The Swiss chard laid out to be cleaned could wait, as could the tomatoes from his garden, still unsliced. Cayce did not like Luke being out where he couldn't see him as weather bore down. He didn't like it at all.

He slid into a pair of flip-flops he kept by the kitchen door. "Oreo!" he called, and a black-and-white mutt about the size of a boxer, with bright brown eyes, bounded into the kitchen, toenails clicking on the linoleum. "Wanna go outside, boy? Wanna help me find Luke?" Oreo had been left behind two years ago by Marc, Cayce's "friend and roommate," as his mother put it. Marc couldn't stand the stifling life of a gay man in a small town and had set out for the bright lights and tall buildings—and easy men—of Pittsburgh. Who knew? Perhaps Marc had been swayed by all the *Queer as Folk* reruns he used to watch. Once he'd packed up his Nissan pickup, Cayce never saw the guy again and had never found love again.

But who the hell had time for that crap!

Cayce didn't know why he ever bothered to think of the man, who had never been much help as a parent to Luke...or even as a dog owner, for that matter. Marc had been all about Marc. "C'mon, Oreo!"

Outside, the wind was kicking up. Papers and small pieces of gravel skittered across the road in front of the house. Cars passing by had turned on their headlights, piercing the odd, darkening afternoon light. The maple trees lining the road bent in the wind, like fingers splayed backward. The sky had a funny greenish tinge, and Cayce had seen that weird green color enough times to know what the storm portended.

Cayce made his way down First Avenue, searching from side to side and pausing occasionally to rub a piece of grit out of his eye. "Luke!" He yelled, "Luke!" even louder when there was no response. Where was that boy?

A drop of water landed on his arm, icy. The rows of houses lining the yellow-bricked street had deserted porches—everyone escaped indoors. The lights switched on inside the houses made them look like sanctuaries, and Cayce wished he could be in his own sanctuary with his own son, smells of the Sicilian peasant food he had grown up on filling their little house. Cayce supposed his neighbors had all retreated into their living rooms, where they could turn on the Weather Channel or listen to the radio to validate what was happening before their eyes.

Everyone, that was, except for Lula Stewart, bless her. Lula, who had lost her husband the winter before, still sat on her glider, wispy dyed-black hair being lifted by the wind.

"He went thataway," Lula called, pointing to where First Avenue dead-ended at the woods.

"Great," Cayce whispered to himself, then said to Lula, "Thanks. I'm going to wring his little neck for him."

"Be nice, Cayce. He's only seven."

"I know, I know." Cayce headed for the darkness of the trees at the end of the street. As he picked up his pace, so did the wind and the droplets of water, coming heavier every second.

The sky flashed with white light. Cayce gasped as a crack of thunder ripped through the air, reverberating through the ground and leaving in its wake the smell of ozone. "God, that was close." Why didn't Luke have the sense to come in out of the rain?

The sky ripped open and released the downpour, a sibilant hiss, so heavy it nearly blinded Cayce. In seconds his T-shirt and board shorts were drenched, clinging to him like a second skin. Water sluiced from his curly black hair into his eyes. The sky morphed into premature night, brightened only by the lightning. The thunder's crash upped Cayce's sense of anxiety and fear with each crack. The volume and the bright lightning seemed to have a direct line to his heart, which hammered double time in his chest.

"Luke!" he screamed above the wind that yanked twigs and whole clumps of leaves from the trees above him. An orange drink carton hit Cayce in the back of the head.

"Luke!" He watched in despair as Oreo ran back toward the house, tail between his legs. "Traitor," he called after the dog.

The woods were even darker than the street. Cayce held his hands out in front of him to avoid crashing into trees. Already, his flip-flops were making a sucking sound as he pulled his feet out of the mud.

Annoyed, Cayce wiped the icy rain away from his face, flinging his damp mop of black hair back, trying to see in the storm's murk. In the brief bluish flash of lightning, the woods looked empty, deserted. Why couldn't he see Luke cowering under a tree, or better yet, running toward him, hell, even running *away* from him? Anything but this dreadful emptiness, abandoning him to the woods and the storm.

"Luke!" he yelled again, his throat growing hoarse. He tried to keep his voice even so Luke wouldn't think he was mad, so the little boy wouldn't hear his dad's fear. "Luke, if you can hear me, yell. I'm not mad."

And he wasn't, not at his little boy anyway, whom he pictured trembling under a tree or huddled under a neighbor's porch, shivering, terrified, wet, and cold. But Cayce *was* angry at himself, for not keeping better tabs on the weather and the whereabouts of a seven-year-old.

What was wrong with him? Maybe his mom was right; maybe Cayce was too young (and alone) to take on the responsibility of rearing another human being. She was always telling Cayce to give the boy back to his mother. "Little boys need their moms," his own mom often proclaimed.

Apparently, though, moms didn't always need their little boys. Case in point, Joyce, Cayce's wife of less than a year, who was only too happy to leave the "burden" of Luke with Cayce when she abandoned them both four years ago, heading off without a backward glance for the presumably greener pastures of Portland, Oregon. Like Marc, Joyce apparently believed happiness awaited *outside* the city limits of Fawcettville, Pennsylvania.

"Luke!" he called once more, competing for dominance with the wind, the thunder, the driving rain.

But all that answered him was the roar of the storm and the sound of detritus whistling through the air and smacking against the trees. Cayce was beginning to think his quest was in vain, that Luke was probably already at home, sitting at the kitchen table and wondering where his dad was, hungry for his supper.

It happened so quickly Cayce only experienced the event through instincts, like an animal.

The flash was so bright, Cayce gasped, squeezing his eyes shut.

The scent of ozone filled the air. Hair stood up on the back of his neck, tickling.

The rumble of the thunder deafened, so loud and close it drowned out his scream. And the sharp break of the tree branch above his head was akin to the crack of a whip.

The limb crashing down on his head dropped him to his knees. Everything went dark.

Chapter Two

"Nana? Is Dad over there?"

Sarah D'Amico closed her eyes and clutched the crucifix on her neck. She made a "tsk" sound she hoped Luke hadn't heard. Would her son never change? Never accept responsibility? Here was Cayce's seven-year-old calling to see where his father was. In the middle of an awful thunderstorm!

"No, Luke, your dad isn't here." Sarah never knew what to say to the boy. He wasn't like other kids. He spoke way too clearly, even when he was two or three years old, and his vocabulary seemed too mature for his age. "When was the last time you saw him?"

"He was making supper, and I was in the yard. I went down the street to see if Theresa could come out and play and maybe her mom would let her eat with us." Luke took a breath. "Theresa wasn't home, and when I got back here, the storm had started and Dad was gone."

Sarah twisted the phone cord around her finger, wondering what she should do. Her husband, Sam, in the living room watching *Jeopardy!,* would suggest they go over to Cayce's immediately, if only for the sake of the little boy. But Sam didn't know Cayce like she did; he'd always been too soft on their son. Imagine, up and leaving a seven-year-old boy to fend for himself with no word of where he'd gone. Sarah peered through her black horn-rims out the kitchen window. It looked like night out there, and it sounded like they lived closer to a railroad than they actually did.

"Nana? What should I do?"

Sarah sighed. She guessed she would have to abandon her own dinner of pasta fagioli and walk over to Cayce's. In the process, she would get drenched, and supper would be late. It would serve Cayce right not to— what was the word they were using these days?—not to *enable* him.

Sarah looked to the Dutch oven on the stove, where the beans and red sauce were bubbling, steam rising up from them, and decided she would *not* be used like this. Sam could walk over. Let him get wet. She had dinner to make.

"Nana?"

"Yes, Luke. I'm going to send Pap-Pap over. He'll be there in just a few minutes."

Sarah hung up the phone without saying goodbye or even checking to see if the boy had heard her, then felt guilty. Luke was, after all, only seven and probably scared out of his mind.

*

Sam D'Amico loved *Jeopardy!* He had watched the game show for years, since back when it wasn't electronic and its host was Art Fleming. He liked playing along, especially when the category was geography of some sort, and imagined that someday he would get out to California, where he could be a contestant himself.

Alex Trebek had just announced the category for final *Jeopardy!,* and Sam leaned forward. He would bet a lot on "European Rivers," if he had been playing.

"Sam?"

Sam sighed and ran his fingers through his thick, close-cropped gray hair. He could sense his wife standing in the archway between the dining room and living room, her sizable shadow falling over his shoulder. "What is it, *bella*?"

"Cayce's not home."

"And?"

"Well, it's just that Luke called, and he doesn't know where he is."

"What?" Sam turned in the recliner to regard his wife. "Luke doesn't know where he is? In this downpour? Where could he be?"

Sarah rolled her eyes. "That's what we all want to know, Sam."

Sam stood, abandoning "European Rivers." "I guess I better get over there and see what the hell's going on." He glanced out the picture window. It looked like the wind, thunder, and lightning had died down, and the rain had settled into a steady downpour. It would be good for the lawn.

He glanced at his wife as he headed for the closet and his slicker. She had twisted her mouth into a straight line, indicating her disapproval.

"Cut it out," he said. "Luke probably wandered off, and he's out there trying to find him. Give our son some credit, woman."

Sarah returned to the kitchen, calling over her shoulder, "If Cayce still isn't home, bring Luke over here. He can eat with us."

As he headed toward the back door, Sam thought he'd never given much credit to inexplicable "feelings." Things like premonitions were best reserved for TV shows and movies, not for real life. But he couldn't escape the fact that he felt cold, in spite of the fact that Sarah's yellow kitchen was warm. The oven was on for the biscuits she was baking, and on the stove, the beans, tomatoes, macaroni, and ham were bubbling in the Dutch oven.

So why did he feel cold? Why was there this cloying nausea in his stomach, as if he'd gotten hold of something rotten?

The screen door slammed shut behind him. Even though his son and grandson lived only a block over, Sam ran the short distance to their little house, panting. He couldn't explain it and wouldn't have wanted to try if someone had asked, but he felt in his gut there was something terribly wrong.

His fears were confirmed as he entered the back door of Cayce's rented house. Luke sat quietly at the table, his small face creased with worry. The boy wasn't doing anything, just sitting there, hands folded in front of him and tears welling up in his eyes.

"I don't know where Dad is," Luke whispered, trying with all of his seven-year-old will to put a little breath and bravery behind his words.

Sam saw the plate of burdock on the counter and the bowl of Swiss chard next to it. It was odd that Cayce would just leave in the middle of making supper. He knew Sarah would have accused Cayce of being irresponsible, of going off on a whim, but Sam had seen his son mature a lot over the years as he grew into a responsible father.

"It's my fault," Luke whispered, staring down at the table.

Sam squatted down next to him. "Now, what do you wanna go and say a thing like that for?"

"Because I wandered off without telling him where I was going. He was probably out looking for me." Luke sniffed and searched his grandpa's eyes for disapproval. "He prob'ly got lost in the storm." His eyes grew wide. "Or maybe struck by lightning."

Sam, smiling, pushed Luke's blond hair away from his forehead and let it fall back into place. "Don't be goofy. Your dad's lived around here all his life. I doubt he's lost. But you might be right about him being out looking for you." Sam tried to frown at the boy to show his disapproval but didn't have the heart, especially when Luke looked so upset. "Most likely he's on one of the neighbor's porches, gabbin'...and waiting for the rain to die down."

Why did Sam feel like he was lying? Why did he feel this urgency tugging at him to get out there and look for Cayce? Why did it seem so imperative, as if too much time had already been wasted?

"What do you say we go out and look?"

Luke hopped down from the kitchen chair, and Sam could see he was relieved to have something proactive to do. He started toward the door.

"Whoa there, son. Don't you have a poncho or something? Don't want you to catch your death."

Luke left the room and came back with a yellow slicker pulled over his shorts and T-shirt. Sam took his hand, and the two set off into the rain.

Luke was the first to see him. He let out a yelp, a sound almost identical to the sound a dog makes when someone steps on its foot.

And then he was running.

Sam saw his son lying at the entrance to the wood, and his heart lurched. For a moment, it felt like someone had knocked the wind out of him, and he couldn't move, couldn't speak, couldn't stop the boy from barreling toward his father, who lay, still as death, on a bed of mud mixed with pine needles. His skin was waxy, ashen. His big, strong body looked fallen. A large tree branch lay near his head.

The worst thing about this picture wasn't Cayce's stillness or the pallor of his skin but the huge, bloody gash in his forehead. It was like a dent, raw meat showing through. Sam was certain his son's face would have been hidden by a mask of blood had it not been for the downpour sluicing its magenta alarm away. Cayce looked almost as if he were sleeping.

Sam hurried after Luke and grabbed his shoulder just as they reached Cayce. He tried to turn the boy away, not wanting this gruesome vision to be stamped into his brain.

Oh God, Sam wondered, his mouth gone dry, heart thudding, *what if Cayce is dead*?

Luke whimpered as Sam held him back, fingers clutching the boy's frail shoulder. Sam wasn't sure how to proceed. He couldn't lose his son, not on a summer day. Not when he had just been watching *Jeopardy!* and thinking about the pasta fagioli his wife was in the kitchen making. Cayce's palms were turned up and blackened with mud, as if he had tried to catch himself when he fell and his hands had slid through the moist earth. At first Sam wondered if his palms were burned, if he had been struck by lightning and the electric circuit had escaped through his hands. He was relieved when, stooping, the blackness came off easily at his touch.

He was also relieved to feel the pulse of his son's blood through his wrist. Thank God he wasn't dead. At least not yet...

And then he noticed the tremor coursing through his son's body every few seconds. Cayce needed help. Traumas to the head required quick and certain medical attention.

None of this seemed real.

He tightened his grip on Luke, who was straining against him like a dog on a leash when it spies a squirrel. He couldn't let the boy go.

Could Cayce survive until they got help? Would he suffer permanent harm? Brain damage?

He looked so pale.

Sam felt helpless, watching the tiny rivulets of water break and course across his face. He felt a knot in his throat and wanted to do nothing more than sink to his knees and cry out. He loved his son fiercely, and if he was gone, he didn't know how he would stand it.

Something had to be done.

He squatted down next to Luke. "Listen, boy. Your dad's been hurt. It might be serious... We need to get some help right away." Why was it so hard for him to breathe? "You need to be a big fella for me. Can you do that?"

Luke stared at him, wide-eyed, and nodded.

"I need you to run over to the Wyatts and ask them to call 911 and get an ambulance down here right away."

Luke stared at him. "Is Daddy dead?"

Luke sounded so plaintive, so young, that Sam was afraid he himself would burst into tears, but he knew he couldn't do that. Maybe later, but not now. Not when he had to be the strong one. Not when time was in such short supply. He smacked Luke on the butt. "Of course not, Luke. He's just hurt. Now scoot. We need to get some help."

Luke dashed off without a word, heading toward the Wyatts' green-shingled house. Sam bit his lower lip, gnawing at it until he got the surprise of a squirt of his own blood in his mouth. It tasted metallic, and Sam pushed at the tiny cut on his lower lip with his tongue. "Get hold of yourself, old man."

The ambulance would come soon, and with its flashing red lights and sirens, the neighbors would come out too.

And Sarah.

Sam could picture her running down First Avenue, wiping her hands on her apron, her face creased with worry, knowing that the commotion was for Cayce, knowing, as a mother would, that something very bad had happened to her child.

Sam sucked in a great, quivering breath and thought he could already hear a siren in the distance. Perhaps he did. The hospital was only five minutes away.

And here came Luke, running on little toothpick legs, blond hair blowing back in the wind.

And the Wyatts, an older couple he and Sarah had known since they had moved to the little neighborhood down here by the Ohio River back in '63... They were trying to keep up with Luke.

And behind them, Sarah, running, stumbling. Even in the rain, Sam could see she was crying, tears born of a terrible yet still inexplicable knowledge that something was very wrong.

Sam turned back to his son's twitching form and knelt on the ground beside him, tenderly touching his neck, where a weak pulse beat. "Thank you," he whispered, "thank you."

Chapter Three

Cayce's awakening came by degrees. First the sense of an unfamiliar bed, linens starchy and stiff against his bare back. When his eyelids began to flutter, there were glimpses: metal rails, a tray topped with a box of Kleenex, a vase of daisies, dials and lights, and a long metal pole with a fluid-filled plastic bag hanging from it. The tube ran into a big vein on the back of his hand, and for just a moment he had to resist an urge to yank the tube out.

Then he was back asleep, moving from semi-consciousness to sleep with swiftness, with almost no change at all.

Walking down a dark corridor, narrow, colorless walls pressing in. If he raises his arms, he can touch both sides of the corridor as he moves along, toward a pulsating bluish light and the cry of a child.

The cry is familiar. It's Luke. Comprehension comes full force. Luke is not lost but needs Cayce, needs his father. He moves faster, faster, but it's weird. The boy's crying does not get louder, nor does he seem to get any closer to the light he supposes signals the end of the corridor. It's as if, when he moves forward, the hall stretches. It's as though he's not moving at all. Futile.

"Luke! Luke, honey, can you hear me?"

"Daddy. Come and get me."

A shriek.

And suddenly he was awake again, the sheet beneath him drenched with sweat. His hair stuck to his head, and little beads of perspiration ran from his hairline to tickle the back of his neck.

There was pain, dull, constant, and thudding behind his eyes. Tentatively, he reached up, feeling a mass of gauze at his forehead. Even the slightest pressure on the bandage made Cayce wince, sending bright tendrils of pain spiraling inward.

A nurse came in, stared down. When their eyes met, she smiled. "Can you hear me?"

Cayce moved his tongue around in his mouth but couldn't get it to wrap around any words. He nodded, staring plaintively up at the nurse's moon face, ringed with dark-blonde hair. He recognized her as a girl he'd known in junior high school. Debbie something.

The nurse touched his shoulder. "You don't need to say anything right now. I'm going to go get the doctor."

And Cayce slept once more.

A rainswept landscape, thunder and lightning. So cold. His clothes cling, hair plastered to his head, dripping down his neck.

Ahead of him, a hill, and at its top, Luke.

He tries to run to him, but every step he takes seems to make the hill recede farther into the distance.

And then he was awake once more. A different nurse, or perhaps an aide, looked down. This one was an older woman whose skin had seen far too much sun. Even now it had a rich bronze hue and was the texture of distressed leather. Her hair was frosted, bubble cut. Her brown eyes seemed larger under the thick lenses she wore.

"Honey? Can you hear me?"

"Yeah." It hurt his chest to speak. "Where's Luke?"

"Who, honey?"

The woman's voice was raspy, telling a history of too many cigarettes. Cayce suddenly had a vision of the woman at home, lying out in a floral print bikini too young for her in the tiny backyard of a white aluminum-sided house. There was a little redwood table next to her yellow vinyl lounge, and on top of it was a bottle of Budweiser, beaded with condensation, a black portable radio playing Shania Twain, and a ceramic ashtray, overflowing with Newport butts.

"Luke, my son."

The woman bit into her lip and then smiled. "I'm not sure *right now*, hon, but he's okay. I've seen him in here with his grandma." Her voice was gravelly, deep as a man's.

Cayce glanced out the window. The day was cloudy. He must have been on a high floor, because all he could see was a milky white sky and the tree-covered hills of West Virginia. "Why am I in the hospital?"

The aide busied herself for a moment, checking Cayce's IV. She glanced out the window, then looked back to Cayce. "You took a pretty nasty blow to the head. Looks like a tree branch caught you right in the forehead. Concussion, I guess. Nasty. You've been out for quite a while, honey."

"What are you talking about?" Cayce felt panicky, his heart starting to race. The woman's words were so simple. Concussion? How was he having glimpses into this woman's personal life and yet had no recollection of his own? "You're kidding me, right?"

"No, sweetheart. It happened. Yesterday afternoon. You made the paper." The aide, whose badge said her name was Wilda Carr, smiled at Cayce when she told him this, as if Cayce had accomplished some sort of feat. She fussed with Cayce's blanket, pulling it up tighter around his chin.

Yesterday afternoon? Where had the intervening time gone? Cayce felt too tired to wonder. Suddenly, all he wanted to do was sleep. His eyelids felt heavy, burning, and it seemed like it would take all his effort to just lift his hand to stifle a yawn.

But what awaited him on the other side of consciousness?

And where was Luke?

Cayce forced himself up on his elbows. "Wilda, I really need to know about my little boy. Can I call my mom?"

Wilda wasn't sure what to say, and Cayce knew it. Wilda wanted to get home, because tonight she was planning on meeting up with a guy named Lorenzo, who was all of twenty-six and supposed to be dating her daughter.

How? Why am I thinking these things?

Wilda smiled—falsely, Cayce was sure. "Let me see if I can find the doctor, hon. Then we can see about makin' that phone call."

And even though Cayce was certain Wilda had not spoken out loud, he heard the woman's raspy voice as she left the room. "Damn that guy. Why couldn't he have waited until my shift ended?"

*

"You were lucky you weren't killed." The doctor brushed away a strand of hair from Cayce's forehead and fussed with his blanket, tucking it in at the sides. "That oak branch was heavy. We were worried there'd be serious damage. When they brought you in, the ER folks weren't sure you were going to make it." The doctor, a man who couldn't have been much older than Cayce himself, smiled down. "But here you are. Twenty-four hours and some change later and you seem in pretty good shape. Blood pressure's low, your heart rate is good, and other than a nasty gash on your forehead, you don't look too shabby. We'll want to run a few tests—EEG, brain scan—just to make sure everything's functioning okay up here." The doctor tapped his forehead. "But I'm not foreseeing any problems. I mean, you're looking more bright-eyed every minute." He grinned. "I guess you should count your blessings it was the tree the lightning struck and not you."

The doctor's words, which should have been reassuring, weren't. They caused a kind of queasy panic to rise up in Cayce. He couldn't recall much of the previous day at all. Certainly not being outside when a tree branch, freed by lightning from its connection to a trunk, had fallen on his *head. How in the hell...* Even when he used to drink—more than his share, at times—he had never experienced a blank space as some of his friends did, unable to remember how they got home or how they wound up in bed with a strange guy.

But that's what he had. A blank space. The last thing Cayce could remember was making supper in the kitchen.

And looking for Luke...

"My son. Do you know...?"

"Luke is fine. Your mom and dad brought him in last night. Smart little boy."

Cayce closed his eyes with relief. There was something nagging him about Luke. Something awry. But it seemed like everything was okay with him. He shook his head. "You know, I can't remember any of this. I mean, wouldn't you think that when a person gets hurt like I did, they'd remember? I mean, how exciting." Cayce laughed. "And we get so little excitement here in Fawcettville."

The doctor shook his head, unsure how to take Cayce, and then allowed himself a laugh. "Yeah, I think you're going to recover just fine." The doctor put his hand to Cayce's shoulder and gave it a squeeze.

He lives alone. He's gay too. He's only been in Fawcettville since the spring, and he knows hardly anyone. There was someone. Roger? Peter? Things hadn't worked out. Poor thing. He's about to find out fast this town's no place for a young gay man, even if he is on the run from a broken heart. There are so few of us here. At least for now, he occupies most of his time watching CNN and sports on TV...when he's not at the hospital. Cayce glanced up at the doctor's dark-complexioned face.

He met Cayce's gaze, smiling. "I'm Carlos Soto, by the way." He took one of Cayce's hands in his own and squeezed. "I've been looking after you since they brought you into emergency yesterday."

Gingerly, Cayce felt the gauze mounded on his forehead, the adhesive tape. Underneath the throbbing pain there was a tightness. Stitches? "How long will I have this?"

"A couple more days. I'll write you a prescription for pain. The stitches can come out in about a week. I'm sorry to say you're going to have a nasty scar. You might want to think about getting some plastic surgery down the road."

"Or getting some bangs."

Carlos Soto chuckled. "That would be the economical alternative."

"And that's the kind of alternative I'm always in the market for."

"What kind of work do you do?"

"I wait tables at this shithole's most fabulous diner."

Carlos nodded. "Then you'll need to be getting back on your feet pronto."

Cayce stretched. "Yeah. I can hardly wait." He chuckled, feeling a little more energy.

Cayce looked up into the face of the doctor and felt something akin to warmth. There was a kind of strength to his dark features that Cayce liked and, for no good reason except what he would call intuition, immediately trusted. Carlos's dark hair was cut short, shaved on the sides and sticking up on top. It gave him a childish look that made Cayce wonder if it took away some of his authority with older patients. His face was round, and he had eyes so dark Cayce could hardly distinguish the pupils from the irises. "You're not from here, are you?"

"What gave me away?"

Cayce thought of saying he just knew but realized how stupid that would sound. He didn't even understand it himself. "We don't get many Hispanic people in Fawcettville. Pretty much German or English, bland salt-of-the-earth types."

"And I'm a Mexican spitfire."

Cayce blushed. "Well, no, I didn't mean..."

"It's okay. I'm kidding. My family's originally from Cuba, but I grew up in Miami. Coral Gables, actually." Carlos glanced down at his watch. "Listen, I have rounds to make, but I'll check in on you in the morning. Okay? We should probably be able to release you then. Anything I can get you?"

"I'd love to see Luke."

"I'm sure he'll be in soon." Carlos tapped his watch. "Visiting hours'll start in about an hour. Anything else?"

"How 'bout a paper? I hear I'm a celebrity."

"Oh, I think I can have one of the aides bring you a *Review*. I'm pretty sure you're on the front page: 'Local Man Survives Head Trauma in Storm.' I guess that's big news for Fawcettville."

Cayce shrugged. "It's big news to me, anyway."

Cayce watched as the doctor left his room. He felt a funny mixture of anticipation and consternation. He wished he hadn't asked for the newspaper. He couldn't quite understand why, but there was an element of dread in its imminent arrival.

And that was bad. "Stop it, now," he whispered. Maybe he just realized it wouldn't be the world's most pleasant experience, reading about how he had been taken down in the first round by the branch of an oak tree.

But that wasn't it. Cayce turned to look out the window at the milky sky and waited for the newspaper, knowing it was about to bring him something a lot more jarring than news of his own accident.

But he had no idea where the knowledge came from and why it was causing his stomach to churn.

*

The Fawcettville newspaper was nothing much. It never had been—reporting on the lives of some 15,000 citizens filled usually no more than twenty or thirty pages. The national news occupied the front page and maybe continued on to the second. The remainder was taken up by advertising, editorials about such things as high school activities and earth-shattering decisions like whether local merchants should continue to stay open late on Thursday nights, and reporting who had gotten married, divorced, arrested, been involved in automobile accidents, or admitted to the emergency room of Fawcettville City Hospital. There was a comics page and a crossword puzzle, sometimes a syndicated movie review. If someone wanted something meatier, they purchased the Pittsburgh paper.

Cayce was surprised when his copy of the paper was delivered, not by the nurse who had been by earlier, but by a man. From the looks of him, he seemed to have no connection to a profession in healthcare. He was a handsome, grizzled, and prematurely gray man who reminded Cayce immediately of the actor Sam Elliot. When he spoke, Cayce was even more surprised to hear that his gravelly voice was couched in a British accent.

"Hello!"

"Hello," Cayce responded uncertainly. He noticed how the guy was dressed kind of strange, especially for Fawcettville, where most of the men went in for jeans, shorts, T-shirts, and flip-flops or tennis shoes. This guy wore a gauzy white shirt, loose fitting, and what looked to Cayce to be a pair of earth-colored drawstring linen pants. His junk moved around freely. Cayce didn't need some internal vision to know the guy was going commando.

The man handed him the newspaper, folded neatly.

"Thanks." Cayce laid the paper on the bed and regarded the man, waiting. As if prompted, the guy smiled and extended his hand. "I'm sorry. You're probably wondering who the hell I am."

When they shook, it was like an electric jolt went through Cayce. There were no images in his brain, but he was immediately flooded with heat, exciting and comforting at the same time. Their eyes met, and Cayce felt riveted to the man's deep-brown orbs, as if he were being drawn in.

At last the man yanked his hand away. Cayce realized he had been clinging almost desperately to it.

There was confusion on the guy's face—the wrinkled brow, the heavy lips pulled into a frown.

"I'm Dave Newton."

"Okay. Cayce D'Amico. Is the name supposed to mean something to me?" Cayce thought that sounded rude. "I'm sorry. I just wonder if I should recognize you." He gingerly touched the bandage at his forehead. "The brain has gotten a little scrambled. We're hoping it's not permanent."

Dave laughed. "I should be the one who apologizes, barging in here." He tapped the newspaper. "I wrote a story about you in yesterday's paper. One of the nurses told me which room you were in, said I should come in and say hello."

"So, what? You want to interview me about it? Because I don't remember—"

Dave raised his hand. "No. Nothing like that. Believe me, even in Fawcettville, you don't warrant a follow-up, I'm sorry to say. I just wanted to stop by and offer my best wishes for your recovery." A blush rose to his salt-and-pepper grizzled cheeks. "I don't normally do things like this. I try to be a curmudgeon, actually. I just had an impulse." He took in a hurried breath and moved a couple of steps back, away from the bed and toward the door. "I should be going. I do hope you're well. Or well on the road to recovery."

Cayce regarded him, and still tendrils of warmth moved through him, just from the nearness of Dave. He was good-looking, sure, but there was something more about this man. Call it a sense, an inkling, but Cayce felt an inexplicable connection and a certainty that he would see him again.

Soon.

But not now. Dave Newton was already gone.

Yet Cayce was more than a little intrigued by the newspaper lying at his side. He could count on one hand the number of times he had been celebrated enough to make its pages: his birth; when he had been on the homecoming court in high school—a *Carrie*-like fluke... Cayce had already been deep into his first crush on another boy, a cross-country runner named Kevin, panic about which had forced him to ask Patti Bangham to the dance; when his then-wife Joyce had given birth to Luke; and when he had sprained his ankle and been admitted to the emergency room.

And here he was on the front page. There was no picture, but the headline was identification enough. Cayce had assumed that when people got hit so hard in the head it knocked them unconscious for hours, they eventually died. But obviously that wasn't true, because here he was, feeling better, actually, with every passing moment. The article gave credit to quick action by the Fawcettville Fire Department in saving the "local man's" life. "We were on the scene immediately," paramedic John Fore was quoted as saying, "and were able to administer treatment right then and there." Cayce smiled; thank God for that. He went on to read how he had been rushed to the hospital and was now in stable condition.

Cayce was just about to put the paper aside when another article—and a familiar name in the byline— caught his eye. "Teenager Reported Missing," by Dave Newton. It wasn't so much the headline that got his attention but the picture of the young girl beneath it. Pretty. Long blonde hair. And disturbingly familiar.

Even though Fawcettville was a small town, the girl's name, Lucy Plant, didn't ring any bells. Perhaps Cayce had waited on her at the Elite, the diner where he worked. But still, no specific recollection came back. Cayce couldn't visualize the girl sitting at the counter, nor at one of the booths.

And yet she looked so familiar, as if she were someone Cayce was friends with, or even a relative.

Cayce scanned the story. The girl had been reported missing by her mother yesterday afternoon, just before the storm that had caused such a turn in Cayce's own life.

There were no clues. The girl, at least according to her mother, could not possibly have been a runaway. "Lucy's a good girl," Amy Plant had told Fawcettville police detective JT Simmons. "She wouldn't even go down the block to visit a friend without telling us first."

The last time anyone had seen Lucy Plant was when her mother looked outside the living room window. Lucy had been playing with her Barbie dolls on the front lawn.

Cayce closed his eyes. He remembered, suddenly, the storm coming, and not knowing where Luke was. He sympathized with the girl's mother and the panic she must have felt when she couldn't locate her daughter.

A ceiling fan. Beneath his closed lids, Cayce saw a ceiling fan. He didn't know why. He didn't own one himself, and the one in his parents' living room was an entirely different model from this one, which was white, with a plain globe. His parents' fan had four frosted-glass light fixtures and faux wood blades.

Cayce kept his eyes closed, watching the ceiling fan whirl, its blades blurring and becoming singular. There was something wrong with the fan. It didn't work quite right.

Cayce felt nauseated and opened his eyes. His face was glazed with sweat. His stomach churned, and he was afraid he would vomit. Why was seeing a ceiling fan so disturbing? Or was this some sort of aftershock, an effect of his accident?

Cayce didn't think so.

He glanced down at the face of Lucy Plant and sucked in some air. "Oh my God," he whispered, "she's dead."

The smell of the Ohio River, fishy and damp, suddenly came to him, even though his hospital windows were hermetically sealed and the river was a good four or five blocks away. Why had he said Lucy was dead?

What did he know about it?

He shut eyes again and saw a blinking light: red.

What did it mean?

Part of him wanted to close his eyes again, to see if more of the vision would come. Part of him dreaded ever closing his eyes again. Where was this coming from? *It's just aftereffects, Cayce*, he told himself. *You suffered a blow to your head, brain-jarring. That's all.*

He lay back on the pillows, clutching the newspaper tightly to his chest. When he closed his eyes again, he saw the blinking red light and a shadowy figure behind it: a woman's head. The image, for no objective reason, was horrifying.

Cayce sat up in bed, heart pounding. "No," he said loudly, then whispered, "no."

He forced himself to breathe deeply. He looked down at Lucy Plant's calm, smiling face again. The straight blonde hair, the kind someone more romantically inclined would refer to as "flaxen." The wide eyes, too big for her little-girl face but which would someday be beautiful. The dusting of freckles across the bridge of her nose. The chipped front tooth.

Cayce felt his eyes brim with tears, a lump in his throat. "So innocent," he whispered, rocking back and forth in the bed, unaware that he was even moving. "So innocent. What a waste." He smelled the river again, and when he closed his eyes once more, he had another vision: the murky brown water of the Ohio River, its tree-lined shores and...and... Cayce bit his lip so hard he tasted blood.

A freshly dug grave.

Cayce opened his eyes and batted at his own face, as if he could physically remove the odd imagery. He didn't want to see these things. It was like a dream, a nightmare, but he wasn't sleeping.

The images were so vivid—the knowledge so certain.

Lucy Plant wasn't coming back.

Cayce's gaze fell upon a line of type in the news story about the girl's disappearance. Her mother was making a plea. "Please, if anyone knows anything about my daughter...if anyone has seen her, please, please, let us know. All we want is to know that she's safe. No. All that we want is for her to be home again, where she belongs. Her little brother misses her. I miss her. Her father...we all do. Please, if you know anything about our girl, come forward."

And Cayce wondered what he should do. He visualized himself down at Fawcettville police headquarters, telling them he knew something about the girl's disappearance. "Yes, I had a vision. The girl is dead, and she's buried near the river. I saw a ceiling fan and a blinking red light, like on a video camera."

He would be treated with understanding and pity. Scorn and laughter behind his back. The police would call some mental hospital in Pittsburgh.

But what could he do?

He *did* know something about Lucy Plant. He was sure of it. He wished he didn't, but there it was.

Cayce flung the newspaper to the floor and forced himself to look out the window, where the tree-covered hills of West Virginia stared dumbly back, much as they stared dumbly at the shallow grave Cayce was certain this poor young girl was buried in.

Footsteps. A child.

Cayce sighed with relief. Luke.

"I wanna see Daddy!" he yelled.

And his grandmother was telling him to slow down.

It was the real world. Cayce wondered if he'd ever be part of it again.

Chapter Four

Myra stood at the bathroom sink, appraising her reflection. "Odd," she whispered to the platinum-blonde waif gazing back at her. "So damn odd." The edges of the mirror were rimed with steam, so her reflection had blurred edges, adding to the surreal aspect. It wasn't her. Myra wondered where the girl she had been had gone. Just a few months ago, she had been Penny Landsdale. She had lived across the river, in a small West Virginia town called New Hope, where she had been a senior at New Hope High. Penny looked nothing like Myra, she thought, opening a contact lens case. She slid the lenses onto her eyes, turning them from hazel to an almost electric green. The color was unnatural. Myra hated it, but Ian had bought the lenses for her and insisted she wear them. "Green is the color of the Beast," he had whispered in her ear as he pressed the small plastic case containing the lenses into her sweaty palms. "And the eyes are the window to the soul." He stared into her hazel eyes with his own green-lensed ones. "I want us to have the same window, so the Beast will know we're a pair." Myra hadn't understood him then and wasn't sure she did now. Still, Ian was handsome, with his dark, curly hair and chiseled features. Older. Not many boys had paid her much attention at school, not when she was Penny Landsdale. Not when she was twenty pounds overweight, with thick thighs and a big ass. Not with her acne and the gap between her front teeth. Not with that long mousy brown hair that hung in split ends to the middle of her back, lank and thin.

But a man had paid attention to her. Twenty-four years old and handsome—Myra giggled—as the devil. She picked up a bottle of CoverGirl and began dotting her face with the peach-colored foundation. It hid the acne pretty well. Ian had taught her that. He had taught her a lot of things since school had let out last May and she had left her parents' home—over strenuous objections, but she wasn't about to be dragged down by those scenes right now. For example, he had taught her to cut all fats from her diet and to subsist on fruit and vegetables, both raw, and lots of water. The weight had melted off, and her love for this handsome stranger who had appeared almost out of nowhere, like some Prince Charming, had helped her keep it off. Now, when she looked at her naked reflection in the mirror, she saw the lines of her ribs below her small breasts. Her hips had shrunk; her thighs had gone from tree trunks to willow limbs. For the first time in her life, she was skinny.

And beautiful, she thought, smoothing the foundation into her skin, blending it below her jawline. Ian had cut her hair in the kitchen of his trailer, cut it short and bleached it platinum. The result had been startling. Myra had almost not known herself when Ian finished and finally allowed her to look in a mirror. She had giggled, a nervous, high-pitched sound, equal mixture of glee and wonder. Her blonde hair, the crimson lips, the black lashes framing the green eyes, and her newly thin body transformed Penny Landsdale into Myra Hindley— a name with which Ian had christened her. Where did he come up with such things?

She switched off the bathroom light and headed toward the bedroom, where Ian had laid an outfit on the bed for her: black leather skirt and a leopard print blouse that he had said she was to tie beneath her bust. Next week, he said, they would look into having her navel pierced.

God, she loved Ian. He was the only one who had ever managed to look beneath her exterior and see her for the sexy young woman she was. She had him to thank—and thank him she would.

But the Beast, as Ian referred to him, must also be thanked. According to Ian, the Beast was the source of her beauty. It was the Beast guiding his hand in her transformation.

Beast. Ian. Whatever. Myra knew only that she was happy, and she would do whatever it took to hang on to that happiness.

No questions asked.

She paused in the bedroom doorway, hearing the bass roar of the Mustang's engine as it pulled up to the trailer. She closed her eyes, whispering, "Thank you." Allowing herself one final once-over in the mirror, Myra tied the knot in the leopard print blouse so her navel showed above the black leather and headed out into the twilight.

Their trailer wasn't much, Myra thought as the door swung shut behind her, but what a view they had. There was nothing else here on this hilltop other than woods. The hill behind the trailer banked sharply down, and below them, the village of Fawcettville, where warm yellow lights were just beginning to wink on in the frame houses. The small town was bordered by the greenish-brown curve of the Ohio River. Myra stared at its churning waters for just a second and felt an odd sensation in the pit of her stomach: nausea.

No, she wouldn't think about that.

She turned to the car, where Ian was just emerging. Tall, skin pale against his black clothes. He smiled, and her nausea melted away.

She came to him, silent as a cat, a barely perceptible grin playing about her lips.

He cocked his head. "Are you wearing panties?"

She shook her head.

The next thing she knew Ian had flung her across the hood of the car, its dying engine hot beneath her. He'd crammed two fingers inside her, was kissing her roughly, holding her head by her hair. It hurt, and Myra whimpered, but as she felt the warm wetness growing inside her, sliding down, it felt better, and she found her cries turning to gasps.

Ian unbuckled his pants.

"For the Beast," he whispered, pushing her legs back and, finally, biting her tongue so hard she tasted the metallic tang of her blood.

Later Myra sat with Ian in the living room. It was a cramped space, its furniture thirdhand and threadbare, the kind of stuff one found piled in alleys behind homes that were, at best, considered modest. But with the curtains drawn and the coffee table transformed into a makeshift altar, replete with a dozen candles of varying sizes, shapes, and scents, the room took on a different dimension.

Ian sat close, his arm a comforting weight across her shoulders. The room was silent save for the sound of a low-hanging branch hitting against the trailer. The tree was a dead maple, its trunk stooped like the back of an old man.

This was their quiet time. This was the time when Ian did not speak to Myra of his financial woes, of how they were going to bring money in because he had quit his job as a caster at the pottery in the valley below them. Ian considered himself above working at the pottery, filling molds with the liquid clay called slip, moving down rows of molds, filling, filling all day long. No end to the monotony.

No end to his complaining, Myra thought, no end to the long discourses on how the Beast had better things in mind for him and how they must trust in the Beast to take care of them. Would the Beast come up with the rent payment that was due next week? Would he deliver it to them in a bloodred envelope, left secretly outside their door while they slept, Myra's fitful slumbers interrupted by nightmares of being buried alive?

Ian, as if he had read her thoughts, her doubts, said, "We should pray to the Beast."

The two of them knelt before the coffee table, and each gazed into the flickering light of the candles. Why did Myra feel like laughing? There would be no mirth in the laughter.

Ian intoned, "Green-eyed Beast, master of all that is evil, we pray to you, offering up our bodies and souls in exchange for your sustenance." Myra, not knowing what else to do, bowed her head. Was it right to ape the practices she had learned as a child attending the First Lutheran Church with her parents? Did the Beast require her to bow her head, or would the Beast expect her to hold it high, in defiance of Christian traditions? Christian mythology, Ian would have called it. She glanced at Ian out of the corner of her eye and saw his head lowered so assumed she was doing the right thing.

"In the name of all that is evil, we pray for guidance."

Myra bit her lip. She squeezed Ian's hand and tried, really tried, to believe that what they were doing was right and Ian knew best. After all, he was the one who studied the books: texts by authors with names like Aleister Crowley and Anton LaVey. He was older than she and, of course, far more worldly and mature.

Ian lifted his head and slid back onto the couch. After a second, Myra joined him.

He turned her head to his and stared at her. For the first time, Myra wondered what lurked behind those eyes. There was a deadness to them that belied the handsome face and strong jaw.

"The Beast has spoken. It's time for another sacrifice."

Chapter Five

Cayce was tired as he sat in his kitchen. More than tired, exhausted. Uncertain if he had the strength to make it through the day. Even the thought of work made him ache from head to toe. He had been back at the diner now for three days and had yet to get back into the groove of things. The orders seemed to come in faster than they used to. His coordination was off. His memory didn't work the same way it once had, and he was forced to ask his customers who ordered what as he unsteadily brought their orders to the table, something he had always prided himself on never having to do. Carlos Soto, his new doctor, had told him it would take him a while to completely recover, that the shock his system had taken was significant, and time was the only remedy for the damage it had wrought. The bangs he had carelessly cut across his forehead to hide the wound tickled it, making Cayce want to reach up and scratch, something that would not be good. Unless he wanted to see if he could earn extra tips from his customers by having blood trickle down his face.

Very appetizing.

The trauma to his head had sapped his energy. The two weeks he had taken off from the diner, which he'd thought was plenty of time to get back to normal, hadn't been enough. For one thing, he couldn't sleep. His dreams were filled with phantom images that caused him to awaken sweating, twisted in his sheets, a garbled scream still hot on his lips. He had begun to fear going to sleep, terrified of the nightmares that awaited him. He had seriously considered calling up Casey Williams, an old friend from whom he knew he could purchase some pot, but he didn't want to go down that road again. When it got late enough and his body was aching for sleep, Cayce would have a glass of red wine, and that might help him fall into a fitful doze.

And Luke, the little dear, seemed to have no respect for what his father had gone through. Right now, as Cayce tried to work a crossword puzzle at the kitchen table, Luke was in the living room, the TV volume turned to earsplitting, the explosions, screams, and other sound effects accompanied by his giggles. Perhaps the cacophony would have been cute if Cayce hadn't been so tired, if he could have found it within himself to go in and turn down the TV volume and tell his son that he had only fifteen minutes before bath and then bed. But getting up from the maple kitchen chair would have taken too much effort.

Four letters. Nick and Nora's pooch. Cayce closed his eyes. The clue was a familiar one in crosswords, but he could think of nothing, inane TV dialogue blocking out any thoughts he might have for himself.

He put the Bic down, shoved the newspaper away, and stood. Breathing in deeply, he promised himself he wouldn't be angry with Luke. It wasn't the little boy's fault he was neglecting him lately. Well, not really neglecting, but not paying as much attention as he could have. He took care of the basics, saw to it that he was clean, well fed, looked after. But Cayce had little energy for anything beyond the required child-rearing basics.

In the living room, Luke lay on the floor, a throw pillow from the couch beneath his head, thumb in his mouth, eyes wide as images from the TV screen flickered over his face. Cayce doubted if he had even noticed his father standing over him. Cayce picked up the remote from the coffee table, aimed it at the TV, and watched as the screen went black.

"Scoot. It's time to get cleaned up and then bed."

"But, Dad..." Luke whined. "That program only had about ten more minutes."

"And you've got only about ten more minutes to get a quick bath and into your pj's."

"Come on, Dad." Luke reached for the remote.

Cayce snatched it up. "No, Luke. I mean it. Upstairs. Now."

Reluctantly, Luke roused himself from the floor, put the pillow back on the couch, and started upstairs.

"Make it quick. I'll be up in a couple minutes to tuck you in."

"Okay."

Cayce returned to the kitchen, glanced down at the newspaper, and whispered, "Asta." But he was too tired to bother with filling in the crossword puzzle clue. Instead, he switched on the radio and slumped in a kitchen chair, head in hands.

A song was just ending. One of those hip-hop numbers that he hated. Just as well there was no music. Did music even exist anymore? After an ad for a local car dealership, the news came on. Cayce had started to tune the announcer's voice out, making of it white noise, a background drone, when something he said made him perk up and listen.

Listen with horror.

Another teenage girl had gone missing. Her name was Sheryl McKenna.

*

He read the next chapter of *The Wind in the Willows* on automatic pilot. The act of reading to Luke was more a matter of eye-mouth coordination than of conscious thought. Cayce was surprised when he came to the end of the chapter and could not remember even one word he had read to his son, who lay on his side, thumb in mouth and eyes closed.

Cayce reached down and ran his fingers through Luke's hair, trailing his fingertips across his cheeks, still baby smooth and plump. He tugged his thumb out of his mouth and wondered when he would ever break this habit. "I sure do love you," he whispered to the sleeping boy, pulling the sheet up around his neck. Luke smelled sweet, of the baby powder he had sprinkled on him after his bath and the clean smell of little boy, something indefinable and uncorrupted.

The air coming in through the screen was a little cooler, foretelling the approach of autumn. It had been a hot, miserable summer in so many ways, Cayce was grateful for the change.

For a while, he simply sat in the chair beside his son's bed, staring down at him in the dim light of his Mickey Mouse night-light. Cayce had once decorated the room in a Disney theme, a time that now seemed many more years ago than it actually was. Partly, Cayce recognized the fact that he just wanted to spend some quiet time with his son, who, during his waking hours, was a bundle of energy, impossible to pin down for more than fifteen- or twenty-minute intervals before he was off to something else. The doctor had once asked him if he wanted a prescription for Ritalin for Luke, the drug that supposedly calmed hyperactive kids. But Luke was just a child, Cayce thought, his manic energy just part of his makeup. He had seen enough of drugs in his own days to realize he didn't want to start his son on them when he was a boy of seven.

Briefly, he thought of his ex, Marc, again—his devastating Irish-Italian good looks, his compact yet muscular frame that Cayce had watched go from robust to skeletal as he became more and more enamored of cocaine than he was of him, or of anything else for that matter. He had read somewhere that Ritalin was very similar to cocaine in its chemical makeup. God forbid. So Cayce sat back in the chair, listening to the sound of the dog, Oreo, as he made his way up the stairs, which creaked in all the familiar places. He appreciated being able to just sit for a change and look at his son, recharging his paternal batteries, which had been running on a low current for the past week or two.

Oreo came into the room, giving his owner a mournful look with his brown eyes, and hopped onto the foot of Luke's bed, where he curled into a ball and, after a lick of his lips and a yawn, fell immediately to sleep. "Dog, you don't know how much I envy you," Cayce whispered.

One part of Cayce thought he should get up, brush his teeth, and head for the comfort of his own bed, sheets cool from the night breeze. But the other part of him recognized the fact that he was dreading going into his own bedroom down the hall. News of Sheryl McKenna's disappearance lurked like a stranger behind the door, just beyond his more pleasant thoughts of Luke and the peaceful rise and fall of his chest, the warm air coming out of his mouth. He knew that once he got into bed, the door would close, and the missing young girl would begin, in a way, to call to him. All it took was hearing her name and description on the radio, just that small connection, and it was like igniting something in his brain.

And that call would make Cayce feel helpless…and terrified. He feared the weird, dreamlike images that would rise up, forging a bond with the girl that Cayce had not sought.

Why was this happening?

*

The sound of a car alarm outside Luke's window awakened Cayce. He had fallen asleep in the chair beside Luke's bed. The alarm wound down, replaced by the sound of chirping cicadas and crickets, the distant rumble of thunder. Heat lightning flashed, muted blue-white swatches of color that illuminated the street in front of their little house.

Cayce's neck hurt, and he reached up to massage it, trying to loosen the knotted muscles. He glanced up at the Donald Duck clock on the wall opposite; it was going on midnight.

In spite of the crick in his neck, Cayce thought perhaps falling asleep in the chair next to Luke's bed was a good thing. After all, his body was bone weary, and perhaps he could just drop his jeans and T-shirt on the floor next to his bed, crawl in under the sheets, and fall back asleep.

And maybe he would dream of nothing.

Hell, maybe he'd even have a pleasant dream. Something sexy. Cayce grinned as he padded, barefoot, down the hall to his room.

He slipped out of his clothes, folded them and put them on the rocking chair in the corner, and crawled under the sheet.

He closed his eyes.

*

Someone stood above him. Cayce awakened to see a dark-haired girl staring down at him. He let out a little cry, not too loud, because he didn't want to awaken Luke. The girl held a finger to his lips, leaning over so that the long, dark curtain of hair partially obscured a very pretty, very young face.

The girl motioned for Cayce to follow; Cayce shook his head.

The girl reached down and took Cayce's hand in her own. Her touch was ice cold, and Cayce glanced down at the hand. Even in the dim light, he could see the sapphire ring on her finger.

Cayce got up, following the girl, not bothering with clothes. Eventually, he stood naked in the gravel driveway of his house with the girl, who gestured toward the river. And even though the river was two blocks away, Cayce could suddenly see its brownish curve, the hills of West Virginia along the opposite shore. Up high, at the top of one of the hills, was a red brick house, old, that Cayce had admired since he was a little boy. Fronted by white pillars, the house occupied the only space on the hilltop, and Cayce had often envied the solitude and the panoramic views the house must command.

Cayce stood alone in the driveway, shivering. A light rain had begun, cold needles on his skin. And he knew he had sleepwalked...the touch and vision of the young girl had been a dream. He gasped as he looked down at himself, seeing his silvery-white nude body in the dark, and hoped none of his neighbors had insomnia and had witnessed his unintentional exposure.

He turned and trudged back inside, picking his way through the sparse gravel of his driveway. He could protect his feet, if nothing else.

As he went back up the stairs, avoiding the places he knew would creak, he thought of the dark-haired girl, how beautiful she was. And how cold.

The girl was Sheryl McKenna, the one whose disappearance had just been reported on the radio. Cayce knew this with the same certainty as he knew his own name.

The bed waited. Reluctantly, Cayce made his way back to it and lay down. He closed his eyes, and everything started. There was a reddish color behind his eyelids; Cayce willed it to go away. He begged for sleep, simple, untroubled sleep that did not contain unwanted, mysterious images that seemed to have their own volition and a purpose Cayce wasn't quite sure he yet understood.

The visions came rapid-fire, with no consistency or order. Cayce ground his teeth, knowing he could stop the montage if he would just open his eyes but unable to lift his eyelids. It was as though they were glued shut.

The sapphire ring he had seen earlier, still on the girl's finger. A scattering of earth covering the hand that lay limp against a tree root.

Sheryl McKenna's face, cold in repose, her blue eyes clouded and open, gazing at something only she could see.

A beetle skittering across the porcelain-white skin.

A shift, and Cayce found himself in some sort of pornographic movie, only there was nothing titillating about this one. No lurid bump-and-grind musical score to accompany the sex taking place, the sex to which Cayce was forced to bear witness. He heard only the sounds of the man's panting breath and the whispers of the girl, occasionally interrupted by a gasp, a small cry that didn't begin to describe the pain Cayce knew she was feeling. The girl lay beneath a dark-haired man in the backseat of a car, which was nothing more than a dark hulk in the night, details indecipherable. His back was slick with sweat, and the girl's eyes were wide as the man thrust into her, hard, making her whimper and bite her lip with each thrust.

As if the volume was just switched on, like a mute button pressed to release the sound, Cayce could hear music coming from the dashboard, odd electronic beats, something no radio station would ever play. It created a hellish background score to the rape taking place in the backseat.

Cayce turned, and there it was in the darkness: the blinking red light and a shadowy figure, another woman, peering through the viewfinder of a video camera.

And then he was high on a hilltop, looking down over the Ohio River's rushing, muddy brown current. Skeletal branches reached out over the water like fingers of bone.

Cayce started awake—sweat-slick, heart pounding, twisted up in his sheets like a mummy.

Tomorrow, he had to do something.

Chapter Six

Cayce awakened early, feeling wrung out. But at least he didn't have to go into the diner until the afternoon. And Luke, God bless him, slumbered on upstairs, with Oreo snoring at the foot of his bed. That boy could sleep! Summers, he wasn't often up until noon, which was a kind of blessing for Cayce, who relished the little bit of time he got to himself.

Especially on mornings like this one. The lack of sleep from the night before and the restless images that haunted him when he *did* manage to get to sleep had left him feeling as though he had the world's worst hangover. A glance in the mirror revealed a red-eyed wraith, looking much older than his years. Many more nights like the one prior and Cayce was pretty sure his nights alone would become a permanent condition.

He brewed himself a cup of coffee and slid half his body out the front door to retrieve the morning paper. He threw it on the kitchen table and poured himself a steaming mug of energy, augmenting it with three teaspoons of sugar and a big dollop of hazelnut Coffee mate. He needed a jump start this morning.

He sat down with his coffee and opened up the paper.

And there she was, staring up at him: Sheryl McKenna. A beautiful girl with dark hair and a worldly expression. She wore too much makeup, but one could still see she had about her the air of an innocent.

The images came to him suddenly, hitting him like an electric jolt. He sat back in his chair, eyes shut and the breath stolen right out of him. A young girl, impossibly beautiful, with long black hair. The moon on the river. Two figures, a man and a woman emerging out of darkness. What came next Cayce only felt, as though it was a sense memory, having more to do with emotion than sensation. He experienced, from those shadowy figures, a sense of trust. Somehow he knew this was what Sheryl had felt. And then, seconds later, Cayce's heart sped up because the sense of security morphed quickly to terror.

*

Cayce realized he was whimpering. The newspaper had dropped to the kitchen floor. Sheryl McKenna's face still looked up at him from its front page. It was as though she was pleading.

"What do you want me to do?" Cayce whispered to the newspaper. "What *can* I do?" He had a sense of what had happened to the girl. He knew her fear. But how could he tell anyone and not have it sound like the ravings of a lunatic?

He took a sip of his coffee. His hand was trembling, so some of it sloshed on his chin. Luckily, the beverage had gone cold. Cayce stood and put his mug in the microwave, hit the button for thirty seconds.

"Call the reporter," he said to himself. It was almost as though someone else were speaking to him.

He sat back down with his coffee, lifting the paper up and turning it carefully facedown on the top of the maple table. "Go on, call that reporter." He considered the idea. He had met Dave Newton. Dave Newton was covering the stories. It made sense. "He'll listen." Perhaps if Cayce spoke to him, Newton could use his inside track to the police department to...to...what?

Cayce had an idea, no, a certainty, really, that the girls were gone. It was too late to save them. But it was not too late to give their loved ones closure, to help them find the bodies. He knew, with a certainty he couldn't explain, they were buried somewhere nearby.

He pictured Dave Newton in his mind. He was a kind man; that much he could tell from their very brief interaction at the hospital. What kind of reporter would stop in just to check on a stranger who had been hurt?

Dave Newton was also an attractive man. Very attractive. *That* notion came out of nowhere, Cayce thought. He had been so preoccupied with being a single dad, working his fingers to the bone to make ends meet, that what he had once thought a very powerful sex drive had almost withered away. Become that of a sixty-year-old. A sixty-year-old with no access to Viagra.

Cayce smiled. He supposed he could call Dave Newton. What was the worst that could happen? That Newton would think he was nuts? Cayce shrugged. That would just add him to the list of the ten thousand or so other souls in this riverside burg with whom Cayce had once crossed paths. They all thought he was nuts already; what was one more? For many in their small town, he was the young faggot who had somehow managed to have a son.

But what was the best that could happen? His visions, or whatever one wanted to call them, could help the police at least locate the girls' bodies. Cayce shuddered. And if they could locate the bodies, maybe they'd find the killer or killers. Cayce had watched enough true crime TV to know that murderers often left unwitting clues at the scene of a crime—the errant cigarette butt, carpet fibers, a shoe print. Who knew?

And on a more self-centered note, calling the reporter would give Cayce a chance to perhaps meet up with the older man again, see if he was as attractive as he recalled.

Cayce stood and went to the junk drawer in the kitchen and rooted around for the slim phone book that was thrown in there somewhere, mixed in with half-empty bottles of Elmer's Glue, Scotch tape, pencils and pens, grocery lists, old utility bills, a bag of dog treats Oreo had decided he didn't like, and God only knew what else.

There it was!

He pulled out the directory and located the number for the *Fawcettville Review*. He knew if he hesitated for even an instant, he wouldn't call, so he rapidly punched in the numbers and listened to the distant ringing, clutching the receiver tightly.

When a woman answered, Cayce was almost surprised. He hoped he recalled the reporter's name right. "Could I speak to Dave Newton, please? Is he in?"

The woman on the other end didn't say anything for a moment, and Cayce started to panic. What if she was connecting him right now? What would he say?

But there was no reason to panic, because she came back with, "Mr. Newton isn't in the office."

"Well, uh, do you know when he will be in?"

"He generally works from home, as does most of our staff, if you can call the three people who work here a staff." She snorted. "He comes in when the mood strikes him, to pick up mail or when we have a meeting. He doesn't have a set schedule. He files his stories online."

Thank you very much for lots of useless information I don't need, Cayce wanted to say. "Well, when you see him, could you ask him to call Cayce D'Amico?"

"I could. Or I could put you into his voice mail."

"That's a great idea."

The woman vanished from the line, and Cayce listened as Dave Newton spoke into his ear, his British accent sounding exotic and exciting. Cayce was tempted to hang up, to reconsider, but the beep spurred him on. "Mr. Newton, you might not remember me, but I'm Cayce D'Amico. The guy that got beaned with a branch from a tree you wrote about a while back?" Cayce drew in a breath, realizing there was no way to build up to this. *In for a penny, in for a pound.* "I may have some information about the disappearance of those girls."

Chapter Seven

Cayce waited for three days for Dave Newton to call back. He never did. The three days caused Cayce to worry more and more about what he knew and how he could help those families. He decided he had nothing to lose. He would talk to the police, even though he feared they would think he was crazy.

Fawcettville, Pennsylvania, had only one police station. It was housed in the basement of City Hall in what was still grandly called "downtown," even though the term referred to only about three or four city blocks that consisted mostly of bars, dollar stores, and boarded-up storefronts. As Cayce parked his car near the squat limestone structure that housed the workings of the municipality of Fawcettville, he remembered when he was little and the downtown was bustling, with two movie theaters, a soda fountain, a JCPenney, and assorted clothing stores, along with a few restaurants and bars. But those were the glory days of western Pennsylvania's steel mills, and those days were long over.

Earlier, Cayce had dropped Luke off with his parents and had endured his mother's questions about his whereabouts while their grandson was with them. Now, as he listened to the engine tick down and the cooling fan of the Fiesta come on, he wished he had just told his mom that Mike, his boss at the diner, had called him in to fill in for a sick server.

Cayce's mother had never been much for children, even for him. She was a brittle woman who valued the Hummel and Precious Moments figurines that adorned almost every available surface in her two-story home on Pennsylvania Avenue more than human contact. Cayce could never stand to spend very long at his parents' house, because he would become so stressed watching the tension in his mother's face as Luke moved about, the fear just beneath his mother's olive skin that the little boy might break something. It was a shame, because Cayce loved his dad, the heavyset crew-cut man with the husky voice who had an almost endless capacity for tolerance and love. Someday, when he got him alone and the two of them were enjoying some of the homemade wine he made every year, Cayce would ask him what on earth had ever drawn him to Cayce's mother, who had been high-strung and worrisome even when Cayce was a little boy.

"What do you need to go to the police station for, Cayce?" his mother had asked, slapping at the Formica-topped kitchen table with a tea towel to free it from any evidence of the breakfast she had just shared with her husband.

Cayce stared at the kitchen's gold-and-rust-patterned wallpaper as if he'd never seen it before, as if an answer were buried within its abstract pattern. Luke had already taken off for the living room, where he sat next to his grandfather on the couch, watching Drew Carey and *The Price is Right*. Cayce could hear the upbeat music from the show in the kitchen and wished that he too could be lost in the guessing games of prices and the studio excitement of who next might be exhorted to "Come on down!" Instead, he had to face his mother's interrogation, her searching for some way to show disapproval of whatever it was her son had decided to do *now*. Worse, he had to face the nervousness in his gut as he tried to figure out what to say to his mother and the police about the dreams, and—what would you call them?—*visions* he had been having lately without sounding like a complete lunatic.

"I just think I have some information that could be useful to them," Cayce said softly, opening the refrigerator and desperately searching its shelves for an escape. He knew just such a cryptic statement was opening the door to all sorts of questions, questions for which he wasn't sure he had suitable answers. The desperation almost made him want to give up on the whole thing, but the faces of the two young girls still haunted him.

The expected question came: "What kinda information would *you* have? Information about *what*?" Sarah washed the breakfast dishes, up to her elbows in steaming hot water, while giving Cayce a look that, even under the thick lenses of her glasses, indicated her disapproval of whatever he would say next.

"Nothing, Ma. It's kind of personal."

"This doesn't have anything to do with drugs, does it?"

Cayce rolled his eyes. Ever since his mother had found a quarter-ounce Baggie in his dresser drawer when Cayce was seventeen, she'd been certain her son was a drug addict. She wondered about Luke's safety and pointed out to Cayce articles in newspapers and magazines about the "war on drugs" and how marijuana was a "gateway drug."

"No, Ma, it has nothing to do with drugs." If only he could simply rush out the door, but normal people didn't rush out the door of their parents' home in the middle of a conversation, even if that conversation was doomed. "You heard about those two girls who disappeared in the past few weeks?"

Her mother dried her hands and took off her apron. "Yeah. Who hasn't? Probably runaways."

"Maybe not, Ma. Maybe I know something that might help the cops."

"What would someone like you know?"

"I might have seen them before they disappeared. I just think the police should know."

"Where—"

Cayce cut off his mother's next query with an upturned hand. His salvation came in the form of a small white lie. "Listen, I made an appointment. I don't get going, I'm gonna be late. We'll talk when I get back, okay?"

Begrudgingly, his mother accepted the lie. In his mother's world, one did not arrive late for appointments with official bodies like the police.

And now, as Cayce exited his car, he hoped the interview with the police would go better than the one with his mother. He wanted to find a way to help. But how? How could he tell them what he knew without them making a phone call to alert the men in white coats?

Cayce started up the stone steps of City Hall.

*

JT Simmons was the Fawcettville police force's first and only female detective. She had started back in the 1960s, when she was an oddity, when she had been referred to officially as a policewoman instead of the genderless nomenclature of today, where female cops, like their male counterparts, were simply police officers. JT had endured teasing, practical jokes, and often the kind of behavior from some of her coworkers that would now win her a sexual harassment suit.

The daughter of a police detective in Pittsburgh, JT's only dream had been to follow in her father's footsteps. And she might have had an easier time of it if she had remained in the much larger city of Pittsburgh, but she had followed an older woman, her first crush, here to Fawcettville back in '64. The woman, Terry, was what people unkindly referred to as a bull dyke. But JT had loved her strength, the way she took charge, and how she encouraged JT in her dreams of law enforcement, not finding them unsuitable as her mother did, or even her father, who harbored his own suspicions about JT's relationship with her masculine "friend."

Now JT was alone. A thick-waisted woman with close-cropped gunmetal gray hair and a pair of black-rimmed oval glasses, she made working for the Fawcettville police force her life. Terry had passed away from breast cancer in '77, and JT had never sought a replacement, other than the scarred desk at which she now sat and its mounds of paperwork and its black dial phone. Through sheer persistence, she had made detective, and she fully expected that one day she would run the show here in Fawcettville. She knew more about law enforcement than anyone in the building.

She wanted a cigarette, but smoking in her office had been banned a few years ago, the result of efforts by city council health nuts. She popped a piece of Dentyne into her mouth and imagined what it would be like to step outside and light up her Marlboro and feel its comforting smoke fill her lungs.

But that would wait until she had seen the young man they were sending in. Two figures appeared behind her frosted glass office door, and JT could see that one of them was a uniform and the other a tall guy with a mop of dark hair.

The door opened, and the officer, a young kid with brush-cut blond hair, gave JT a roll of the eyes behind the head of the guy. JT knew what the look meant: *another nutcase*. Whenever anything went beyond the pale of crime in Fawcettville, the nuts came in with their information. The two missing girls had already elicited a couple dozen phone calls, all claiming to have seen one or both of them at various locales between here and Pittsburgh.

But this young man was the first to have bothered to make the trip in to actually speak to someone in person. He didn't *look* like a nutcase, but JT's years of experience told her appearances counted for little. This guy had a pleasant demeanor, an easy smile, and a firm handshake when they were introduced. Yet JT knew the most normal-seeming people often harbored secrets at odds with their bland exteriors. This one was handsome, with broad shoulders and the black hair, strong nose, and green eyes indicating a southern Italian heritage. The guy was a little frightened, his gaze darting about JT's cluttered office, looking anywhere but at the detective.

Officer Hyatt spoke. "Sir, this is Detective Simmons. She's one of our best. You can tell your story to her." He gave JT a look that was almost a smirk and said, "JT, this is Cayce D'Amico. Says he might know something about the missing girls."

"Why don't you have a seat, Mr. D'Amico? You can close the door on your way out, Matt."

JT found it was often best to let other people begin. When they started first, it kind of put them on the spot, and their true feelings were more likely to emerge. JT picked up a Bic pen and began to chew on its plastic cap.

"Well—" Cayce D'Amico swallowed. "—this might be a little hard to believe, but I think it's important." He looked out the window at the day, which had turned sunny and bright. "See, you might have heard about me. A little while back, I was, um, caught in a storm... I just missed getting struck by lightning." Cayce paused, staring down at the scuffed Linoleum. "But I didn't miss getting struck by a tree branch, about the size of a small tree." He pulled aside his hair to show the detective the scar, still painfully red and bordered with purple, yellow, and green. He let the hair fall back over the wound. Cayce grinned, then stopped. "It was on the front page of the papers."

JT nodded. Although she didn't recall the incident, she said, "Yeah, I do seem to remember something about that." She took the pen out of her mouth and leaned forward. "But I'm a little confused. What would that have to do with the missing girls?"

It was obvious Cayce didn't want to go any further. To JT, Cayce looked like he wanted to do nothing more than run from her office. Cayce's face slickened with sweat, and his olive complexion went a shade paler.

"You know something about Sheryl McKenna and Lucy Plant?" JT sat up straighter.

"Well, maybe..." Cayce's voice trailed off. "Maybe not. Believe me," he said and gave the detective a lopsided grin. "I do know how, um, incredible what I'm going to say might sound."

The detective nodded.

Cayce bit the inside of his lip and swallowed audibly. "I know this sounds ridiculous, but since my accident, I've had, well, for lack of a better word, visions. And some of those visions have had to do with the girls."

JT smiled and tried to put on a sympathetic face, but it was an effort. "Well, what did you see?"

Cayce let it all out, everything, from a vague description of the man and woman he had seen with the girls, to the blinking red light of the video camera, to the visions of the fresh dirt by the side of the river, even down to the detail about that dirt being across the river from a red brick hilltop house in West Virginia. "I think there's some validity to what I saw."

"Why's that?"

"Because I knew what Sheryl McKenna looked like before I had ever seen a picture of her in the paper." Cayce explained the dreams he had the night before and how those dreams meshed perfectly with what Sheryl McKenna actually looked like.

The detective asked, "Where do you work, Mr. D'Amico? Do you have a job?"

Cayce cocked his head. "Down at the Elite Diner. Mike Bailey's place?"

"Oh, I know it," JT said. "Great burgers and fries, but my old stomach won't tolerate that crap anymore." JT laughed. "More's the pity."

"Why are you asking me about where I work?"

JT leaned back in her chair, picking up the pen off her desk again and gnawing at its tip. She consulted the ceiling. "Well, it's just that sometimes we see people and don't remember that we have...but our brain files it away. I'm just saying that it's possible young McKenna was in your restaurant before, and when you saw her picture in the paper, it might have come together for you."

"Even if that was true, why the hell would I dream of her the night before the story came out in the *Review*?"

"So you knew nothing about her disappearance when you went to bed last night?"

Cayce blew out a sigh. "I heard about her disappearance on the radio."

The detective nodded, folding her blunt-nailed hands in front of her. "So maybe Ms. McKenna was in the diner with some girlfriends, you heard her name, and your brain filed it away. This kind of thing happens all the time."

"I'm sure," Cayce said, staring down at the floor. "Couldn't you just check things out? I mean, take a look down by the river where I said?"

"Of course. I'll add your information to the other information we're building on these cases. Believe me, we check them all out." JT waited for Cayce to say something more. "Now, I do have a lot of work to do, Mr. D'Amico, so if you don't mind."

Cayce stood on trembling legs. "Please...check things out."

"Will do." JT picked up the phone.

*

In the lobby of the police station, Cayce sat down on one of the hard wooden benches. He felt disoriented, out of sorts. He thought Detective Simmons could actually do what she said and have things checked out, or she could be back there right now, regaling the other cops in the building about the "medium" who had just come into the station, ready to solve some crimes. He imagined their laughter.

He shook his head, the doubt like a cloud hanging over him. Would Simmons pay *any* attention to his hunches, visions, dreams? More likely, she would file them away under "lunatic ravings" and continue plodding through an investigation the tried and true way, the way that might yield no results until another girl turned up dead somewhere, in a shallow grave in the woods, maybe. Or down by the river…

Cayce had a horrifying image then, one that was so alarming it felt like an electric jolt to his heart. Luke. In a shallow grave by the muddy Ohio. He clutched his chest and closed his eyes, trying to still the pounding of his heart.

Cayce shook his head to clear it. The prospect of Luke being missing, or worse, dead, brought hot tears to his eyes.

"Cayce?" The familiar deep voice with its British accent caused him to look up. The reporter stood in front of him. "Do you remember me?"

"Sure, sure." Cayce swiped at his eyes and knew he failed miserably in an attempt to smile. "You're Dave Newton."

"That's right." Dave sat down next to Cayce, and Cayce noticed how warm his eyes were. "Are you all right? You look a bit upset."

Cayce drew in his breath. *This is what you wanted, isn't it? To talk to this guy?* He just didn't know if he had the fortitude to go through it again, spilling out a story that seemed like something out of maybe a book by Stephen King.

He leaned back against the hard wood of the bench and eyed Dave out of the corner of his eye. "Wanna go for coffee? Or do you prefer tea?"

Dave Newton grinned and rolled his eyes. "Actually, I prefer whiskey, but coffee will do nicely."

"We can go anywhere but the Elite Diner," Cayce said. "I don't have that much time. I have to get back to my son."

"And I am supposed to be working."

Cayce stood. "Well, this could be called work, since it has to do with the missing girls."

Dave stood next to him. "Really?"

"C'mon."

The two made their way around the corner to Lill's, a Fawcettville institution that specialized in chili, hot dogs, and fries, either separately or together. Coffee was an afterthought, but they had it.

Cayce led Dave to a table near the back, and after they had ordered, he plunged in, spilling out essentially the same story he had just told JT Simmons. When he had finished, he regarded Dave Newton with a wary eye, certain the reporter would laugh or say something overly supportive to humor him.

But what he said was "I believe you."

Cayce felt as though he had entered some alternate universe. "What? That wasn't what I expected to hear from you."

"What did you expect?"

"I don't know. That I'm crazy or, like the cops, you'd check into it. And I'd walk away, knowing you were humoring me."

Dave stirred his coffee, even though Cayce was certain it had long gone cold. "I don't know that I can do anything. That's the problem. But I grew up with parents who believed in such things. We went to Stonehenge and the Glastonbury Tor all the time. My mum believed in the power of ley lines. We were kind of low-rent spiritualists."

"Great." Cayce thought he should be getting back to Luke.

"What? I was just trying to let you know that I believe there are things in this world we don't perhaps have reasonable explanations for. Plus, you don't seem like the kind of man who has the time or, and don't take offense, the imagination to make this shit up."

Cayce smiled reluctantly. He realized he liked this man. He'd never met anyone like him, especially not in these parts. Dave Newton had a brain and an open mind to go with it. How rare was that?

And he was cute, in a grizzled sort of way. Cayce found himself imagining how the stubble on the planes of Dave's cheeks and chin would feel under his fingertips.

Stop it, he told himself. *Get home to your son.* "So my telling you really hasn't changed anything?"

"If you're asking if I'll write a story about what you've seen, the answer is no. Not yet, anyway. Like the police, I'm afraid the newspaper would want something more concrete to hang our hats on."

Cayce shook his head. He pulled out a few dollars from his wallet and put them on the table.

"Don't be angry," Dave said.

"Oh, I'm not. I understand. I just can't help but wish I didn't have these feelings, see these things. It doesn't help anyone, yet I know." His head slumped, and he said, very softly, "I just know."

Dave reached out and covered Cayce's hand with his own. His touch was hot, tender, and Cayce turned his palm upright so that their two palms met. There was something arousing and raw about the connection, almost as if they were doing something intimate, like sharing a deep tongue kiss. Cayce stared into Dave's eyes. Dave didn't look away, not for a long time. Something passed between them.

"I have to go." Cayce stood suddenly.

"Will you be in touch? I'd like to see you again." Dave reached into his pocket to grab his wallet and took out a business card. He extended it to Cayce.

Cayce nodded and took the card. "Maybe next time, we can meet under better circumstances. Talk about something else."

"I'd like that."

"Would you?" At this point, Cayce didn't even know for sure that Newton was gay. Although the language their eyes spoke and that little thing they had done with their hands sure seemed to confirm it.

"Yes."

"Okay, then." Cayce hurried away from the table, thinking how his life had gone from boring and pedestrian to complicated and confusing at the drop of a...tree branch.

Cayce hurried to his car and got inside, wincing at the hot vinyl interior. With shaking hands, he brought the key to the ignition.

The police weren't ready to do anything; he knew it. And as much as Dave Newton might like to help, he couldn't. Not yet.

But what could Cayce do? He couldn't just let things remain as they were, not with what he knew.

*

Later, after Luke was tucked into bed and the little house was silent once more, the darkness pressing against the windows like something palpable, Cayce sat alone in the living room. He had flipped through TV channels, but as usual, there was nothing he wanted to see. Besides, he didn't know if he could concentrate on a movie, and a sitcom would just be too absurd in light of the thoughts that were racing through his head: thoughts of getting in touch with the parents of the missing girls himself.

Chapter Eight

Cayce and Luke were in the kitchen.

"But what if my teacher doesn't like me?"

"Your teacher will like you."

"But what if the other kids don't remember me from first grade?"

"They'll remember you."

"What if it's too hard, Dad?"

"It won't be too hard. Everything you learned last year will come back, and then you build on that. Trust me. In a way, school gets easier every year. *If* you pay attention. You'll see."

Cayce took the empty cereal bowl away from in front of Luke, set it in the sink, and went into the dining room to get the new red nylon backpack he had just bought for him at Walmart. He had loaded it up with fat pencils, the sixty-four-count box of Crayolas, three spiral-bound notebooks, safety scissors, a red plastic ruler, and a small bottle of Elmer's Glue. If he needed anything else, Cayce could pick it up later. *Anyway,* he thought grimly, *shouldn't my second sight help me make sure my son has the right stuff for his first day of second grade?*

Cayce helped Luke slide the backpack on and walked him to the screen door. Cayce watched him walk down the driveway, knowing he wanted to look back, knowing his green eyes were moist, and knowing that, already, the older side of him was kicking in, for better or worse, and that he was being brave, fighting the urge to run back to his father.

He fought back his own urge to run after him, to give him one more hug and kiss before he joined a group of kids heading up the street in front of their house.

After Luke was gone, the house seemed unnaturally quiet, eerily empty, as if Luke had taken more than just his physical being with him.

Cayce sat for a long time in the kitchen, staring at the telephone, a cup of coffee going cold in front of him. Oreo came in, gave him a glance, then made a circle before settling himself on the braided rug in front of the sink.

"Great. How am I supposed to do the dishes?"

He had already looked up the McKennas' number in the phone book and had scrawled it in the margin of yesterday's newspaper. The blue-inked number faced him, as if it were waiting. Cayce didn't have to be at the diner until three, so he had plenty of time to do what he felt needed to be done.

The day was a warm one, suffocating even early in the morning, with a dirty white sky and the angry buzz of insects filling the air, spilling in through the kitchen's screen door.

Cayce stared out at the day for what seemed like hours but was in fact only fifteen minutes or so. Like a scared actor forcing himself to take the stage, Cayce lifted the wall phone from its cradle and pushed the buttons rapidly for the McKennas, preventing himself from backing out. He knew, if these were the days prior to technological advances like Caller ID and *69, he might have lost his nerve and hung up.

But someone did answer. A woman, the youth in her voice obvious, gave away her West Virginia "down the river" origins when she said hello with a slight drawl, the twang of a country western singer.

She had to say hello twice before Cayce spoke. It was as though Cayce needed the shove of that second hello, slightly annoyed, to get himself going.

"Mrs. McKenna?"

"This is her. Who's this?"

"You don't know me. My name's Cayce D'Amico. I live not too far from you." Cayce felt a trickle of sweat run down his back. "I was wondering if I could talk to you."

"That's what you're doin', isn't it? What's this about, anyway? I'm not in the market to buy anything, mister."

Cayce laughed, but it came out closer to a squeak. "Oh, believe me, I'm not trying to sell anything here. I just wondered if I could stop by and see you for a little bit this morning."

"About what?" Suddenly, wariness crept into the woman's voice, and just as suddenly, Cayce knew that the thought that someone was calling about Sheryl was dawning on her. It was almost as if she spoke the words, spoke her trepidation that this odd man was calling out of the blue to make a ransom demand, although from where the money would come Sheryl McKenna's mother had no idea, or to tell her that Sheryl was dead.

And Cayce knew he should be honest but wondered how much to say over the phone. This would all be easier if he could face the woman, look into her eyes, reassure her, parent to parent.

But what reassurance did he have? That bag was empty.

"I need to talk to you about Sheryl."

"What about her?" The West Virginia twang turned to ice.

Cayce sighed. "It's so hard to explain over the phone. I think I might know something about her...about her... disappearance. Maybe not. I'd just like to talk to you in person."

"What could you possibly know?"

"Can I just come over? I can be there in fifteen minutes."

"Why don't you just tell me what you're calling about right now? Why can't you do that?"

"It's just easier to explain in person. Please, Mrs. McKenna."

She sighed. "Whatever. Fine. You know where I live?"

"Yes. Give me fifteen minutes."

And now, as Cayce knocked on a weathered, green-painted door, again he questioned why he was doing this. Could he really help, or were his nightmares the result of the lightning strike? Some sort of mental aftereffect that had nothing to do with reality?

He looked around the yard, trying not to think. Sheryl McKenna's home was a study in grim. The tiny wooden house had scabs of white paint that clung stubbornly to it, trying in vain to hide the black and rotting wood beneath. The yard was balding; only a few patches of dry grass, mixed with weeds, grew. A black-and-tan dog, looking like some sort of pit bull/German shepherd mix, was chained to a tar-papered dog house. The animal stared at him with rheumy eyes. Cayce was sure if he reached out a hand to pet it, that hand would be bitten off. Absurdly, the name painted in crude white letters above the doghouse door was "Peaches."

The smell of the Ohio River, just a block away, was strong, brackish: fish with an undercurrent of mildew. For an instant, Cayce detected something rotting, akin to the odor of spoiled meat, and wondered if it had simply been borne up by a wind from across the river or if it was another of his premonitions, or whatever it was they were. He shut his eyes and saw a shovel making impact with dark, damp earth and shuddered.

When Sheryl McKenna's mother opened the door, Cayce felt as though he had already seen her. And maybe he had. Fawcettville was, after all, a small town. Cayce could have passed the tired-looking woman on the street downtown or served her in the diner. The woman stared at him with red-rimmed gray eyes, looking him over as though Cayce was something she had discarded in the yard that had managed to make its way back to the porch. Mrs. McKenna was small, with no fat on her bones. She looked almost skeletal. Her skin was weathered, the result of too much sun, too much smoke. Her skin, combined with straw-like bleached blonde hair and hard eyes, made her, Cayce was sure, look older than her years. She held a cigarette in her hand, and the smell of tobacco smoke came out of the house like a wave when she opened the door.

"You Cayce?"

"Yes. I'm Cayce D'Amico." Cayce was uncertain whether he should extend his hand. In the end he decided that the woman would just stare at his hand, so he didn't bother.

"Janet McKenna. What do you want?" Her voice was dead.

"Can I come in?"

"Who is it, Jan?" A man's voice came from the back of the house, and Cayce, upon hearing it, immediately stiffened. He didn't know why. He felt cold.

Janet turned her head, took a drag on her cigarette, and called, "It's that Cayce, the one who called." She turned back around. "I guess you may's well step in."

Cayce followed her into a cluttered kitchen: stacks of dirty dishes in the sink, an old stove covered in grease and food stains, counters filled with newspapers, magazines, and overflowing ashtrays. The centerpiece of the room was a wood-grain laminate table with four mismatched chairs. A man with a crew cut and a beer gut glared at him from behind a caul of cigarette smoke.

"That's Rick," Janet said, sitting down.

Cayce nodded and took a seat. He rubbed his forehead, staring at the pack of Kools on the table. Even though he had given the habit up seven years ago, he wanted one, wanted the calm the smoke would bring.

But he didn't dare ask.

"You said you knew something about Sheryl."

Cayce nodded, hating the bile moving around in his stomach and splashing against the back of his throat. *Why did I come here*? "Well, yeah. I think I might. But it could be nothing."

"What the fuck are you talking about?" Rick continued to stare, suspicious, as though Cayce had materialized out of thin air at the table.

Cayce sucked in a breath when it hit him like a flash on a movie screen: this man on top of a young girl. A young girl who peered over his writhing, sweaty back with dead eyes.

God, no, Cayce thought.

"I... I..." How could he put this? "See, I kind of have these visions? I know it sounds silly, but—"

"Oh Lord." Janet McKenna regarded the ceiling.

"I don't know if it's worth anything at all. But I've seen Sheryl, and I think I might have seen something that might help you find her."

"Get out."

"What?"

Janet McKenna stood, and the hand holding the almost-burned-to-the-filter cigarette trembled. Her other hand was balled into a fist. "I said get out."

"Okay." Cayce stood, holding on to the table for support. "I just thought I might be able to help."

"Do you know how many lunatics have called, driven by, showed up at our doorstep since my daughter disappeared? Do you?"

"No," Cayce whispered, backing toward the door.

"A lot. A whole lot. And not a one of them could help. Do you know why?"

"Why?" Cayce's mouth was dry.

"Because none of them had been sent by the Lord. And you have the nerve to come in here with your devil's visions and try to tell me you can *help*? I don't need your kind of help. What do you call yourself anyway, some kind of psychic? Psychics come straight from Satan, mister. You don't fool me. Only through the power of Jesus Christ will my Sheryl come back to me."

Cayce closed his eyes for just a second. When he opened them again, both the man and the woman were staring at him, hatred as plain on their faces as their noses. Cayce forced himself to press on. "I just think you should listen to me for a minute. If you don't like what I have to say, forget it. But maybe it can help."

"I don't think so." Janet McKenna had begun to cry.

"Now you go on, get the hell out of here." Rick dragged angrily on his cigarette and blew the smoke at him.

"I know about you," Cayce whispered, leaning toward the man. "I know all about you. Listen. I can see the truth. I know what you did."

When he said those words, Cayce knew he was right and knew, for the first time, his visions had validity. Rick sucked in some breath, held it, his eyes widening. Cayce saw the truth written on his face, the way it had gone ashen.

But Janet McKenna was picking up a food-encrusted plate from the sink and preparing to fling it at him. "You get out of my *house*!"

The plate broke just over his left shoulder, against the wall.

Cayce turned and ran from the house.

Chapter Nine

"This isn't what I ordered!" the old woman called out, the irritation in her little old lady voice heightening her pitch, making her sound like a harpy. "Young man, I didn't order a grilled cheese. I ordered a…"

Cayce hurried over to her table, hoping his boss, that prince among men, Mike Bailey, didn't hear the old lady's cries. "Ma'am, I'm very sorry." Cayce picked up the plate. "Now, what was it you had?"

"I shouldn't have to tell you again. I already placed my order. You wrote it down." The old woman toyed with the paper napkin on the table, not giving Cayce the benefit of eye contact. She said, in a much softer voice, "You figure it out."

Cayce consulted his pad and went back to the kitchen. The old bitch's tuna melt was, fortunately, still waiting under the heat lamps. But who got the grilled cheese?

Cayce hurried over to the woman and set the plate before her. "Listen, ma'am, I'm very sorry."

"Mm-hmm." The old woman lifted a slice of bread to peer at the tuna and American cheese underneath. "Don't worry. It'll come out of your tip."

"You do what you have to." Cayce sighed and hurried away. He glanced up at the clock for what seemed like the fiftieth time tonight. It was ten o'clock, one more hour until the end of his shift. Cayce's feet ached. Worse, he still stung from his visit to the McKennas'. How could they have been so cruel? He had only been trying to help.

The frustration simmered just beneath the surface of his consciousness, a consciousness he needed to devote to his work, however menial it seemed in comparison to what he knew. Sheryl McKenna, he was certain, had been buried on a hilltop, somewhere overlooking the river. He wished there was something he could have done *before* that fact became reality. And God, how he wished he could have convinced Janet McKenna to listen. Cayce was certain that just knowing what happened to her daughter would give the woman some closure, a release. At least that's what would have been true for Cayce had he been in the woman's shoes.

This line of thinking led Cayce to wonder how Luke was doing. He had left him with his parents and knew they indulged the boy too much, letting him stay up far past his bedtime, feeding him ice cream and candy—and making his next day at school a useless one.

Cayce stepped toward the back door of the kitchen, pulling his cell out of his apron pocket.

"And where do you think you're going?" Mike glared at him from his position behind the cash register.

"I have to call my parents, Mike. Luke is with them. I just want to check in, make sure he's okay."

"Cayce, you have two tables still waiting for you to take their orders."

"I know. I'll get right on it. Just let me make a quick call. Two minutes, tops."

"Yeah." Mike scratched his bald pate. "I hope your customers won't mind waiting while you take care of personal business."

Somehow Cayce managed to get through his shift without any more major errors. Somehow he managed to get Luke home, give him a glass of Alka-Seltzer, and tuck him into bed.

"I want a story," Luke whined.

"It's too late. You have to get up at seven o'clock for school in the morning." Cayce glanced at the clock on his nightstand. "Seven will be here before you know it, and then I'll have to drag you out of bed, stick your head in the toilet to wake you up, and flush, flush, flush."

Luke giggled and didn't press the story issue. Cayce lay beside him for a moment, taking some solace from the warmth of his little body. He sighed. "Dad's pooped." He tousled Luke's blond hair. "I love you, buddy."

The two lay quietly for a while; then Cayce sat up. "You need to get to sleep, little man." But Luke had already dropped off.

Cayce went downstairs and into the kitchen and poured himself a glass of milk. He stared out the screen door at the darkness. Cars whooshed by on the street in front of their house every couple of minutes. Otherwise, it was still. The air coming through the screen had an undercurrent of cool to it; fall wasn't far behind. He wondered if this night, after the trauma of the day, would be one in which he could find some sleep. Sleep uninterrupted by visions.

The phone ringing startled him, sounding like an alarm in the still night. Cayce raced to it and snatched the receiver from its cradle.

"Hello." *Who could be calling now? It's almost midnight.*

"Is this Cayce D'Amico?"

A woman's voice, unfamiliar. He immediately wondered if he would pick something up from her voice, get a mental picture of the woman. But there was nothing.

"Who wants to know?"

"I'm sorry. I should have introduced myself. My name's Amy Plant."

Cayce's heart made a small leap. The name Plant meant something. It took a minute for his conscious mind to catch up with his thudding heart. Lucy Plant, the first girl who disappeared. That was where he had heard the name before.

"Oh, hello. Yes, this is Cayce. Can I help you?"

"I'm sorry to be calling so late. But see, I just got a call myself from this woman, Janet McKenna? She said you talked to her today."

Oh God. Cayce wondered where this was leading. Was this Amy Plant about to chastise him? Tell him he was nuts? The spawn of Satan? She didn't sound upset. Her voice was calm, husky. It had a velvet quality that made Cayce feel at ease, even if he didn't have a clue why she was calling him.

"Yes, I did speak with her earlier. What's this all about?"

Amy Plant paused. There was silence for a moment or two. "She called to warn me about you. See, I'm Lucy Plant's mom. Our daughter disappeared a while ago."

"I know who you are. And I'm really sorry about your daughter. But why are you calling me? I'm sure I can't help you. Didn't Janet McKenna tell you that?"

"Janet McKenna, if you'll pardon the expression, sounds like a nutcase. I thought you might be able to help my husband and me. Lucy disappearing has just about destroyed him, and I'm ready to try anything that might help us find her."

"I don't know what I can do for you." It seemed the air was being sucked out of the kitchen. Cayce was having trouble breathing. *Please don't make me get into this. I never asked for it. I don't want it.*

"But Janet McKenna told me you've had some sort of psychic visions concerning her daughter."

"Yes." Cayce's stomach churned. "That's true. But I don't know that they really mean anything. I... I've been sick."

"Whether they mean anything or not doesn't matter so much to me. We have nothing to go on right now, nothing. And what you might know is better than that. It has to be."

A long silence followed. Cayce didn't know what to say. It seemed Amy Plant didn't either; Amy Plant was indeed waiting.

"I never said I knew anything about Lucy."

"I think you might. Do you?"

Cayce swallowed, breathed in deeply. He had no choice. He remembered lying in the hospital bed, Lucy Plant's face staring up at him from the front page of the paper. "Yes... I may have seen something. I don't know." Cayce rubbed his forehead, trying to force away a dull throbbing that was beginning just behind his eyes, trying to force away the vision of a crookedly whirring ceiling fan. Cayce couldn't account for the nausea and the dread this prosaic image evoked.

"Look, Cayce, I've heard of cases where psychics have been able to help find missing people. It happens enough that sometimes police departments use them in their searches."

Except the one here in Fawcettville. "I don't know if I'm psychic, Mrs. Plant." *But you do know... You do.* "What do you want from me?"

"Just to talk to you. To see if you can help. You're right, it may amount to nothing, but it's more of a shot than we have right now."

"I don't know."

"Please." Amy Plant's voice dropped to a whisper. Cayce could hear the pain in her voice. "Please. Don't make me beg." She went still for several moments, then said very quietly, "I don't have anywhere else to turn."

"Okay. I guess we can talk. But I can't promise you anything. When would be a good time?"

"Can you come over right now?"

"My little boy's in bed right now. I can't."

"How 'bout tomorrow? In the morning?"

"Yes. Tomorrow. In the morning." Cayce got Amy Plant's address and hung up the phone.

It would be a long, sleepless night. He stepped out onto the back porch, sat down on the stoop, and stared into the darkness.

Chapter Ten

The first thing Cayce noticed, as he headed down Ohio Street, was that the Plants weren't far from the McKennas. They lived in the same run-down neighborhood, referred to rather grandly as "Little England" because of some vague historical connection. Perhaps early settlers had first come here, building homes on the banks of the Ohio River and setting up the industrial potteries that had once given the area its prosperity, but that prosperity was now only a memory. Out of a couple dozen such enterprises in the tristate area—Ohio, Pennsylvania, and West Virginia—only three remained, a representative business for each of the three states. The area was the first to be flooded whenever the Ohio River got bloated because the small neighborhood was at, or maybe even below, river level.

The second thing Cayce noticed was that, though the Plants were obviously poor, they were not trashy like the McKennas. Their small white clapboard house was well maintained, with a close-cropped green lawn fronting it, its white-and-green trim impeccable. The windows were clean, the shrubbery trimmed, and the lawn edged.

Cayce pulled over to the curb in the front of the house, put his Fiesta in park, and sighed as it chugged down to a stop. The car had nearly 140,000 miles on it, and Cayce didn't know what he would do if it decided to become one of the dearly departed. Out of the corner of his eye, he saw a blonde-haired girl with long legs playing with Barbie dolls on the front lawn. The image was comforting, so normal, but as Cayce turned his head to get a better look, he discovered, with a jolt to his heart, there was no one on the lawn.

Lucy Plant. Cayce felt something sharp-edged and mean gnawing at the pit of his stomach. He briefly fingered his keys, still in the ignition, tempted to restart the car and pull away from the little well-kept house. He wouldn't have to look back. He owed the Plants nothing. Perhaps, he rationalized, his visions would only compound their grief, raising hopes where none should blossom and making even more of a mess of their lives.

But Cayce couldn't do that. He had never been the kind of person to shrink from helping anyone. He remembered briefly his years of trying to "help" Marc with his cocaine addiction and how long it had taken him to give up on a situation everyone he knew felt was hopeless. Cayce had been the only one who believed Marc's "this time will be the last" promises. Cayce put faith in Marc every time he dumped the straws, the screens, and the mirrors in the trash, tearfully telling Cayce he was through with the stuff *for good*. Marc had seemed so convincing, and perhaps he too hoped his resolve would be stronger than the last time.

Cayce shut out the memories, pulled the keys from the ignition, and stuffed them in the pocket of his cargo shorts. He took a few deep breaths, unsure how he should handle this new role. Glancing in the rearview mirror, he pushed the hair on his forehead around, arranging it so he was sure it hid the shiny red scar. He shook his head. The guy staring back at him seemed older. The signs of age—hollow cheeks, a flatness in his green eyes, and even how his lips turned down—were all recent developments.

Someone peered out quickly from behind a curtain as Cayce walked up the front sidewalk. This, Cayce was sure, was no illusion.

He knocked and swore he could hear footsteps and then a staccato burst of urgent whispering. Again, Cayce had the urge to turn and run back to the safety of his car. But empathy for other parents' suffering caused him to remain rooted to the spot on the concrete front stoop.

Amy Plant answered Cayce's knock. She was a big, raw-boned woman with thick dark-blonde hair. Her eyes were wide spaced and large, so pale blue they were almost startling. Her teeth were slightly crooked, and her lips were thick. There was something solid about her that was immediately reassuring to Cayce.

"Cayce?" Amy's voice had a velvet quality, deep for a woman but soft enough to make Cayce lean slightly forward to make sure he heard her.

"Hi. You must be Amy. We spoke on the phone."

Amy Plant swallowed, and the way her eyes darted around told him she was nervous. Cayce wished again he hadn't come, wished again he hadn't been drawn reluctantly into this vortex of murderous insight.

But...maybe he could help.

Amy stepped back, gripping the brass doorknob tightly enough, Cayce noticed, to whiten her knuckles. "Come on in," she said hoarsely. "I really appreciate you coming by."

Cayce walked into the almost blinding darkness of the little house. It took his eyes a couple of minutes to adjust to the dimness after the brightness of the September day outside.

"Sorry about the dark. Kevin likes it that way. Or he has, anyway...ever since Lucy, um, went away." Cayce followed Amy into a small living room done in shades of brown and gold, maple wood, and "country" touches on the wall, like straw wreaths with hand-painted wooden geese figures on them. There was a fireplace along one wall, and Cayce saw that it wasn't a working one. Someone had placed an arrangement of pillar candles in the hearth.

Cayce perched on the edge of a brown vinyl recliner, and the two said nothing for a minute. Cayce looked around at the knickknacks on the occasional tables, Precious Moments figurines, ceramic testaments to times gone by. There were schoolgirls dressed in long dresses, little boys on tractors, an old-time country church. He noticed the framed school pictures on top of the console TV. A towheaded boy in one, a preteen boy with darker hair in a second, and a freckled girl with long blonde hair in another. *Lucy, oh Lucy!* In between these, there was a family portrait taken years ago, when the children were still small. Amy sat proudly with her three children, husband behind her. Kevin was smaller than his wife, chubby, with thinning blond hair but a nice smile. Cayce felt something stir within him, a recognition of people who lived for their kids.

"That's Kevin and the kids," Amy said, noticing Cayce's gaze. "That was taken a few years ago." Amy stopped for a moment, looking away. "He's nuts about those kids." She pulled back the curtains covering the picture window to peer outside. "So am I," she said softly, voice breaking, speaking more to the glass than to him.

She finally turned back and went to the photo of Lucy on the TV. She held it out to Cayce. "This is our Lucy." Cayce didn't want to take the photo, was afraid of what touching it might inspire, what visions and terrors, but he had no choice.

The brass-framed photo sent a jolt through him. Cayce felt an almost electric surge, and it made him sit back suddenly. His hand jerked, and he dropped the photo on the floor, cracking its glass. Lucy's face appeared, for just an instant, in his mind's eye, ashen, milky open eyes staring up at nothing, a contorted mouth in a final scream or perhaps gasping for air. And then a shovelful of dirt obscured the image.

"Oh, I'm sorry." Cayce stooped to pick up the photo. "Look... I broke it. I'll buy you a new frame."

Amy knelt beside him. "It's okay. The picture still looks fine." Amy set the photo back on the TV. A large diagonal crack ran across Lucy Plant's smiling face.

Cayce's heart was thudding, and he was afraid that, in a moment, he would find it hard to breathe. "Do you think I could have a glass of water?"

"Sure thing." Amy hurried out of the room, and Cayce heard her in the kitchen, running water from the tap. He took a few deep breaths. What was he going to say to these people?

When Amy came back with the water, she grinned sheepishly. "Sorry, we're all out of ice. But I ran it for a while to get it nice and cold." She sat across from Cayce while he drank, staring at her hands.

Cayce took a while, drinking the water slowly, trying not to think, staving off the inevitable. He didn't want to discuss Lucy, didn't want to tell this kind woman he thought her daughter had been killed, that her last moments were filled with terror and pain. Why had he been chosen to bring this message?

"Do you work, Mrs. Plant?"

Amy looked up and smiled. "Please. Mrs. Plant's my mom. Call me Amy."

"Okay, Amy."

"Fawcettville Ceramics. Down the river a bit?"

"Oh yeah, I know it. One of my girlfriends used to work there, in the color room. She was a dipper. Do you know what that is? She would dip the ware in different colors before it was fired…"

"I know what it is. I work there, remember?"

Cayce laughed. "Stupid of me. What do you do there?"

"Caster. I work with the liquid clay. We call it slip. I fill the molds, time it, and out comes a piece of pottery. A jug or a decanter. Vases. Stuff like that." Amy stretched. "Been there fifteen years, ever since I graduated high school. I was one of the first girls in the job. How 'bout you?"

"The Elite Diner. Waiter." Cayce smiled. "It pays the bills. Barely."

"Great fries."

The two fell silent, neither looking at the other. Cayce went back to studying Amy Plant's knickknack collection, and Amy to the study of her careworn hands. Making conversation when Lucy Plant was out there somewhere, missing, bordered on insanity. But Cayce needed Amy to bring up the subject of her daughter first. If he did so, it seemed too cruel, almost as if he was eager to deliver his hopeless intuition.

"Would you like to meet Kevin?" Amy said finally.

Cayce was surprised; he had just assumed Amy's husband was at work. "Sure. If you think he's, um, up to it." Cayce looked around. "Where is he?"

"Upstairs."

Kevin Plant was no longer the man in the Sears family portrait downstairs. Gone were the laugh lines around his eyes, the alertness in those dark brown irises. Kevin Plant lay in bed, skin so sallow it almost blended in with the cream pillow supporting his sagging head. He stared at a TV set on a stand in a corner of the room, its volume so low it was barely audible. When Amy and Cayce entered the bedroom, his eyes registered only the barest flicker.

How was this man managing to get by? How were the brothers Lucy had left behind coping?

Amy knelt beside the bed and took one of her husband's hands in her own. "Cold." She rubbed his hand, then spoke in a louder voice. "Honey, this is Cayce D'Amico. He's stopped by to visit. Don't you want to say hello?"

Kevin moved his head slowly to Cayce, who stood in the doorway, shifting his weight from one foot to the other. It was as if the man saw him for the first time. He lifted colorless lips in a glimmer of a smile, then resumed staring at the TV screen.

Amy looked helplessly at Cayce. "Kevin's taken this really hard."

"I understand." *Oh God, why do I have to bear witness to this*? Cayce moved a little farther into the room. "Hello, Kevin." Cayce didn't know what to do with himself.

But Kevin wasn't speaking. Whatever was on the flickering TV screen required all of his attention.

"I should be going," Cayce said in a barely audible voice. There was just too *much* here: too much despair, too much hopelessness, too much loss, too much pain. He didn't know if he could bear it for another minute. He turned and hurried down the blue-carpeted stairs.

Outside, he stood gasping, wanting to cry, wanting to bring Lucy back to the Plants, whole and smiling, the victim of some youthful misunderstanding. But even though he had no provable evidence to back it up, he was certain such a homecoming was no longer a possibility.

He was about to dash for the safety of his car when the door opened behind him. He felt Amy Plant standing in the doorway, eyes pleading.

"You know something. I've heard about people like you. Psychics. I've seen on TV where they've helped people find...lost...loved ones."

Cayce turned to look at her, took in her reddened face and moist eyes.

"I don't know."

"I think you do."

Cayce walked back toward the house, feeling pulled by a force beyond his control. He stood in front of Amy Plant, staring down at the sidewalk, where a horde of ants busied itself with the sticky residue on a discarded Popsicle stick. He breathed in, raised his eyes to the woman, and tried to rally himself. He just let the words tumble out.

"She's somewhere down by the river. When I see her, the bridge to West Virginia is in the background, due south I would guess."

Amy took one of Cayce's hands in her own, squeezing so tight it hurt. But Cayce did nothing to withdraw his hand from her grasp.

"Will you help me look for her?" Her eyes were wet, and Cayce knew she had nowhere else to turn.

Cayce tried to swallow, but there was no spit in his mouth. He wanted to give Amy's shoulder a sympathetic squeeze and then turn and run. He wanted to say no, this wasn't his business.

But what he said was, "Of course."

Chapter Eleven

Cayce stared out the window of Amy Plant's car, a late-model American. Maybe a Ford Taurus? Cayce didn't know cars. The radio played softly, tuned to one of those "smooth jazz" stations out of Pittsburgh. Dulled brass instruments tried, without much success, to bring to life Duke Ellington's "Take the A Train." The piece was an abomination, Cayce thought, something that would have the late Duke spinning in his grave.

Cayce wanted to think of anything but the woman beside him. The two had not spoken since he had gotten in the car. Cayce had gone home from the Plants' long enough to greet Luke when he came home from school and to give him a quick supper of what he called white trash pasta—Kraft Macaroni & Cheese blended with a can of tuna and a box of frozen peas—and chocolate milk. Cayce's stomach had not allowed him to eat anything. He downed a cup of black coffee for fortification, but all the caffeine did was up the jangling of his nerves. After Luke had finished eating, Cayce had taken him over to his parents'.

*

The moon was full, a big silver orb setting on the hills towering above the Ohio River. Its pale light gave everything a silver glow, and Cayce was grateful. At least they would be able to see as they searched. Gratitude, however, might quickly be usurped by horror, if Cayce's intuition about Lucy Plant was right.

But Cayce didn't want to think about that. In fact, Cayce didn't want to think about anything. He continued to stare out the window, trying to keep the visions that danced just below consciousness at bay. Visions of a small pale hand on a background of rich black river soil, the pink nails besmirched with grime.

Amy pointed the car toward the river. "This way, right?" Her voice came out just above a whisper, shaky.

"Right." Cayce tried to think of Luke and other, more conventional, worries. The Ohio River curved along the town of Fawcettville, and even though Luke had been warned, over and over, to keep away from its muddy banks, Cayce was certain his admonitions wouldn't keep him away. Parental warnings had failed to blind generations of boys, including Cayce, to the river's allure. As a child, he had explored its banks, searching for discarded treasure among the rusting metal cans, abandoned tires, and other detritus that the river expelled, even wading into its brackish waters when the weather turned hot. And he was still here.

And yet Cayce couldn't calm himself with thoughts of his own survival. Almost every summer, the river claimed another life, usually a young boy who ventured out into the water and found himself flailing against the strong currents away from the shore, currents that carried him toward an unexpected yet certain oblivion. And there were always the older women whose husbands had vanished, either through death or desertion, who would wash up, free from loss...free from everything.

Such cheerful thoughts! Cayce reprimanded himself.

And then thought of the alternative. *Lucy. Will we find you tonight?*

Amy steered the car down a bumpy road filled with potholes and headed toward the river. In the distance, cooling towers from Fawcettville Power, one of the nation's first nuclear power plants, rose up against the night sky, tiny lights on the towers blinking in the darkness. The towers, sentinels against the silvery night, gave an almost surreal feel to their venture. Wafts of steam came off the tops of the two towers, to be snatched up by the wind. Cayce thought of how a girl back in grade school had thought the towers manufactured clouds. He wished he could be back there among such innocent thoughts.

"This the right way?" she asked. Her mouth was set in a line, her stare intent on the bouncing twin lights illuminating the road in front of them.

"Yeah, this is what I've, um, seen. See the New Hope Bridge? It's south of here. Just like in..." Cayce's voice trailed off. Just like in what? His dreams? His visions? It all sounded so full of hocus-pocus. He cleared his throat and simply said, "I think this is the right way."

The road grew narrower, bumpier, and dustier as they neared the water's edge, until finally it petered out altogether. Ahead of them lay a large, grassy field and beyond that a copse of trees, already beginning to shed their leaves with the approach of cooler weather.

Amy switched off the ignition. Cayce didn't need to look at her to know her large blue eyes were pleading with him to shoulder the burden, to lift from her this cloak of doubt and anguish, even if it meant getting the worst possible answer to her questions.

Amy swallowed hard. Cayce knew what she was thinking: if Lucy was in this field, there was no way they would find her safe.

Cayce longed for some optimistic words to give the woman, some reassurance. He hoped to find Lucy Plant cold and shivering, hiding behind some trees, a runaway too scared of parental wrath to come home but grateful to fall into the arms of her mother.

Even with the windows rolled up, Cayce got a sudden whiff of dark earth, its smell telling a tale of something recently buried. There, he knew, near the water's churning edge, where the soil would be easy to dig. That's where they would find Lucy.

And finding Lucy that way, Cayce thought with horror, was the last thing he wanted tonight.

He wanted to be wrong.

Wordlessly, the two got out. The air had a slight chill.

"It's going to be okay," Amy said, her shaky voice belying her words. "It's going to be okay, isn't it?"

Cayce said nothing as the two of them stepped over a chain that supposedly barred anyone from entering the field.

The ground beneath them squished with each step they took, and as they progressed, their feet sank deeper into the mud, sometimes causing them to have to pull their feet out with a loud sucking noise. An odor of fish wafted up from the river.

"She's not here," Cayce said. "This is pointless. You should be home...in case the police call, in case Kevin needs something."

"Is that what you really think?" Amy stopped and regarded Cayce, her blonde hair lifted by a gust that smelled of something rotten. "If that's what you really think, let's go back to the car."

Cayce swallowed hard. For a long time, he stared out at the black water, its surface splashed with the silver of the moon. It would be so easy to just go back to the car. Wouldn't it? He could return—guilt-wracked but ignorant—pick up Luke, take him to their own little home, put him to bed, drink some wine, and try to put this behind him. *Yes...that would be so easy. So simple.* He turned back to Amy. "No." He sucked in some air, exhaling slowly. "Give me a second."

Cayce had never tried to make a vision come before. The visions themselves were unwanted, intruders to his psyche that he would have excised from his brain if given half a chance. Gladly. But he wanted to help, even if that meant ending this family's suffering by replacing it with a new grief. At least there would be the comfort, if he could call it that, of knowing. He closed his eyes, breathing in the cool, damp air, and made himself go limp, opening himself up, in a way, to whatever his newly found vision might bring.

For a while—nothing. Just random thoughts, then a hope and a dread that this bizarre gift had departed as mysteriously as it had come.

And then a flash, a wash of red, dark like blood, across the inside of his eyelids. "Near the water," Cayce whispered. "She's near the water." He didn't open his eyes, not wanting to see the pain on Amy Plant's face and wanting to be more certain of where they might find... something. He saw himself walking closer to the pebbled, sandy shore, a place where the grassy surface of the field dropped off to meet a littered beach. In his mind, he made himself look up, peering across the dark water to the opposite shore, West Virginia.

And across the shore was a house, its yellow lights like a beacon in the darkness. The moon gave just enough light to supply details: a one-story ranch constructed of light brick. Run down. The drainpipe broken and falling off the side of the roof. There was a doghouse, and outside it, a mutt was chained. Dark, big, with pointed ears. A shepherd mix.

Cayce attuned his senses, and far off but still close enough, he heard the barking of a dog. Its bass woofs were barely audible and coming from somewhere downriver.

He took Amy Plant's cold, callused hand in his own. "This way." Cayce led her along the shoreline.

It wasn't long before they came to what he had envisioned. The brick ranch was the only house occupying this part of the West Virginia shore. The barking of the dog had led them ever closer, almost as if the animal were a guide. Cayce stopped and looked at Amy then, her eyes bright with tears in the darkness. He didn't need to say anything.

Before them, the grass had been trampled.

They trudged forward, on through the darkness and the damp, silent. Cayce stumbled and fell. He grunted as the fall knocked the wind out of him. "What the hell?" he groaned when he had found enough breath to put behind his words.

But he knew. He knew.

The two looked down to see a mound of fresh dirt. Some tin cans had been pulled over it, along with some drying weeds, but the dirt looked freshly dug. Nothing could hide that. All around them, weeds and various grasses grew unchecked. But there was this spot, a rough rectangle in shape, about as long as Cayce was tall.

Cayce dropped to his knees in the mud and began digging.

Amy grabbed his shoulder, her nails painful. "Maybe we should go back and get the cops."

"I can't!" Cayce cried. "I can't wait that long. I have to know." He threw up clumps of wet dirt behind him as his hands plowed deeper and deeper.

Amy couldn't wait either. She fell to her knees next to him and began to dig.

They dug for about a half hour before Cayce's hand hit on something. He recoiled, wanting to vomit, yanking his muddy hand back from what he had just touched.

It felt like cold flesh.

"Amy, stop."

Amy pulled her hands out of the dirt. Cayce turned to her, his lower lip quivering, breathing hard.

"What is it?"

"I hit something."

"What?"

"I don't know," Cayce said, lying. He knew all too well what he had felt: flesh and bone. "You're right, let's go call the cops. I think we need to."

"I won't stop. I can't." Amy buried her hands in the earth once more, near Cayce's. He knew what she would find and didn't want her to experience the icy touch he had just felt. He pushed her away, hard. Turning from her, he dug some more. Maybe what he had felt wasn't really human flesh...

Only seconds passed before he stopped as if stunned and let out a scream.

"It felt like hair! It felt like hair!" He closed his eyes, trying to hold down the acid bile rising up to splash against the back of his throat.

Amy was behind him, wheezing, gasping. He thought it would be only moments before she began to wail. He bent over and dug more.

The moon appeared from behind a cloud and revealed a silvery whiteness in the dirt.

It was a human hand. A small heart-shaped ring glinted on the third finger.

Amy whispered, "It's Lucy."

Cayce brushed away more dirt. Long blonde hair emerged and a face that made him turn, finally, and retch into the weeds.

The face of a young girl, decomposing and half eaten, stared up from sockets devoid of eyes. Lucy Plant. Even though insects and decomposition horribly disfigured the face, Cayce would have recognized the blonde hair anywhere. He remembered, with a jolt, Lucy's school photograph: a smiling young girl on the brink of womanhood with the same long blonde hair. Hair that was now streaked with mud.

Cayce turned his head. He reached out to touch Lucy's cheek, looking blue-white even in the darkness, already mottled with mold. He snatched back his hand, biting his lower lip so hard he tasted blood. "Oh God, why?"

Chapter Twelve

There was little Dave could do to escape this shithole of a town. Fawcettville, Pennsylvania. God, in his wildest of wild dreams—and he'd had more than his share of those— he'd never thought he'd find himself in such a place. Foothills of the Appalachians. A little town, population 15,000, clinging desperately to the banks of the Ohio River and an economy, once buoyed up by steel mills and industrial potteries, in rapid decline. The people downriver a bit were called hoopies, with vague origins in the Mingo Indian language, Indians who had once occupied this fertile land, now home to nothing more than the smell of decay and better times gone before. *How in the hell?*

Oh, he knew. He knew all right. It was a man, always a man who led him astray. When would Dave Newton ever learn he was better off alone?

Ten years ago he came to Fawcettville, hot on the scent of another handsome man, full of promise, with a side serving of disappointment. Dave had been happy then, back in the West Midlands of England. It was there he had met the guy who would change his life.

Wasn't it funny how a chance encounter in the woods surrounding Cannock Chase could alter the course of one's life forever, irreparably? Dave tried to remember some short story he had read once, by Ray Bradbury maybe, in which someone had stepped on and killed a butterfly—and that tiny action had somehow changed the course of history.

Meeting Jack had been like that. Jack with his fair hair and blue eyes so pale they startled, daring you to look away. He had been backpacking his way through Europe that summer, after graduating from university. He had a body stolen straight from Joe Gage porn, but he was a pure mind, an untainted spirit. Jack had lost his way on Cannock Chase, a large, unspoiled area of trees, meadows, and creeks, the whole of it covered in pale purple heather. It had been the perfect meeting, like something out of a Jane Austen novel, updated for the twenty-first century. Dave had gone there to be alone to write in his journal. Back then, he had dreamed of being a great novelist, someone whose words would change the world.

Once he met Jack, though, in his jeans and crisp white T-shirt, it was all over for Dave. At thirty, the anarchist and cynic had fallen hopelessly in love. All the silly love songs he had poked fun at took on resonance. Fucking morphed into making love. Two weeks was all it took. Two weeks of traipsing around his little island of a country, showing Jack everything from Stonehenge to the Glastonbury Tor, to the Roman baths in Bath, to the pebbled beaches of Brighton, to the houses of Parliament and the bright lights of the West End of London.

Ten years ago, it had taken only two weeks for Dave to find himself on a British Airways plane, bound for New York City, then Pittsburgh, then riding next to Jack in a beat-to-shit Nissan Sentra to Fawcettville.

It took only ten months for Jack to disappear. His vanishing mysteriously coincided with the appearance of Dave's love of mind-altering substances, the most innocent of which was single malt Scotch and the most nefarious of which was crystal methamphetamine, which could keep him going for days. Jack never understood why Dave couldn't sleep—and why he no longer had any interest in making love.

And so Jack had not exactly vanished but had run back to parents in Warren, Ohio, leaving Dave alone, an alien with no funds to get home and an appetite for destruction.

Dave fell back on his blessing and his curse—his power with words—and found himself living in the sad little burg with neither the resources nor the energy to escape. Over several varieties of malt in a local bar one hazy, half remembered night, Dave had "interviewed" with the editor of the *Fawcettville Review*, Fawcettville's only newspaper. Sean Green and Dave Newton found reciprocal needs in each other. Sean Green needed a reporter. Dave needed a job.

Thus his journalistic career was born. Intending at first only to make enough money to get back to England, Dave, at least in the first few years, never achieved his goal. The funds went up his nose, down his throat, up in smoke.

As he grew older, the substances lost some of their allure, and Dave was able, with no small amount of difficult starts and stops, to put them behind him. By then, he was yet another player in this fucked-up postmodern version of Sherwood Anderson's *Winesburg, Ohio*. He became another character on the periphery and a byline people recognized. He was a familiar face at domestic disturbances, courtrooms, and jail cells. Dave Newton became a resident of Fawcettville and eventually a citizen of a country he had never even intended to visit.

Was Dave settled? Was Dave happy? In a word, no. But the pull of life's orbit was too strong for him to resist, and like so many going-gray-at-the-temples, middle-aged men, he had lost the route out of a life that only chance, and certainly not he, had chosen.

So on nights like this one, Dave sought oblivion. Gone were the jangling highs of crystal meth, but the Scotch had hung around, an old amber lover, warm at night though ruthless in the morning, eating away at Dave's liver but rescuing him from having to think too hard about the mess he had made of his life—a life spent alone in a shabby one-bedroom apartment in Fawcettville's in-critical-condition downtown, where the downstairs neighbors were an interchangeable family of hoopies from down the river in West Virginia.

He had his music too. Dave favored bands of his youth: the Ramones, the Kinks, Cockney Rebel, early Bowie. He could down half a fifth, listen to the music at ear-splitting volume, and fall asleep with all the lights on, thinking this life wasn't so bad after all.

Until the next morning.

He was about to fall into just such a stupor when his phone rang. Dave sat up, heart pounding for all it was worth. The music had ceased about an hour ago, and the phone was like an alarm. "Bloody fuck," he whispered, rubbing his salt-and-pepper hair with one hand and reaching for his cell with the other.

"'Lo?" Why hadn't he just powered the damned thing off when he'd come home?

Because Dave, in spite of it all, was an eternal optimist, and every time that telephone sounded, it just might be good news, a savior come to call, to whisk him away from a life he certainly had no control over anymore and that he had no means to escape.

It was Sean Green on the other end, former drinking buddy, editor, only friend, and pain in the ass.

Dave lit a Marlboro and looked at the blue display on his DVD player. A little after eleven. The call couldn't be good news. Not at this hour. Green had found himself a wife somewhere along the way, and the days of hours-long drunken late night calls were long past.

"Dave. You awake, buddy?"

Once Dave would have bristled at being called anyone's "buddy." Now he scarcely gave it a second thought. "Barely. This better be good."

Sean sucked in some air, making a noise that sounded half between a gasp and a chuckle. *What the hell?* "It is good, at least in the way you mean it. But it's bad, bad news."

"Listening to your police scanner again?"

"Right." There was a long pause then. Dave's stomach lurched. He knew something bad was about to be said. Something really awful.

"You know how you've been writing about those missing girls?"

"Yeah, yeah." *Oh shit, no...*

"Well, they found one of them. Down by the river. Lucy Plant. I think you need to get down there."

Dave saw the photo of the little blonde girl in his mind's eye—sweet, uncorrupted—and shook his head, drawing in deeply on his cigarette. "Christ, no. She's dead, right?"

"Afraid so."

Dave was amazed at how quickly trauma and despair could clear his head. "Murdered?"

"Looks that way, Dave. Listen, go down, get the details, write it up. I'll hold tomorrow's edition until you get the story in. Think you can turn it around in a couple of hours? You up for a big byline?"

"Don't try to tempt me with fame, mate. It's too late for that. I'll get my skinny ass down there, but for the girl's sake, not mine."

"Whatever. This is front page, and once it hits, you're going to be elbowing for a place at the table with the big boys from Pittsburgh and the like."

"Right. I'm on my way." A cold shower and a clean set of clothes, assembled in less than ten minutes, would transform him from lush to ace reporter. At least that was the ruse he had pulled on himself for the past decade. "Who found her?"

Another pause. "The girl's mom."

"Christ."

"And an unidentified man. Don't have all the details. But I want you to find out."

"I'm off, then." Dave hung up the phone, stubbed out his cigarette, and headed for the bathroom.

*

The night had turned cold. Cayce wrapped his arms around himself, thinking the chill creeping into his bones was so much more than meteorological. It seemed that no matter how much he hugged himself, he could find no warmth. Amy Plant stood near, face gone blank, ashen in the moon's silver light. After trying to offer some useless words of comfort to the woman, he had given up. Lucy Plant's mother had turned to stone. No tears. No furrowing of the eyebrows. No screaming to the heavens. Nothing. Amy Plant's zombielike demeanor was more disturbing than any expression of grief could have been.

Cayce wished there was something he could do. He tried to hug her; it was like hugging a statue. He did all he could think of, wrapping his denim jacket around her shoulders. It was too big for her, but Cayce knew a little about shock and knew that a person headed into that numb condition needed warmth. He had given her all he possibly could.

Cayce shivered and wondered what more he could do. He could admit only to himself that a part of him wanted to give Amy a hug, stare into her eyes, and tell her he would find a way home on his own. The police and the medical examiner would be there soon. Amy would be in capable hands. Cayce, even though he knew it wasn't true, rational, or logical, felt like kicking himself for bringing this poor young mother this pain.

But he was a young father, and somewhere Luke waited. He longed to hold his little boy in his arms, to feel his solid, small warmth, the reassurance of his soapy-smelling hair and the satin of his skin, still like a baby's. He wanted to bury his nose in Luke's hair, make him uncomfortable by holding him too tightly, and revel in the reality that *his* child was still there. *His* child was alive.

Was that selfish? Awful? Cayce wondered if any parent, thrown into such a bizarre, horrifying situation, wouldn't have exactly the same desire.

Cayce wished he had never been the instrument that led this shell-shocked mom to the body of her daughter, a sight no woman should ever have to endure. Why did Cayce have to be a part of it? Did God pick him? Curse him? Or did some other dark power force this new "gift" upon him? Sure, at the very least, this gruesome discovery had put an end to one family's questions about their missing child. Yet it also put an end to hope and marked a beginning of a grief that would remain with them throughout their lives.

The police arrived. Squawking mechanical voices and rumbling engines filled the chill of the night. Whirling blue lights and strobes of white gave a surreal, carnival feel to their discovery.

Lucy Plant's murder no longer dwelled in the realm of the private; it was rapidly becoming public domain. The thought made Cayce sick. He realized why the police needed to be there. They were beginning the relentless hunt for clues that would lead them to the person or people who had done this terrible thing. And with that thought, a vision of a platinum-haired woman, her face obscured by the red-blinking light and bulk of a video camera, came chillingly into focus.

Would Cayce, in the supermarket, on a walk downtown, or on his way to work, recognize the people who had done this to Lucy Plant? And if he did, would anyone believe him when he tried to convince them of their guilt? Would any court accept his visions as evidence?

Cayce knew the answer to those questions. He stared out at the shiny blackness of the Ohio River. What good was having this gift if no one believed him?

He turned back to where the assembled officials were setting up spotlights, impossibly bright. They were cordoning off the area where the body had been discovered with yellow crime scene tape. They would invade Lucy Plant, lying lifeless and white, with tape measures, camera flashes, and the stares of the grimly fascinated and the concerned.

Why, Cayce thought, stomach churning, the scene had turned almost festive.

But what other choice was there? Let the killers go free? And Cayce knew, somehow, that there were killers in the plural: two, not one, a man and a woman. He knew it as surely as he knew his own name.

Cayce watched as an older woman with gunmetal gray hair, a man's trench coat, and the orange glow of a cigarette's tip in her fingers, made her way through the uniformed police and others gathered on the scene. The woman looked familiar. It didn't take Cayce long to realize who she was. And once Cayce remembered she was the detective he'd tried to convince that he knew something about the then-missing girl's disappearance, the woman's name came back to him: JT Simmons.

Oh, JT Simmons, will you believe me now?

Why didn't you listen when I came to you before? Why couldn't you open your mind to all the possibilities?

Cayce shrugged. What difference would it have made? When he spoke to Simmons, it had already been too late. But still...the detective could have listened with less of a scornful look in her eye, with less ridicule brimming at her lips.

Cayce slipped farther back into the shadows, closer to the dark river, watching as JT Simmons made her rounds, speaking to a uniformed cop here, a black-suited man there, gathering the concrete information she needed to solve this atrocity. No whims or ethereal visions for her. Cayce could see that much just watching. There was nothing tentative in the woman's demeanor. JT Simmons, it was clear through even cursory observation, was hard, all business. Cayce should have known the moment he first encountered her that JT Simmons would never be the kind of woman who would put any stock in the pronouncements of *psychics*.

Just thinking the word made Cayce's stomach leap. *Psychic.* Was that what he was now? Was that how he would become known? Instead of the gay single father, as he was known around town, would he now be labeled the town seer? And if he was psychic, why hadn't he known that a trip to the police station would be fruitless, a mission destined to fail?

Why didn't he know, if he had second sight, what he should do now to make things better?

They would want to talk to him. JT Simmons, others. Hell, they might even suspect him. He could imagine what they'd ask.

"And how did you know exactly where to find the body, Mr. D'Amico?"

"Can you account for your whereabouts when Lucy Plant disappeared?"

"Is there someone who can verify those whereabouts at the time of the girl's disappearance?"

"Maybe you should come along with us."

"You have the right to remain silent."

Perhaps remaining silent would have been his best course of action.

Cayce shook his head, feeling sicker with each passing moment. Why, why, why had he been so *blessed*?

Before he could ponder these fears and questions further, he felt a hand on his elbow. Cayce jumped.

"Cayce D'Amico? I'm sorry to bother you. Remember me? Dave Newton, with the *Review*? We met before; we had coffee. Do you think I might have a word?"

Both Cayce and Amy turned at the same moment. There stood Dave Newton, shifting his weight from one foot to the other and looking as though he couldn't decide whether to offer them a brave smile or solemnity. His dark eyes, behind round wire-framed lenses, were bright—and trained on Cayce. He couldn't help but feel drawn to this man. It was more than just his looks, although they brought the word "fine" to new levels, but an undercurrent of caring Cayce could feel deep within his bones.

Cayce didn't know what to say. He hadn't thought yet of the press, of their interest in such a gruesome and sensational story. Of course they would want to talk to him. Talk to the grieving mother...so the rest of the world could rest easy. *At least it wasn't us...this time.*

Amy Plant said nothing. There was a calming fascination for her, it seemed to Cayce, in staring at the dark, churning waters of the Ohio River. He touched her arm gently, and she looked up at him as though she didn't recognize him. It took a second for some understanding to show in her eyes.

Cayce leaned in, whispering, "You don't have to talk to him. Why don't you go wait in the car?"

He watched as Amy Plant made her way to the car, stumbling once. This night, Cayce thought, was really a nightmare that would never end for her. He turned back to Dave. "Of course I remember you."

Dave waited expectantly, digital camera bag at his hip, mini tape recorder in his hand. Cayce didn't like to think of Dave Newton as the press, as a vulture, really, preying on the unfortunate to sell a few papers. Instinctively, he felt there was more to this guy.

"Do you think we could talk? Could you tell me about what happened?" Dave asked.

"I don't know." Cayce looked away, toward the crime scene techs, trying to make some sense out of a situation about which there could never be any logic or reason. Talk to the press? He wasn't prepared. Again, he wondered why his second sight didn't ready him for such things, why the gift—*curse*—was so selective in what it did or did not reveal.

If he told Dave Newton his story, what he had witnessed, it would put him and his name on page one tomorrow. He didn't need ESP to know that giving Dave Newton even a bit of his story might thrust him into an unwelcome scrutiny. The public was hungry for such peculiarities, especially when those peculiarities had something to do with something as exciting as murder.

But if he didn't talk to Dave Newton, the reporter might go after Amy Plant, and one thing that woman did *not* need right now was the prying of reporters.

And then a chilling thought came to Cayce. So chilling, in fact, it was literal, feeling like a cold breeze on his skin. Two of the public reading a story with his name in it would be the killers themselves, most likely. They would know who Cayce was and wonder how he knew so much. They would know where Cayce lived. Cayce gasped. They would know where *Luke* lived.

Cayce eyed Dave Newton. "You probably want to talk to the police...and there are plenty of them around. Why don't you go bother one of them?" Cayce turned away, hoping the reporter would do the same.

Of course, that wish was not granted. "Please," he heard from behind him. "You're the man who helped Mrs. Plant here find the body, aren't you?"

Wow. He's no slouch in the investigation department. How could he find out so much so fast? It was less than an hour ago that they had discovered Lucy's body. Amazing how quickly the discovery set things into motion.

The reporter waited, hands at his sides. "Look. You have no reason to believe me, but I'm not looking to sensationalize this. It's a job I have to do. I don't do it, someone else does. Maybe someone who isn't as ethical as I am. Maybe someone who's just looking for a story that will draw attention to themselves, rather than elicit sympathy or understanding for what's happened here."

"And you're someone I can trust, right?" Cayce wanted to believe; he really did.

Newton smiled. "I don't know about that. But I'm not some fame-hungry reporter, looking to make a name for himself no matter what. Could you talk to me, please?"

"Promise me one thing."

"What?"

"That...at least for now, you'll leave Amy Plant alone. She just lost her daughter."

There was silence, save for the whispering of the trees.

"Thank you, Cayce." Amy Plant had returned silently, and Cayce turned to see her standing behind him. Her voice had lost any confidence it once had. It was a watered-down version of its former self. "You don't have to look out for me."

Cayce put his hand on her shoulder, looked up to see the tears standing in her eyes. "Look, why don't you go talk to the police. I'll deal with Mr. Newton here."

He watched as the woman lumbered away toward the lights and activity. Years had been added to her gait in the span of an hour, and all Cayce could think was: *Don't look at Lucy again. Whatever you do, don't look at her again.*

Cayce turned back to Dave Newton tiredly. "What is it you want to know?"

Newton clicked the tape recorder on. "Tell me how you and Mrs. Plant happened to find the girl."

Cayce debated. He could walk away, but two things held him back. One, he wanted to help the investigation in any way he could. If getting what he knew out there could help lead police to the killers, he wanted to talk to the reporter. Two, he wanted to know this man better. So he reached out to turn the tape recorder off and said, "Do you have everything you need here?"

"What do you mean?"

"Gotten all the info you need from the cops? The scene?"

"I suppose."

"Then maybe you and I could go somewhere else, someplace private, where we could talk in peace." Cayce peered at him, knowing that the word *pleading* probably rose to the reporter's mind when he looked at Cayce's face.

"Sure. My car is over here."

*

They ended up driving only a few miles down the road. As they drove, Cayce noticed other cars and a van headed toward the crime scene. More media, already on their way. Cayce thought the description *vultures* was apt. He turned to Dave. "How did you get to be so lucky?"

"What do you mean?"

"You beat all the other reporters to the scene."

"My boss listens to his police scanner obsessively. And I have the advantage of being closest. These others have to come from places like Pittsburgh, Youngstown."

Cayce fell silent. The images from the night rose up to torment him, and as they crested the top of a hill overlooking the river, he said, more calmly than he felt, "Stop the car."

Again with a calmness whose origin he didn't question, he walked to the back of the car. He was heaving, and acid splashed the back of his throat, yet nothing came up. Once he thought things had settled, he closed his eyes and tried to take a few deep, calming breaths. When he opened them again, Dave Newton stood nearby, his face half-hidden in shadow.

"Are you all right?"

"Of course I'm not all right! What's wrong with you? I just helped dig up a dead little girl!" Cayce's final two words were mixed up with a sob. He pressed his fists against his eyes, trying to force the tears back in. He shook his head. "I'm sorry. I shouldn't have snapped like that."

"It's understandable," Dave said. He moved forward and, as naturally as though they had known one another for years, took Cayce in his arms, squeezing him tight. He moved his hand in a gentle circular motion on Cayce's back, saying nothing for a long while.

At last they pulled away. And Cayce felt he knew this man better, just from his touch. He also felt this wasn't some extrasensory perception on his part but simple intuition. You could gather a lot about a person from the way he reacted in a crisis, from the way he just instinctively knew to hug another lost soul when they needed it. There was something real, something genuine in the gesture.

Cayce also felt some things from when their bodies touched that may or may not have been psychic perception. He knew Dave Newton was not only gay but also lonely. There was something in the hug that felt just as eager to take comfort as it was to give it.

Cayce looked into Dave's eyes in the dark for only a moment and allowed himself to do something very impulsive—he leaned in and kissed him. The kiss was hungry, a sealing of lips and tongues, a desperate need to validate life in the presence of such horrific loss.

The kiss lasted until their eyes were pulled open and their bodies yanked apart by the sound of a car engine and flashing blue and red lights upon them.

Cayce squinted into the light, seeing a large woman emerge from the police car. It was JT Simmons. "Cayce D'Amico?"

"Yeah."

"I need you to come down to the station with me."

Chapter Thirteen

By the time Cayce returned to his little green-shingled house, the sky in the east was brightening with dull gray light. Fog shrouded his yard, transforming Luke's swing set into something dark and geometric: a sinister machine, its intended purpose vanished under the mist. It had been a night like no other, the darkness not just an absence of light but a feeling, a descriptor, a summing up of events that went beyond human comprehension.

He tried to simply keep his mind blank. His eyes burned. His limbs felt heavy, weighted down. But Cayce knew that too much had happened in the past several hours to allow his racing mind the oblivion of sleep. Going to bed right now would be an exercise in futility. It was the old conundrum of being too tired to sleep. He plopped down heavily on the back stoop, determined to watch the slowly rising sun, an orb of orange in a milky gray sky. It would work its magic on the fog, burning it away, bringing the day to life.

He didn't want to but couldn't help replaying the events of the previous night over and over, a Technicolor nightmare on endless loop. Starting with the horror of the discovery of Lucy Plant's body—the image he most wanted to banish from his mind—and ending with JT Simmons's cool, incredulous interrogation in her office at City Hall, the night was one he wished he could simply permanently excise from memory.

Save for that tiny oasis, that stolen kiss, with Dave Newton. *That* was like a gift from above.

*

Cayce remembered sitting in JT Simmons's office, Styrofoam cups of coffee on the scarred desk in front of them, a tape recorder bearing silent witness to their talk, the detective regarding Cayce with obvious disdain and suspicion. Cayce knew the look, the slightly down-turned mouth, the rheumy eyes staring with neither sympathy nor compassion.

Before they had even begun talking, Cayce felt intimidated. He wanted to banish any outward signs of fear, thinking those telltale gestures might make JT Simmons more suspicious than she already was. But he couldn't help broadcasting signs of his anxiety: crossing and uncrossing his arms, shifting restlessly in his chair, gaze darting everywhere but the detective's face. When he caught himself doing any of these things, he'd stop, staring out at the black night that pressed in against the detective's grimy window like something palpable.

"I didn't realize you and I would be meeting again so soon," Simmons said, lighting up a cigarette. "I know I'm not supposed to do this." She held the cigarette up. "But it's late. What are they gonna do? Arrest me?" She didn't smile, squinting through the smoke spiraling up in front of her craggy, bespectacled face. Cayce was, by turns, repulsed by the smell of the cigarette and wanting to ask Simmons if he could have one of the Marlboros lying in a box atop her desk.

"Yes. It was only a little while ago." Cayce looked around the office and thought how little of the personality of its occupant showed: bare white walls, a beige metal credenza with an empty top, a desk piled high with reports, a black telephone, a plain green cup filled with pencils, and nothing else. No photographs. No commendations. Not even a cheap framed print on the wall.

"Remind me about the content of our last discussion." The detective squinted at Cayce through a spiral of smoke.

Cayce stared at his shoes, noticing how muddy they were, beyond cleaning. Even though he couldn't afford it, he would have to get himself down to Walmart and buy himself a new pair. The only thing these shoes were now good for was the garbage. "I, uh, thought I might be able to help you with the disappearance of those girls."

"You mean the disappearance of Lucy Plant?"

"Yes." Cayce was about to add "And Sheryl McKenna" but then thought better of it. He glanced briefly at Simmons, who had leaned forward in her chair, regarding Cayce with undisguised distaste.

"Did you know Lucy Plant? Her family?"

"No, not until just recently."

Simmons nodded. "Just recently," she repeated. "And how did you come to make their acquaintance?"

Something small with razor-sharp teeth began to gnaw at Cayce's gut. What should he say? How could he make this woman, who it seemed had already made up her mind that Cayce was a nutcase or, worse, a murderer's accomplice, take him seriously? Cayce didn't know. He plunged forward. "Amy Plant, the girl's mom, got in touch with me. She'd heard I might know something about Lucy's disappearance, and she begged me to help. They were at their wit's end. They were willing to try anything to help them find out what had happened to Lucy." Cayce paused. "Even talking to me."

Simmons nodded slowly. "I see. You said that Amy Plant had heard you might know something. Where would she have heard something like that?"

So it would all come out. What did it matter? "I had talked to the McKennas. You know who they are. Their daughter, Sheryl, is missing. I wanted to tell them that I might be able to help them locate her. Might. I don't know. I just wanted to help." Cayce looked up at Simmons, meeting her eyes. "The McKennas told the Plants about me. Warned them, actually. They thought I was nuts—just like you do."

Simmons ignored the comment. "Just so I'm sure I understand: Mrs. Plant got in touch with you to see if she could find out what you thought you knew. Having such information might help her find her missing daughter."

"That's right."

"Refresh my memory. How would you happen to know where either of these girls had gone?"

"As I told you when I was in here before, I get visions, if you will. Kind of like waking dreams. Lately I've been seeing things about the girls. I don't know why. They just come to me."

"So, you're like a psychic."

"I don't know what I am. I was out looking for my son, Luke. I got hit on the head. A concussion, a little time in the hospital. When I came to, I seemed to know things." Cayce shrugged. "It sounds unbelievable, and I really wish it wasn't so, but that's the way things are. Maybe, if there's a God, he gave me a gift for a reason. I have to try to help. I can't keep these things to myself. Obviously there's some validity to what I see in my head. Don't you think?"

Simmons ignored the question. "And so you *saw* Lucy Plant's grave, down by the river? In your head?"

"Yes. Sort of. I knew something to do with her was down by the river. I knew where it was because I would see the house over in West Virginia and how close the bridge was to where she had been buried."

"And you never knew the girl before?"

"Never. I swear." Cayce felt a lump form in his throat but didn't want to give Simmons the satisfaction of seeing him cry.

*

The sun came up, burning the last wisps of fog off Cayce's damp lawn. Cayce leaned against the house, eyes closed. JT Simmons had told him he shouldn't leave town; the police would certainly want to talk again. Cayce thought that was funny. Where would he go? With what money?

Cayce rose on weighted legs and went inside. The kitchen looked like someone else's, its stack of newspapers on the kitchen counter, the little radio, the dishes in the sink and the sunflower place mats on his maple kitchen table all unfamiliar, as if he had stumbled into the house of a stranger.

And maybe he had. Who was Cayce D'Amico? Certainly no one *he* had ever met before.

Ah, he was just exhausted beyond reason, traumatized beyond belief. A little sleep, fetching Luke from his parents, getting him off to school, cleaning up the house, and going back to his routine at the diner would put things back to normal quickly enough.

Cayce wondered if normal was a territory to which he could ever return. He shook his head, wondering what the future would hold. Shouldn't he know that? Wasn't that what psychics could do? Read the future? Why was his so uncertain?

He got up and went inside. In the living room, Sheryl McKenna sat on the couch, waiting.

"Oh," Cayce mumbled, his hand rising to his mouth. Part of him wanted to turn and run from the house. But he didn't.

The girl, sitting cross-legged on his living room couch, was as real as the tan Berber carpeting beneath his feet. There was no ghostly aura surrounding her. She was just a girl, clad in jeans and a black tank top. Her black hair, straight, shone in the morning light. Filtering in through Cayce's miniblinds, the light made slats across the girl's face, which showed no reaction to Cayce's entrance to the room. Sheryl McKenna stared straight ahead with an intensity that made Cayce look to where the girl's gaze was focused. But there was nothing there save for the little cart upon which sat his TV, its screen rolling and static filled.

And then Cayce understood. This wasn't a psychic vision. Sheryl McKenna was alive. Cayce didn't understand why the girl would come to him or how she had gotten into his house, but this was no vision. The girl was as real as Cayce himself. Cayce was certain that if he sat beside her on the couch he would feel warmth emanating from her body. If he reached out with his hands, Cayce could feel the silk of her hair, the smoothness of her skin.

Sheryl stared at the flickering images on the TV screen. Cayce looked to where the girl had focused her gaze. The TV, which usually got pretty good reception, was snowy; little white lines rolled across its surface. It was like a blizzard and almost impossible to make out what was on the screen. Then he saw it: a view of the river. The camera looked down on the flowing muddy waters, as if the shot was taken from high up, on a hilltop. The camera moved back to reveal a few trees and...a trailer? With all the snow and static, it was hard to make it out, but there it was: a big rectangle. Even through the snow, Cayce saw that it was an old trailer, set up on concrete blocks.

The screen went black.

Cayce shook his head. The girl remained on his couch, as real as the quivering hand she held in front of her. She had to be real. Somehow, she had made it to Cayce's house...

But these thoughts were wiped out in an instant when Sheryl McKenna focused her dead gaze on Cayce and said simply, "Help me."

Cayce was left staring at an empty couch. There was no fading away. No puff of ethereal smoke. The girl was just there one moment, gone the next.

Cayce ran from the room, whimpering without realizing it, and headed straight for the bathroom. He felt as though he might throw up again, but managed to hold back. He splashed some cold water on his face and looked at his ashen countenance in the medicine cabinet mirror. A wraith stared back, thin, hollow eyed, frightened.

Cayce jumped as he heard the thud of the newspaper landing on his front porch. What would the morning edition bring? Would he be front page news? It seemed that even though he had never sought fame, it was suddenly seeking him.

Chapter Fourteen

Myra was awake first. She lay for a while, listening to Ian's even breathing and wondering what would happen next. She turned with all the stealth of a thief to look at him.

He looked the same as always. Handsome. His dark face stubbled with black whiskers. The eyelids appeared vulnerable, the thin flesh veined, the quick movements of his eyes underneath the skin apparent. What was he seeing? What grim horrors? Was he dreaming of murder? Suffocation? Watery, moist earth that gave easily under the shovel, digging a shallow grave to bury what he called a sacrifice, hiding the corpse of a girl not much younger than herself? Is that what he was seeing?

And in his dreams, did he justify his killing with the regimentation of a bizarre religion to which only the two of them belonged? Or were his dreams more honest?

Myra turned away from the gorgeous face, the hairy, muscular chest, and stared at the opposite wall, covered in cheap paneling. Was Ian really obsessed with making sacrifices to some "beast," some "devil"? Did he really believe that making these sacrifices would help them find some sort of power, or peace, or wealth?

Or—and she had to be honest here, alone in the wan light of the morning filtering in through vinyl miniblinds—did Ian really have a taste, rooted in sex, for snuffing out the lives of young girls?

She recalled how wound up he was after each killing. How the blood pumped into his penis, making it stiff and almost insatiable. She thought of how the only response to his lust after killing was dumb acquiescence. To say no would not be tolerated.

And so she would let him do what he needed to do. Violate her right there on the floor beside the body on the bed. Push into her before she was ready and expel himself into her before she even began to feel the queasy satisfaction of his so-called lovemaking. It was ugly.

Myra sat up, gooseflesh rising on her naked body. She reached over to the chair next to the bed and grabbed her pink chenille bathrobe, a remnant of more innocent times when she was Penny and not Myra, and quietly shrugged into it.

She went into the kitchen and measured Maxwell House into the receptacle of the Mr. Coffee, added water, and waited for it to brew. A mundane start to a morning. She could be anyone. A housewife getting up to make coffee for her husband before he set off for work at the industrial pottery down by the river, where he worked as a caster or a waxer in the color room.

Did she want such a life?

She did.

While the coffee was hissing and turning out its black sustenance, Myra went to the front door and opened it. More mundane stuff. The daily newspaper lay on the concrete blocks that comprised their front stoop. She bent to pick it up and opened it to the front page.

When she saw what awaited her there, in black and white, Myra would have sworn her heart stopped. Hands trembling, Myra took the newspaper to the kitchen table, where she set it before herself and simply stared at it, waiting. Waiting for the jolt to come into her system that would allow her to begin reading beyond the headline—"Missing Girl's Body Discovered"—and find out how it could have happened so soon. How they had found Lucy Plant's body already, when Ian had assured her it would be months before anyone would come across the physical evidence of their deeds.

And there was the photograph, a grainy black-and-white testimony that bore witness to their actions. The heaped-up dirt, the blinding lights, the men and women in action around the makeshift grave, the medical examiner, the police in their uniforms, detectives.

The coffee was ready. Perhaps a strong black mug of the stuff would propel her into action, help her focus on the smaller type below the headline.

*

Janet McKenna had been up all night. Many nights lately, Janet had been unable to sleep. Ever since Sheryl had gone missing.

Rick slept. No problem there. Sometimes Janet wondered if he was glad Sheryl was gone. Glad because now he would have Janet all to himself—to beat her, to fuck her, to make her his slave in a way kept secret from her family and friends.

And when the night grew dark and Fawcettville silent, no whoosh of passing traffic outside, no quick conversations overheard as people passed their little house, Janet wondered if Rick had had anything to do with Sheryl's disappearance.

But she quickly squelched those thoughts. They died before she let her brain give them much sustenance. They were too horrible to contemplate. And so they lingered in the back of her mind like hulking shadows. Giving them form and shape would have been more than Janet could bear.

And now it was morning. Janet was on good terms with how the darkness of night moved to a washed-out gray and finally to the brightness of day, how the sounds of activity all around her would grow in intensity.

A thud against the front door made her jump. The newspaper had arrived. She stood on legs she was always amazed continued to support her and went to the door.

The paper's front page confronted her like an accusation. "Missing Girl's Body Discovered," the headline shouted, kicking her legs out from under her so that she dropped to her knees where, weeping, she leaned across the threshold to begin reading.

"Lucy Plant, thirteen, daughter of Mr. and Mrs. Kevin Plant of Fawcettville, has been discovered in a shallow grave on the banks of the Ohio River."

Janet picked up the paper, walked backward into the kitchen, and kicked the door closed behind her. She sat and covered her face with one hand. In the other, she held the paper, like something scorched and bad-smelling.

This didn't mean anything. *This did not mean anything.* Janet trembled, unable to even hold the paper still enough to read the printed words. She shoved aside some dishes and pulled an ashtray toward herself, groped behind her on the counter for her Kools and her Bic. She lit up and inhaled a huge lungful of smoke, almost enough to make her choke. Her eyes watered, and she smoked the cigarette down to its butt in less than a minute.

She felt better. Her hands had slowed to just a little shakiness, hardly noticeable. She pulled the paper in front of her and read the article, by a reporter named Dave

Newton. There weren't all that many details, just the fact that the girl's mother, Amy Plant, and a man named Cayce D'Amico—it didn't immediately register on Janet's foggy brain why that name should be familiar—had discovered the body late last night in a shallow grave on the banks of the Ohio River. She read on, about how the medical examiner had ruled the death a homicide due to ligature marks around the girl's wrists and ankles and broken blood vessels in the lungs, indicating suffocation. She read about how Lucy had disappeared a little over a week ago from her front yard in the part of Fawcettville known as Little England. Janet checked the address and saw that the Plants lived only a couple blocks over, on Etruria Street. That knowledge made her close her eyes, trying to will away the tightness in her chest. She lit up another Kool.

The article had less to say about how the girl was found, keeping the details to a short statement about how investigation into the case was "continuing."

Janet closed the paper and thought about making some coffee. Instead, she went to the freezer, where she kept a bottle of Kirov vodka. She pulled down a glass, filled it halfway up with the viscous alcohol, added a splash of orange juice, and sat back at the kitchen table, where suddenly the light coming in through the window seemed too bright. It felt like the muscles underneath her face were vibrating. Her stomach churned.

"This wasn't Sheryl." She began talking to herself. "This has nothing to do with Sheryl. Sheryl ran away. You know how wild that girl can be." Janet was no stranger to the girl's nocturnal comings and goings, even if her daughter thought different. There was a lot Janet knew about her daughter that was easier to ignore than to confront. Growing pains. She would pass through this phase, just as Janet had, and move on. With her mother beside her, she too would one day find Jesus and see how he could be her personal Lord and Savior.

She just had to wait.

So Sheryl had run off. Pittsburgh, with its bright lights, tall buildings, and fast pace, probably called out to her. Soon enough, she would show up on the back porch, tail between her legs, begging to come home.

"This was not Sheryl. Lucy. Lucy Plant. This was not Sheryl."

Janet downed the orange juice and vodka and stood to make another. Maybe she would skip the orange juice this time.

She pulled the newspaper closer again, letting eyes already getting blurry scan across the columns of type, and saw the name Cayce D'Amico again.

She sat down hard as it all came back to her. Cayce. The weird visit yesterday. Janet replayed it all in her mind, forcing herself into a corner of the kitchen to watch it with bated breath, listening, looking harder at Cayce D'Amico's features: handsome face, wide green eyes, black hair. Everything contorted, Janet now saw, into a kind of desperate fear. It was obvious now that the guy hadn't wanted to be there in the filthy kitchen with two hostile people who could only stare at him, cruel words poised on lips drawn into thin lines.

What was it he'd said? That he might be able to help them find Sheryl? And then he had gone out and found this Lucy Plant, with her mother dragged along.

Janet went cold. Her skin felt clammy. She felt a line of sweat bead up on her forehead and trickle down her face.

How did this man know where to find Lucy Plant? That's what Janet wanted to know. What had he said? Something about a vision? Visions were the devil's work...and so was murder.

Janet sat stock still in her chair. She was humming something tuneless and didn't even realize it. She didn't want to think anymore. She didn't want to remember the conversation she and Rick had had with the D'Amico man, the hateful words, the hurled plate.

She didn't want to wonder if he could help them. She didn't want to wonder if he had information that could help them find Sheryl before it was too late. She didn't want to think Cayce knew something because he was sick, a twisted creature who preyed on young girls... He seemed so good-hearted, kind. Who would suspect?

No! No! She couldn't think that way. If she thought that way, it would mean Sheryl was dead. It would mean she and Rick were part of some devil-inspired game.

But that didn't make any sense. Why would a murderer come to the loved ones and offer to lead them to the body? How stupid was that?

Everyone would be asking the same questions. How did Cayce know?

Janet lowered her head to the table and watched as the tears began to drip, hot, onto its greasy surface. She couldn't think anymore, could she?

She downed the second glass of vodka in one swallow and rose to pour another, then jumped when she saw Rick standing in the archway to the kitchen, hair sticking up all over, grimy T-shirt just barely covering his hairy belly. He was grinning. Ignorant bastard.

"Party time? This early? That's my girl." He moved toward her, and Janet just stood there, still, as his arms went around her and his stink rose up to engulf her. She reached out blindly with one hand and knocked the newspaper to the floor as she followed her husband back into their bedroom.

*

Myra didn't know what to do. She had read the article about Lucy twice, because the first time her eyes drifted over the lines of type, her nerves jangling so much that she comprehended none of it. The second time, she sipped half a cup of coffee, forced herself to take several deep breaths, then made herself go slowly. She knew all the details already: the ligature marks, the location of the grave, the identification of the girl. There were no surprises in the news story. From that, she took some solace. There was nothing about the perpetrators. It seemed that if there were any clues to their identities—"*our* identities," she murmured—none had been released. There wasn't even any speculation. The story was all about the body being discovered.

But how? Myra searched, during a third reading, for a clue of how the girl's body had been found, when she and Ian had so carefully hidden it. Had they been seen by someone in the woods on the banks of the river? Was there some silent observer watching, taking notes as to the exact location—which, Myra admitted, even she would have been hard-pressed to find mere hours after the burial.

She remembered the night they'd buried the girl. It was hot, muggy, the mosquitoes swarming from the river, diving for their skin and eyes. Little mean pinches and bites that made her gasp. "Over here," Ian had said, motioning her to a place just back from the water's edge, where tall grass and garbage mounded in equal profundity. "This is the place the Beast has chosen."

Myra looked around her, straining to see through the thick pitch of the night, the moon obscured by clouds and no city streetlights penetrating. She stumbled over a rock as she came near him, her nostrils flaring at the fishy smell rising up from the water.

"Are you sure?" she had whispered.

"I don't have to be sure. We can rely on the guidance of the Beast."

Oh please, Myra had wanted to say, casting looks over her shoulder, but there was no one around, the only movement the branches and leaves of the trees that stood like sentinels on the banks, whispering as the wind soughed through them.

"We need to go back to the car," Ian had said, "for the sacrifice and the tools."

Myra traced the crime scene photograph with a red-lacquered nail. It was so prosaic. If she looked closely, it blurred into a bunch of dots, meaningless. She remembered making their way back to the car, which was parked several hundred feet away, where the dirt road leading down to the river abruptly ended in grass and pebbles. Ian had made her carry the shovel and spade they had brought, while he slung the girl's body over his shoulder, expelling a breath as the body draped itself on top of him. She must be heavier now, with all the life sucked out of her. Myra had thought before they left home that they should at least wrap her in a sheet or fashion some garbage bags around her, but Ian was having none of it. "I trust in the Beast absolutely," he had told her. "He will protect us." Ian panted as he made his way down to the riverbank, using one hand to wipe away the sweat from his brow.

She didn't know about trust. What if someone saw them carrying a young girl, obviously dead weight in the most literal sense? What would they say? They would be caught like rats in a trap.

But no one had seen. Or at least, thinking back, it seemed no one had. The woods and riverbank were utterly silent in the moist heat, the rush of the river and wind the only sounds.

But someone must have been there, Myra thought. Someone had to have been hiding and watching. How else would they have known where to find her...and so quickly?

She noted the name of the man who had been with Amy Plant when she had discovered her daughter's body: Cayce D'Amico. Who the hell was that? Was he the one who had guided Lucy's mother there? The newspaper gave no clues. The story concentrated merely on the body being discovered, no hows or whys. Maybe this D'Amico man was out for a walk on the banks high above where they had buried Lucy Plant and had watched them?

But Myra distinctly remembered looking up, searching all through the darkness from every vantage point on both sides of the river, and she had seen nothing, other than the maddening swarms of mosquitoes as they drew near for another attack.

Myra wondered what she should do with this information. Should she keep it from Ian? Stupid idea. This was big news, made bigger by the fact that it had happened in Fawcettville, where almost nothing ever occurred. Ian would find out, even if she shredded the newspaper and burned it in the rusting can outside their trailer. It would be in other newspapers, on the radio, on the TV news.

No, she would have to let him know. Have to inform him that the Beast, for whatever reason, had failed them. She alone would have to endure what she was sure would be his rage at all his hard work come undone. She flashed on images of his filthy, sweaty face as he dug, his eyes lit up even in the darkness as he glanced over at the body lying in the dirt.

Sleep peacefully, my love, she thought, crossing the short distance from the trailer's kitchen to the bedroom. *Your slumbers will no longer be untainted. Now we have to deal with suspicion and fear.*

Maybe now we will have to run. Myra smiled at the thought; it wasn't such a bad idea. She wrapped herself around thoughts of romance, of being on the lam with her hero. Perhaps they could settle down somewhere warm, and Ian would finally put all of this behind him. They could transform into new identities, ones that didn't involve sacrifices, strangulation, suffocation, and sex.

Perhaps not.

She stood frozen at the bedroom's threshold. Ian was beginning to stir; slowly, his eyes opened to regard her.

"Sweetheart," she said, her voice coming out barely above a squeak. She paused to gather the breath and spit to say the words that would put all the rest in motion. "I have something to show you."

Ian sat up in bed, grumbling. He wiped sleep from his eyes, complaining of the "heaviness" he felt. "I need more sleep."

"But you have to see today's paper." Myra sat gently on the edge of the bed, holding out the newspaper like an offering.

He snatched it from her hands, sighing, and unfolded it so the front page fell open before his sleep-clouded eyes.

He skimmed the type for a moment, then sat up, spine stiffening. He leaned back against the headboard, scanning the story Myra had just read. His only reaction was a quickening of his breath. After he was finished, he handed the paper back to her. "We have any coffee?"

Myra wanted to scream "That's all you have to say?" Instead, she hurried to the kitchen, poured a cup of the dark liquid, and brought it back to him the way he liked it, black and steaming. She handed it to him, and he gulped, heedless of the heat.

After downing almost half the mug, he patted the bed next to him, and Myra sat. Her nerves tingled. She didn't know what to expect. She never knew what to expect.

"How did this happen?"

Myra looked at the wood-paneled walls, as if an answer might be secreted there, in the grains of the paneling. "I..." she began. "Honey, I don't know. We were so careful. Or at least I thought we were."

"I was so careful. The Beast was careful, but I wonder if you let something slip." He took her chin in his hand, roughly, so it hurt, and turned her head toward his face. His beautiful face, eyebrows now scrunched together. "But what did you do? Did you talk to someone about this? Maybe someone in that hoopie family of yours across the river?"

Myra was stunned. Since they had been together, Ian had made certain that Myra had effectively cut off all communications with her "former" family, the ones who knew her as Penny and who, today, might pass her on the street unrecognized.

"No, of course not, sweetheart. You know I don't talk to them anymore."

"Then how did this happen? And so soon?"

Myra's heart began to pound. It was as if Ian expected an answer, as if he believed she must know why their efforts to conceal their crime—sacrifice, he would call it—had failed. She searched her mind for some way she could have given away a clue to the girl's whereabouts, but there was nothing. She had literally talked to no one but him since they had brought Lucy Plant back to the trailer. "I couldn't tell you. For me, there has only been you. I haven't even seen any of my family in months."

Ian flung the sheets off angrily. Normally, Myra would have been excited by this unveiling of his body, so solid and packed with muscle. Ian never wore anything to bed. But now she only felt fear, felt it as an unpleasant sense of dread that made her innards go cold. The fear made a need to flee rise up; she wanted to leap from the bed and hurry outside the trailer.

"Someone must have seen us." He looked down at the newspaper. "Maybe that guy the article mentions. What was his name?"

Myra looked down. "Cayce D'Amico." Her voice was barely a whisper.

"Cayce." He turned to Myra, quickly and unexpectedly, and hit her, the back of his hand connecting hard enough with her cheek to make her head swivel. She raised a hand to her stinging cheek and stared up at him, stunned.

"We have to do something. The Beast would want us to do something about him." He stood from the bed, heading toward the bathroom. "Good thing you're already dressed. I'll be ready in a minute, and we'll pay a little surveillance call on this fucker. Find out just how he knows so much."

"All right." Myra wanted to cry but held her tears in check. She knew enough to know her tears would do no good. They would only excite him.

Chapter Fifteen

It was the second day after the discovery of Lucy Plant's body. The phone had not stopped ringing all morning. Cayce sat in the living room, staring straight ahead, and wondered what he had set in motion. Reporters, stringers, and assorted nutcases had all picked up their phones and punched in his listed number, all hoping for a few minutes of his time. Reporters had traveled from newspapers in nearby places like Pittsburgh, Steubenville, and Youngstown and as far away as New York City and Orlando (this a tabloid he had often seen as he checked out at the supermarket), all desperate, they said, to help. "We want to hear your side of the story. We can get that across to the world. Let us be your pipeline, your voice. We'll be sympathetic and can act as your spokesperson." Some of them wanted exclusives. Some hadn't bothered to ask.

The phone had begun ringing at 5:00 a.m. The day's newspaper hadn't even been printed yet, but Cayce knew word would travel fast. The night before last, he had stood, shell-shocked and dry-eyed, next to Amy Plant, not knowing that reporters, TV and print alike, were already on their way. Cayce hadn't thought about it at the time, having been unfamiliar with this world of preying on the lowest, basest news that occurred, but realized now there were whole legions of people with police scanners in their cars, offices, and homes, poised and ready to pounce.

Giving his imagination free rein, he could imagine how the lights and cameras would assemble, like what he would visualize would take place on a movie set. He saw reporters running restlessly from official to official, looking for comment. He could tell himself it was like something out of the movies, but that illusion was quickly squashed when he thought of the body of the young girl lying behind him, being measured, prodded, and photographed, no longer a some*one*, but a some*thing*, transported into a realm that only days before she didn't even know existed.

When JT Simmons had summoned him to her office downtown, Cayce had felt bad about leaving Dave Newton behind. He had felt safe with the man, even though he had no rational reason for feeling that way.

The phone wasn't ringing now. He had ripped the phone cord from the box on the wall after someone (not a reporter) had called, wanting to know what it felt like to kill Lucy Plant. Had the girl cried at the end and begged for her life, the soft male voice wanted to know.

That call had sent him over the edge, but he couldn't let himself fall apart. He had responsibilities. So he pulled the blinds shut and roused Luke.

"Honey, it's time to get up," he whispered to him as gently as he could, trying to pull himself together, to dry the tears on his face, to stop himself from trembling.

Luke looked up, his expression dazed, sleep in the corners of his eyes. It was still dark, and the little light on his nightstand gave a glow that was all wrong to his bedroom. He sat up and rubbed his eyes, more alert. Cayce could tell from his wary expression he sensed right away something was wrong.

"What's the matter, Dad?"

"Nothing. I just have lots to do today. How would you like to go see Nana and Pap-Pap today?"

Luke looked confused.

"Don't you have to work? What about school?"

Cayce didn't know what to tell the boy; he had completely forgotten he had just returned for second grade. "I just have lots to do," he said and made it clear with his tone that this pronouncement would be the end of any further questioning. "Nana and Pap-Pap can get you off to school when the time comes."

*

They slipped out the back door as a grayish light was just beginning to fill the sky. A caul of mist still lay above the dewy grass. There was a chill in the air, a bite. A couple of vans were parked outside, and Cayce was already learning what it was like to be a celebrity. He wore dark aviator glasses and had thrown on a baseball cap.

"Let's play a game," he whispered to Luke, kneeling down just outside the back door. "We're spies, and we have to make it to the border, where Nana is, without anyone seeing us."

Luke, even at seven, wasn't falling for this. He eyed Cayce with the suspicion of a mental health-care professional and wordlessly followed his father through the backyard and the network of other backyards that would lead them to his parents' house, ignoring the barking of dogs and curious eyes glancing out of kitchen windows. At least they were able to make it to their destination without someone running after them, microphone, tape recorder, or notebook in hand.

*

Dave Newton watched Cayce D'Amico emerge from his back door, a sleepy little towheaded boy clinging tightly to his hand, blinking as dawn's pinkish light began to illuminate the day. Dave kept his eye on them as they headed through their backyard, casting glances behind them, and finally watched as they knelt and then crawled through the bottom of the hedge bordering the southern end of the little yard. Their heads popped up seconds later, and the two of them continued running through the yards, a pair of jokers on the lam.

Dave tucked his notebook into his back pocket, not about to pursue a father and his kid obviously trying to make an escape from prying types like him. There would be time enough to talk to Cayce. Dave had a feeling it wouldn't be long before Cayce would return to the house alone, after safely depositing his son somewhere out of harm's way.

Was Dave capable of insinuating himself into Cayce's life? Was he no better than one of the vultures he had already seen around town, hungry for a story at any cost? Could he lie, wheedle, and cajole this obviously terrified young man into giving him a story? And for what? Fame? Fortune? A scoop? Dave laughed bitterly. His days of chasing such dreams were past.

So why was he watching Cayce like a spy? Watching and waiting...

He didn't know. To date, his biggest stories had been sentimental features on the triumphs of local handicapped kids, the scintillating activities of the Fawcettville city council, and features on topics as world-heavy as the first baby born at City Hospital in the New Year.

But Dave Newton, for everything he was tired of, for all the failures and upheavals in his life, was not stupid. He knew an opportunity when he saw one, and he knew he might never be handed one like this again. Not here in this sleepy little river town in a place called Pennsylvania, where he had never expected to be finishing his days, doing work he never thought he'd be doing. If he didn't at least try for this fleeting moment—and for the sake of so many, he hoped it was fleeting—then he didn't see much point in continuing with much of anything.

Besides, there was something about Cayce, something that touched his heart and made Dave want to know him better and, yeah, maybe to help him.

Dave turned, looked at the TV vans camped outside Cayce's house, and walked farther down the block, waiting.

*

The knock on the kitchen window startled him. Cayce sat, feeling like a trapped animal in his living room, looking up only occasionally through the sheer curtains on the picture window to see the white TV van with its big rooftop-mounted antenna sitting in front of his house. A few times, there had been knocks at the front door— knocks that had made him jump—but Cayce had kept quiet, and they stopped after a while.

Finally, he heard the ignition of the van rumble and then fade away, as he assumed its inhabitants moved off to more willing quarry. He prayed they would leave the Plants alone.

But the knock at the kitchen window set his nerves to jangling all over again. Just when he was starting to think maybe he could go into the kitchen, put on the kettle for some tea, and pop some raisin bread into the toaster, that infernal tapping on the glass had started.

For a moment, Cayce had sat frozen, still stuck, as if by glue, to his living room sofa, the light from the TV washing over him. *The View* was on, that much he knew, but who their guest was and what they were discussing today, he had no idea.

He stood and crept through the dining room. He allowed himself a quick peek through the archway leading into the kitchen. What he saw made him flatten against the wall, gasping.

There was a man framed by the window, just peering into his kitchen, taking in Luke's cereal bowl and juice glass, still on the table, Oreo's food and water dishes lined up on the Linoleum floor. Cayce stepped back so quickly, there was no time for details to register about the man, other than the fact that he was male and white. He didn't even know if this was someone with whom he might have been acquainted.

His heart began to thud as things snapped into place. This was the killer. Cayce's name was in the paper and listed in the phone book, along with his address. How easy it would be to find him! Cayce's mouth went dry, and he tried to rein in the fear that was causing his stomach to churn and sweat to form at the nape of his neck and in his armpits.

No, no. It's probably just another reporter, or one of those nutcases, hungry for details about the killing.

He stepped out a bit and looked again. The face was still there and soon was accompanied by a hand on the right side, rapping on the glass again. And then he put it together and felt sheepish for not knowing at once who was out there. He shook his head, whispering the word "fuck" to himself. His sheepishness quickly morphed into anger.

It was Dave Newton, the reporter he'd spoken to. *And kissed, don't forget kissed.* Why hadn't he just come to Cayce's front door like a normal person? Then he thought of the news van, the other reporters who'd been outside, circling like vultures over a fresh kill.

Dave didn't seem like the predatory type. He rapped again.

Cayce's breathing returned to normal, and he wondered if Dave would go away quicker if he just told him to get lost. He liked the man, he really did, but right now he was just too shaken to talk to him or anyone else, especially anyone connected to the media. *I still have the right to call the police and report a trespasser on my property, don't I? That's just what I'm gonna do.*

Fear replaced by a slow-burning anger, Cayce moved to the kitchen and cranked open the little window, having to reach over the stove to do so. In another context, this whole encounter might have had comic overtones.

The warm air washed in, and Dave smiled and closed his eyes with a kind of defeat.

"What do you want?" Cayce knew the question telescoped all the exhaustion he felt.

"I know this is a bad time. And I know every reporter literally on the block might try the same line, but I really would like to talk to you, to help if I can."

Cayce shook his head, frowning. "Tell my side of the story?" Cayce rolled his eyes, reaching toward the pull that would close the window. "I have nothing to say. Last night was a mistake."

"I don't blame you."

The two stared at one another for a moment. Dave took a breath and said, "Do you think maybe I could swing round to the kitchen door? We could chat through the screen. I'm not sure how much longer this wooden door's going to support my weight." Dave glanced down at the wooden cellar door upon which he stood. "Damn Krispy Kreme for coming to town." Almost sheepishly, he held up a waxed paper bag of glazed donuts. "These are for you. They're still warm."

Cayce let out a short burst of laughter. "You sure know the way to a guy's heart. You can come around to the door. But you can keep your donuts, and you're not coming inside."

"Thanks."

Dave clambered down off the cellar door, and in a second, his full frame stood at the screen door. Cayce noticed again how handsome Newton was, with pale skin and dark, dark eyes, the fire of which his tiny glasses could not conceal. Cayce wondered if he was Welsh.

Cayce reached out to flip the lock on the screen door handle. "As I said at the window, I really don't have anything to say. This whole thing has been a nightmare..." Cayce caught himself, fearing he was already giving away quotes that could be used in that evening's edition of the *Review*. He could imagine the words "this has been a nightmare" in a headline.

Dave Newton smiled, and Cayce noticed the yellowing teeth of a smoker. "Cayce, I know it's hard. And I know you don't want to be drawn into this. But it's too late; you already are. Now, you can tell me to go away, as you're doing, and I will go. I'm not the kind of reporter who gets persistent. Hell, I'm barely the kind who can be bothered to file a story on time. But sooner or later, *your* story will come out. And it can come out one of two ways: with or without your authorization. Do you know what I'm saying?"

Cayce considered, soothed by his sensible words, the warmth of his raspy, velvety voice, and his accent, which, rather than being foreign and strange, had a calming effect. It seemed like Dave Newton was in charge, and that was something Cayce needed right now—someone to take over. He played with the catch on the door's lock. "I don't know," he said, with barely enough breath to make his voice register.

Dave licked his lips. "Look, I'm not from around here, but I've been here more years than I care to mention. I can work with you and make sure what you want to say gets out the right way. Those other reporters from the cities can't make that claim, and if they do, they're liars. They're going to try to make you into something you're not. All I want to do is make sure I have your side of things right and report that as accurately as I can."

"I'm not sure I should talk. What about the police? They've already raked me over the coals. I bet they wouldn't like me talking to you." Cayce could feel his heart rate quicken, just a bit, and was determined not to let panic take over.

"There's no law against having a word with me. And maybe if you share things with me, it will make things easier when you eventually do have to give the police a formal statement, or whatever they want."

Cayce sighed. "You make sense, Mr. Newton. But I'm really torn. All of this happened so fast, and I don't even know why I got caught up in it...or how, really. I don't know what's going on." Cayce paused, breathing just a little harder. "How do I know I can trust you?"

What difference does it make? Cayce wondered. *You trusted him last night. You would have talked to him then if that detective hadn't come along when she did.*

Dave shrugged. "Trust is the same thing as faith, in a way. You just have to let go and believe. I can give you my word that I won't distort what you have to say. I can give you my word that I will try to be as faithful a mouthpiece as I can for you." He smiled. "I'm sorry I can't give you more than that. Ultimately it's up to you whether you trust me or not."

Cayce unlocked the door. "All right. I'm probably doing the wrong thing, but come on in." Cayce leaned back to let Dave Newton in. "You can sit down if you want, over there at the table. I was going to make some tea." He laughed. "Oh, that's right, you like coffee."

"Tea is just fine. Are you sure you won't help me eat these donuts?" Dave slid out a chair, sat, and pulled a tape recorder and a notebook from his bag. "Why don't you just start at the beginning? I'm still not sure I understand how you came to help Amy Plant discover her daughter's body."

Cayce's spine went rigid as he stood at the sink, where he was filling the kettle with cold water. He sucked in some air and moved to the stove, listened for the click of the pilot light, and watched as the blue flame emerged from the burner. He looked out the window.

Finally, he turned and sat, thinking he had forgotten to take down the mugs from the cupboard and get out the tea bags.

"It started when we had that storm last week."

Dave clicked on the tape recorder and sat back.

"I was fixing supper, and I noticed that Luke—that's my son—wasn't in the yard, where he was supposed to be."

*

Dave couldn't believe what he was hearing. Cayce led him through the events of that day last week when a summer storm had gathered in bruised clouds over the hilltops of West Virginia, moving across the river to douse the little town of Fawcettville with rain that felt like warm hail: big hard drops applauded by thunder and lit up by lightning. Dave wasn't sure of the connection he should make between Cayce getting hit in the head with a tree branch and his discovery of the Plant girl's body, but the man sitting before him seemed to think there was one.

Cayce led him through the visions, from the tiny ones—how he knew the evening plans and thoughts of his nurse in the hospital—to the bigger ones that had shown him what he now thought was a vision of Lucy Plant's murder—the blinking red light, the whirring ceiling fan— and the location of her shallow grave.

*

"It all just came to me. I didn't ask for it. In fact, I tried to push it away." Cayce looked desperately at Dave, searching the lined oval face for understanding. He wasn't sure he found it. The reporter simply stared, implacable, unaffected, waiting for him to continue. He supposed this was part of his reporter's bag of tricks, being silent and letting the subject talk. Well, it was working. Cayce felt a curious kind of relief course through him as he unburdened himself, hoping Dave wouldn't see him as nuts. Or worse, as a killer. "I admit, I even drank a little to try to push away the visions. They were so horrible...and so insistent."

As he talked, Cayce remembered the visions of the grave and of Lucy being tortured. They were no longer like visions but like memories, as if he had been there, watching it all, helpless.

"I had to do something. I have a kid too, you know. If something ever happened to Luke, I'd be out of my mind with worry. In fact, I *was* out of my mind the day this whole damned chain of events got started." Cayce blew out a big breath. "I *had* to try to help these people who had lost their children." He gnawed at his lower lip, still uncertain if he wanted to reveal what he knew about Sheryl McKenna. Maybe he should just keep quiet about the second girl, end all of this right here, as best he could, remove himself from a limelight he'd never sought.

He really knew very little about Sheryl McKenna, at least nothing that would be useful. He had felt a painful certainty that the girl was dead but now wondered if his vision was correct. Was she too buried in a shallow grave down by the river? Were the killers that stupid? Maybe the vision was incomplete. Maybe Cayce had seen only the location where she was killed, not where she was buried. These things he saw in his head weren't an exact science. He could be wrong. Anyway, if Sheryl McKenna had been buried on the banks of the Ohio River, wouldn't that have occurred to the authorities? Shouldn't they be searching right now, without any help from him? Maybe some revelation was still in store.

Cayce had a flash of the flickering TV screen with its image of a hilltop trailer and shivered; he had already had a revelation. He was torn about being the recipient of such knowledge and wondered what he should do with the information. Put himself out there again, setting himself up for suspicion and ridicule? Or just keep quiet and hope the authorities would find the girl on their own? It was tempting to take the latter route, but again, Cayce wasn't sure he could, not when there was at least one grieving parent out there who might be removed from the unendurable torture of not knowing.

Dave Newton brought him out of his reverie, sounding like he was repeating a question.

"So you just saw, like in your mind's eye, where the grave was?"

Cayce nodded. He didn't want to do this anymore. He felt sick and just wanted this man with his notebook and tape recorder to go away. He blew out a big sigh, realizing the quickest way to get his wish fulfilled would be to simply cooperate.

"I know it sounds crazy, but yes. That's just what it was: my mind's eye. I just saw the area where she was, the river, the bridge. I don't know why it came to me."

"So, are you saying..." Dave Newton licked his lips. "That your injury might have given you some sort of extrasensory perception? That you're now psychic?"

Cayce shook his head. "That sounds insane. I'm not the kind of person who ever put much stock in things like the occult or astrology or even supposed mental abilities like clairvoyance or tele...tele..." Cayce searched for the word.

"Telekinesis? Telepathy?"

"That's right. I never even read Stephen King. Horror movies and thrillers scare me. I know I shouldn't admit that, being a guy. And I probably shouldn't admit what I really like are romances and comedies." Cayce stirred his tea, gone cold in the mug. "I don't even know what I'm saying here. I don't know if it was a coincidence that I got a bad blow to the head and suddenly could start seeing things or if those things were connected. Even if the blow to my head had nothing to do with things as they are now, I still wish I could go back to before I had visions of those girls." Cayce caught himself. He had done what he thought was unwise to do: revealed that he knew something about the other missing girl, Sheryl McKenna.

Dave Newton looked up from his notebook, where he was jotting something down. "Girls? You said girls. Plural."

Cayce laughed. "I know. I meant to say 'girl.' I'm a little frazzled, as you can imagine, with all that's gone on." He laughed again, a high-pitched twittering sound that he knew sounded completely stupid and might as well have been a translation for the sentence "I am a liar." "Anyway, as I was saying, I'd just like to go back to being what I was: boring. Waiting tables in a diner, trying to make ends meet and raise my little boy." He looked at the reporter, eyes wide, hoping Dave wouldn't pursue his earlier slip.

But that was not to be.

"You said girls." Dave bit his lip. "Please don't take this the wrong way, Cayce, but I'm not sure I'm buying that it was a slip. See, the fact is, there's another girl missing. We even printed something about it in the paper. Her name was..." He began to shuffle around in a fabric briefcase, looking, Cayce supposed, for the name of the missing girl.

He closed his eyes and said, "Her name was Sheryl McKenna." Cayce noticed that, without thinking, he had referred to the missing girl in the past tense.

"So you know something about her disappearance?"

Cayce gave out another stupid little laugh. "I didn't say that. I get the *Review*. I could have seen her name in the paper."

"Yes, you could have. Or you could have heard it over the radio. But I think there's more than you're saying."

Cayce felt jittery. He couldn't stand this anymore. And why did he have to? There was no law compelling him to talk to this guy, sympathetic as he seemed. "Well, what you think and reality might be two different things," Cayce snapped. "*I think* I'm ready to call this interview quits. I hope you got enough. Now, if you don't mind, I have a splitting headache and would like to lie down before I have to go pick up my son."

"If you know something, Cayce, you should talk about it."

"Please!" Cayce shouted, surprising even himself. Dave Newton's jaw dropped. But the volume and the shrillness had their effect: he was gathering up his things.

"I apologize. If there's anything you want to talk further about, you already have my card. And, as you know, it even has my cell phone number, so call me anytime." Dave met his eyes. "Anytime at all. I mean it."

Cayce listened as Dave put his things away, the scrape of his chair along the linoleum, the sound of him taking a few paces. "I'll just see myself out, then."

Cayce looked up, nodded.

"Thanks very much for your time. Keep the donuts. Maybe your son would like them."

Cayce didn't respond.

"Right." And Dave Newton left him alone.

Chapter Sixteen

"We have to leave."

Myra ran a hand through her hair. She sat at the tiny, scarred kitchen table with Ian, the accusing newspaper spread out on its surface. "They're going to find us out, Ian." Myra's hands trembled. Something ferret-like, with razor-sharp teeth, gnawed at her insides.

Ian stared at her. His pale-green eyes, which she usually found so seductive and alluring, regarded her with disbelief and a kind of haughtiness best reserved for someone with insufficient intellectual capacities. She hated those eyes and that gaze right now, wished she could just stand, go outside, start up the car, and drive herself back to West Virginia. She saw herself returning to her parents' home and heard their questions about her whereabouts, what she had been doing with herself over this blank period when she had disappeared.

Why hadn't they even bothered to come looking for her?

"Are you even thinking about what the Beast wants? I haven't gotten the slightest inkling from him that we need to flee."

"Damn the Beast!" Myra was tired of the game. She'd assumed all this talk of the Beast and praying to its evil was just part of their sex play. She'd always wondered if even Ian believed all the talk, all the mythology about the Beast that she knew was created in his twisted mind.

"They've found the first girl. I don't know how, but it seems this guy, this Cayce D'Amico, knows something. And that could mean he knows something about the other one. Ian..." Myra tried and failed to keep her voice from rising with hysteria. "Ian, if they can find the bodies, maybe they can discover a trail back to us. I don't want to go to jail." Myra gnawed at a hangnail on her pinky. She knew if she started crying now, she'd end up with her face slapped—or worse. "Can't we just go away, just for a while, until the heat dies down? There's nothing keeping us here. The Beast won't mind. He'll understand." Myra looked wistfully over Ian's shoulder, through the window. A dead-white sky indicated the heat and humidity of the day. In so many ways, Myra felt trapped. Even the air itself closed in on her.

Ian rose and leaned across the table, towering over her. He looked menacing, and Myra sharply sucked in her breath, cringing. She put a hand over her face, and he snatched it away.

"How does the likes of you know what the Beast will or will not mind? You don't. I am his conduit, and he's telling me we have to remain. So what if they found a body? There's no connection to us."

"How do we know that?" Myra regretted the words as soon as they left her lips. She knew she had no right to speak them. Yet Myra remembered how they had plucked the girl right from in front of her house...in the same car that sat outside the trailer. Who was to say that a neighbor hadn't been watching from behind a curtained window as Ian got out of the car and talked to Lucy, luring her into the car? Who was to say that person wasn't down at police headquarters right now, giving a description of the car and the handsome young man who'd urged the girl to get inside? A child getting into the car of a stranger might put a caring neighbor on the alert, might even make that same neighbor jot down a license plate number. Myra tried to comfort herself with the weak conviction that if someone knew their license plate number, the cops would already be outside, pounding on the door, guns at the ready.

Ian sat thinking for a long time. He smoked a cigarette, wordless. Myra wished she could read him. His voice startled her.

"The Beast is telling me there's a way out of this. We have to silence this D'Amico guy, once and for all."

Myra understood what he meant and began to weep softly. "I don't want to kill anyone else." She caught a sob in her throat, thinking of the look on the McKenna girl's face as the life ebbed out of her, how her blue eyes had connected with Myra's, accusing. "I don't think I can do it, Ian." She covered her face to hide the tears.

Ian pulled her hands away and held on to her wrists so hard it hurt. "I said nothing about killing."

"Then what?"

"The Beast wants us to find out more about him. He says we have to discover what it is this man holds most dear."

"I don't know what that means."

"You wouldn't. Just trust in me." Ian stood. "As I told you before, we're going to pay Mr. D'Amico a visit."

Myra sat quivering in her chair, imagining them in a car. Imagining whirling blue lights behind them. She wished she was Penny again—fat, acne-scarred, but safe, safe in her girl's bedroom, writing in her journal and listening to Shawn Colvin. She feared Penny was as dead as Sheryl McKenna. At least Sheryl McKenna didn't have to live out a nightmare. At least Sheryl McKenna had the comfort of a shallow grave, just outside the door.

*

Cayce sat at his parents' kitchen table with Luke, who was eating a bowl of pastina with butter, egg, and grated Romano cheese. A salad of dandelion greens in oil and vinegar was next to the pasta, ignored by Luke. "Too sour." He had twisted his face into a grimace after taking a bite of the greens.

"I need you to stay here with Nana and Pap-Pap for a couple days."

Luke kept his head low, the act of eating suddenly requiring intense concentration. Finally, he raised his head. "Why? Why can't I be at home? Who will take care of Oreo? You said I was responsible for his food and water."

"I can do it."

"But you said—"

"I know what I said." Cayce sighed. He looked out at the Indian summer day. His skin was damp; strands of hair clung to his forehead and neck. He had endured his mother's questions earlier, when he had decided it might be best to keep Luke out of the limelight, what with all the calls—and, unfortunately, visits—the media was paying. He decided that now, since his name was public knowledge, it would be best to shield Luke from more than just reporters. The thought sent a chill through him in spite of the heat.

"Listen, honey." Cayce took his son's hand in his own, forcing him to look up at him. "I'll come see you every day. And I'm just down the street." Cayce frowned right along with his son. "This is hard for me too. But it's just for a little while."

"I still don't understand *why*," Luke whined.

What am I supposed to tell him? That he needs to stay away from the house because there are some killers out there who know his daddy's name? That the press might want to interview him about his crazy psychic father? There was nothing more to say to the boy appropriate for his level of understanding. Cayce stood. He put a hand on Luke's head, messing up his hair. "Buddy, we can talk more about this later, but I have the afternoon shift at the diner, and if I don't get going, I'm going to be late. And we both know how Mike hates it when I'm late."

Luke lowered his head close to the pasta and began shoveling spoonfuls of it into his mouth, refusing to look at him.

He knew he was dismissed, and even though it hurt a bit, Cayce was relieved. For once, he was glad he had his job to go to. He knew it would be busy, and at least for the hours of his shift, he wouldn't have to think about murders, visions, or why his son was suddenly feeling rejected. Where would he find the time? And that was a blessing.

Outside, heat shimmered off the pavement, and Cayce hoped he'd be left alone. The news vans parked outside earlier—he was glad to see—were gone. In their place was the simple to-and-fro traffic on Pennsylvania Avenue: the eighteen-wheelers lumbering by, cars with bad mufflers. In the trees, gypsy moths weaved intricate webs. Cayce breathed in, but the air was like smoke, thick and unsatisfying, unable to reach the areas of lung he needed it to reach. The sun beat down, and he longed for the shower, the cool spray of water over his body. He could just close his eyes and let it flow. Peace...for just ten minutes or so. Was that too much to ask for?

And then he felt it.

For a moment, everything seized up, and Cayce was afraid he was going to have another vision of a murdered girl or a shallow grave. But this wasn't the same. Cayce slowed, looking out of the corners of his eyes to try to place this feeling of being watched. The traffic on the two-lane road flowed by, the faces behind steering wheels blank.

Yet the hair on his neck rose up. He could feel eyes on him. He stopped and turned, a hand to his forehead shielding his eyes from glare, and looked up and down the street. There was a green pickup parked a few yards away and a red Mustang just behind that. Both vehicles appeared vacant, though with the glare on their windshields, he couldn't be sure. The street was otherwise empty.

Cayce started to walk toward the Mustang, its faded red paint job almost calling to him. He didn't understand why he wanted to draw near. His breathing came faster as he got closer to the car and saw two people inside.

Cayce wanted to scream. Just stand on the quiet street and scream. He had no idea why, but the two silhouettes filled him with dread. His feet kept pulling him forward. The rational part of him wondered what he would say to the people in the car once he came abreast of it. The intuitive part was repelled and drawn at the same time. Cayce felt sick, and he didn't think it was the heat making him feel that way.

As he neared the car, there was movement, and he hurried closer. The engine roared to life, tires squealed, and the red Mustang raced down the street, kicking up pebbles and leaving the smell of exhaust in its wake.

Cayce tried to catch his breath, to slow his thundering heart.

It was them.

*

"That was close." Ian peered into the rearview mirror at the dark-haired young man standing on the sidewalk, staring after them. Ian would swear he could smell the fear coming off him.

Myra sat tight-lipped, rigid, body language betraying nothing, eyes hidden behind oversized sunglasses.

Ian slowed the car as they traveled east. "He almost walked right up to the car! We could have just grabbed him, found out what he knows, and then gotten rid of him. But that would have been too easy."

"You said we wouldn't kill anyone else."

"I said nothing of the sort. The Beast decides who dies and who lives. And that includes you, so lighten up." He pulled into a little frozen custard stand. "Ice cream?"

"Am I allowed?" Myra asked. "It's a lot of calories."

Ian rolled his eyes. "Live a little."

"Okay, a cone, then."

Ian took the keys from the ignition and turned to smile at Myra. "Good work back there."

Myra said nothing.

He put a hand on her shoulder. "You know, with the neighbor? Getting the goods on that D'Amico guy? What was it you said?"

Myra sighed and looked out the window. "I said I was from the insurance company and that I was trying to track him down because an uncle had left him a small amount of money." Myra continued to stare out the window, voice dead. "The woman volunteered the stuff about his son, about the grandparents."

"Still, it was a great job. You got her to trust you. I'll be right back with your cone. You deserve sprinkles, and you, my love, shall have them."

*

Cayce went into the house, slammed the door, and leaned up against it. He was as breathless as if he had run a mile. *It was them. It was them. It was them.* He saw the car with Sheryl McKenna in it, could see it in his mind's eye clear as memory.

He hobbled into the living room and collapsed on the sofa. *I need to get ready for work. I can't do this.* He wanted to run into the street, screaming and flailing his fists, telling anyone who would listen to chase the red Mustang. It was the car that had taken the girls to their deaths.

But who would listen?

Cayce closed his eyes, giving himself a moment to compose himself, but it was impossible. Along with the certainty that he had just seen the killers also dawned the knowledge the killers had been parked almost in front of his house—and they were watching.

Thank God Luke wasn't with me. Thank God Luke is at his grandparents' and not here.

Cayce rubbed his forehead, thinking maybe he should just call the police, get that Simmons woman on the phone and lie to her. Tell her to forget about the visions. The truth was he *had* seen the red Mustang and seen both Lucy Plant and Sheryl McKenna in it. Just look for a beat-up old red Mustang, he could say, and you'll be well on your way to solving these crimes.

Easy enough...if you hadn't already told your "visions" story to practically anyone who would listen. Why were you such a fool? Cayce paused, ready to kick himself, to take a fist to his very own face. But then he continued the monologue he was conducting with himself. *How were you to know? How were you to know how to deal with this gift, this curse? You only wanted to help people, and you never wanted to be involved at all.* He sighed. *Get ready for work. You still have a child to support, a living to make.*

Cayce headed for the shower, dropping a trail of clothes as he went.

Chapter Seventeen

The crowd at the diner was a nightmare—and in its own way, a blessing. Cayce had known that construction on City Hall a few blocks over was going to bring in some workers but had no idea how much of an impact the work would have on the diner. Right now, the place was filled with men in dusty work clothes and boots, baseball caps, and sunglasses, toothpicks between their teeth. They were a noisy bunch, and the small diner was filled with their husky voices and the clatter of their cutlery against Fiestaware dishes. The few regulars vied for his attention, all of them working his last nerve and all of them God's blessing. For the past three hours, he had not had a minute to spare to think about missing girls, the danger he was in, or the couple in the red Mustang. He was simply a machine, balancing three and four plates up his arm, a glass of iced tea in each hand, scurrying from counter to booth to table, refilling coffee, water, and soft drinks, asking "How is everything? Can I get you anything else right now?" His body had worked itself into an almost mindless rhythm, and it felt good to be on automatic pilot, to have his brain barely engaged. Maybe, he thought, a lobotomy would be the answer to all his woes.

But there was one thing he couldn't ignore: a vague nausea growing in his gut. The smell of the grill and the grease splattering in the back as Rosie, the short-order cook, fried up hamburgers and set trays of potatoes into bubbling grease didn't help matters much.

He hoped he wasn't getting sick, but in the back of his mind he knew this queasy feeling wasn't coming from any bug or greasy food but from fear.

And he didn't want to examine why he was afraid. *Although ignoring it might be a very stupid thing to do. Fear usually means pain, or it's a warning.* He thought suddenly of Luke. He didn't know why, but it made him gasp. He wanted to drop the plates he had picked up—hot turkey and hot meatloaf sandwiches with mashed potatoes and lots of gravy—and run from the diner. He had even begun lowering them toward the counter when one of the Creche sisters piped up, "Hey, Cayce, this coffee ain't gonna refill itself." The woman was smiling to indicate she meant no harm and holding up her mug to indicate she really did want it refilled...*now.*

Cayce grabbed the pot and hurried over toward Isabelle Creche. "Sorry, ma'am. We're just swamped in here today."

"Yeah...too many men."

"You got that right," Cayce answered and walked off, laughing, the gaiety belying the fingers of dread continuing to massage his insides. Cayce cleared tables, took orders, his nervousness increasing. Faces blurred; he grew confused. Had he served that four-top yet? What about the back booth; was it cleared?

When Cayce saw her, he almost dropped the plates of banana cream pie. Instead, he picked up his pace and set the pie in front of two of the workers so he could pause for a moment, to try to understand why seeing the woman in the booth at the back made his heart nearly stop and a sheen of clammy goose bumps break out.

He stopped near the counter and pretended to look down at his order pad, keeping his peripheral vision trained on the woman in the booth. Just seeing her sent prickles up and down Cayce's spine, ratcheting up the nausea to the point where Cayce was afraid he would have to run into the restroom to throw up the little food he had managed to eat so far today.

Mike bustled by behind him, brushing up against his back. "Customers. Customers," he whispered.

Cayce took in a deep breath, trying to slow his heart rate, the rise in his blood pressure, and the awful sickness just seeing this woman engendered.

He didn't know why the woman should bother him so. And wasn't it more and more the way, ever since his accident? For one thing, the blonde was barely a woman. She was a young girl, perhaps still in her teens. Never mind the glamour she attempted to project: the platinum bleach job peeking out from under a silky leopard scarf, the oversize tortoiseshell sunglasses, and the sixties-style sleeveless dress Cayce's mother would refer to as a "shift." She looked fresh out of high school. The foundation on her face did little to conceal a rash of pimples on her chin.

Cayce loaded up on plates and headed to another table, but he couldn't get the image of the girl out of his head. *Why? She's just sitting there, looking at a menu. Is it because Mike always tells us to kick singles out of booths when we're busy and to tell 'em to sit at the counter? Hardly.* Cayce's hands trembled, sloshing coffee into saucers as he set down food and drinks for yet another table of construction workers.

The nausea in the pit of his stomach peaked. He found an empty stool and—even though Mike would give him hell for it—collapsed into it, trying to hold down the bile burning the back of his throat, to stop the room from spinning. He took several deep breaths.

"What's with you?" Brenda Smart leaned close under the pretense of wiping off the counter. "You're white as a sheet."

Cayce managed a sickly smile. "Just felt a little weak in the knees is all. Maybe I'm just tired. Hey, could you get me a glass of water? I need to get back to work or Mike will can my ass." Cayce rubbed his head, regarding the girl out of the corner of his eye.

Brenda set a glass of ice water before him. Cayce gulped it down and wiped his mouth on the back of his hand. "Thanks." Brenda started to walk away. "Say, do you know that girl in the booth at the back?"

Brenda ran a hand through her red hair and squinted. She shook her head. "Nah. Never seen her before. Why? You interested?" Brenda winked, and Cayce attempted to manage a smile. Brenda knew he was gay. They had discussed his man-woes, or lack thereof, many a slow night at the diner.

Fortunately, Cayce was relieved of the responsibility of coming up with an answer because Brenda was called away by an old woman who wondered where the iced tea and tuna salad she had asked for were.

I need to get myself back to normal. A pulse was pounding in Cayce's temple; something twitched behind his left eye. When he closed his eyes for only a moment, he saw the blonde without the scarf, holding a video camera and moving slowly in a circle, keeping the camera trained on something Cayce couldn't quite see...but was sure he didn't want to.

Cayce hopped from the stool and ran to the restroom, where he threw up. When he came back, the girl was gone.

I have to get out of here. I have to get out of here and get home to Luke. Cayce felt the imperative with a certainty that went beyond reason. He trembled with the need of it. Getting out of here had all the allure of a shot of heroin in the vein of an addict. He'd lose his job over it if he had to. *Something is very wrong.*

Mike Bailey was in his tiny office at the rear of the diner. The room was little more than a closet, with space enough for a battered green metal desk, a chair, a couple of shelves, and a cork bulletin board. Mike had a mound of papers before him, and his fingers were manipulating a calculator.

Cayce stood in the doorway and stared at the sunburned bald spot on the top of his boss's head and took in the stained white shirt and the too-short tie stretched over his paunch. "Mike?"

He looked up. There was no sympathy in his eyes; if anything, all his face revealed was a slight trace of irritation. He had never been the kind of man Cayce felt he could turn to with a problem, but now he felt he had no choice. *Something is happening out there. Something I need to stop. They're coming for Luke. I have to get out of here. Now!* Mike's face went blank, and he returned to looking down at the papers spread out before him.

"What do you want, Cayce?"

"I don't feel so good, Mike. I don't think I can finish my shift."

Mike blew out a big sigh. "I feel for you, Cayce. I really do. But have you taken a look at the lunch crowd we have out there today?"

"I know, but..."

Mike held up his hand. "I'd really appreciate it if you could buck up for just another hour. Then me and Brenda can prob'ly handle things. Can you do that?"

Cayce found it difficult to swallow. A line of sweat trickled down his back, crawly. *No! No, I can't do that. In an hour, it will be too late.* "What will be too late?" Cayce blurted out without even thinking. *I'm not psychic, I'm just fucking crazy.*

"Huh?"

"Nothing, Mike." *Be strong. If you can't be strong now, it's all over.* Again Cayce wanted to ask "What?" but caught himself before he spoke the word aloud. "Listen, I gotta go. I'm sorry to leave you like this, but man, I can barely stand up." For emphasis, he added, "I just threw up. I don't wanna make anyone else sick, you know?"

"So be it!" He turned his full attention back to his calculator, sighing.

Cayce hurried away with Mike calling after him, "Your paycheck's gonna be docked for this."

"Thanks, Mike," Cayce called out and then whispered, "You're all heart."

*

Myra stood outside the restaurant. Her palms were sweaty, and she found it hard to catch her breath. She walked over to the area of downtown where several streets came together with a little fountain in the middle, called, rather grandly, "the Diamond." She sat by the fountain, trying to concentrate on the burbling water, to think simple thoughts like how hot it was and how the air was heavy with humidity and car exhaust.

But it didn't take long for her mind to wander back to why she was sitting there in the Diamond, across from a little magazine store called the Smoke Shop, with people hurrying by her to the few stores left in downtown Fawcettville. Oblivious. All these people and not one of them was aware she was sitting there waiting for her boyfriend to pick her up. Innocuous enough, sure, but not so innocuous when you factored in the awful truth that the same boyfriend would have with him a little boy he had just kidnapped.

My God, what am I doing? Murder, kidnapping, rape... How have I sunk so low so fast? Myra had never felt more trapped in her young life. Earlier, she had gotten up the courage to stage a full out-and-out argument with Ian over his plan, a plan that was still sketchy in her mind. She understood why he wanted the boy—to buy the father's silence—but how long were they expected to keep him? If the ransom was the dad's silence, would they ever give the boy back?

She had tried to tell Ian all the good reasons for not doing what he was proposing: they were already in far over their heads, they had already committed enough crime to send them both to prison for the rest of their lives. They could die by lethal injection or whatever they used. She would have to check to see what the capital punishment laws were in Pennsylvania, she thought, because it might be a future she would be facing very soon.

And then there was the whole issue of having this little boy around to take care of, for however long. She didn't think either of them had the ability to take care of themselves, let alone a child. But Ian wouldn't listen. Of course he invoked the name of the "Beast," saying that he would protect them and it was out of his hands. "I am only carrying out orders," he intoned, a glazed look coming into his eyes.

Ian was crazy.

And she was trapped.

Myra had not gone to the restaurant because Ian had wanted her to. He probably would have been furious at her for showing her face. His plan was that she just sit tight downtown while he went to the grandparents'. He would swing by and pick her up once he had the boy. Then they could plot their next move. Myra needed to see what Cayce D'Amico looked like. She didn't know why. She *did* know that seeing the man up close would make things even harder.

Oh shit, Myra...Penny...whatever...come off it! You can be honest with yourself just sitting here on this fine summer day. You went to the restaurant because you wanted to tell Cayce D'Amico that he needed to get home, that he needed to protect his boy. You should have told Cayce what was going down. By doing so, you could have saved a little boy's life. Because, my dear—don't kid yourself—you know Ian and you know the Beast and you know, sure as anything, that the little boy is going to end up just like the two girls. And you'll be expected to get it all on tape.

Myra swallowed hard, the bile and acid from her stomach splashing up at the back of her throat. She turned on the bench, bit her knuckle hard enough to draw blood, and tried to hold back the sobs. *You're a coward. You could have helped that guy. Thank God he at least left. I hope he went home—fast.* From across the street, Myra had watched Cayce D'Amico hurry out of the diner and run down the street to a beat-up car, then watched as the car roared by, muffler chugging and transmission whining. But the car wasn't going so fast that Myra couldn't take in the panic on Cayce's face. *You could have run after him. He stopped at a light just a few yards away. You could have made it the short distance and stopped him. It's what Ian would have wanted.* A grim chuckle escaped Myra's lips at her next thought. *It's what the Beast would want.*

But you didn't. And hopefully God was watching and winning the battle with the Beast, and Cayce D'Amico would make it home in time to save his son.

"Penny? Penny Landsdale!"

Myra was shocked out of her reverie by a familiar voice. She looked up into the squinting eyes of Tammie Blankenship, former classmate and, once upon a time, one of the few people she called a friend back in New Hope in a different time, in a different life. She and Tammie had spent many nights at each other's houses, had sneaked their first cigarettes together, had sworn each other to secrecy over what they would be willing to do with certain boys at New Hope High, had played Barbies together when they were far too old for it, experimented with marijuana. She hadn't seen Tammie in ages. It seemed like a different person altogether who had had those experiences with the pudgy dark-haired girl standing before her, pulling down her cropped blouse over a belly that should never have been exposed. But Tammie was like that: she saw someone different in the mirror than everyone else did.

Myra pulled the sunglasses down low, squinting at Tammie, then replaced them. She knew she looked very different from Penny. Different enough to get away with it. "I don't know a Penny Landsdale. You must have me mixed up with someone else." Myra studied her fingernails.

"Oh come on! Girl! You're looking good, but don't play games with your old best friend. I—"

"No, really. My name is *not* Penny...and I wish you'd leave me alone." Myra scanned the street for a red Mustang, thinking this would be exactly the perfect time for Ian to show up, the car screeching to a halt with a screaming kid in the backseat. A perfect witness. Just to get rid of Tammie, Myra added, "I don't even know why you'd think I'd even know someone like you. Why don't you cover up that gut? It's disgusting."

Tammie froze as if Myra had shot a poison dart directly into her heart. Myra could see her swallow, see her face begin to crumple. Tammie hurried away, head down.

Myra sat back against the bench and blew out a big sigh. *Ian, where are you?*

*

Sarah thwacked the veal cutlets with a wooden mallet. It was going to be a good dinner. She would at least see little Luke eating some nutritious food for once in his life. She gave the last cutlet one more thwack with the mallet and held it up. "Almost paper thin, good work." Dinner was going to be simple: dredge the veal in a little flour, dip it into some beaten egg, then a pile of bread crumbs seasoned with garlic, parsley, oregano, basil, and thyme. Then the cutlets would go into a pan already searing hot, the olive oil on the surface shimmering, almost smoking. A quick sear, first one side and then the other, and...delicious. A squeeze of lemon on top, a few sprigs of parsley, and they would be eating like kings. Accompanied by a side of boiled red potatoes and some Swiss chard sautéed with a little olive oil and garlic, the meal would be the kind of thing, Sarah was sure, Luke didn't get to see much of. Hadn't he told her once that Cayce fed him cereal sometimes for dinner? Sarah shook her head, shaking the flour off a piece of veal. *I didn't raise my son that way. I taught him how to cook just like Mama taught me, even though he was a boy.*

And now here was Luke, coming in the door. "Shoes off! Shoes off! I don't want you tracking dirt on my clean kitchen floor."

"Yes, Nana." Luke dropped his schoolbooks in a heap next to him, then unbuckled and removed his sandals— *Sandals! What kind of school lets kids wear sandals?*— and placed them near the baseboard. "Where's Oreo?"

"Tied up outside, where he belongs. I don't know how you let that smelly animal in the house with you."

"Oreo's nice." Luke went over to the table and pulled an orange from the fruit bowl in its center. Sarah snatched it out of his hand. "Na-ah! You'll spoil your supper. We'll be eating in about ten minutes. Go upstairs and wash your hands."

"Yes, Nana."

She listened as he shuffled away, heard his quick exchange with Sam in the living room.

"You winnin', Pap-Pap?"

"Oh yeah, up to $30,000 now."

Sarah heard the slap of a high five and the theme music from *Jeopardy!* Boys, she thought, sticking a fork into the new potatoes boiling on the stove.

Sarah was just giving the Swiss chard a final shake in the colander when a tap came at the back door. Sarah shook the colander once more, then turned to look through the screen door. She wasn't expecting anyone. She lifted her head a little to peer through the glasses perched on her nose.

A young man stood there. Handsome guy, big, with dark hair and a dark complexion. Maybe he was Italian. He was dressed nicely, not like most of the guys his age you saw around town lately in their uniform of jeans, ball caps, and NASCAR T-shirts. This guy wore a white button-down shirt and nicely pressed black pants. He looked presentable. Sarah wiped her hands on her apron and smiled. The man was holding something behind his back, and it made Sarah think, for a moment, that he was bringing flowers to surprise her with. What nonsense!

"Hello?" Sarah came to the screen door, still rubbing her hands on her apron. She reached out to unlock it, then pulled back her hand. These days, you couldn't be too careful. Things weren't like they used to be. But this man looked so nice! So trustworthy. Still, she would keep the screen door locked until she found out what he was doing, standing on her back porch.

"Hi." The young man's voice was deep and warm. He had such an honest face.

"Can I help you?"

"I'm afraid I might have some bad news." He finally pulled his hand out from behind his back, and Sarah's eyes widened.

"I think this might be yours?"

"Oh jeez..." Luke would be a wreck. The man was holding out Oreo's collar and the length of clothesline she had used to tie him up in the backyard. She didn't know how he had done it, but it looked like that dog was some kind of escape artist.

Finally, Sarah unlocked the door. "Come on in. That belongs to my grandson's dog." Sarah shook her head. "Did you see the dog at all?"

"Actually, I did. That's why I stopped. He ran out in front of my car." The man smiled, but there was a bit of sorrow in his eyes. "I just missed hitting him, really had to slam on the brakes."

He moved farther into the kitchen, sniffing the air. "Smells like you're a good cook."

Sarah blushed. "A little veal. It's nothin'." Sarah noticed Luke had come into the kitchen. Well, actually, he was hanging back near the entrance. He regarded the man with wide eyes, and Sarah could see his eyes moving from the man's face to the collar and rope.

"That's Oreo's."

Sarah looked to the man then back to Luke. "It looks like Oreo got away."

Luke started shaking his head, and his eyes brightened with tears. "*Nooo.*"

"This is..." Sarah cocked her head.

The man gave Luke a huge smile. "I'm Ian. I saw your dog running away. He went down First Avenue. I bet he hasn't gotten too far. Maybe you and your grandma could take a walk down there?"

"Nana? Could we? C'mon, we need to move before Oreo gets too far." He tugged at her hand.

Sarah looked over to the stove, where her supper was simmering, bubbling, and sautéing. "I can't leave supper right now, Luke."

The man squatted down and put his hand on Luke's shoulder. "Want me to help, sport? I saw where he went. With my car, we could probably track him down in a few minutes." He looked up at Sarah and gave her a winning smile. "That is, if it's okay with your grandma here."

Sarah didn't say anything, rubbing her hands on her apron.

"Never mind—it's probably not a good idea. These days, you can't be too careful." Ian turned toward the door.

"But Oreo!" Luke whined. He looked ready to burst into sobs.

"I don't know…" Sarah glanced out the window.

Ian stood and put his hands up. "It's okay. I understand. You don't know me from Adam. Better to be safe these days." Then, to Luke: "I'm sure Oreo will come back, tail between his legs and hungry for dinner." He smiled at Luke.

"Please, Nana. We'll have a better chance if we can go in the car. Please!"

Sarah swallowed hard. He certainly looked like a trustworthy young man. Why would he have bothered to even go to the trouble of coming to the back door if he wasn't someone who wanted to help, a Good Samaritan? He could have just driven on. That's what most folks would have done.

She took in a big breath and let it out quickly. "I guess it's okay. But just for a little bit, Luke. Supper's almost ready. If you don't see the dog in—" Sarah glanced at her watch. "—ten minutes, I want you to come home. Ian here is probably right; Oreo will be back. If you don't find him now, he'll find you. He has a good home with you. Dogs know." Sarah turned back to the stove. "It's okay if you want to run around the block in your car, but please don't spend too much of your time. If you don't see him, I'm sure he'll be back. If not, I'm promising Luke right now I'll take him over to the pound first thing in the morning." She looked down at Luke. "It'll be all right. Now you better run along, before he gets too far." Sarah smiled. "Or too dirty."

"If you're sure…"

"I think it'll be fine." Sarah sniffed. "Now, my food's gonna burn if I don't get back to it."

She watched as the kind young man put his hand gently on the back of Luke's head and led him out the door. In a minute, she heard the roar of an engine coming to life. She turned to grab her tongs to take the Swiss chard out of the pan.

She heard the closing theme music from *Jeopardy!* and then Sam's shuffle into the kitchen. He paused in the archway, raising his eyebrows. "Where's Luke?"

"Oreo got away. Lucky for us someone spotted him before he got too far. A very nice young man who took the time to stop his car and come and tell us."

"That was nice, but where's Luke?"

"The young man, Ian he said his name was, is taking Luke around the neighborhood in his car so they can find Oreo." Sarah turned to the stove and began lifting the veal out with a spatula, transferring it to a platter.

"And you let him go?"

Sarah turned back to her husband. His grizzled face didn't look happy; his heavy eyebrows were pushed together, and he was frowning.

She tried to smile, but already she was questioning if she had done the right thing. "He was very nice. I'm sure it's fine."

"For your sake, I hope so." Sam turned and went back into the living room. She heard him call over his shoulder. "For Luke's sake, I mean. For Luke's sake."

Sarah turned back to her supper. Suddenly nothing looked or smelled so good anymore. *Everything will be fine. He was so nice!*

*

Cayce sped down Hill Road toward Pennsylvania Avenue. He could see his parents' green-shingled house in the distance. *Something is not right. Something is not right.*

He almost collided with the car to his left when he saw the red Mustang pull away from the curb. "No!" Cayce shrieked and pressed down hard on the accelerator. The sick feeling in his stomach that had begun at the diner was now in full bloom. His stomach churned; there was a thin sheen of sweat covering his face and trickling down his back. He could barely swallow, and when he succeeded, the sharp tang of bile came back up. He had to white-knuckle the steering wheel, his hands were shaking so badly.

The car was heading east toward Pittsburgh. Even now, he was talking to himself and trying to rationalize. *It's just a car. It might not even be them. And if it is... Oh God, what if it's them? What about Luke? Surely Ma would never let him go with... But what if they just grabbed Luke as he played in the yard?*

There was a traffic light up ahead, at the corner of Pennsylvania and Mulberry Street. It was changing from yellow to red, and a car was pulling out from Mulberry Street. Cayce cried out, "Damn!" and beat his hand on the steering wheel. The red Mustang picked up speed. Cayce watched, twitching, as it continued north and then rounded a bend and went out of sight. "No," he whispered.

"Come on, come on." Cayce drummed his fingers on the steering wheel, waiting for the world's longest traffic light to cycle through back to green. A voice very much like his mother's began to whisper. *Now, Cayce, wouldn't it make sense just to stop for a minute at Ma and Pop's?*

Just see if everything's okay before you go tearing off after some strangers that you might scare half out of their minds? Most likely, Luke will be sitting at the kitchen table, playing with one of his X-Men figurines and waiting for supper. Ma will be wondering why you're home from work early.

It wasn't the voice of his mother, Cayce thought, burning some rubber as he screeched through the intersection once the light changed. It was his own voice, the one he had before the accident. Before he had begun having the visions and inexplicably knowing things.

He remembered Lucy Plant in her shallow grave down by the river, and he knew Luke was in trouble. *That voice—the one telling you something's wrong—is right, Cayce, and you know it.* He sped by his parents' house, laying on the horn as someone started to cross the street at First Avenue. He wasn't about to slow down. He would round the bend up ahead, and the Mustang would be in view. He would be able to catch up. He had to.

They have Luke. I don't know what story they gave to Ma, but it wouldn't have been hard. God bless her, she isn't the brightest of souls. Cayce let his mind drift, and he saw him at his mother's back door, smiling. *Him.* He had seen him in visions before, and the thought that he might now have Luke made Cayce want to throw up. He pushed the accelerator to the floor and glanced down to see he was doing almost eighty.

He rounded the bend at Pleasant View Drive, tires squealing. He clung to the steering wheel, almost losing control. The car felt like it was going to go up on two wheels, but he managed to keep it together. The red Mustang was probably about a mile ahead. There was a beat-up Ford pickup, rusted green, and a brand new SUV in a bright metallic blue between them. The Mustang was going pretty fast. Cayce swore he could see Luke's face peering out of its back window. His arms were extended, the way he used to do when he was a baby and wanted to be picked up. He was crying, his little mouth open in a silent howl. Cayce knew he was too far away to see any such thing in reality. But still, he knew his vision was right. It was true.

What if they get away? Cayce's heart thudded. *Is this what it feels like when you have a heart attack? What if I get stopped at another light and they turn and head up the hill, get lost in the maze of streets? How will I ever find them?* Cayce sped up, and his front bumper came dangerously close to the back bumper and hitch of the pickup in front of him.

He then had a flash so real it almost caused him to run off the road. He struggled to hold on to the steering wheel, as if it had a mind of its own. He burst into sobs and, without warning, found himself wailing.

He saw Luke being led by the hand by the girl with the platinum hair. They were heading toward that trailer he had seen in his visions. Low, ominous clouds— nearly black—gathered on the horizon.

"Oh God," Cayce whimpered and whipped the car out left of the center line in a desperate effort to get around the pickup and the SUV before the light ahead—at Erie Street—changed.

All he could think of was Luke. *He's going to die if I don't catch up. He's going to die...* Cayce might as well have been dreaming. He didn't see the little silver Sentra coming toward him, didn't even notice it, in fact, until he heard the shriek of its brakes, the bright alarm of its horn, and saw its grille rising up, huge, in front of him. Too late.

He slammed on the brakes, pushing them to the floor, gripping the steering wheel and throwing himself back against the seat for leverage, but there was no time to stop.

Cayce didn't even have time to scream as the two cars collided head-on.

Part two

Chapter Eighteen

His shoulder hurt. In a few hours, Cayce knew, he would have one hell of a bruise. When his car and the Sentra collided, the air bag saved him from any real damage, but he had somehow twisted in his seat upon impact, going up and to his side, slamming into the driver's side window hard enough to crack it. But the only injury was a bruise. The paramedics told him he was lucky as he sat by the side of the road, head in hands, shaking. The hood of his car pointed toward the sky; steam rose from the engine compartment. Everywhere, the smell of antifreeze. A teenage boy had been driving the Sentra and paced nearby, on a cell phone. Cayce tuned out his urgent, fast, and broken-voiced chatter. Cayce couldn't join him in the panic over this car accident.

Yes, they had told him he was lucky. Both cars had been totaled in the collision, and both vehicles looked like no one should have walked away alive. And perhaps no one would have in the days before air bags. But the collision was head-on, and the air bags had saved both of them from flying through the windshield or being forced down and into the engine.

Cayce didn't feel lucky. He kicked at some gravel and whispered, "Fuck." The red Mustang was, by now, long gone. There was no way to ever catch up. Luke was inside. He knew it now with the same certainty that he knew his own name and that he waited tables in a diner in

Fawcettville, Pennsylvania. He saw again Luke's terrified face looking out the back window of the Mustang, the way he seemed to know Cayce was behind him, his despair at his dad not being able to save him. Every child wants a father who can rescue him. He had failed as a dad; he had not been able to help Luke when he needed him most. And now God only knew what was happening to Luke. Cayce could only hope that God would watch over him, because he had done a shitty job.

He wondered if the image of Luke reaching out to him from the car would be the last he'd ever have of his little boy. A snapshot of despair, burned into his brain for eternity. A sob, like a cough, escaped him.

He knew—again, with complete certainty—this image was not the hallucination of an overprotective father, but reality. *Luke was in the car with a person or people who had killed two girls.* Cayce could barely work any spit down his throat. He didn't know how long he would have or even if it was already too late, but he had to find his boy. *The only reason they would want him is because they know about me. They know about me because my name was in the paper, and in a town this size, it's not so hard to find someone. They realized I know something, and Luke is their insurance that I don't lead someone to another shallow grave or, worse, to wherever it is they're living.* Cayce had a quick flash of a view from a hilltop, a view he had seen many times before, but the image stayed in his mind's eye only long enough to tease. He wanted time to look down from the hilltop, to see how the river curved and what landmarks were on the other side. Already, he was learning how to use this gift or curse. The knowledge that they had taken Luke as some sort of insurance to buy his silence was cold comfort. Who knew how they would treat his little boy? Who knew when they would tire of having Luke around and do to him the same things they had done to those girls and then move on? Cayce balled his fists in impotent rage and looked up to the sky, as if God was looking down and would tell him what to do.

But all he saw were banks of clouds moving in, threatening rain.

The cops had asked if he had someone to call who could come and pick him up, if he wanted the city to tow his car or if he wanted to call a private company. Cayce couldn't think. There was only worry about Luke; they could have set the car on fire for all he cared. "Let the city tow it," he had said in a dead voice, barely above a whisper. "I don't care." They had explained the car would be put in the city lot, and he would have to make arrangements to get it out. There would be daily storage fees. Was he sure he didn't want to call a tow company? Cayce just shook his head, feeling shaken and empty. Even the boy whose car he had hit offered Cayce his cell phone. He just waved him away and ran after the officer who had stopped to write up the details about the accident.

Cayce caught up to him and tapped him on the back. He knew his face must look crazy, a mask of anguish. He didn't know what the officer would think about what he was about to say. That he was in shock? He couldn't tell him the truth. He'd have to lie.

"Officer! Officer, please! Do you know why I had this accident?"

The officer was young; this might have been his first job out of school. He couldn't have been more than in his early twenties. His dark brown eyes regarded Cayce, and he could tell the cop wanted to be compassionate. He could also tell his guard was up, and he was on the alert for the ravings of a crazy man who had just been in a head-on collision. Cayce didn't know how he knew these things from just a glance at a young and impassive face, but he did.

"You were going too fast?"

Cayce nodded. "That's right. I was going too fast. But do you wanna know why?" Cayce fought to keep his voice level. He could feel it struggling to go up higher, into the realm of hysteria. "Do you know why?" Cayce moved in close to his face. "Because my son was kidnapped."

The officer cocked his head. His expression changed from one of concern to one of alarm, and his dark eyes brightened.

Cayce swallowed and nodded. "That's right, Officer..." He glanced down at his badge. "Officer Rivera. I was chasing a car—a red Mustang—my son was inside. Someone took him from my parents' house. I was trying to catch up with the car. I could see Luke—that's my son—in the backseat. He was reaching out for me. Oh God, we have to find him!" Cayce couldn't hold on. He clutched frantically at the officer's arm and chest.

"Calm down, sir. Let me take care of this."

A short while later, he found himself sitting in JT Simmons's office once more. They had gotten Cayce some water, and Simmons had been surprisingly sympathetic. Where the older woman had once been cold to the point, Cayce thought, of cruelty, she was now suddenly compassionate, her dark eyes filled with concern. She had made sure Cayce was comfortable, offered him a drink, and was now sitting back in her chair, a phone receiver to her ear.

Cayce watched her. JT Simmons was calling his mother. Cayce had managed, between sobs, to tell most of the story, though keeping to himself that the image of Luke in the backseat was only a vision and not an actual sight.

"Well, let's just give your parents a call. Maybe they know who he went off with, and it's not as sinister as you think."

Cayce knew it was probably even more sinister than he could possibly think but humored the woman. He needed her on his side.

Simmons punched in the number and listened, smiling at Cayce. "Don't get too worried just yet. These things sometimes resolve themselves very quickly, often without any problem. We've seen—" Simmons stopped when she made a connection. "Hello? Hello, is this Mrs. Sarah D'Amico?" Simmons paused. "This is Detective JT Simmons, from the Fawcettville Police Department." Simmons stopped, and Cayce could hear his mother's voice, sounding tinny, broadcast through the receiver. She was talking fast, panic making her voice higher. *God, I already know how this is going to go...and it's not going to go well.*

Simmons put up a placating hand, even though Sarah couldn't see it. "Mrs. D'Amico? Mrs. D'Amico, could you please calm down for a moment and let me finish? I have a couple of things to tell you, and I want you to know up front that your son is all right."

A surge of unintelligible words issued out of the receiver again. If the situation wasn't so dire, it would have been funny, like some comedy routine. Cayce could tell JT Simmons was trying to keep her cool by the way she drummed her nails on the desk, just waiting for Sarah to say what she needed to say. Cayce concentrated on the blunt fingers and square-cut nails, noticing how some of them were stained yellow from tobacco.

"Mrs. D'Amico? Mrs. D'Amico…. Cayce is sitting right here with me. He's been in a car accident." Simmons paused. "No. No, he wasn't on drugs. I just wanted to reassure you that he's okay." Simmons paused again. "It was on Pennsylvania Avenue, just up from your house."

"C'mon, Mom, let the woman finish," Cayce whispered.

"Anyway, Cayce is fine, although he'll probably be needing a new vehicle. What I'm calling about is your grandson. Is he, by any chance, there with you right now?" Simmons looked at Cayce over the top of her glasses. She looked down at her desk and nodded. "I see." She looked up again and frowned. "Did you get the man's name?" Simmons pulled a yellow legal pad in front of herself and poised a pen above it. "Ian?" She scrawled. "You didn't get a last name? Okay. How long ago was this?"

Cayce's heart had begun to thud uncomfortably, feeling like it might break through his chest. He was finding it hard to breathe, and the room was beginning to spin. He could barely hear JT Simmons saying, "And did you get a look at the car they left in?"

Cayce felt everything flicker, like the lights going dim in a power surge. He whimpered, "A red Mustang," before collapsing to the floor.

Chapter Nineteen

"Come on, there's nothing to worry about." Myra held out her hand, *again.* But the boy would not get out of the backseat of the car. It was as though he had planted himself there, an immovable force. Myra knew even if she reached in and grabbed him, he would cling to whatever hold he could find in the cramped interior. Even if she could loosen him, he would kick and scream loud enough for people at the bottom of the hill to hear him.

Ian wasn't helping. He stood by, simply watching, smoking a cigarette. *Damn him.* Myra would have liked some help. At least Ian could have used brute force, but he was leaving it all up to her. The more she failed at her task, the angrier he got. She felt like he almost wanted the anger, wanted her to fail so the rage could build and he could later take it out on her. She knew from past experience what her "punishment" would entail: violation and pain. And Ian could be very creative in delivering those things. She could pull back her clothing and reveal the scratches and bruises to prove it.

She wanted to cry herself as she looked at the little boy in the backseat, sobbing, his lower lip out like a comic caricature of a child's despair. Along with his panic and sadness, though, she could see how resolute he was, one hand clinging to the armrest so hard his little knuckles had gone bloodless. He stared at her as if he was challenging her.

Myra sighed. She offered the boy a smile and wondered for the first time if she looked scary, garish with her platinum hair, too much eye makeup, and bloodred lipstick. "Honey, aren't you hungry? Just come into the trailer with us, and I'll make you a nice peanut butter sandwich." Myra put a hand to her forehead. "We have cable. We can watch cartoons on the Cartoon Network."

"I want to go home," the boy managed to get out between sobs. "I want my dad."

"I know you do, honey, and we'll call him a little later."

Ian blew out a harsh sigh. "Get on with it," he whispered between clenched teeth.

She wanted to whirl on him and tell him he wasn't helping. She wanted to ask why he was just standing there anyway. Why didn't he at least go into the house and let her deal with this her way instead of making her feel more pressured and stressed than she already was—which was pretty stressed and pressured. They had, after all, just added kidnapping to the other felonies they had committed this summer. If they were ever caught...

But she couldn't say anything. She knew if she did, the best result she could hope for was to earn herself a bloody nose or lip. Lately, Ian was quicker and quicker to reach out and harm her in any way he could. She trembled at the thought of it.

Myra ducked her head into the car. "Please, sweetheart." She reached out with her hand and whispered frantically, hoping Ian wouldn't hear. "He'll beat me if you don't get out of the car." She wanted to weep. "He'll really hurt me. And he might hurt you too. He wouldn't even think twice about it. Is that what you want?"

Luke suddenly stopped crying, and his face went white. She knew she had scared him, and she hated to do it, but this was about survival. She did not want to help dig a grave for this sweet little boy. She didn't want to stand by with a video camera while Ian did unspeakable things to him. "Please." Myra held out her hand and bit down on her lower lip to hold back her own sobs.

And Luke scooted over on the seat, took her hand. Myra breathed a sigh of relief, smiling at the boy. "Thank you," she mouthed.

The pair walked by Ian, who stood silent, arms folded across his chest, watching their progress across the trash-choked weeds they called a front yard, up the two cinder blocks they called a front porch, and inside.

The interior of the trailer was dark and close, as if the heat and humidity outside had made itself a home there, stretching out its heavy, sweaty legs. The little boy held fast to Myra's hand, his own small and clammy. She knew he was having as much trouble seeing as she was. It would take a moment for their eyes to adjust to the darkness inside after the glare outside.

The boy said nothing, and neither did Myra. She was waiting. She knew Ian was just outside and wondered why he wasn't immediately behind them. She had left the door open a crack. Quickly, she squatted in front of Luke. "Look, honey, there's a couple of things I want to tell you before my boyfriend, Ian, comes inside. One is, don't disobey him. Do whatever he asks, and do it immediately. There's no gain in backtalk or not obeying. Do you understand?" The little boy stared back at her. Even in the darkness, she could see his eyes were vacant, his skin pale. He had gone, in just a few instants, from terrified to numb. She supposed it was how one coped. She had seen the same thing happen to Sheryl McKenna after Ian… Well, she didn't want to think about that now. That was in the past. And she had the present before her that she needed to deal with—urgently. "The second thing is you might hear Ian talk about the Beast. The Beast, just so you know, isn't real. It's just Ian and his imagination. So don't be scared when he talks about the Beast. The Beast is just like those monster movies you see on the TV. It's all just made up, just for fun. It's—"

Ian walked in, and it seemed the temperature in the trailer dropped, like the air had been sucked out of the space. He blocked what little light was coming in through the crack in the doorway. All the curtains had been drawn. He stood for a moment, looking down at the two of them.

Suddenly, Myra felt silly—no, disloyal—crouching before the boy, and she stood and faced Ian. She was waiting to take orders.

And the orders came. "Tie him up."

Ian went off to light candles, to put on some weird music he had discovered in a used record store—mostly vinyl; Ian was the only person Myra knew who owned a turntable. The record was called *Hands of Jack the Ripper* and was by the British guy who called himself Screaming Lord Sutch. It was just a lot of screaming—that much was right—horrible music about death and monsters. Myra didn't like it and was sure it scared the boy.

"Why are you still standing there?"

Myra jumped when she felt Ian draw close. Shadows danced around the tiny living room, almost alive, changing with the flicker of the candle flames.

Ian put his face right up to hers. "I told you to do something. I didn't mean to do it in five minutes or when you're damn good and ready. I meant for you to do it immediately."

Myra nodded. She looked down at Luke, who stared up with wide eyes, looking first at her, then at Ian. She could see his lower lip trembling, just a tiny bit, and he was trying to hold it in, to be brave. It made her feel even more protective of him.

"It's not me asking, Myra. The Beast needs it. We have to be able to control him. Now get busy." He took her face in his hand, squeezing too hard on her jaw. She gasped. "Or would you prefer I tie him up? I can do it, but it will be a lot less pleasant for all concerned."

Myra sucked in some air and moved her head very gently and very slowly to free herself from Ian's painful grasp. She rubbed at her jaw. "I can do it. But..." She gnawed at one of her nails, staring up at him. "I can do it, but do you really think we need to, Ian? I can keep an eye on him, make sure he doesn't get in any trouble."

"I told you. The Beast commands it. Let's not question him."

Myra nodded. "It's just that we don't know—" Almost before she could see it, Ian's hand flew up and slapped her so hard across the face her head swiveled and she saw stars.

He groped in the kitchen drawer and drew out a tangle of bungee cords and handed them to her. "No more chances. Are you going to do this, or shall I?"

Myra clenched her teeth to keep from weeping. "Right away," she whimpered.

Ian stalked out of the trailer.

Myra hurried back to the boy, who was sniffling. He was trying not to cry. She squatted down before him, a tangle of bungee cords in her hand. "You don't want Ian to tie you up, right? I'll make sure these won't hurt...and I'm sorry, but we have to do what Ian says."

Myra began wrapping the first cord around the small boy's frame, grateful that he sort of stood there like a dummy, like some sort of mannequin. She didn't know if she had the strength to fight him if he had chosen to be obstinate.

Ian came back into the trailer, flinging the door open so hard it slammed into the wall. With him came a burst of brilliant light so bright it hurt Myra's eyes. She turned to squint up at his dark figure, a silhouette with a sickly whitish glow surrounding him. Her throat was dry as she fumbled with the second of the bungee cords. "I'm going as fast as I can..."

Ian shook his head. She looked to his hand and saw what he had gone outside for: the video camera. "I thought we should have a memento of the occasion. Just hold on."

Myra bowed her head and knelt before the boy, staring at the floor. She wanted to say something to reassure him but found there were no words left in her head. She felt as numb as the little boy looked, his skin sweaty and ashen, breathing through his mouth. She simply waited.

Ian held the video camera in front of him. "Smile for the camera." Even an innocuous comment like this one held a kind of threat in it, a veiled implication of terror. She looked up at him, barely able to open her eyes against the punishing light. "Do we have to?" she whispered.

She wasn't sure Ian heard her. He didn't respond, just began moving the camera up and down the two of them, the lens caressing them, framing them in a forced embrace.

"Get busy, Myra. What do I have you for if you can't even carry out the simplest tasks?"

Myra gritted her teeth and wished she had something, anything—an ice cube, a piece of chewing gum—to alleviate the awful dryness in her mouth and throat. She busied herself with the cords, wrapping them around the boy's limp form, wishing now he *did* have some fight in him. This deadness, this *just standing and waiting* was sad. It made her want to cry. It was as if the boy had given up already and knew what was in Myra's head: visions of torturous death and a shallow grave.

"It's gonna be all right." Myra tried to put a little breath behind her words. "Would you like to lie down in the bedroom?"

Ian snickered. "What did you have in mind?"

Myra looked up at him, trying to make contact with the eyes behind the camera. "Don't." She shook her head.

Just then, all three of them froze, a weird, almost family-like tableau.

Someone was knocking at the door to the trailer.

Chapter Twenty

Cayce stood at the door to JT Simmons's office, feeling numb and weak from his earlier collapse. Everything had an aura of the surreal about it, like if he just shook his head hard enough, all of this would go away and he'd be back at the diner, serving up big platters of burgers and chili cheese fries.

The visions about the girls were horrible enough. But at least he didn't know them. At least it wasn't personal.

JT's voice came at him like it was traveling through a tunnel. Cayce could imagine how his face looked to the detective: dull, eyes without brightness, mouth partly open, a cow chewing its cud.

"Now you go home and get some rest. Let us get the wheels in motion so we can find your boy. Don't worry, there will be plenty for you to do later. Right now, I need to get on this."

Cayce took small comfort in the fact that Simmons was taking Luke's disappearance—abduction, really—so seriously.

"Before you *do* start to get some rest, though, I need you to go right inside your house and find the best and most recent picture of your boy you can find and give it to the officer to bring back here. We'll take that, scan it, and send it out over the wires so we can have people looking in the whole tristate area, instead of just here in Fawcettville. We can also make up some flyers." Simmons smiled. "Cayce, a lot of times, kids come back within the first couple of hours. Try not to worry too much."

Cayce let loose a sob. "Try not to worry? Try not to worry? Are you crazy? This isn't a case of some little boy wandering off. He was *taken*. Do I have to remind you? I saw him in a car with someone I don't know." Cayce looked down at his watch, its face blurry through his tears but still clear enough to see that two hours had already elapsed since he saw the car speeding away, two hours since it had pulled away from in front of his parents' house on Pennsylvania Avenue.

Simmons shook her head. "I'm sorry, Cayce. I was just trying to comfort you."

"I don't want comfort! I want my son back!" Cayce was trying to rein in his terror, his wildly beating heart. He knew he was just a few inches away from crossing the border into hysteria. His gut wrenched with panic and loss.

Simmons put a hand on his shoulder. "We're going to plaster this town and all around with that picture of Luke you're going to go home and get right now. Soon there will be hundreds—no, *thousands*—of people looking for Luke. If anyone has seen him, we'll know. Right away. And we can act on it."

Cayce sniffed. "You even believe that?"

Simmons took his face in her large hands and forced Cayce to meet her gaze. "We *have* to believe that, Cayce. We can't give up hope already. Now let the officer take you home, give him that picture, and then give yourself permission to lie down... even if it's only for twenty minutes. Stress like you're under is draining, and we need you to be strong. We need your energy so we can find him." She got right up in Cayce's face. "Understand?"

Cayce nodded.

"Now go," the detective said gently. "I'll be in constant touch."

Cayce followed the officer, a young guy with broad shoulders and curly dark hair, down a corridor and into the bright sunshine outside. Cars passed in front of City Hall. Strangers walked along the street, laughing and talking. An older man with gray hair paused to light a cigarette.

It was as if nothing had happened. *Don't they know my son has been kidnapped? I don't even know what's happening to him! What they're doing to him! And no one even cares!* The bright sunshine of the day was completely inappropriate. Cayce felt sick, like his legs were going to go out from under him. He sat down suddenly on the concrete steps.

The young officer squatted next to him, dark eyes alive with concern. "I'll give you a minute, sir."

Cayce shook his head, trying to draw in some air. He didn't know if this faintness, this queasiness, would ever go away. "Never mind." He grabbed on to the other guy's arm and used it to hoist himself up. "Let's go. I need to get you a photograph."

*

He had given the officer—Justin Garcia—Luke's first-grade school photo. Other than growing a shoe size, he looked essentially the same. Cayce knew from memory what the photograph looked like: Luke's somber expression, as if he knew there was no way some silly kid photographer could make *him* smile, the green-and-blue plaid shirt he had worn that day, the cowlick sticking up, and the openness in his big green eyes. Today, he could not bear to look at the photo. He had simply gotten it from the junk drawer in the kitchen, where it had lain in a plastic bag for months with others just like it—he had exhorted Luke to trade his photo with classmates, but Luke had insisted the whole idea was silly: "What do I need to do that for? I see those same old faces every day anyway."—and handed it facedown to the officer.

He tried to reassure Cayce. "This is really going to help. Getting his face out there."

He took a quivering breath, and Cayce suddenly realized the officer was almost as scared as he was. He didn't want to think about that.

"I'll get this right down to HQ. Now you listen to what Detective Simmons said. Get some rest. I'll come back for you in a little while." He gave Cayce a sickly smile, entirely unconvincing. "Maybe I'll even have Duke with me."

Cayce frowned. "It's Luke."

He closed the door on the officer's apology.

The deadness, the numbness washed over him. *Why am I not having any visions now? Why isn't this thing showing me where my son is?* Cayce's mind was as empty as a blank slate. He went into the living room and made himself lie on the couch, in spite of the sheen of sweat covering him from head to toe. His stomach churned. He forced himself to close his eyes, hoping that blocking out images from the real world might make some images come.

But there was nothing. This gift—if that's what one could call it—was contrary and stubborn. It called the shots, and it was mostly a bastard. Impulsive. Demanding. Cayce felt he no longer had any control.

Yet he kept his eyes closed, hoping that—like a movie—images would begin to appear on the backs of his eyelids, like some sort of screen.

He drifted, thinking of nothing.

Later, he dreamed of awakening groggy. He didn't know how much time had passed. His head pounded. The couch beneath him was damp with sweat. He swallowed, trying to get some spit going, and swung his legs over the side of the couch, planting his feet on the floor. He was thrilled to discover that nausea and dizziness, constant companions, had left his side. Outside, it was still light, and the sky was a brassy white. The temperature must be in the nineties, but Cayce felt cold. *Fall is just around the corner. When's it going to start feeling like it?*

It hurt to stand. His whole lower body felt as if it had been beaten, bruised. *Luke is here. While I slept, they brought him back.* The thought just popped into his head, as they had a way of doing these days. He smiled a little but still felt shaky. *It could be a lie. A false impression.*

Cayce hobbled to the foot of the stairs. He needed a drink of water, but he would deal with thirst in a minute. Right now, he had to see if Luke was upstairs in his room, as a feeling deep in his bones told him he was.

Holding on to the wall for support, Cayce began to mount the creaking staircase up toward Luke's room. Luke had his own portable TV in there, and Cayce closed his eyes when he heard it. He let out a little yelp of laughter, relieved. *It's not just an image.* Canned laughter came from the room, and Ricky's and Lucy's voices, telling a tale of comic marital discord, wafted out from behind Luke's closed door.

Cayce paused at the tinny sound. "Thank you," he whispered. "Oh God, thank you."

He managed to get himself down the remainder of the hallway and paused outside Luke's door to listen, hand on doorknob.

"But Ricky, you promised!" Lucy whined.

Cayce turned the handle and went inside.

There was no scream. The voice had been stunned out of him.

Luke lay on his bed, illuminated by the harsh glare of the sun outside. His bedclothes were covered with soil, as was his naked body. Clumps of dirt littered the bed. He had been opened up from navel to neck with some kind of knife, something that cut jaggedly, leaving pieces of skin and muscle in pieces on his too-white skin. His green eyes were still rimmed by the black lashes his mother used to say were too long, "like a little girl's," but they stared dully at the ceiling, covered with a milky white substance. His mouth hung open, a trickle of blood seeping from one corner. All his teeth had been broken and stuck out of his gums, jagged stumps.

And his tongue, ripped or cut from his mouth, lay on the pillow beside his head.

Cayce sat up suddenly, the shriek ripped from his throat. His heart pounded so fiercely, he was afraid it would explode. He couldn't breathe. "Oh God, oh God. No!"

He hurried into the kitchen. He couldn't stand this. He felt so helpless and alone.

I have to find Luke.

He groped around on the kitchen counter, where he thought he had left Dave Newton's card. Yes, the guy was a reporter, and undoubtedly he would want a story, a scoop, or whatever they called it, but right now, Cayce needed someone next to him. He needed to feel he wasn't by himself in this. And for some reason, the warmth of Dave's brown eyes seemed like the comfort he needed. That, and the sad state of affairs that made him realize he really had no one else—other than his mom and dad—to turn to. He knew his parents would be as hysterical as he was. He needed someone objective and removed, someone who could help him.

How would he help? Cayce didn't know, other than maybe getting Luke's picture on the front page of the paper, which might help if someone had seen his little boy.

He punched in the number and was relieved to hear the deep, British-accented voice on the second ring.

Cayce was so tired and desperate, all he could manage to say was "I need help."

He didn't know if it was the magic of Caller ID or what, but Dave didn't trouble himself with asking who precisely needed help but said only, "I'm on my way."

*

When Dave Newton arrived at Cayce D'Amico's run-down little house in the east end of Fawcettville, he wasn't sure what to expect. Even the house, with its faded green shingles and its white trim in need of painting, looked depleted.

He was about to raise his hand to knock on the front door when Cayce opened it. He simply stood there before Dave, appearing more lost than Dave could ever remember having seen anyone. Cayce said nothing. His black hair was plastered to his head with sweat, and he looked older than what Dave would imagine his age to be, somewhere in his late twenties. Still, Cayce managed to look, somehow, attractive. Under other circumstances, this was a man who might pique Dave's interest, an interest he thought he had long ago buried.

He stepped inside the living room and closed the door behind him.

There were no words. Cayce all but fell into his arms and began to cry. Dave rubbed his hands up and down Cayce's broad back, trying to make calming noises but thinking how silly calm of any sort was with the situation at hand.

He pulled away slightly and looked into Cayce's eyes. He leaned in and kissed him. "I'm sorry. I shouldn't have done that. I don't know what got into me." And he really didn't. He hadn't thought about kissing Cayce at all. It just suddenly seemed right. Natural.

"It's okay," Cayce said. He took Dave's hand and led him to the couch, where the two of them sat for a long time in silence.

Finally, Cayce looked at Dave and said, "Maybe you kissed me because you picked up somehow on what was in my head when I was in your arms."

"Which was?"

"I had a vision. Not of anything bad. The opposite." Cayce rubbed his forehead, and Dave was sure he was about to start crying again, but he didn't. He continued, "I don't usually see things, I think, if I have any handle on this at all, in the future, but this time maybe I did."

"What did you see?" Dave brushed some hair away from Cayce's forehead, feeling strangely protective of the young man.

"I saw us—you, me, and Luke—all together at a park somewhere, maybe that one down by the riverfront. It was just a simple scene. We were walking along a trail, and Oreo—that's our dog—walked along behind us." Cayce's face clouded with even more worry for a moment. "Oreo's missing too." He shook his head. "Anyway, that was about it. Stupid."

"No, not at all. I hope it *was* a vision. I hope it does come true. For all of us. I'd like to spend more time with you."

Cayce let out a whoosh of air. "I can't think about things like that now!"

"I know. I know. I was just saying. The important thing is that Luke and Oreo were with us."

"It was probably just wishful thinking. That's all." Cayce sat up straighter. "Would you be willing to take me down to the police station? I can't just sit around here, waiting."

Dave stood, held out his hand. "Of course. I'll be with you, through whatever happens." He looked into Cayce's eyes. "And saying that, you have my promise that, while I may write about this, I am not wearing my reporter's hat. I'm here for you to lean on."

"Let's go." Cayce urged him to the door.

Chapter Twenty-One

All three pairs of eyes went to the door, where the knocking sounded again. It was tentative at first, but now it came more forcefully. Ian looked from the door back to Myra, questioning. She was certain her own expression was one of panic. Luke struggled a little in her grip, perhaps seeing an avenue of escape in the knocking on the door. Myra held fast, digging her fingers deeply enough into his arms to make him wince.

"Who is it?" Ian demanded, facial muscles tightening in rage.

Myra shook her head, shrugging, and whispered, "How should I know?"

The knocking continued. A voice came from behind the door. "Hello? Anybody home?"

Myra kept looking quizzically at Ian, as if to say she was as baffled as he was, but there was a queasy knowledge growing in her gut. The voice had the ring of familiarity about it. *Oh God. No.* A few more raps on the shaky metal door, and then the next words from the person on the other side confirmed Myra's fear.

"Hello? Penny? Are you in there? Open the door."

Ian's face clouded over. His eyes flashed, as if they had been sparked on flint. "What the fuck?" he mouthed.

Luke struggled harder, and Ian moved toward them. There was such threat in the simple action that Luke froze. Ian roughly shoved Myra away from the boy, so hard she landed on her ass on the floor. Ian snatched the boy up in one arm, clamping his other hand over the boy's mouth, and hurried toward the back of the trailer, to the bedroom.

"Take care of this," he said over his shoulder. Veins popped out on his forehead, and he spoke through clenched teeth.

Myra put a hand to her head, feeling woozy, like she might faint. She braced herself on the floor and forced herself to stand. The pounding continued.

*

Tammie Blankenship was mad. She would say she had a long fuse, but when that fuse finally ignited—watch out. She rapped once more on the cheap imitation-wood trailer door, sweat trickling down her side, knowing she would not be satisfied until she faced that bitch Penny Landsdale and gave her a piece of her mind about what she had said downtown. True, Penny had lost a few pounds, but it gave her no right to talk to Tammie that way, telling her her stomach looked *disgusting* under her crop top. What a thing to say! Worse was when the bitch pretended she didn't even know her. Where did she get the nerve? They had gone to school together, had slumber parties, traded secrets, been *best friends,* for Christ's sake. How in the world did Penny expect Tammie to believe she didn't know her?

It was outrageous is what it was.

When Penny had said those awful things and pretended not to know her, Tammie had been so stunned she was literally speechless. She'd walked around the block in a daze, not sure if she wanted to cry or bite someone. As she walked, her rage grew, so that by the time she got back around to the Diamond, she was ready to give that bitch a piece of her mind.

But she was gone. Tammie was shaking with rage. She had to sit down on a bench and light a Virginia Slim to try to calm down. She smoked the skinny cigarette down in about three puffs, scanning the people walking by, hoping Penny would show up again. Tammie wasn't sure if she could keep from slapping her. She almost smiled. *Almost. Oh*, she thought, *this could be a scene right out of* Jerry Springer.

Reluctantly concluding that Penny would not return, Tammie had gathered herself up, angrily yanking the stretchy black blouse down over her stomach. *I'm not that fat. I've been working out. I look good.* Still, she was furious at Penny for shaking her confidence, for harshing her good feelings about herself. She had started up the street, intending to stop at CVS to see if they had any more of that lip gloss she liked and then to maybe head home across the river, where she could drown her anger in a nice cold bottle of Michelob.

Lucky for her and unlucky for Penny, Tammie had a chance meeting. Up ahead, she saw someone familiar coming out of Clutter's Meat Market, the little butcher shop that had been in downtown Fawcettville for years, though she didn't know how it stayed in business or why anyone would want to go there when they had the Walmart superstore out by the highway. Penny's mother. Tammie smiled. Perfect. She quickened her pace to catch up with Penny's mom. *Talk about fat! That bitch must make the scales twirl around twice.* The cotton fabric of Mrs. Landsdale's housedress was soaked with sweat. Her broad back was hunched with the brown paper shopping bags she carried from the butcher's. *Probably just bought lunch.* Tammie snickered.

"Mrs. Landsdale! Mrs. Landsdale!" Tammie hurried to catch up. Mrs. Landsdale slowly turned around, her features pinched and pink, sweaty. A lock of graying hair fell over her forehead, and she blew it out of her eyes. She looked quizzically at Tammie, and then Tammie saw recognition dawn. She smiled.

"Is that you, Tammie Blankenship?"

Tammie caught up to her. "In the flesh. I'm glad *you* recognized me."

Mrs. Landsdale cocked her head.

"I just saw your daughter, and do you know she had the nerve to pretend she didn't know who I was?"

The older woman shook her head. "That sounds about right. Our Penny hasn't been the same since she met that man."

"What man?" Tammie took one of the bags from Mrs. Landsdale.

"Oh, I forget his name. She moved out a while back...to go live with him in sin. I've never been so ashamed. How's your mother?"

"Mom and Dad are good. Dad's gonna need a heart transplant, they say. We're just waiting to hear from the VA."

"Oh, I'm sorry to hear that, honey."

"He's gonna be okay. Don't you worry."

The two women regarded each other for a moment. "Did Penny say where she was living?" Tammie tried to act casual.

Mrs. Landsdale's features darkened. "She didn't want us to know. But it's hard to keep a secret around here. You know what I mean?"

"Uh-huh."

"A friend of Penny's dad told us just a couple weeks ago they was living in a trailer up on a hill. You don't need to take that. I can handle it." Mrs. Landsdale took the bag back from Tammie. "He was the one rented it to them. I wouldn't have even known that if he hadn't gotten in touch with Frank because they haven't paid any rent in about three months. The man was fit to be tied."

"I can imagine. Whereabouts are they? Maybe I could drop by and let her know she better get that rent paid."

Mrs. Landsdale shook her head. "Oh, I don't know. The girl's not our daughter anymore." Mrs. Landsdale frowned, and her eyes brightened with tears just a bit. She took in a big breath. "The trailer's up the Hill Road, all by itself, on a bluff. Me and Frank thought about going over, but we just don't know what to do with her anymore. I'm kind of afraid of her, tell you the truth. And I'm afraid Frank would wring her neck. He doesn't need that. Not with his heart. He's got a bad ticker too. Bypass surgery last year, you know."

Tammie nodded. "Well, let me tell you. I'm not going to take my old best friend pretending she don't know me lying down. So I just go up the hill..."

"All the way to the top. The trailer's the only thing up there."

"I think I'll run up there right now."

Mrs. Landsdale grabbed Tammie's hand. "Tell her to come and see her mother, would you?"

"Oh, I'll be sure to tell her that." *And a few other things.* Tammie started away. "It was nice seeing you again."

"Let me know what she says. Okay, Tammie?"

"Sure thing."

She'd gone directly there. Now, she pounded once more on the door, and finally, it opened. Penny peered out at her, just sticking her head around the side of the door. Tammie's anger dissolved. Penny looked terrified.

"What are you doing here?"

*

Myra didn't know what to do with Tammie Blankenship. She thought the best course of action would be just to get rid of her, quickly. And pretending she didn't know her was no longer an option. She forced a smile. "I'm sorry about before. I don't know what got into me. Things are a little, um, complicated right now."

Tammie nodded, leaning over to try to look into the dark trailer.

"What's going on, Penny?"

Myra smiled again, hating the sound of her old name, hating the fact that this poor fat girl was putting herself in way more danger than she knew. "Nothing. I just found a boyfriend, and you know how that goes. We're having a few problems."

"Well, I'm glad you're off pretending you don't know your own best friend." Tammie leaned in closer. "You sure you're okay? Why's it look so dark in there?"

"Keeps things cooler. This old trailer gets hot." Myra knew there was an edge to her voice, and she struggled to keep her words from coming out sounding shaky. She wanted so desperately to see this girl leave. "Listen, honey, I have a ton of stuff to do. Maybe we could meet up sometime? Have a Coke and catch up?"

"Can I come in? I'll only stay a minute." Tammie moved up and pushed her way right by Myra, before Myra even had a chance to stop her. She stood inside the trailer, looking around at its dirty, weird interior, illuminated by a dozen flickering candles. The video camera still lay on the kitchen counter. Myra saw the place through her eyes: the filth, the skull on the coffee table, the poster of Anton LaVey above the couch.

"Listen, I'm kind of in the middle of something here. Really, I need to get back to it. I'll call you." Myra touched Tammie's flabby arm, urging her back toward the open door.

She could tell Tammie was about to resist, but then she just kind of let go and allowed Myra to lead her to the door. "I saw your mom downtown. She's worried about you."

Myra got her to the threshold. "I'll have to give her a call too."

Tammie was just about to step back out into the sunshine when there was a loud scream from the back of the trailer. "What was that?" Tammie's mouth dropped open.

And Myra didn't know what to say. She was too tired to think fast, to come up with a plausible story explaining why the shriek of a young boy had just issued forth from one of the bedrooms.

"Help!" The little boy's voice came out, the "p" ending in a strangled muffling. *Oh God.* What was going to happen now?

Tammie stepped back in. "There's something wrong here." She seemed determined. She started toward the back of the trailer, and all Myra could do was watch helplessly as she passed through the living room into the little hallway, disappearing into the bedroom where she knew Ian was holding the little boy. "Don't..." she whimpered.

She could only imagine what fate awaited her old friend once she passed into that room.

Chapter Twenty-Two

When they got to the police station, Dave went to talk to the detective. Cayce had begged, "You go. I don't know what I'll do if there's bad news." Cayce sat down heavily on one of the benches near the front door.

Dave returned after a few minutes and sat down beside Cayce. He pulled a sheet of paper from the battered bag over his shoulder. Cayce looked down. Luke's somber face stared up at him. He couldn't get past the large type that said "Missing."

"Oh God." Cayce fingered the small face on the paper.

Dave gripped his hand. "They're doing everything they can to find him."

Cayce pulled his hand away and covered his face. He felt dizzy, sick, like he could actually faint. Maybe that wouldn't be such a bad thing. Blissful ignorance. *It's sad,* Cayce thought, *when you find unconsciousness preferable to life. If something happens to Luke, I'll kill myself.* He leaned over, placed his hands on his knees, brought his head down, and tried to take a few deep and even breaths. He pulled in some air, sat up, and looked at Dave Newton, who remained by his side.

"So they're already putting out flyers? Getting the word out?"

"Yes, word has gone out over the wires. The police department is being really great about this, Cayce." Dave reached over as if to grasp Cayce's hand again, then stopped just short of contact. "A lot of people already know, and that means a lot of people are already on the watch. That's a good thing, don't you think?"

Numbly, Cayce nodded. "Why are you bothering?" he whispered.

*

He pondered Cayce's question. Why *was* he here? The first thought that leaped to mind—and this one very unpleasant—was that he was here to stick with Cayce until his son was found…so he could be on the scene with the father. A sick feeling inside told him he would not be reporting on a happy moment. And he felt ghoulish for wanting to be there when a father found out his son was most likely dead. In fact, wanting to be present at such an event turned Dave's stomach. To want to get a "scoop" like that was just sick, and it made him want to throw away his career—if you could call it that—and apply at the McDonald's out by the Walmart.

But there was more to it than that. For one thing, he knew he could also witness a happy story. He could just as easily be reporting on a father reuniting with his unharmed child. Happy faces and tears. All recorded in his journalist's words and with his trusty Nikon digital.

He also knew there was yet another layer to wanting to share this story with Cayce, whatever its outcome. When he looked at Cayce, something was aroused in him, and it wasn't necessarily sexual. Although he did find Cayce very attractive—and stirrings like these, weak though they were, had not been coming to him for a while now—Cayce seemed vulnerable and alone. Dave wanted to protect him, to shield him from the hard times he knew Cayce was going through. He hadn't felt this way about any man since, well, since Jack, whom he had followed here from England. And Jack was gone, had been gone for many years. Dave had chased him away, with his demons backing him up, and he would never return. Until recently, Dave had thought he didn't miss Jack. And he didn't. He had even thought he didn't miss what they shared. But since meeting Cayce D'Amico, he wondered if that was true.

He wished he could put aside his reporter's tools—the notebooks, tape recorder, camera—but knew he was too much of an old dog working a beat to do that. But he wanted to somehow demonstrate that he was Cayce's ally, someone he could count on, who would not only not exploit him but who would be there for support.

He knew that confessing these feelings at the moment would seem insincere. So he was left with trying to be the dutiful reporter with a heart and hoping Cayce bought it. He did not want to see him alone.

"I'm here because I want to be with you during this difficult time. Yes, I want to report on it. We get so little news here in Fawcettville. Unfortunately, willingly or not, you're a star, and people want to know what's going on. But Cayce, remember, people care. I know there are people all over town already organizing search parties to help find your son. So it's not just about sensationalism, about wanting to know the worst. People—myself included—are rooting for you. In addition to being a reporter, I'd like to offer my hand and my shoulder for your use right now."

Dave smiled, because he knew his words were so corny. Corny or not, they were heartfelt. Even his smile felt odd, out of character. His face wasn't used to contorting into the upward motion. The muscles required for smiling had been long out of use, rusty.

*

In spite of himself, Cayce smiled back at the man sitting next to him. One thing he'd had before the "event," as he now thought of it, was intuition. He knew immediately when he liked someone or when he didn't. When someone was "real" and when someone was putting on an act. He used to think his feelings of intuition were fallible. But years of experience had shown him they weren't. Time and time again, he was right about people he encountered; initial impressions were always on the mark.

As he felt the smile creep across his features and the tears brim in his eyes, he knew Dave Newton was absolutely truthful when he said he was also there as a friend. It wasn't his words that convinced Cayce; it was more the expression in his dark brown eyes. They were eyes, like his, that were tired and had seen a lot. But they were also caring eyes. And Cayce could see that he wasn't just chasing a story when he said he wanted to help him through this ordeal.

Cayce wondered how much people relied on instinct and wondered further whether people shouldn't trust those instincts more.

"Thanks." He reached out and covered Dave's hand with his own. "I appreciate it. Now would you mind going back and talking some more to the cops? I need to know what they're doing to find my boy. Can you do that for me?"

Chapter Twenty-Three

Luke listened to them in the other room. The woman cried, and the man said short, angry words. He couldn't make out more than a few of them, but some filtered through and scared him: *please, trouble, kill,* and *stop.*

He shifted onto his back, trying to get comfortable, but it was hard on the floor. The carpeting was cheap, and the hard floor dug into his back. But there wasn't much more he could do to make himself comfortable. She had tied him up, put duct tape over his mouth, and the man had carried him in here to toss him on the floor like a doll. He wished he hadn't screamed. For one thing, maybe he wouldn't have the tape over his mouth, which made it feel like he was smothering. But the second reason was the one that made it really bad: he had gotten someone else in trouble. If he had just been quiet, she wouldn't be here now.

The big girl lay across the room from him, also on the floor. Like him, they had tied her up. Unlike him, they had not used bungee cords but thick rope, like clothesline, first tying her wrists together, then her ankles, and then using rope to pull the two areas together so her body was bent into what looked like a painful little bow.

The man with the dark hair had done it. At first, she'd hit him and spit at him, but then he beat her, punching her face and hitting her so hard he started losing his own breath. Luke had to close his eyes when he saw the blood on the man's knuckles. At first she screamed, but by the time he was done, all she could do was make these little panting, grunting sounds. Luke rocked himself so he could turn away. After the man started punching her, Luke didn't want to watch, but there wasn't anything he could do to stop up his ears.

Luke had scrunched up his shoulder every time the man's fist made impact with the girl; it was almost like he was the one getting hit. He had felt funny and sick, even though the man hadn't touched him.

The girl was crying on the other side of the room. Luke heard her trying to sniff the snot back up in her nose, trying to pull herself together, but there would only be silence for a minute, and then she would start crying all over again. Luke wished he could tell her to stop, because he knew her crying would only make things worse. Her sobbing and sniffling would make the man madder, and then maybe both of them would get hit. The worst had been just before he left the two of them in the room alone. The man had kicked the girl, and she had let out this great big whoosh of air and then moaned. He slammed the door, but not before he said, "The Beast will be back later."

Luke knew from the blonde-haired lady the Beast was just imaginary, like a made-up monster. So his saying that didn't scare Luke too much. What really made him shake and want to suck his thumb—which he couldn't do because of the duct tape over his mouth—was when he had kicked her.

He wished he could scoot over to the girl and comfort her, but he couldn't move. He hoped the man wouldn't beat her anymore. He also hoped his dad would figure out where he was and save them both.

He swallowed, thirsty, and listened to the sobbing and yelling going on in the other room. What else was there to do?

*

Myra closed her eyes and pulled in a deep breath, forcing herself to exhale slowly. She had to get "ahold of herself," as her mother would have put it, had to stop the hysteria and the crying. Honestly, she could have sworn such behavior only made Ian more aroused. He enjoyed it; she could tell from his eyes. He would do whatever it took, say whatever needed to be said, to keep her upset and crying. Myra knew she might never be able to reason with him, but the only chance she would have to make headway would be if she could do it calmly and rationally.

And she needed to talk some sense into him! She felt like she was living in a house of cards, one ready to collapse at any moment. This was a small town. One person had already found them. Another out there (and they had *his* son) already knew—Myra didn't know how—they had killed at least one young girl. Myra was smart enough to realize the Beast wasn't going to protect them much longer.

She remembered learning one thing back before she dropped out of New Hope High after meeting Ian, who claimed he could educate her better than any school. The knowledge was passed on during psychology class with Mr. Shamus. He had talked about how the mind and the body react to an emergency. She could picture standing before the bank of windows in their classroom, windows overlooking the tree-covered hills on the other side of the river. She didn't know why she had listened that particular day, when most days she would have been doodling in her notebook or checking and rechecking her cell to see if she had any messages, but right then what he had told them seemed critical. "Human beings, and animals too, usually have two responses to an emergency: fight or flee." He had looked down into the textbook they used, *Beginning Psychology: a Primer for High School Students*, and read from it. "Fight or flight is an ancient sympathetic reaction to stress characterized by accelerated heart rate, elevated blood pressure, and an increase in adrenal gland secretions, preparing the animal to either fight or turn tail and run."

Myra knew things had progressed beyond them having any chance of fighting what was certain to come down on them. She knew they needed to flee. Every fiber of her body and mind told her this was the truth.

But convincing Ian was another matter. He really believed the Beast had put some sort of protective force field around them; they were invincible. *When you believe something like that, it's pretty hard to get you to consider other options. Why should you?*

But she had to try. Maybe persistence was the key. She opened her eyes, forced herself to count, in her mind, to ten, and began trying to get through to Ian, to tell him why they should make sure their captives were okay, then load up the car with whatever would fit—whatever they *must* have with them because they were never coming back—and get as far away as possible.

She grabbed his hands in hers and looked into his eyes. "Ian? Ian, could you listen to me for a few minutes? Please?"

He grinned and leaned his head back, as if shocked at her nerve.

"I'm not kidding, Ian, five minutes. I really need you to hear me."

He sighed and shook his head. "Whatever. Go ahead."

Myra swallowed and blew out a big breath. "Things are bad, sweetheart. And they're going from bad to worse. I know the Beast has the perfect plan for everything, the ultimate design, as you say, but we have to look at all the facts. We have to look at everything going on around us." Myra scooted closer, gratified that he was listening and that his features were open. Scared as she was, she tried to keep her eyes on his, forcing the contact and not giving him a chance to look away or to begin forming arguments against what she was saying, using flawed logic about the damned mythical Beast. "The facts are...the way I see it, the facts are that, very soon, we're going to get caught. Ian, Tammie Blankenship found me in a matter of an hour or less. That D'Amico guy somehow knows about us. He has to. He knew exactly where we buried the Plant girl. And after we were so careful! Honey, everything is crumbling around us. I'm telling you it won't be long before the cops are pounding on that door. And then where will we go? Our chance will have gone. And you know as well as I do there's enough right outside this trailer to send us to prison for the rest of our lives...or worse." Myra lowered her head and stared at the floor. The silence seemed to stretch on infinitely. She knew, with a sinking feeling, what Ian was going to say. More bullshit about the Beast protecting them. She felt like a cow being led to slaughter. *You can get out yourself, girl. Nothing stopping you.* Myra thought of how easily Ian had bound the two people lying only a few yards away; he could do the same to her. She would probably hold up her wrists and ankles to make it easier. Leaving by herself was not an option, even if she had the guts to do it.

She was ready to scream because Ian wasn't saying anything. It was the same way she always felt, waiting for him. Like having her eyes closed, shoulders scrunching, bracing herself for a slap or a punch she knew was on its way, and part of the whole deal was wishing he would just get it over with and end the anticipation. But Ian let out a breath and began to talk. His voice had none of the animation it had earlier. It was low, slow, and deep. Resigned.

Myra listened.

"You're right. I know it too. I didn't want to admit it. I thought the Beast would give us something in exchange for our sacrifices, but so far, we've gotten nothing but into deeper trouble." Ian scanned the dark interior of the trailer, and Myra wondered if he was thinking about the Beast overhearing his disloyal words. She watched as his Adam's apple bobbed. He was just a man. "I know we need to get away."

She grabbed his hands; she couldn't resist. "I'm so glad you're finally seeing sense."

His eyes flashed and he frowned; she wished she could take back the words.

"It's not you convincing me, my dear. It's the situation." He looked off into the darkness, and Myra could see his face shifting, changing in the candle's flickering light. She'd known it was too good to be true, or she should have. "It's not you convincing me of anything. It's the Beast. He's telling us we have to move on. Because we made those sacrifices, he's going to make sure we have safe passage out of this hole." He smiled. "Where do you want to go, Myra? Someplace warm?"

She hugged him. She didn't care if he was listening to the common sense she was dispensing or the delusional voice in his head, as long as the end result was the same. They needed to *flee*.

"Yes! I was thinking Florida. We'll be happy, there, Ian, you'll see…"

Ian pondered. "Florida might be good. There are a lot of Satanists there. People like us. Maybe we could work for a while, get our passports, and then get over to England. I would love to see Manchester. And the moors."

Myra knew nothing about Manchester, England, or why Ian would even want to go there, but the relief coursing through her was enough to block out any doubtful thoughts. She pulled away. "We should go now, Ian. We can throw a few things in bags, just the important stuff, and be on our way." She stood and looked out the window. It was now late afternoon. The sky was bright white, promising a hot, oppressive night. She wished the Mustang had air-conditioning, but then she wished for a lot of things she was pretty sure would never be. It was enough that Ian was seeing things her way, and they were on their way out of Fawcettville. Finally. Gone. Without a trace.

"We just need to make sure to call someone once we get on the road and let them know about Tammie and the boy." She chewed on her lower lip, thinking. "No, that won't work. We have to take them with us, Ian. If we let someone know they're here in the trailer, they can connect us to them, and then they'll be after us. They'll track us down, and we'll be just as trapped as if we'd stayed here." She sat back down on the floor next to him. "Once we get out of town, we can let them go somewhere…in the woods, somewhere remote, where it will take some time for them to get back." Already Myra could feel herself growing sick, knowing this plan would not work either. Aside from the fact that both Tammie and the boy had seen them, Tammie knew who Myra was and knew the trailer's location. She would need a new identity. Still, didn't people do things like that all the time? Wasn't there a whole market that dealt in phony birth certificates and stuff like that? She didn't know how to tap into it, but she was sure Ian could. He was so smart. They should probably get new identities anyway...

She was so busy with these thoughts she didn't notice, at first, that Ian was glaring at her. She stopped speaking suddenly, as if she had run out of steam. In a way, she had.

"Are you even listening to yourself? To how stupid you sound?"

"I'm sorry, Ian." Myra's voice was tiny.

"The Beast has been talking to me while you prattled on." He took her hands in his, and this time, it wasn't gentle. It was a rough grasp that hurt. But this hold didn't scare her as much as the face he showed her, the intensity in his eyes. It was almost like an electric current passing through him to her. His face was beaded with sweat, and he seemed on the brink of a delirious joy.

"The Beast says we can't leave witnesses. The Beast says we must kill the child and the sow and then burn the trailer with them in it."

Myra's eyes grew wide.

"Don't worry. He says we have all night to take care of it. I think it will be particularly fun to take the sow slowly, while you tape it. The boy we can dispose of quickly." He took Myra's chin in his hand, forcing her to look at him. "It will be merciful and quick. I know you'd like that." His smile was almost tender.

Myra tried to swallow but had no saliva. She tried to breathe, but there was no air. She just nodded, dumbly.

Chapter Twenty-Four

Cayce couldn't imagine feeling more exhausted. His bones ached. His eyes burned. He was so tired, he didn't think he could lift his arms. Yet he couldn't imagine a time when sleep was more of a foreign concept.

"Wait a minute." He grabbed Dave Newton's arm after practically stumbling down the front steps of City Hall. If anyone had seen him, they would have assumed he was some lush freshly sprung from the drunk tank.

There was a small part of him that would have liked to escape into the oblivion that lived in the very bottom of a bottle. But Cayce knew no amount of alcohol could quell the terror coursing through him. There were things to do. *What's the quote?* Cayce wondered, allowing himself for a moment to go back to his high school English classes at Fawcettville High. *Miles to go before I sleep?*

"Wait. I just need to sit…for just a second." He looked up at Dave, who nodded. He could see Dave was worn out too. But Dave had stuck by Cayce's side through everything, even when JT Simmons objected to a reporter being along for the ride. Cayce needed someone beside him. If he had to pay for this luxury with having his name in the paper again, well then, so be it. Cayce didn't think he'd survive this alone. And Dave Newton was there. Nobody else was. "Can we?"

Dave sat beside Cayce and took his hand, squeezed.

In the station, Dave had been there with Cayce as he checked over the minutia of unimaginable terror—making sure they had details like the red Mustang correct, that Cayce didn't break down at the thought of reading about his own little boy as the subject of an Amber Alert. Dave had stayed beside Cayce while JT Simmons talked with someone in the Pittsburgh office of the FBI. This was, after all, a kidnapping, and kidnapping was in the purview of the bureau. The department had made sure anyone who might know something about Luke, or anyone who had seen him, would know what he looked like and would know how to contact the proper authorities immediately. The only time Cayce had taken a break was to go into the bathroom, to take a piss and to splash some cold water on his face. He had pulled his dark hair back with a rubber band to face TV cameras from Pittsburgh and Youngstown and managed to get through an impassioned plea to come forward if anyone knew anything about his son. He was determined not to let people see him cry. He knew if Luke was somewhere watching, he needed to see a strong dad, one who could save him, even as Cayce stuffed the hopelessness he felt deep down inside.

In fact, as he leaned against Dave in front of City Hall, he thought it was curious that he hadn't cried in hours. What was wrong with him? Sure, he was a guy, and men weren't supposed to cry, but this was his *son* here, a little boy gone. Plus, he had managed to cry earlier, sobbed hysterically, and now it was all gone, replaced by a dull numbness, making him feel like he was a robot going through the motions of life: movement, speech, respiration...

He peered up at the starless night sky. When had darkness fallen? He didn't know how he was going to face the night alone. What if other nights followed and still his little guy's room stayed empty? *Stop it! You can't give up. Luke is alive out there somewhere, and you need to find him.* Cayce knew that somewhere deep inside, psychic or not, as a father he would know if Luke was dead. He would just know it. He could feel Luke's presence, alive, within him. But he could also feel Luke's peril. He didn't have much time.

It was this last thought that made him feel useless. Desperate.

After sitting in silence for a long time, just watching the occasional car roll by, Cayce turned to Dave. Dave had been so patient, not saying a word, not asking questions, just giving Cayce time after all the fuss inside. "What are we going to do?"

Dave shrugged and shook his head. "Maybe we start by going back to your house."

"And do what?" Cayce wondered. "Shouldn't we be out there searching, going street by street? Calling Luke's name?"

"If I thought that would work, I'd be right there with you." Dave eyed Cayce. "Have you seen anything? I mean, about your son..."

Cayce shook his head. "Nothing." He rubbed the back of his neck restlessly. "Other than that moment when I saw the three of us together in the park—" Cayce cut himself off with a sharp intake of breath. He felt he couldn't say the words crowding his brain that needed to logically follow. "Other than that time, the only vision I've ever had is of someone who's already dead." The last two words came out in a whisper, and for the first time in a long while, he could feel a lump growing in his throat, the hot burn of tears at the corners of his eyes. He made himself breathe and finally stood up, brushing the dirt off the seat of his jeans. "I suppose going home's as good a plan as any. I don't know what we can do there, though."

"We'll think of something." They walked together toward Dave's car, parked a few yards away. "We can at least listen to my police scanner." He pulled a small device that looked like a walkie-talkie from his bag, showed Cayce, and put it back. "We'll be the first to hear if there's a break in the case."

Cayce snorted. "Break in the case? You sound like one of those crime shows on TV, *SVU* or something like that." Even though he laughed, the sound escaped his throat dry and hollow.

"You know what I mean." Dave unlocked the doors with a little button on his key chain. They slid inside the seen-better-days Honda Civic.

Cayce stared out at the dark night, which pressed in, almost like a shape, rather than an absence of light. "There ought to be something *more* we can do." He waited for Dave to start the car. "It's fucked that here I am, supposedly some sort of psychic, and I don't get one tiny little image to help myself or my son when I most need it." He rubbed his eyes. "It's fucking pathetic."

"Just close your eyes now. Put the seat back. Try to rest. Let me drive you home." Dave pulled away from the curb.

*

At his house, Cayce kept his panic at bay by offering Dave a seat in the kitchen and making coffee. The house seemed empty, a shell, without Luke and Oreo there. The silence all around them seemed foreign, disconcerting—as if Cayce were floating through a dream. It was just plain unnatural to walk in the kitchen door and not have Oreo there to greet him, tail wagging, practically knocking him over to jump on him and cover his face with canine kisses. And that was the lesser of the two evils. Luke not being there to prattle on about something he'd seen on TV or to beg for a bowl of Froot Loops before bed—well, that was heart-wrenching.

Coffee brewed, he set a mug before Dave and sat across from him, staring into his reflection in the dark liquid. Even Cayce would admit, from just this distorted reflection, that he had aged a decade in a single day.

The darkness outside the kitchen window had a different quality than what Cayce was used to. It had more of a presence, closing in, like it was alive. *Stupid thoughts. Concentrate.* Cayce closed his eyes. He took a deep breath, willing an image to come, but there was nothing. The emptiness that came back to him was mocking. It was as though his intuition, his ability—whatever name one chose to give it—was teasing, capricious, only there, really, to torment him. He cursed the day he'd felt those first inklings.

Dave—God bless him—seemed content to simply sit across the table quietly. For someone for whom words were his stock-in-trade, he certainly seemed to know the value of silence. Cayce liked that he seemed to know instinctively how to simply be here with him and to let things come. There was no pressure. Cayce hadn't seen Dave open a notebook or flick on a tape recorder the entire evening. This absence of action made Cayce trust Dave even more.

He imagined himself getting up from the table without a word and moving over to Dave. He would take his hand and lead him up the creaking staircase to his bedroom, which had been shared with no one, save for Oreo or Luke, since last summer when, in a flight of drunken fancy, he had brought home a bartender from a gay bar in Pittsburgh whose name Cayce couldn't recall— the bar's or the tender's.

They would move into the darkness. Cayce would throw back the sheets and undress slowly, seldom losing eye contact with Dave as he did the same. There would be no words. Only touches, caresses, kisses, and sighs. Cayce would shut down his mind and let his body take over, let physical sensation release calming and healing endorphins. He would feel the heat of Dave's body, taste every inch of him...

Maybe someday.

Now he opened his eyes and looked up from his coffee. "It's funny. Before Amy Plant and I found Lucy down by the river, the images were coming to me without warning. I hated them. I didn't want to see what I was seeing. If someone had offered to cut those images out of my brain, I would have sat back and let them do it.

"Now I want nothing more than to *see* those images. I want something to go on."

"What brought the images to you before?"

"What do you mean?"

"I mean, was there anything that triggered you seeing something? Did anything happen just before?"

"No. Not really." Cayce thought back, and something connected in his tired mind. "Wait a minute. Usually, I would see things when there was some sort of, I don't know, some sort of prompt." Cayce thought about the nurse in the hospital, how the touch of her hand had made him see the woman in her backyard, had let him peer into the nurse's desire to get with the young man she was seeing later that night. A pounding started behind his temples. He remembered the first time he had seen anything about Lucy. Cayce nodded without realizing he was doing it. "When I started seeing Lucy, it happened right after I saw her picture in the paper."

"Did the picture come to life or something?"

Cayce gave a mirthless smile. "No, nothing as dramatic as that. It was like, I looked at the picture, and there was a flash...and I was seeing stuff about her. About her death. I kind of knew how she had been killed." Cayce took a quick gulp of coffee; it had gone cold. "Later, when I met with the Plants at their house, I got a really clear image of Lucy when Amy showed me her school picture. It was so strong, like a jolt of electricity." Cayce remembered how the shock caused him to drop the framed photo on the floor.

"Did the same thing happen with Sheryl?"

"Kind of. Being in her house, I saw all sorts of things."

Dave scratched his chin. "It seems like you need something from the person to trigger what you see. Or at least an image of that person. I've heard of psychics picking up on stuff from personal items."

"You mean like a bloodhound sniffing some clothes before it sets out to find the person who's missing. Is that what I am? A dog?"

Dave shook his head. "It just makes sense. There's a lot about the mind we haven't yet begun to understand, and I don't claim to know why seeing a picture or touching something the missing person has touched would make a difference, but it has a kind of logic to it."

Cayce nodded and then frowned. "But Luke is all around me in this house. Why can't I get anything from him?" He slammed a fist on the table, causing some coffee to spill over. He got up and went to the "junk drawer" and rifled through it. When he found what he was looking for, a photograph of Luke, taken just this past Christmas, he clutched it tightly in his hand. He sat down at the table with it and closed his eyes willing something—*anything*—to come.

But nothing did. "I don't see him. I don't get anything," Cayce whispered softly.

Dave didn't say anything in response for a long time.

Cayce searched his hard yet warm features, wondering how old Dave was—*Forty? Fifty? Too old?*—and tried to figure out what he was thinking, what connections he was making. He felt he could make the connections himself if he wasn't so exhausted and stressed.

Finally, Dave put his hand over Cayce's. "Maybe." He stopped and sighed, looked toward the kitchen window above the stove. Cayce looked toward it, wondering what he was seeing. But only blackness pressed in, almost hard enough to break the glass.

"Maybe you saw stuff from the girls because they were already gone." Dave's voice was soft, barely above a whisper.

"You mean..."

Dave stared hard at the table's surface. Finally, he raised his head to chance a look at Cayce. "I'm sorry. Yes. Dead."

Cayce felt as though someone had just delivered a punch to his gut, as though his breath had been taken away. If that was true, he didn't want any images to arrive from Luke. He wanted to *never* see his little boy in his mind's eye—not like that.

And maybe the fact that he could get nothing about Luke was a sign that he was still alive.

If, as he believed, the killers had taken Luke—which was the logical explanation and the one that resonated—then maybe finding Sheryl would lead them to finding Luke. Cayce squeezed his eyes together tight; his breathing came faster. He bit his lip hard enough to taste blood.

"I need something of Sheryl's. I'm not sure, but if I could get hold of something of the girl's, it might lead somewhere. It might take me to Luke." Cayce knew there was logic to the plan. He also knew his visions had logic of their own he had yet to figure out, if he ever would. There wasn't *always* a trigger for seeing something. Sometimes the visions just came, unbidden. But it did seem that the stronger ones came when there was some sort of connection.

All of this is hopeless. But I have to try.

Dave smiled and nodded. "I know nothing about this psychic rot. But it makes sense. How can we get something? Would a newspaper photo do?"

Cayce shrugged. He thought a newspaper photo might work, but if he wanted to feel something really strong, it would be better to have something with a more direct connection. He then thought of his visit to the McKennas and remembered how he'd been treated. He had practically been thrown out bodily.

"We don't have a lot of time." Cayce scratched behind one knee. "We need something of the girl's." He would face them again if necessary; he would do anything if it would bring his Luke back. The problem was, would he even be able to speak to them, let alone convince them to part with something, like a photo of their daughter or a piece of her clothing? "But I don't know if I can get it."

"Why not?"

"I'm not exactly the McKennas' favorite person." And Cayce told Dave about his visit. Everything.

After he finished, Dave said, "I could go. I could get something. I don't have to say I even know you, but what I could say is that I might be able to help publicize the fact their daughter's gone missing. I could tell them the more people who know about Sheryl, the better chance she'd have of being found."

Cayce still felt helpless. He remembered the McKenna woman and her horrible husband. Would they be more or less forthcoming or helpful to a reporter, even one who said he wanted to help them find their daughter? Cayce had offered the same help, and they had thrown him out of their house.

"I can be very persuasive. Do you want to wait here? Or do you want to come with me?"

What Cayce wanted was for all of this to be over. He stood. "I'll come with you. But I'll stay in the car. I can't just be here by myself."

"Then let's go."

*

"I don't think you should do any more of that." Janet McKenna had just come out of the bedroom, down the stairs, and into the living room, where her husband, Rick, sat on the couch. A porno was playing on the thirty-two-inch plasma screen. A naked woman—a girl, really; Janet wondered if she was even eighteen—with cartoon-sized breasts was on her knees between two men.

Rick looked up at her. His eyes were bloodshot, the pupils so dilated all color was blocked out. His nostrils were inflamed. Covered with a sheen of sweat, his naked body looked oily in the flickering light from the TV screen.

"What the fuck do you have to say about it?" As if to show her who was boss, Rick lit another cigarette, took a long drag, placed it in an ashtray, then leaned over with a dirty straw to snort up another line of cocaine. Then another. A third. The coffee table was littered with white dust, cigarette ash, beer cans, and a jar of her hand cream.

Janet worried the bottom of her nightgown, wondering where the days had gone when Rick wanted to come to bed with her. Now it was going on ten; they both had to get up early for work. They should both be in bed, whether it was for blissful cuddling or turn-the-shoulder stony silence, she didn't care. She just didn't want him doing this. "I just think you should save some for later." Her voice was small.

"Why? You gonna join me later?"

"No." Janet tried to force her gaze away from the screen. Ever since Sheryl had gone missing, Rick had seen no reason to hide his habit, and evenings like this were becoming way too commonplace. She ran a shaky hand through her hair; it felt like straw. Maybe she should lay off the L'Oreal for a while. "It's just that, honey, you're never going to get to sleep if you keep doing that." She tried to smile and failed. "It looks like you're already pretty wired." She didn't want to look down at his hand, which was pumping and pulling at himself. His penis was small and red, limp. Janet wondered where he was getting the money to buy all the coke. She knew he had sold his Malibu and wondered if the proceeds had already gone up his nose. She wondered how many cash advances would be on their next credit card bill. He was going to kill himself. And then who would she have?

"Go on back to bed." Rick dismissed her, his gaze returning to the screen; a third man had joined the other two. Rick pulled harder. "I'll be up in a little bit. Just give me one more hour." He turned his head. "An hour? Okay? Can you give me that?"

Janet swallowed hard, wondering if she should just give up and sit next to him, snort a line or two, let it all fall away. She had been a party girl once...before she found Jesus. But where had Jesus gotten her? Stuck with a cokehead drunk and a missing daughter? Oh yeah, her prayers had been answered. *From my mouth to God's ear.*

But she knew how the drug reneged on its promises of euphoria and energy. And she knew, somewhere, that her faith was not just something she had taken up to quell the loneliness of living in a house where she was ignored by the people she loved.

"Okay. I'm going to go back to bed and try to get some sleep. Could you at least turn the TV down? I can hear that moaning all the way upstairs." She didn't wait for Rick to say anything, just turned and started trudging back up the creaking staircase. She also didn't wait for the volume to be lowered. The best she could hope for was that he wouldn't turn it up.

When had her husband started hating her?

Just as she was to the last creaking step and resigned to the lonely bedroom, where her only company was a noisy box fan in the window, something happened that made her spine stiffen.

Someone was knocking at the door. *Oh God, no. The cops.* Her breath came a little faster. It was bound to happen sooner or later, what with all the cars pulling up to their house at all hours and Rick running outside, sitting in the cars for a minute, then running back in. *This is just what we need. What with Sheryl missing... What if they take Rick away?* Janet couldn't stand the thought of being alone, even if she was desperately lonely.

The knocking sounded again, a little more insistent. Janet placed a hand on the wall for support. She was steeling herself for the next sound she expected to hear: "Open up! Police!"

But there were no voices, other than Rick shouting, "God *damn* it!"

The TV went off, and she heard him hurrying around the living room. She imagined him sweeping the baggies, straws, credit card, and mirror into the coffee table drawer, hurrying to throw on his jeans and wifebeater. "Fuck!" he shouted again as the knocking sounded a third time.

"Who the hell is it?" Rick hollered up the stairs, where Janet stood, frozen.

Janet hurried down the stairs, saw her husband standing, shirtless, in the living room, his grizzled and flushed features bewildered, sniffling, wiping angrily at his nose. There was a little blood on his fingers.

"Just sit down." She made a waving motion to him. "I'll get the door. Just keep quiet. I'll get rid of whoever it is." Janet hurried through the hall. *Unless it's the cops. Then we're fucked. Excuse me, Jesus.*

Janet opened the door, heart pounding, blood beating hard behind her eyes. She worried about fainting.

There was no one in uniform standing on the porch in the dim light from the sodium vapor lamp on the street. The only person out there was a guy, not too tall, with salt-and-pepper hair and dark eyes behind wire-rimmed glasses. He looked like a professor. He wore a sheepish grin. What the hell was he doing at her front door?

*

Dave Newton stood in the deepening twilight, waiting. His ears perked up at the sound of scurrying around inside, muffled words. He felt like he was conducting a raid.

He peered through the dirty glass in a small window to watch as a shadowy figure emerged from a room off the front hallway and then disappeared back into it. Finally, a woman came down the stairs quickly.

Dave wasn't sure what to say when she opened the door. The only word that came to mind was "slag," the British term for a prostitute, but used more familiarly as a woman who looked as though she'd been rode hard and put away wet. Dave had learned, over the years, to combine his British and American colloquialisms. The woman had bleached blonde hair that had seen one too many "beauty" treatments, so it looked like straw. Her face was a network of fine lines spread across a surface of dry, artificially tanned skin. Though Dave was sure the woman wasn't even out of her thirties, she looked much older. The eyes that peered out from under the platinum fringe were rheumy and not kind.

Her face screwed up into an expression of distaste, as if she had something bitter in her mouth. She said nothing. Dave knew it was late, but this undisguised hostility was more than he'd expected. No wonder Cayce was afraid to return to this house. Rancor and meanness radiated off her just as much as the smell of cigarettes and alcohol. Her thin lips were drawn even thinner by the way she held them in a tight line. Before Dave had even said a word, this woman was already furious.

"What do you want?" she finally asked. She kept the door half closed in front of her, peering around its edge. "This better be good."

Dave attempted a smile and tried to remember the skills he had honed over the years, interviewing people who didn't want to talk to the press. He took a quick breath and began. "It's about your daughter."

The words brought about a dramatic shift in the woman's demeanor. She softened, almost deflated, when he mentioned her daughter. The rigidity drained from her form. Her features relaxed, but not in a good way, shifting from hostility to sadness in an instant. Her lower lip trembled, and she started to nod. "She's been found, hasn't she?" She shook her head. "I knew this would happen." Her breath started coming faster, and Dave was afraid she was going to burst into tears. Belatedly, Dave realized what she must think—why else would a stranger come to call late at night?

He put up a hand. "Can I come in?"

Though obviously traumatized, the woman took a moment to look behind her, back into the house. She shook her head. "I'll come out." She stepped barefoot onto the porch, closing the door behind her.

Her face got close enough to Dave's for him to sense the sour smell of cheap vodka on her breath. Dave was an expert in cheap liquor. "You know something about my Sheryl? Tell me."

Dave once again attempted a smile, a winning expression. He again raised his hands in a gesture that he hoped conveyed *I mean no harm.* "Listen, first off, I don't have news about your daughter."

The woman's expression was amazing in the speed at which it could shift. The sadness and shock disappeared, to be replaced by wariness. Her eyes narrowed. "Then what the fuck are you doing here? Who the hell are you, anyway? It's a little late to be peddling Amway."

"Let me start at the beginning. I'm Dave Newton, from the *Review*."

"Oh God! You're a reporter. You've got some nerve, asshole, showing up here at all hours when decent people have to get up for work in the morning! *Decent* people who're just trying to get on with their lives when a family member has gone missing." She stuck out her lower lip, her eyes bright, even in the dark, with outraged tears. "I can't believe you people. Why can't you just leave us alone?"

Dave put a hand to his forehead, feeling a throb behind his temples that signaled the beginning of a headache. "Listen, we've gotten off on the wrong foot. I'm here because I want to help you."

"Right." She spat the word out. "How can someone like *you* help? Do *you* know where I can find my Sheryl? Do *you* know where she is? Can *you* tell me what happened to her?"

With each question, she poked a finger, hard, into Dave's chest. Her gaze was intense; Dave thought it bordered on madness. This might not be as easy as he had thought. Now, faced with the very real grief and terror of a flesh and blood human being, Dave wasn't sure he could continue. But he had to; Cayce depended on him. And very likely, another young life hung in the balance.

Dave shook his head slowly. "Mrs. McKenna? Is that right? Mrs. McKenna, I really wish I could. I want nothing more than to stand here in front of you and give you some answers, to lessen your pain. But I think with the *Review* and me on your side, maybe we can get those questions of yours answered sooner rather than later. Now, it's hard to talk out here. Would you let me come inside?"

Again, the woman's gaze shifted warily behind her. "I don't think so. My husband is—asleep—on the couch in the front room. You get me? I don't want to wake him up." She smiled uncertainly.

Dave nodded, although he couldn't fathom why she *wouldn't* want her husband to be part of this conversation. Wasn't Sheryl his daughter too?

"Let's go sit down over here, then." Dave led her over to a couple of plastic laminate chairs. They sat.

Janet McKenna got back up suddenly. "Just a minute."

Bewildered, Dave sat on the porch and waited. In a moment, Janet McKenna returned, a cigarette dangling from her lips and a pack of Marlboro Lights and a disposable lighter in her hand. She sat, removed the cigarette from her lips, and blew the smoke into the air.

Maybe it will keep bugs away. Dave began his pitch. "There are usually two ways missing people turn up. One is simply that they return on their own. Some have stories to tell. Some keep quiet." He glanced over at Janet McKenna. At least she was listening. "The other way is through a lot of work by the public. Searching. And that's how I can help you find Sheryl. She's out there, right? And even though there's been coverage in the paper, on the radio, and even on TV, you can never have too many people looking for a missing person." Dave paused. Janet McKenna smoked silently. He hoped what he was saying was sinking in. "What I'd like to do is this: write a big feature on Sheryl so even more people know she's missing. And with the feature, I'd like lots of pictures of Sheryl."

Janet McKenna nodded. She flicked her cigarette into the yard, which roused an old cur that had been chained up not even fifteen feet away. He howled once, then lay back down. Dave had hardly noticed.

He waited for Janet McKenna to say something. When a couple of minutes had passed in silence, he asked, "Do you think you can get me some pictures of Sheryl? I bet you have lots of them. And I promise to take good care of them and get them back to you straightaway." Dave paused, thinking. He had what he thought was a good idea. *There's no harm in asking.* "Maybe you even have some favorite thing of hers, a T-shirt or a stuffed animal. I could take a shot of that down at the *Review* and add it to the pictures." He gave his kindest smile to Janet McKenna—and felt like a ghoul. He had to keep reminding himself he was doing this for a good cause. He was trying to save the life of a little boy out there somewhere right now with people who cared a lot less for his welfare than his father did.

Dave thought of Cayce sitting in the car, hidden in the shadows of the McKennas' front yard. He probably watched them right now, wondering what Dave was saying, hoping he would find success, and wondering if all this would be in vain.

He had to get Cayce something. Nothing else mattered.

Dave said, "Really. The more people who know, the more chance we have of someone having seen Sheryl. That's what we want—someone to come forward with the answer." Dave put a hand, gentle, on her shoulder. The woman didn't flinch, and Dave thought that was a good sign. "So, what do you think, Janet? Will you let me help you find your daughter?"

Chapter Twenty-Five

Dave and Cayce sat huddled over his kitchen table. Spread out before them were five photographs, showing Sheryl McKenna from the ages of twelve to her current age, sixteen. Two of the pictures were school photos, one was of Sheryl and an older boy at a dance, and the last two were snapshots taken at home: Sheryl outside on a tire swing; Sheryl frowning at the camera in her nightgown, early morning light streaming in a window behind her. Cayce shuddered, remembering what he knew about Sheryl's stepfather and wondering if he had been the one who had taken the picture. Dave had also managed to get a charm bracelet and a Pittsburgh Pirates jersey from Janet McKenna. These were set next to the photographs.

Cayce stared at them, feeling queasy. He was terrified, not wanting to begin, because beginning could mean failure, and he couldn't, didn't, wouldn't accept failure. He had made Dave lay the photos and keepsakes out on the table. He refused to touch them, had hardly even glanced at them.

What if nothing came to him? What if he touched these things, stared at these photographs, and nothing came? What if his gift/curse was only temporary, and the part of his brain that caused his visions had somehow healed? The trauma that caused him to have the visions was a fleeting thing. Maybe now, without even being aware it was happening, he was simply back to being

Cayce, with nothing special, an ordinary gay single dad, trying to make ends meet and raise a boisterous son.

Just a few hours ago, it would have been a dream come true.

But now he so desperately wanted the images to come he was afraid to even try. He put his hands over his face, breathing hard. *You have to try. Luke. Think of Luke. You have no choice. Get busy.*

Dave spoke. "Cayce? You need anything?"

Cayce looked over to where Dave sat across the table. He knew the guy wanted to help, but he needed to concentrate. It was kind of a life and death thing. "Yeah. I need to be left alone. Can you go outside? I'll come and get you in a little while."

"Sure."

Cayce watched as Dave went out through the screen door, listening as it slammed, as his footfalls crunched in the gravel of the driveway, the *thunk* of his car door closing. He hated pushing Dave away, but if this was going to work, he had to give it his all.

"Okay." Cayce let out a trembling breath. "It's time." He turned to the photographs, willing himself to relax, to be open.

He picked up the first photograph, of Sheryl when she was twelve. He smiled. It was summer, and Sheryl was on a rope and tire swing, hung from a big maple tree. Her face was slightly obscured in shadow, but Cayce could see a little girl on the cusp of womanhood. Her tanned legs were long and skinny, sticking out of a pair of too-short powder-blue terry-cloth shorts. She wore a tiny white eyelet lace top with spaghetti straps. Her black hair hung to her waist; bangs hid her eyebrows. Cayce could make out the little buds on her chest, just beginning to blossom.

There was something gazelle-like about Sheryl. "Why, you're beautiful," Cayce whispered, his voice catching in his throat. He set the photograph down and looked away, breathing hard. Yet, other than a feeling of tenderness, nothing came to him.

He picked up the next photo, an almost thumbnail-sized portrait—Sheryl's school picture, most likely taken during the last term. This one was probably the most recent. Cayce took in the details—and the transformation. Sheryl's hair, still glistening blue-black, had changed only in the fact that the bangs were gone. She wore too much makeup. The black eyeliner was almost raccoon-like, and the bubblegum-pink lip gloss just looked, well, *gross*. And cheap. She wore large, thin gold hoop earrings and stared out at the camera with her head cocked, a souped-up defiance in her eyes. Cayce wondered what had brought the sweet girl from the tire swing to this slutty-looking reject. He knew his thoughts were unkind; he also knew girls abused like Sheryl often ended up acting out in ugly ways. Sheryl was still young enough in this photo to look pretty, in spite of the effort she'd made to mar that beauty, but Cayce could see the future, though this vision was born of common sense, not psychic power. Sheryl would continue to use these same tools to adorn herself, continue to be self-destructive, and ten or fifteen years from now would look as hard and old as her own mother. Cayce shook his head and sighed. While it was interesting to have this look into Sheryl McKenna's life, it was not helping with what he needed to do. It was not helping him find the girl, and then, hopefully, Luke. He placed a hand over his face when he realized that Sheryl McKenna would not be seeing the future he had just imagined. Sheryl McKenna now lived only in the past and most likely only in the memory of her mother.

He scanned the dance photo and the other school portrait, feeling increasingly helpless. Both aroused feelings of tenderness, but both had the same disappointing results: a complete lack of connection. *Where is the switch I need to flip? How do I make it come?* Cayce felt a kind of love for Sheryl McKenna. His heart ached for the girl he knew was dead. That kind of certainty, Cayce felt, was part of the power he had gained that day when the tree branch came down. With a trembling hand, he picked up the last photograph, though his sight was too blurry to see the image he held. Sheryl was dead. Cayce felt it—knew it—and knew too that his gift had not left him utterly.

This one was also pretty recent, Cayce guessed. He glanced down at Sheryl's pure and beautiful face, even frowning as she glared at the photographer. Here she looked innocent. Without makeup, her skin was porcelain. Cayce imagined sleep in her eyes. It was plain this photo had been taken without the subject's approval, and Cayce was filled with an odd anger. The fear and violation were clear in her eyes.

And then it started coming to him. Finally, a vision.

A man stood just outside her bedroom, holding one of those Instamatic cameras people had years ago, the kind with the flash built in. The man smiled, and his teeth were stained yellow. His eyes were alive. He giggled like a little boy. "Come on, honey, smile for Daddy." He giggled some more, the laugh finally bottoming into something deep, almost threatening. "This is your wake-up call." Click and flash, blinding.

Cayce shook his head, trying to clear the image. He had seen this man before. It was, as he suspected, Sheryl's stepfather, Rick. This wasn't the kind of vision he wanted to have. This was painful. And it led nowhere. He turned the photograph facedown on the table, hoping to block out more of the vision. None of it could help. *The man taking the picture was naked.*

Cayce picked up the Pirates jersey, weariness washing over him like a wave, depleted. Having these visions was like going through a strenuous workout or running several miles. Even though he sat completely still, the process of the visions reached deep down inside, stealing energy. "Please, let there be something." He held the shirt, fingering its nylon weave, lifting it to his nose to sniff—and got nothing. He set the jersey down and reached for the charm bracelet. It made a tinkling sound, and the heft of it surprised Cayce, but then there were a lot of charms on it. Cayce went through them all, the bears, the letters, the hearts, the cheap imitation gems, and got nothing. He clutched the bracelet hard, squeezing it, hoping to wring some essence of Sheryl out of the gold electroplate.

He wanted to cry. "No," he whimpered. He thought of this as his only chance, other than going out and getting in the car with Dave Newton and blindly combing the countryside, hoping they would see something that would trigger a mental connection. That could take days. The police might get there before him, and they might be pulling a body bag with Luke in it from a shallow grave or a car trunk.

A car trunk... Something clicked.

And then he saw Oreo. "Come here, boy, come here." A tall dark-haired man squatted down in his parents' backyard beside the dog, gesturing with his hand, holding it out like he had something in it. Then things went black. There was nothing for several minutes, and Cayce felt the pain of loss burn through him. *They got Oreo.*

Then another flash—Oreo's teeth bared in a growl. A lunge and then the dog's mouth connecting with a pale hand, drawing the crimson alarm of blood. Another flash, Oreo yelping as a booted foot kicked him as he ran away. The trunk shut, without Oreo in it. "You got away," Cayce whispered, tears at his eyes. "You got away." *Please find your way home, boy. Please.*

A jolt ran through him. A swirl of red, like blood into oil, swam on his inner eyelids. Cayce gripped the bottom of the chair until his knuckles went bloodless. The red Mustang was parked next to a rusting trailer, dingy white and harvest gold. Cayce stuffed a fist in his mouth when he saw Luke's head pop up in the back window. He looked scared, eyes wide, searching. *He's looking for me. He doesn't understand.* Cayce's heart ached. "My boy," he whimpered, feeling helpless and vulnerable.

Another jolt went through him as his mental gaze moved to the left of the car, to the weed- and trash-choked yard of the trailer. There was a mound of fresh dirt. There were a few old leaves, branches, and rusting tin cans placed strategically over it, but it was clear that the space was a grave.

Cayce knew.

Sheryl!

Cayce wanted to weep, to shut out the images he had encouraged. He wanted to put his head down on the table and cover the surface with snot and tears. Sob for the loss of a young girl, barely into her teens, sob for Luke...

Where is Luke?

There's no time for that now. Concentrate. Go back. Look around. See where you are.

Cayce closed his eyes, trembling because he was afraid the vision wouldn't return, or it would come back to a different place. He didn't know how fragile these images were, but he did know how precious they were. Their very value made it easy for Cayce to worry they would scatter and leave him with nothing useful. And then what would happen? Would Luke end up part of a graveyard on the bluff?

But when he breathed in, it all came back: a shovel breaking through the dirt, the rusty skirting around the bottom of the trailer.

Cayce realized he could move, just a little, when he concentrated really hard. He couldn't move much in the vision, but he could turn himself so he got a clear perspective from both directions on the bluff upon which the trailer sat. First, he could see he was high up on a hill; the Ohio River curved below, flowing on its muddy journey to the Mississippi. *Think, Cayce, think. What do you see? What's at the bottom of the hill? What's across the river*? He narrowed his eyes, both in the kitchen and within his vision. Across the river were two houses, one a red brick ranch and the other a two-story box, sheathed in dingy white aluminum siding, black shutters, a run-down colorless car in the driveway. Down below, he could see the three or four blocks that constituted downtown Fawcettville. He allowed himself a sigh of relief. He had his bearings.

He made himself turn and saw, in front of the trailer, a dirt and ash driveway leading out to a pothole-filled two-lane road. The vision was dimming, the images flickering. Cayce knew he didn't have much time. *Find something unique. There, a sign along the road, blurred.* Cayce squinted, trying to bring the black-and-white marker into clarity. At first, nothing; the sign stayed out of focus as if to confound him. He ground his teeth together, unconsciously angling his head one way and then another, squinting, squinting harder.

And he got it! *Route 14.*

Cayce stood, heart pounding. He had everything.

He hurried out the kitchen door, racing toward Dave Newton's car. Without a word, the reporter turned the key in the ignition and the engine roared into life.

Cayce swung into the passenger seat. "Let's go. I'll navigate."

Chapter Twenty-Six

Dave burned to ask Cayce all sorts of questions. When he rushed out of the house, screen door slamming behind him like a shot, Dave saw a man possessed, a man on a mission. Jubilation, terror, and impatience combined on Cayce's dark features. Hopped-up, jerky, trembling were all terms Dave thought he could use to describe Cayce's movement.

Once in the car, before he even uttered a word, Cayce laughed, smiled, and wept a little. Dave wasn't sure whether he should do as Cayce said or drive him to Fawcettville City Hospital, where they could begin an IV drip of some serious psychotropic drugs.

"I know where he is." Cayce stared straight ahead, as though what was outside the windshield was not the night sky and his little one-car garage but his son, standing with arms outstretched, waiting for his father to lift him up and carry him off to bed.

Dave wanted to ask how he knew, what had happened in the kitchen, what he had seen, and how it all worked. But he knew from everything about Cayce that there was no time. There was urgency in his words and body language. Dave felt compelled, under the spell of a force greater than his own will.

He wanted to help Cayce, wanted him to be right.

Dave wondered if this caring he felt for Cayce, this beam of hope, portended something larger, something he had thought he was no longer capable of.

Love. It had been so long since Dave had felt such stirrings that he wasn't sure if he'd recognize feelings of love if they came up and tweaked the tip of his nose.

Thoughts like these had to be shelved; Dave could take them out and examine them later. He understood Cayce's urgency and desperation. It was late, after midnight. Dave had sat by himself in the car, waiting, for almost two hours, wondering if Cayce had fallen asleep but knowing instinctively not to disturb him.

He had to have had some sort of breakthrough. Dave didn't need psychic ability or even intuition to know that much.

Dave threw the car into gear. "Tell me. Tell me where to go."

Cayce breathed out, as if preparing himself for a difficult physical task. "Head for Hill Road. You're going to take that up to Vermont Boulevard and then make a right and then another right at the first road you come to. It will go almost straight up."

Cayce shifted in his seat and stopped speaking. There was no more to say. Dave thought he looked like a thoroughbred waiting for the starting gate to open.

Dave knew this was not the time for following speed limits. He pushed down on the accelerator and goosed the car up to eighty, checking the gas gauge to make sure fuel was not going to be a problem. Everything was good. They had enough to go for miles and miles, even though Dave already had a sense they weren't going very far.

Excitement surged in him like something electric, pulsing. Something big was going down. Somehow, Dave would help Cayce. And that was good, because he couldn't deny the tenderness and protectiveness blooming within.

He didn't allow himself to think of bad outcomes. *Of a little boy's body...*

Stop. We are not *going to be too late.*

Dave almost missed the left that would take them onto Hill Road. "Here! Here! Left! Left!" Cayce cried, and Dave jerked the wheel left, cutting off an oncoming pickup. Amidst the blaring of a horn and the squealing of tires, they began to ascend the road, climbing, climbing, the dark tree branches above them reaching out like ghostly fingers, silhouetted against a crescent moon.

"Get ready. Vermont's just ahead."

Dave hung a right on Vermont. The little car continued to climb, its headlights and his gaze in synch, searching for the first road on the right. There it was, nearly hidden between sentinels of pine.

Dave took the road up as carefully as he could, given his speed. At last, they were on top of the bluff. One side sloped down, revealing the silent progress of the Ohio River, the commercial district of Fawcettville nestled along its shores. The other side was bordered by woods. The car hit pothole after pothole, the undercarriage squeaking and whining in protest.

Dave did not slow down.

"Watch for a sign."

"A sign?" Dave thought at first Cayce meant some sort of image from God might burst into life on the road before them or the dark, cloudy sky part to reveal a giant flaming hand, pointing to the spot. He stifled a laugh.

"A road sign," Cayce said impatiently. "Route 14. There will be a trailer across from it."

It didn't take long for a scene matching Cayce's description to rise up, as if Cayce's words had conjured the trailer and the road sign.

Dave slowed. They craned to peer at the trailer, looking forlorn and lonely at the edge of the bluff. A good wind would knock it right down into the valley.

"Pull over." Cayce's voice was hoarse. Despair and fear, Dave supposed, stole all the air from him.

The car crunched on rocks and dirt at the side of the road.

"I don't know if I can do this." Cayce gripped the dashboard. "What if he's..." Cayce obviously could not utter the words.

"We have to. I'm here, Cayce. With you every step of the way. There's a flashlight in the glove box." Dave glanced over at the trailer. It was all dark, no lights shining from within. He bit his thumbnail, pulling at it. He wasn't sure he wanted to continue either. The place looked forbidding, dangerous. But Dave knew he needed to be strong. Cayce needed that, needed him, he told himself. Dave's motives, he realized, had nothing to do with providing a story for the *Review*.

Cayce flipped open the glove compartment and removed the flashlight. He flicked it on and off quickly, pointing its beam down at the floor. He whispered, "We should keep this off, at least until we really need it."

Dave understood and shivered. If there were people in there, they were monsters, the kind who killed young girls. The element of surprise was crucial. This encounter could be life-or-death. He hadn't yet had time to be afraid, but now the terror hit like a great wave rolling in—sudden, concrete hard, and cold. Sweat broke out on his back to trickle in a crawly stream down his spine. His heart hammered.

What waited inside that dark trailer?

*

Cayce gripped the flashlight so hard his knuckles were white. He glanced over at the dark, hulking rectangle just feet away.

Is Luke in there? He wasn't getting a sense. Everything that brought him visions, images, whatever they were, was quiet. Part of him hoped he was wrong. He couldn't imagine being inside that awful place. Imagining Luke in there caused Cayce's stomach to flip-flop.

"Why is it so dark?" he whispered to Dave.

Dave's voice came out with a bit of a quiver, but Cayce could tell he was trying to make things less menacing. "They're asleep?"

Dave gripped Cayce's hand. "Cayce, do you think maybe we should phone the police? I have my mobile right here." Dave tapped his pocket.

"And tell them what? They're not going to come rushing up here because I saw the trailer in a vision. We're on our own. You're welcome to stay here in the car if you want, but if my son is in there, I'm getting him out and bringing him home."

"Of course I'm coming with you. What do you think I'm here for?"

"We need to be very quiet. Let's open the doors at the same time, and let's not close them. I don't want anyone knowing we're on our way."

"Okay. One, two, three," Dave said, and both of them opened their doors at the same time. Both put their feet gingerly on the rock-strewn and weed-choked ground and slipped from the car. The two picked their way through trash and weeds, moving silently toward the trailer. Cayce both wished there was more of a moon and, at the same time, was grateful there wasn't. He wondered about the high grass and weeds brushing his ankles. Did they hide snakes or rats? He grasped Dave's hand so tight he knew it must have hurt but couldn't pull back.

Cayce tried to comfort himself as they crept toward the trailer. *Just think: in a few minutes, you could be seeing Luke. You could be holding him in your arms.* The thought made him quicken his pace, helped him forget what horrors might lie in wait. But what if what he held in his arms was no longer alive? He realized they had to be purposeful. There was no time for fear or hesitation.

They stopped just outside the trailer. Dave whispered, "Do you think there's a back door? Maybe one of us should go that way and the other go in through here. If we can get in..."

Cayce looked around and then noticed something odd. There was no red Mustang parked near the trailer. In fact, there were no cars at all. This trailer was the kind of place where, if you lived here, you needed a car. His heart sank.

He grabbed Dave's shirt, clutching. "What if they're gone?"

Dave shook his head. "We can't stand here and wonder. Let's not worry about the back door either. Let's just see if we can get inside."

The trailer's front door was unlocked. Dave went in first, and Cayce followed.

It smelled bad inside, like rotting meat. The air was close, damp, like being inside a steam room. But a steam room where someone had left pounds of hamburger out to spoil in the heat. Cayce covered his mouth and tried not to gag.

"This is an old trick I learned from covering crime scenes." Dave pulled a small blue jar from the pocket of his jeans. In a moment, he placed an oily smear above Cayce's upper lip. Right away, all Cayce could smell was eucalyptus.

Dave did the same.

"Vicks?" Cayce asked, not wanting to think why Dave had brought the stuff along; he hoped it was because he had a cold.

Dave nodded.

In spite of the smell, the trailer had an air of emptiness. Cayce switched the flashlight on. "Come on." He moved quickly out of the kitchen area and into the living room, where the stubs of dozens of dead candles stood. He took in the skull on the coffee table and shivered.

He moved down the hall, peeking first into a bathroom, filthy, with dark smears on the floor and by the tub, some of the smears still recalling what had made them. In the light of the flashlight, Cayce knew what these were: bloody footprints. He felt dizzy and gripped the wall for support.

Blood was smeared all around the bathroom. There were handprints, Cayce now noticed, on the wall and splatters and pools of it in the tub.

Cayce's mouth was dry. *No. I cannot be sick now.* He backed slowly out, breathing in deep the scent of the Vicks. Dave was silent, never removing his hand from Cayce's shoulder. It was a comfort, but it was David-sized comfort in the face of Goliath horror.

Cayce peered into the first bedroom. There was a twin bed with rumpled sheets and a small nightstand. Nothing else. The room was tiny, Cayce guessed no more than eight feet by ten. *Did Luke stay in here? Is Luke in the other bedroom?* Cayce didn't know if he wanted to see. He sat quickly on the edge of the twin bed, knees gone weak. "Will you go look in the other bedroom for me? I can't... I just can't do it." He let out a trembling, choked sob.

Dave knelt before him. "Of course." He touched Cayce's cheek and, with his other hand, gently pried the flashlight from Cayce's fingers. "I'll take a look through the closets, too, if I don't find anything."

Cayce didn't like his use of the word "anything." It was like he was already talking about Luke in the past tense. Cayce's stomach was churning as he watched Dave leave the room. He flopped back on the bed and shut his eyes tight, afraid of the news that might be on its way.

*

Dave made his way down the short distance to the next bedroom at the back of the trailer. He was glad Cayce had stayed put; the smell was growing worse, in spite of the Vicks. Sour, sweet, it made him want to retch.

He paused at the dark entrance to the room. The smell hung over the room like a miasma, a fog of stench. Dave held his nose, breathing through his mouth, and moved forward.

The room's interior was dark, and part of Dave hoped his eyes wouldn't adjust. He stood frozen, panting, heart pounding, and realized these next few steps would be the hardest steps he had ever taken. He didn't need to be able to see to realize something horrible was here.

It crossed his mind that he could simply reach out and grope along the wall until his hand connected with a light switch. But then the room would be flooded with light, and he wasn't sure he wanted that much illumination.

For just one moment, he contemplated simply turning around and going back to Cayce. He could tell him there was nothing in the room and they should move on. They could call 911 from his mobile in the car.

No, he couldn't do that. Even without playing the flashlight's beam over the interior of the room, he knew, from the heavy smell in the air, something dead awaited.

But if he was that certain, why not go back to Cayce and tell him there was a body in the room and they should call the police? Why face the horror that surely waited just a few steps away? He didn't know if he could bear it.

Come on now! This man brought you along because he thought you were strong, thought you could help. This is not the time to turn tail and run.

Dave took several deep breaths and then reached down and flicked the flashlight on.

He let the beam play first on the opposite walls, ignoring the bed. There were more blood spatters and bloody handprints.

Something must be on the bed. Go on...you must.

He lowered the beam of light and couldn't stop himself—he screamed. Forcing himself to look, he fought down the bile rising up. "No, no, no..." he whispered over and over, a litany, not even aware he was speaking. He stood like that, frozen, for minutes, simply staring at the mess on the bed.

Then he turned and went back to Cayce in the other room. He had to tell him what he found. He had to tell him the bad news.

*

Cayce was getting something, but only snatches, coming rapid-fire, like nightmare slides projected by someone with no patience. A girl he didn't know, her mouth in an O, a silent scream. A bloody butcher's knife raised high. Pale hair in the dark, a face obscured by a video camera. Cayce rocked on the bed, saliva dribbling from the corner of his mouth, not wanting to see yet unable to stop the parade of gruesome imagery. He was just about to get up and go to Dave so he wouldn't be alone, whatever horrors waited in the other room be damned.

And then he heard the scream. Bloodcurdling, it made him want to do the same.

Cayce sat up, squeezing his eyes shut and opening them rapidly. Panting. Trying to make himself concentrate on the here and now. The cheap miniblinds at the tiny window, the room's only view to the outside, the clothes scattered on the floor... He didn't want to think about Dave's shriek and his mumbled "no-no-no."

He leaped from the bed and cried out when he noticed Dave standing in the doorway. Dave's face, even in the dark, was a mask of fear: eyebrows drawn close, lips pulled low in the deepest of frowns, little breaths escaping.

"What?" Cayce asked dully, already beginning to cry, already bracing himself for the news.

"I'm afraid I have some very bad news. We need to call the police. *Now.*"

Chapter Twenty-Seven

Luke could not stop shaking. It wasn't cold in the car, but still he couldn't stop trembling, as though it were zero degrees outside and he was dressed just as he was now, in shorts and his Steelers T-shirt. He lay across the small backseat, knees drawn up to his chest, wishing he could suck his thumb, but they hadn't removed the duct tape when they left the trailer. They hadn't even taken off the bungee cords that bound his hands and wrists, even though the lady told the man they could; it would be all right.

The man wouldn't listen. He was very, very mad.

But at least he had let the lady put him into the backseat. And at least she had been gentle about it, almost like when his dad would put him on his bed after he fell asleep downstairs.

She had smiled and whispered, "Just don't make any fuss. You don't want to upset him more than he already is." She ran her fingers through his hair and trailed her fingertips along his cheek, smiling. "This will all be over soon."

She had gently rolled him toward the back of the seat, and Luke tried to calm himself. He was afraid if he got too upset he would have trouble breathing. He would smother.

The lady had left him alone in the car. Here was his chance! He tried—really hard—to get himself free, but the cords were tight, and he couldn't scream through the duct tape. He heard her running after the man and could hear her voice but not her words. It sounded like she was crying—and begging. Luke heard the word "Don't!" several times.

There was the man's voice, angry. Luke heard the f-word and something about "the Beast" and then the trailer door slamming. It almost sounded like a gunshot. The lady must have stayed outside, because he could hear her sobbing like her heart was broken.

And then Luke heard screaming. Terrible hollering. Wails. The angry voice of the man. Luke tried to scrunch his shoulders up to his ears to block out the high-pitched shrieks, but it wasn't possible. There was nothing he could do but listen. He knew the sounds were coming from the other lady, the fat one. And she sounded like she was in horrible pain!

He wished he could stop the man from hurting her.

Luke sniffled and tried to forget what he'd heard. He told himself to just think about the steady *thrum* of the road rolling by under the car. It was hard, though. If they would just be quiet, maybe he could calm himself, but every time he tried to go somewhere else in his mind, they would start fighting again. Sometimes, the man would reach over and hit the lady or grab her cheeks and force her to look at him while the words shot out of him, scalding and mean. Those times, the car would swerve all over the road because the man wasn't paying attention.

Luke wished they would crash, wished they would hit another car. Then maybe he'd have a chance. It was funny: having a car accident was better than staying in the car with these two bad people. At least if they crashed, the police would come...and he would be rescued, even if he did get hurt.

Luke also wished he had not rolled himself over. He figured the lady put him down facing the back of the seat for a reason. But he had managed to get himself facing the other way, and now he was forced to be a witness to everything in the front seat. Maybe if he didn't have to watch, it would be easier. He had managed to go away in his mind when lots of stuff had been going on. He would imagine himself climbing one of the hills across from his house. He would start by walking down the driveway, then checking to see if the street was clear of traffic to cross, then up the retaining wall sidewalk that kept the hill from coming down onto the road. And then he would start climbing, losing himself in the green leaves and golden sunlight of the woods, listening to the crunch of his own footsteps on the dirt and dried leaves and the birds crying out to one another.

He didn't want to hear them arguing, because they were arguing about him.

*

Myra tried one more time. Common sense was the only tack she could take, and she wasn't even sure that worked anymore with Ian. What he had done to Tammie... She sniffed, thinking of her friend in the trailer. Tammie hadn't deserved to die.

Myra's cheeks stung from Ian's slaps. Soon he would probably pull over and start punching her. He would pummel her just so she would shut up. He'd done it before. A part of Myra told her: *Just shut up and let him do what he wants. It will be easier. One more death won't make any difference.*

But she couldn't. The girls had been bad enough, but this little boy! He was like a little angel with his blond hair, his green eyes ringed by those impossibly long and black eyelashes, even his dirty face—they all made her heart ache. She had wondered at times over the past summer if she even had a heart. Now she knew she did.

She started again, cringing, waiting for Ian's hand to fly out and connect with her face painfully. "Ian, please, honey, just listen. Can't we just pull over and put him out by the side of the road? He's just a little kid. When we get to where we're going, we can change our appearances. We'll be no worse off if we let him go. They'll find Tammie. They know we rented the trailer. Ian, honey, they know who we are. All that boy can do is give them a description. He's little. He won't even be good at that. And by the time he tells them, I'll have black hair and yours will be blond. We can get you a pair of glasses at the drugstore. You can grow a beard. I'll start wearing different clothes."

Ian took his eyes from the road to glare at her. "You stupid cunt. Can't you just listen to what the Beast says? Can't you just trust in me? Everything you say is true, yet the Beast says we'll still be safer if we leave a corpse instead of a kid." He smiled, and Myra wondered how a monster could look so handsome. His face was sweet, the stuff of romance novel covers. But underneath, Myra knew, something diseased and monstrous lurked, belying the pretty exterior.

Myra stared at the floor, chewing on her lower lip. "Couldn't you just do this for me? I love you, sweetheart, but I don't think I could bear..."

"I'll take care of it," Ian snapped. "I won't make you record it. You won't even have to watch."

"I don't care about that. He's just so young. It seems a shame." Desperate, Myra thought of another angle. "We could take him with us, make him our kid. Show him the way of the Beast. How would that be?"

Ian was quiet for a long time, and she knew he was thinking, imagining what it would be like to have a young, impressionable mind at his fingertips to mold, a disciple. She used his contemplation as an opening, and she spoke quietly. "We could teach him all about the Beast, and he would come to believe." She swallowed. "Just like we do. He'll be the Beast's first real convert, after us. Just imagine bringing him up, like some reverse of Jesus. I'll take care of him, just like a mother... All you have to do is train him in the teachings of the Beast." Myra felt everything she was saying was stupid and groundless; even she didn't believe a word of it.

Yet she could see the wheels turning in Ian's mind. He had a small smile on his face. She wondered if he saw making Luke their son as some sort of beginning. He shook his head. "I don't know."

Myra smiled. "I don't know" was better than "We need to kill him. We can't leave any witnesses."

She decided not to press her advantage. She thought of the Wicked Witch of the West. What was it she said in the movie? "These things must be done delicately." For now, for maybe even the next hour, the boy was safe.

She peered over the seat back. He lay trembling, almost spasming on the backseat, his green eyes wide. She reached back to touch him, to reassure him, and he flinched at her hand drawing near. She mouthed "It's gonna be okay" and smiled. He nodded.

She turned back to Ian. "We can talk more about this when we get to Pittsburgh. Okay?" Myra put a gentle hand on his thigh. "Can you just think about what I said?"

"I am thinking about it, my love. And it seems like a real stupid idea. But it amuses me to listen to your vain efforts at salvation. Who are you really trying to save, though? Him? Or yourself?"

Myra looked out the window at the dark landscape racing by, wishing she could just leap from the car and run into the woods or one of the yellow-lit houses that would come up every so often, a blur.

Chapter Twenty-Eight

The night was alive with light, squawking voices, people running. Cayce stared dully at the chaos: all at once a crime scene, a burial ground, and a circus.

Why is everyone running? It's too late to do anything for them.

They had just unearthed Sheryl McKenna's body. And finally, the visions came together in one unbroken tapestry of horror—Sheryl McKenna's final night.

Cayce found a big old maple and sat down, legs splayed out, back against the rough bark. The vision came with clarity, like watching a movie, almost unreal. If only...

*

It was a quarter to eleven on a Thursday night, and Sheryl was due to meet Mike in forty-five minutes. She looked at herself in the mirror, knowing Mike would like what he saw. Sheryl had inherited her late father's black hair, so dark it possessed almost a bluish sheen, straight and silky and hanging to the middle of her back. It was her best feature, a stamp of her father's Irish heritage. He had died when Sheryl was five. Her blue eyes ranked a close second, contrasting wonderfully, sexily, with her dark hair. Pale-blue eyes that were ringed in black lashes that needed no mascara, even though Sheryl reached now for the Maybelline and began brushing at those same lashes, lengthening and thickening. It was important she look especially good for Mike tonight. Sheryl was a girl with plans.

The rest of her bore traces of her mother, a one-time alcoholic who had lately found religion. Sheryl knew that her mother, Janet, had been far wilder than Sheryl would ever dream of being. She had heard the stories. Fawcettville was a small town, and its secrets could never be buried very deeply. Janet McKenna was the kind of girl boys snickered at when she walked by them at Fawcettville High. But their snickers were absent when they showed up late at night outside her house, tap, tap, tapping on her window, exhorting her to come out and play. Janet was a girl who just couldn't say no. Even now, her mother endured winks and stares from men on the downtown streets, at the grocery store, in the Laundromat. All of them, Sheryl assumed, had been "suitors" at one time or another.

But Sheryl managed to retain, at sixteen, the youthful beauty to which her mother had long ago bid a reluctant farewell. The button nose, the full breasts, the small waist, the hips that flared out seductively, perhaps too big for a modeling career but definitely attractive to boys...and men. Like Mike. Mike was twenty-five, a fireman with the Fawcettville Fire Department and all man: buzz-cut blond hair, a moustache, and blue eyes that rivaled her own, framed with the same thick black lashes. And his body...good Lord! The most serious weightlifters at Fawcettville High couldn't compete with Mike's hard body, which had almost no fat and was blessed with perfect definition.

Sheryl applied lip gloss and then dusted her cheekbones with a little blush and looked at herself. She was beautiful. Never mind that all she wore on this warm night was a black camisole and ripped jeans. She slipped on the ring Mike had given her shortly after they had met, early in the summer: a tiny, perfect sapphire set in sterling silver. Mike said it reminded him of her eyes.

Sheryl walked to the window. She gently removed the screen and box fan and placed them silently on the floor. Tonight would be a big night. An important night. A night that would change Sheryl's life forever. Mike would be crazy not to take her up on her offer.

She swung a leg over the windowsill and then slid down the side of the house, wriggling her toes for purchase in the moist earth. Once on the ground, she reached up, felt around, and located the screen so she could put it back in the window, loosely enough to get back in later, when the first pink rays of dawn peeked over the hilltops. This return was a scene Sheryl had repeated many times since she had first met Mike last summer, when she had been out with a bunch of kids from school, drinking beer and smoking weed on the banks of the Ohio. She had never been caught.

Well, she thought as she started away from the house, lighting a Marlboro Light with a pink disposable lighter, she had, in a way, been caught, but not by her parents. It had been two months since Sheryl had any use for the tampons stashed beneath the sink in the bathroom.

At first there had been worry, a kind of sick anxiety when a week, and then two, had passed with no period. Mike had used condoms off and on but despised them so much Sheryl hated forcing him. He had always pulled out, squirting his seed on Sheryl's flat belly.

Apparently, he hadn't always pulled out soon enough.

Sheryl moved down the cinder road in front of her house that led toward the bank of the river, keeping close to the trees so as not to be spotted by a neighbor who might tattle. The river, not far from the little one-story she shared with her mother and Rick, had a definite smell, fishy, but Sheryl liked it. There was something clean about its smell, and its waters, in the darkness. The river had fascinated her since she was a little girl and would ride in the backseat of her mother's car along Route 7, coming home from visiting relatives in Wellsville, Ohio. Sheryl would watch the moon on the water, watch as it seemed to follow them all the way back home to Fawcettville.

After tonight, Sheryl thought, turning down a path bordered by oak and pine trees that led her down to the water's edge, she might not need to sneak around anymore. After tonight, she might find herself making all sorts of changes, leaving home and setting up housekeeping with Mike, getting ready for their baby.

It was going to be great.

She paused for a moment, on top of a rise. Below her the river flowed heavily. She listened to the water as it made its trip toward the Mississippi—she had paid attention in geography, contrary to what her mother thought. And just upstream a ways, Mike's car, a dark-blue Honda Civic, was parked, headlights extinguished, on a flat, barren piece of land that jutted out into the river.

This was their spot. Sheryl made her way down the little rise, gripping tree roots for support. After reaching the bottom, she brushed her hands off, clapping them together to free them of dirt, and started toward the car.

Mike waited inside, his CD player on low. Strains of Led Zeppelin drifted out. Mike loved the "classic" stuff, which Sheryl had known nothing about until she met him. Her mother liked old music, too, but favored disco from the seventies when, Sheryl supposed, she was getting screwed in dance hall parking lots up and down the Ohio River between Fawcettville and Pittsburgh. This was the *II* album, the song "What Is and What Should Never Be."

Sheryl opened the door and slid in wordlessly beside him. Mike glanced over, giving her one of his lopsided grins, mouth turned up at one corner. He smelled of cigarettes and beer, a little aftershave. Old Spice. They didn't say anything, and Sheryl leaned back against the seat as Mike took her in his arms, a little roughly, and began kissing her, forcing his tongue deep inside her mouth. He pushed her shirt up slowly, sliding it over her bare skin.

It didn't take long. It never did. As the two of them silently pulled their clothes back on, Sheryl decided that this moment, when he was satisfied and so surely in love with her, would be the best time to bring up her news.

She shrugged her shirt back on and left her jeans in a bunch on the floor. She stroked his face, the stubble rough beneath her fingers.

"I've got some news," she whispered.

Mike lit a cigarette and blew the smoke out the window. "What?"

"Guess."

"C'mon, Sheryl."

"Just guess."

"You've made it for cheerleading." Mike reached down and cracked open a Bud, drank greedily from the can, and belched.

Sheryl mock-slapped him. "It's nothing like that. I wouldn't want to do something like that anyway. Bunch of losers, little girls."

"Well, what is it, then?"

"I'm gonna have our baby," she said, making her voice come out singsongy and whispery, kind of like that actress. What was her name? Jennifer Tilly.

Mike stiffened. She felt his muscles bunching. He stared out the window for a long time. Sheryl had imagined a big smile, a hug. This was not what she wanted. But still, she supposed the news must come as a shock. There would be time for celebrating later. After they had their own place...

"Shit." Mike stared out the windshield, not looking at her. "I thought we were being careful. I always pulled out or wore a rubber. Every fuckin' time." He frowned, and Sheryl recoiled at the way his eyebrows creased together. "You sure it's mine?"

"What?" Suddenly, the whole scenario she had envisioned earlier that night as she got ready to meet him vanished like a wisp of smoke. "What do you mean?"

"I mean I always fuckin' pulled out, little girl. No come. No baby. Not from me, anyway."

Sheryl swallowed, trying to get a little spit around the lump that had formed in her throat. Her eyes filled with tears. "But you're the only one I've been with, Mike. I thought you knew that."

"You're sure?"

"Of course I'm sure."

"What were you, some kind of virgin?"

Sheryl thought sickeningly then of her mother's husband, Rick, and his late-night visits to her room, which had begun when Sheryl was twelve and had yet to end. But this baby wasn't Rick's, couldn't be. Rick had had a vasectomy. Her mother had mentioned it several times, and so had he, when he assured her that "no harm" could come from what the two of them had done. Sheryl shook her head. "No, I wasn't a virgin." Then Sheryl lied. "But no one else has been with me since last winter." She tried to look him in the eye, but Mike stared straight ahead, at a starless, murky night thick with humidity. "The baby is yours. There's no doubt." Sheryl felt herself begin to tremble in spite of the heat and tried to move closer to Mike, but he shrugged her away.

"We gotta do something about this, then."

Sheryl blew out a sigh. Mike was a good guy, deep down. "I knew you'd want to do the right thing."

"I can scrape up some money for an abortion. That won't be a problem."

Sheryl bit her lip to hold back the tears. "I don't want an abortion!" Her voice came out shriller and louder than she had intended. "I was thinking maybe we could get married." Clutching...desperately. "Or at least live together. Give our kid a mom and dad."

"Are you serious?"

"Yes! Yes! Of course I'm serious." She wanted to pound on him with her fists. What had she done? Made up some guy in her mind? She suddenly felt as though Mike was someone she didn't even know.

"Can't do it, babe."

"Why not, Mike? Don't you love me?" And the tears and the snot started coming now. She felt pathetic and stupid.

"Of course I love you, honey. But I can't..."

"What's the problem, then?"

Mike looked at her for a long time. Was that a stupid grin playing about his lips? What was going on? A line of sweat formed at her hairline, trickled down her back. She felt sick.

"I probably should have told you, babe. Should have been up front from the start."

"What? What is it?" Gorge rising, Sheryl was afraid she already knew.

"I'm married."

She reached out to hit him, then checked herself.

She had to get out of the car. She pulled her clothes on, struggling, jumped outside, where the night air was heavy, and ran halfway down the riverbank. Her dinner came up, and she fell, retching on and on until she felt dry heaves.

Surely Mike would come after her.

But all she heard was the bass thrum of his engine starting up and the decreasing hum of that same engine as it headed away, leaving her alone.

She sat on the bank for a long time. At first just to catch her breath, to try to quell the queasiness and the shock. Then she stared out at the water for a long time, letting the minutes slip by, feeling numb. The night was oppressive, too warm, and Sheryl longed for a cleansing rain, wished, almost, that it would come down so hard it would drown her. But the air hung heavy around her, a cloak, enveloping her in moist air. Gnats dived for her eyes. Night insects hummed in the trees. Sheryl felt nothing, not even the sandy earth beneath her hands that, without thinking, she dug into, fingering and discarding pebbles that had once been on the river's bottom.

The moon glinted off the water. For a while, Sheryl expected to hear Mike's car, the sound growing louder as he returned. But that sound never arrived, and Sheryl knew it never would.

The water, she noticed, didn't smell good at all. Brackish. Dead fish. A slight chemical undertone.

She put her head in her hands and wept. What was she to do now? She imagined getting up, brushing the mud off the back of her jeans, and heading home, where, silently, she would pack a bag and then, at dawn, walk swiftly to Route 60 and stick out a thumb. Maybe someone trustworthy would pick her up and deposit her just a little to the east, in Pittsburgh. She could start a new life. Just her and her baby.

Yeah, right. What would she do for money? How would she secure a home for the two of them? Sheryl was certain there were endless numbers of employers in Pittsburgh just looking for a pregnant sixteen-year-old girl, a high-school dropout with no skills.

Oh yeah, it would be quite a new life.

She would have to tell her mother, endure her Christian wrath. It was ironic that the town sinner had become the town saint, converted by her so-called "born again" husband, who was raping his stepdaughter on a regular basis.

Why not just wade into the river and get it over with?

"You look like the saddest little girl in the world."

Sheryl jumped at the sound of the voice behind her. For a moment, she thought her mother had discovered her sitting here, close to 2:00 a.m., on the banks of the river. But although the voice was feminine, it definitely was not her mother's. Too deep, too raspy, too young.

Sheryl turned and saw her standing there, a vision. A girl, really, not much older than she, with platinum blonde hair, wearing a leather skirt, some sort of animal-print shirt, bare feet, and holding a pair of heels in one hand, a cigarette in the other.

"What's the matter, honey?"

Sheryl stared. "Who the fuck are you?"

The girl laughed. "My name's Myra. Myra Hindley. No need to get snippy. I just saw you sitting there and thought you could use a friend." She snickered. "Or two."

Sheryl stood up. "What are you talking about?"

Myra came closer, and the moon revealed Sheryl's first impression as correct. She wasn't much older than Sheryl's own sixteen years. There was something creepy about her, but Sheryl couldn't understand where that feeling was coming from. Maybe it was just the fact that someone was staring at her when she thought she was down here alone. Maybe she was just embarrassed that this girl had seen her crying.

Myra smiled. "Don't be weirded out. I just happened to be down here with my boyfriend." She laughed. "We were parking." She nodded toward upstream. "He's up there now. I just needed to take a little walk, and I saw you sitting there, and, oh, I just felt sorry for you."

Sheryl wanted to cry again. Just someone else recognizing her pain touched her in an odd way. God, she did need a friend, did need someone to turn to.

Myra moved back. "Look, I'm sorry if I interrupted or something. I should leave you alone. Get back to Ian. He'll be waiting. I just thought you might want to talk. I thought I saw you crying, and, well, I've been there myself. A guy?"

Sheryl nodded.

"I knew it. Fortunately, I have my Ian now." She grinned. "He's one in a million."

Sheryl didn't know what to say. All she knew was that she did want to talk to someone. Maybe Myra being here now was sort of a gift. It would be easier, she reasoned, to tell her problems to someone she hardly knew.

"You wanna come back to the car, chat for a little with Ian and me? We've got some wine. No pressure."

"Yes," Sheryl said, trying to keep her voice even. "Yes, that'd be nice." She twisted Mike's ring around her finger, and Myra noticed her fidgeting. Reaching out, Myra took Sheryl's hand in hers. She held the ring up to the moonlight. "Pretty. From an admirer?"

"A former admirer," Sheryl said. "Let's go meet that one-in-a-million guy of yours."

And Sheryl followed Myra into the darkness.

*

Cayce shook his head, trying to clear it of the images and their deadly portent. He forced himself to focus on the activity around him, wondering why he saw these things *now*, when they were useless.

They had discovered Sheryl's body. The policemen and the medical examiner, all of them shouting about the "female" and the "victim," as if Sheryl had never had a name in the first place. There was excitement in their voices. Cayce wanted to close his ears when one of them matter-of-factly said something about the body being pretty far gone in decomposition, "what with the heat." He squeezed his eyes closed, hoping to blot out the persistent imagery of a rotting face, half eaten by insects.

Cayce watched everyone scurry. He felt dull, senses rubbed raw. *What am I doing here*? He looked around, confused, as if he had awakened from sleep and been plunged into nightmare. *It's not supposed to work that way*. Cayce felt like some kind of black magic had transported him from his living room to the bluff. It was hard to remember, at the moment, what had brought him here. Touching the ground, the bark of the tree, he tried to get his bearings, to tell himself once again what was going on, what had brought him to this grisly scene in the heat of an Indian summer dawn. He knew he was experiencing shock. The chill and shivers running through him every so often only confirmed the diagnosis. So did the numbness, the sense of unreality, and the inability to remember...

Thank God, Dave had stayed by his side throughout. If it hadn't been for him, Cayce thought he would lose his mind. Just go—what was the word?—catatonic or something. Maybe it would be a relief.

But Dave had remained, doing most of the talking when the police had arrived. Dave had been the one who led them into the trailer, drawing the cops straight into a chamber of horrors. He had been the one who had discovered the shallow grave behind the trailer. Cayce didn't know if speech was a faculty he had anymore, but Dave had told the authorities about the dead girl in the bedroom and how someone had tried—and almost succeeded—in severing her head from her body. He didn't know how Dave could describe what he had seen without screaming, but he had managed to keep a level tone and give good directions to whoever had answered the phone at the Fawcettville Police Department.

And now Cayce was having unpleasant flashbacks—real ones this time—of the night they'd found Lucy Plant's body. The area around the trailer—just hours ago quiet, still, dead—was now alive with lights, people, cameras, voices. Dave had set the activity in motion with the simple act of pressing the screen of his smartphone and calling the police. It was only moments before they heard the wail of sirens in the distance.

The déjà vu was not welcome as Cayce watched, still amazed at how *busy* everyone seemed. There was a disconnect from the horror of what was actually here and people going about their jobs. It was as though they were working on a construction site, putting up a building, or they were in a restaurant, like him, waiting tables. Didn't any of them realize that young women were dead, their brief lives snuffed out by crazy people? Didn't any of them want to collapse in terror or fight back in rage? Yet they were all snapping photos, taking measurements, chattering amongst themselves with ghoulish excitement. Didn't any of them share his concern for his son, who was still out there somewhere with the same monsters who had viciously killed these girls? He let out a long, low sound, something between a moan and a wail. It was the kind of scream that would awaken him from a nightmare. *But this is real. This is really happening.*

Dave squatted down beside him. He placed his hands gently on Cayce's shoulders, staring into his eyes. He removed one hand to caress Cayce's face. His dark eyes were filled with concern. "Cayce?"

Cayce shook his head, surprised he had made the noise, and wondered how loud it had been. He looked over Dave's shoulder to see if anyone else had heard, though he wasn't sure he cared. He swallowed hard, a raw lump painful in his throat. He didn't know whether he could talk. He wasn't sure if speech was a faculty he still retained. He wondered, if he opened his mouth, whether all that would emerge would be guttural sounds.

He grabbed Dave's hands, clutching, trying to get his tongue around some words, finally saying hoarsely, "They're all so busy. Hurrying, scurrying..." His gaze followed all the people, moving from group to group rapidly, never really focusing. He whimpered again, loud, and caught the next sob in his throat like a hiccup. "They're all so damn busy with the dead. And not a one of 'em is out there looking for my boy!"

Dave knelt in the dirt and wrapped his arms around Cayce. "Shhh. That's not true. I know for a fact they're working on it. You led them here, Cayce; they know their names now—"

Cayce cut him off. "Myra and Ian?"

Dave looked at him strangely, "Yes, but those aren't their real names. They're the names of serial killers back in the 1960s where I'm from." Dave went on, "They have their names, their license plate number. We'll find him. We have to."

The two of them rocked back and forth while Cayce cried; the dam of grief finally bursting. Dave stroked his hair, whispering, "Cayce, you need to be strong. Don't let yourself collapse, not now. We have to find Luke, and you have to be ready to help. Do you understand?"

Cayce cried for a long time, cried until his throat was raw and his eyes burned. Cried for Sheryl and the girl Dave found inside the trailer but most of all for Luke, who was somewhere with these demons who took innocence and slaughtered it. He felt vulnerable and helpless. Every minute that ticked by was one more minute without Luke, one more minute to worry about what was being done to him, and he, the one who was charged with protecting him, nurturing him, caring for him, could do nothing. His sobs slowed, and he shook his head, looking up at Dave. "You've been good to me. Thank you. Thanks for not being a reporter." He managed a wan smile, rubbing at his eyes. "I know. You're right." Cayce felt a deep urge—completely inappropriate—to lean into Dave's face and kiss him. And not just a peck either, but a hungry, devouring, openmouthed kiss with lots of tongue. He shook his head, trying to free it of the image—and the shame and guilt it induced. *Don't be so hard on yourself. That kind of connection is natural. It's stress. Release.* He reached out to touch Dave's wiry salt-and-pepper hair. *There's a little more than stress at play here. But there's no time to think of that now.*

With his thumbs, Dave brushed the tears off Cayce's face. He tried to smile. "I care about you, Cayce."

Cayce was about to say something when there was a flurry of excitement. Cameras flashed, and everyone talked all at once. Then, almost as if on cue, everyone fell silent as the door of the trailer opened and three paramedics emerged, hoisting a black body bag in their hands. Cayce covered his face.

"I don't know how much more of this I can take." Cayce felt there was nothing else to do but remove his hands from his face and watch as the uniformed men loaded the body into the back of an ambulance. Cayce thought it looked like they were carrying a piece of cargo, a sack of cement. Was there no respect for the dead? At least a hush had fallen over them when the door opened and they came out with the girl. *At least they did that much*, Cayce thought. Behind them, there were still bright lights and squawking voices, yells, even laughter as the insanity around the unearthing of Sheryl McKenna continued. Cayce wondered how someone could find humor in a scene like this. *Be kind, Cayce. Understand: sometimes people laugh at the most horrible times. It's also a release. You want compassion. Show compassion.*

The yellow crime scene tape and wooden horses that had been erected on all sides around the trailer looked like macabre decorations. Every minute the crowd grew larger as word spread about the horror on the hilltop. Every minute someone else made the grim pilgrimage up from the valley of Fawcettville to witness the biggest news story the area had ever seen. Every minute, as the sky lightened in the east, someone else would push and jockey for position at the crime scene barriers, hoping to get a glimpse of a body or a splash of blood. What drove such morbid curiosity? Would he have been part of the swelling crowd if things had been different? He liked to think he would have been above it, but who knew? Life had a way, especially lately, of being out of control and full of unpleasant surprises.

It made him want to vomit. All the faces! It was as if they were at a carnival. Everyone laughing, talking, pointing, smoking cigarettes. He wanted to stand and scream at them. *Listen! Listen to me, you assholes. Don't any of you have a sense of decency? Who brought you up? Apes? Go home. Let the police do their jobs. Show some compassion.* But he stayed mum, continued staring wide-eyed at the crowd, who seemed ready for a good show.

And then he noticed another familiar face in the crowd, this one desperate to get through the barriers, this one real. The woman's frizzed blonde hair was pulled away from a leathered, overly tanned face. Her eyes were practically bulging with terror or outrage; it was hard to say which. She pushed against the crowd with her hands, thrusting her chest out to get to the front. She started to climb over the wooden barrier, and a policeman held her back. She began to wail.

"You let me go, you son of a bitch! That's my daughter over there! That's my daughter!" The woman collapsed into sobs, inconsolable, dropping to her knees in the dirt. She hit her head on the bottom of one of the blue horses stenciled *Fawcettville PD*. She didn't notice. Scrambling to her feet again, she pushed and clawed at the young officer who tried to hold her back. "You have to let me see her. That's my baby! That's my baby! Oh God."

People around her were quieting, making room, leaving a wide circle around the hysterical woman. Most just stared. Some whispered behind their hands.

Cayce remembered being in this woman's kitchen. Janet McKenna. She wouldn't listen to Cayce. Cayce wondered if it really would have done any good even if she had. Wouldn't the result have been the same? Cayce didn't get the vision that might have made a difference until it was too late. She had thrown Cayce out of her house, in fact, calling his visions evil, the product of an association with the devil. Cayce winced at the memory of a plate smashing against the wall, just missing him.

And yet Cayce bore her no ill will. The poor woman was nearly insane with grief. Cayce watched as JT Simmons moved close to the officer attempting to hold Janet McKenna back. She whispered something in his ear and then moved into his place, putting her hands firmly on Janet McKenna's shoulders, leaning in close to talk to her. Janet stopped struggling as the detective spoke, nodding dumbly. Cayce didn't know what Detective Simmons was saying, but her words were having an effect. The fight went out of Janet, and she shrunk into herself, her head hung low, staring down. Finally, JT Simmons walked away, leaving Janet to grip the barrier with bloodless knuckles, watching. Someone came over and put an arm around her, whispered to her. A neighbor, maybe? Friend? Relative? Janet slumped even more; it was as if all the rage had ebbed out, replaced by a dull numbness.

Whoever it was, what they said next obviously brought Janet out of her numbed state. Janet shrugged their hands away and snapped at them. She sunk back into the crowd then, and Cayce couldn't see where she had gone. Cayce looked up at Dave. Dave nodded. "Yeah, I just sat on her porch for an hour trying to convince her to give me some of her daughter's things. Poor woman."

Cayce couldn't imagine what Janet McKenna must be going through. Well, that wasn't quite true. Maybe a better way to say it would be that Cayce *didn't want* to imagine what Janet was going through. He could fear the worst about his son, but as long as Luke still hadn't been found, there was hope. Sustaining hope. Cayce knew that was something Janet had had up until a short time ago. Janet could have told herself, over and over, that Sheryl had run away. She was a wild girl, rebellious. Who knew what she could get up to? But all of that, Cayce imagined, had been wiped out by a single phone call, or maybe a bulletin on the TV or radio. Every ounce of hope that woman had felt had just been cruelly extinguished with the discovery of her daughter's body in an undignified grave on a hillside. Cayce didn't know how she could bear it. He would be ripping his own hair out with grief; he would want to die himself.

Please let Luke be all right. Please, please, please...

Cayce was just about to ask Dave to go talk to her when he noticed Janet standing off to the side, not three feet away. Cayce's muscles tensed. He looked up at Janet and reached to grasp on to Dave's hand. Cayce was too raw to weather an encounter with the woman right now; he didn't know if he could bear her rage if it were focused on him. He couldn't fathom how he might respond if the woman started in on Cayce's "evil," on the part he had played in Sheryl's death. Maybe Janet knew something the police ought to know? Cayce gripped Dave's hand so tightly he was sure it must hurt. But Dave bore the pain with grace.

But there was no anger coming from the woman, no harsh words. Janet simply stood close by, staring and wringing her hands.

Finally, she moved a little closer to Cayce, tentative. "I remember you. You were at my house."

"Yes, I... I just wanted to help." Cayce looked desperately up at Dave. "I really didn't mean any harm. I just thought I could help you find her."

Janet nodded and moved closer. She stretched her hand out to Cayce. "You're just like me. Someone who's lost their baby." The woman's eyes glistened with tears.

Cayce didn't know what to say. He stood, so that their faces would be at the same level. He moved closer to Janet McKenna and, without even thinking about it, drew Janet into his arms, letting the simple act of this touch, Cayce hoped, be a comfort.

After a minute or two, Cayce pulled away. Janet was quietly weeping, and Cayce realized he was too.

"I shoulda listened to you." Janet's words came out choked, broken. "But Rick..."

"Shhh. It doesn't matter now." Cayce touched Janet's cheek, smoothing away the tears. "Now you listen to me. I know you think what I see is the devil's work, but it's not." He leaned in close, so close their noses almost touched, and spoke very softly and very quickly.

"I have seen Sheryl." Cayce nodded as the woman stared at him, eyes bright. He was about to tell the woman all about his detailed vision, to let her know how the last few hours of her daughter's life had gone. But as soon as he opened his mouth, something different came out. "She was here tonight. Not her body. But Sheryl. Your girl. The girl you love. I saw her in the crowd. And Janet—Janet—I want you to know, she was happy. She was okay. For her, the worst of it is over. She's in a good place now." Cayce swallowed, wishing he could stop crying. "She's in a good place. Safe. You remember that. Okay?"

Janet McKenna simply stared, her lower lip quivering. And then she turned and walked away. Cayce watched her. Dave came up behind him and wrapped his arms around Cayce. "That was a good thing you did just now. A very good thing."

Cayce looked back. "It was too little. Too little, too late." He pulled away and watched as Janet McKenna turned around and waved.

She called, "I hope you find your boy."

Cayce mouthed a thank-you and turned back to Dave. "I hope I do too. And not like she found her baby." Cayce buried his head in Dave's chest.

He clutched at the gauzy fabric of Dave's shirt. But he didn't get much time with his grief. Suddenly, someone tapped on his shoulder.

Cayce turned and saw JT Simmons waiting.

"No," Cayce whispered.

The older woman looked tired. Her tough features were marred by fatigue, as though gravity had pulled everything down. Her skin looked gray, her eyes lackluster. Cayce remembered their initial encounter in Simmons's office and how the woman had been condescending and skeptical. Now, somewhere in the craggy features and lines of fatigue, he saw real concern in the woman's eyes. Or maybe Cayce simply sensed it radiating off the detective like an aura.

The detective held up a hand. "Don't worry, Mr. D'Amico. I don't have bad news. Unfortunately, I don't have good news either. But I wanted to let you know where we are with the case, where we are with finding your boy. We do have some information..." She paused and glared at Dave, then looked back at Cayce. "Do you want him here?"

"He's okay. He's been a great help to me."

Simmons gave Dave a long look that said "Watch yourself." She then turned back to Cayce and shrugged. "Whether he listens or not is your choice, but some of this information is sensitive. We can't have this getting out to the general public. It could hamper our work. Is that understood?"

Dave spoke up. "I'll be honest with you. I'm a reporter. But I'm here first for Cayce. I would never do anything that would jeopardize him finding his son. I may report on this, but only when you say it's appropriate."

Simmons blew out a big sigh and paused to light one of her Marlboros. "I'm going to trust you, Mr. Newton, in spite of my better judgment. But I'll go with Mr. D'Amico's faith in you." JT Simmons smoked, thinking. "Okay. It's like this. We know who was renting the trailer. We know the car they drive—"

Cayce cut in, "An old red Mustang?"

"Right. Just like you said. We have the license plate number. We have their names."

Cayce started shaking. "Who are they? What are their real names?"

Simmons stared at Cayce for a moment, eyebrows together in confusion. "Their real names?" She waved the question away with her hand and continued, "The girl is Penny Landsdale, from New Hope. The man is named Ethan Craig, and he grew up in Pittsburgh. From a wealthy family. Steel, I think." Simmons leaned close.

"He's been in and out of mental institutions since he was a kid. Very bright, though. And very, very dangerous." Simmons shook her head. "I'm sorry. But we've got APBs out all across the tristate area. There's the Amber Alert. State Highway Patrols in Ohio, West Virginia, and here in Pennsylvania are looking for them. They won't get far."

Cayce toed the soft dirt, trying not to be negative. He couldn't help himself. "But what if they switched cars? What if they're holed up somewhere?"

"Then we try to find out what happened to the old car. We try to find places where they might go. Craig has credit cards. We have watches on them. Cayce, we can only do our best. More than anything, we want to find your boy. We're doing everything we can."

"Right. I know." Cayce's voice was barely above a whisper.

"Why don't you head on home and let us look for that red Mustang?"

Chapter Twenty-Nine

Paul and Virginia Reese had gotten up early that morning—4:00 a.m.—because Paul liked to get an early start, avoiding "those crazy bastards on the road. They get worse every damn day." They were traveling from their home in Chagrin Falls, Ohio, a suburb of Cleveland, to visit their granddaughter, Emily, on the occasion of her fourth birthday. In the backseat was a stack of presents, all elaborately wrapped and beribboned by Virginia, who loved doing it.

Emily lived in Fawcettville, Pennsylvania, about a three-hour drive. Virginia had tried to tell her husband that leaving at four o'clock would get them to their daughter and her husband's home at seven. "They might not even be out of bed," Virginia had chastened, but Paul wouldn't listen. The older he got, the more he wanted to avoid Cleveland's traffic at busy hours. Virginia was convinced it was because he couldn't see so well anymore and his reflexes weren't what they once were. But would he see a doctor or get anything checked out? No. He would rather crawl along at ten, twenty miles below the speed limit than admit to himself he might be getting too old to drive safely.

Still, Virginia hoped her daughter, Shellie, and her husband, Adam, would be up and about and happy to see them so early. They were now only about fifteen minutes from Fawcettville. Maybe if it looked like everyone in the house was still asleep, Virginia could convince Paul to take her to McDonald's for breakfast. She loved those Egg McMuffins, even if she knew they set her cholesterol and blood pressure soaring.

"Emily is going to be so thrilled to get that doll," Virginia said as Paul veered off on yet another back road to avoid traffic. She was glad he still had a good sense of direction and could read a map like nobody's business. "Shellie said she really wanted one, but they couldn't afford it—" Virginia bit her lip, realizing she might be saying too much. Even though Paul was hunched over the steering wheel, eyes intent on the road, she rolled her eyes and attempted to cover up. "How silly! I don't know where my daughter got her cheapskate ways. Must be that husband of hers. The doll wasn't that expensive," Virginia lied, patting her silver upsweep and glancing nervously into the backseat to make sure the doll was still there. The bright red foil-wrapped rectangle lay on the seat, reflecting the sunlight. Virginia smiled.

"What the hell?"

Virginia turned around quickly. Her husband hardly said a word anymore, so just the fact he was speaking made Virginia take notice, even before she registered the annoyance in his tone.

She didn't know what he was talking about at first; then she saw. A young girl with Marilyn Monroe-blonde hair stood by the side of the road, waving both arms over her head, obviously in distress. She practically walked out in front of their moving car!

But Paul just drove on, shaking his head and mumbling to himself.

"Paul!" Virginia punched her husband in the arm. "Aren't you going to stop? That girl was in trouble."

Virginia didn't care about the girl as much as taking advantage of an opportunity for delay so they would get to her daughter's house at a more reasonable hour. "How can you just leave her standing there by the side of the road? It's not like we're in Cleveland now. She looked perfectly nice."

"Let someone else help her. Somebody else will be by in a minute. She's a pretty gal; she won't have any trouble getting someone to stop." Paul looked over at his wife, forcing his sagging jowls into a smile. Virginia noticed how the sun glinted off his bald pate.

"What? Out here in the middle of nowhere? It could be an hour before anyone else comes by, and how do we know that person won't be another old meanie like yourself and won't even slow down?" Virginia blew out an exasperated sigh. "Now will you please go back and see what that poor girl needs?"

"Come on, Ginny. We're almost there."

Virginia looked down at her watch. Six forty-five. She shook her head. Dully, she said, "I know. Please, Paul, we won't have to spend too much time. But we can at least give her a lift somewhere. What good is this nice big car if we can't at least do that?" Virginia looked around at the flawless interior of the brand new Buick LaCrosse. Paul spent hours keeping it looking exactly as it had when it rolled off the showroom floor, just two months ago.

"You're not gonna shut up until I do what you want, are you?"

Virginia rolled her eyes, but she was smiling. Smugly, she said, "No, sir, I am not." She reached over and patted his knee. "So you might as well turn this boat around and make me happy."

Virginia listened to the car tires crunch as Paul executed a U-turn. In just a couple of minutes, she was relieved to see the girl still standing by the side of the road. Pretty young thing, almost waifish. How could Paul have wanted to just drive by someone who looked so helpless?

Paul slowed the car to a halt on the opposite side of the two-lane road. The girl watched them, smiling, but Virginia could see there was a hint of panic in her features.

*

Myra was almost sorry to see the old couple pull over. But she knew Ian was waiting just a ways down the dirt road behind her. He had told her they needed another vehicle. The police would be looking for the Mustang, and it wouldn't take them long to discover to whom the car was registered. Quickly, turning down the dirt road, he had outlined his plan to lure an unsuspecting motorist off the road and then take their car. "How do we do that?" Myra wanted to know, since they had no gun or other weapons they could use to force someone to give up their car. The nausea rose up in her gut. She already knew Ian's intentions, his "leave no witnesses" policy. Ian didn't need a gun or a knife, not when she helped him out by choosing people as old and feeble-looking as the ones across from her, ready to get out of their car to "help" her.

She wanted to wave them off, the old couple who looked like they could be someone's grandparents, he pudgy and she with silver hair. But if she waved them off, she would simply have to find someone else. If she failed, God knew what Ian would do to the little boy. She rationalized: *At least they're old. At least they've had some time to enjoy life, to do what they want to do with it. At least they don't have that much longer to live anyway.* She smiled as the older man emerged from the car, looking exasperated. Myra wanted to clutch at her heart when she saw the polyester slacks, the plaid shirt, and the loafers. He was real. And so was the woman getting out on the other side. She was smiling and waving, and Myra wondered if this was some sort of adventure for her. *If you only knew...*

"What's the problem, honey?" the woman called across the road.

"My car. It's stuck."

The man immediately took on a guarded expression. "I don't see a car."

The old man and his wife crossed the road, and Myra did her best to look distressed. "I know, I know. I did a really stupid thing."

The man continued to look around, searching for a car Myra imagined he thought he'd missed earlier. She wondered if Ian was watching them from the bushes. She knew she didn't dare warn them away. What good would it do, anyway? She would only have to flag down the next car, and that one might contain a young couple with a new baby, so she continued. "I turned down that road there." Myra pointed to the dirt road just behind her, its entrance almost concealed by leaning maples and pine trees. She laughed, but it came out high and watery, almost panicked—a silly giggle. "I was thinking maybe I could find a shortcut. I was running late, you see, and..." She looked off toward the road, hating herself, just wanting to lean in close and whisper "Get out of here now, while you can" and "Take me with you." But she couldn't bear the thought of leaving little Luke behind with Ian. "So anyway, I start down this dirt road and it's full of bumps and ruts and potholes, and before I knew it, my car slid off into a ditch." Myra lowered her head. "Now I'm really going to be late."

"Where you headed?" the man asked kindly, peering around Myra to look down the dirt road.

"Fawcettville."

The woman clapped her hands together and smiled. "That's exactly where we're going, dear. We could give you a lift, and you could call a tow truck from town." She looked to her husband. "Couldn't we, Paul?"

"I guess so." He glanced down at his watch. "But I'm not sure anything will be open yet."

"Oh, for heaven's sake! If nothing's open, she can just call from Shellie and Adam's place. It won't be a problem." The old woman smiled at Myra. "I suppose all of this would be much easier if we had a cell phone." She indicated her husband with a jerk of her head. "But this one here is too cheap to get one."

"I don't see what we need more bills for when we have a perfectly decent telephone at home."

The old woman gritted her teeth. "For times like these, dear. What if it had been us who were in this predicament?"

"We've had this conversation before, Virginia. Let's just get a move on." He looked at Myra. "We can take you into town."

"Oh, thank you. I'm ever so grateful." Myra thought it would be so easy to just cross the road and get into their car, speed away. But what would happen to Luke? What would happen to *her*? The police had to be onto them by now. They would be waiting in Fawcettville with handcuffs.

"Listen, I hate to bother you even more when you're being so nice and all, but I have some stuff in the car I need to get, and, well, I have a couple boxes that are kinda heavy. You don't suppose we could take them with us? I'm afraid to just leave them in the car. Someone might break in."

Paul rolled his eyes, but Virginia said, "Of course, dear. That's a very smart idea. I hope the boxes aren't too heavy. Paul here has a bad back, but if it's not too much, I'm sure the two of us can manage."

Paul blew out a sigh. Myra wondered if he felt affronted, his masculinity compromised. "I'm just fine, Virginia." He glanced at the dirt road. "How far down did you get?"

"Oh, not too far at all. Are you sure this is okay?"

"Positive," Virginia said brightly.

And the three of them started down the dirt road. Myra hoped they were far enough off the beaten trail that no one would hear their screams.

*

Luke saw the blonde coming down the road with an older lady and man. They looked nice, and Luke felt bad for them. He was still tied up—though Ian had allowed him to sit up—and still had the duct tape over his mouth, so he couldn't cry out a warning...or call for help. But, oh, how he wished he could tell the old people to run as fast as they could back to where they came from! He knew they were in trouble now. Luke watched as the old couple suddenly stopped in the road, realizing they must have seen him and Ian sitting in the car. He could hear the man say, "I thought you said you went into a ditch."

The blonde lady laughed like she was embarrassed.

"No, really. I thought you said the car went off the road. That car looks perfectly fine." Luke watched as the old lady began to back up. She looked a little afraid. Luke thought she should be scared; they were being led straight into a trap.

Ian opened the car door. Everything happened so fast after that.

Luke scrunched down into the seat. Seeing Ian begin to chase the two old people was enough. He didn't want to see what would happen next. The old lady was really scared; Luke could see that much in her big eyes and hear it in the little strangled cry she gave before she turned and started to run. When she tripped and fell, Luke made himself fall over so all he could see was the back of the red vinyl seat.

The blonde lady slid into the car with him, and Luke edged up against the back of the seats, into a corner, drawing his knees up to his chest as best he could. Already, there was hollering and arguing going on outside. Luke didn't want to think about what he had seen the man take with him before he got out of the car: one of those thingies his dad had used one time when he got a flat tire. He had loosened the bolts with it. Luke remembered how hard he had to work to get them free, his sweat. Oh God, he didn't want to hear what was going to happen next...

The blonde lady moved closer. Her eyes were bright with tears, and her lower lip quivered. She had a big frown on her face and was nodding. Luke didn't know why she kept nodding. She reached out with both hands, and Luke screamed under the duct tape, wriggling himself around within the confines of the cords binding him. She moved closer and grabbed hold of him, but gently. She was crying a little now as she drew him toward her chest, covering his ears with her hands. He could hear the hitting, and the screams, and the dull groans.

The lady pressed down harder on his ears and started singing a song Dad sang to him as a lullaby: "You are my Sunshine".

A scream, a terrible plea: "Please, no! Don't hit her again!"

The lady sang louder. Luke at last couldn't hear anymore and was grateful. He leaned against the lady's chest, wishing he could suck his thumb as she continued at the top of her lungs.

When she pulled her hands from his ears, all was quiet. The man opened the door, and Luke wanted to scream. His white shirt was splattered with blood.

The man just stared at the two of them for a moment, panting and trying to catch his breath. Finally, he said, "C'mon. We just got a brand new car."

The lady said, "Just a minute." She pulled the scarf from around her neck, saying, "Honey, this is for the best." She then tied the scarf around Luke's eyes and lifted him gently from the car.

Chapter Thirty

Cayce lay in bed, staring at the ceiling. The idea of sleep was absurd, one of those notions you know from the outset is impossible. Every bone, every muscle, every joint felt weighted down with weariness, and yet he knew closing his eyes would do nothing. They would only spring back open a second or two later, almost as if of their own accord. Both the cordless and his cell were on the nightstand beside him. They were cruel things, taunting him with their refusal to ring. Cayce didn't want to look at them, almost as if staring would prevent them from ringing. Still, he couldn't help imagining their ringing and his answer, hearing JT Simmons on the other end, saying two words: "He's safe."

He clutched Sheryl McKenna's charm bracelet in one hand, hoping the contact would cause some sort of psychic fusion and he would get the answers that would lead him or the police to Luke. With all his heart, he prayed his son was alive and unhurt. But he knew also that if he wasn't, it would be easier to know that.

He turned on his side, looking at the dull morning light filtering in through the miniblinds, and wondered where Luke was right now, if he was crying out for him, if he was being taken care of. Thoughts like these made him want to vomit. He could see him with the blonde woman and the dark-haired man, imagine him trying to understand why his daddy wasn't there to protect him.

Were they hurting him? Did they have hearts that maybe opened just a tiny bit for a little boy? Was he lying somewhere, covered with dirt and some hurriedly gathered old leaves?

He just needed to know.

He shut his eyes once more to block out the glare from the window, knowing it was futile to try to sleep. Color swirled on the insides of his eyelids, tones of red, like blood expanding into clear water. Clouds of blood. The red swirled and churned, polluting, growing. His breath came faster. Sweat trickled from his armpits and down from his hairline. He ground his teeth. His body stiffened, trembled.

He saw Sheryl McKenna again, running through the crowd at the crime scene. She was beautiful, young, healthy, and vibrant. She stopped and turned to Cayce. When their eyes met, it was as though all the people around them went into a blurred state, the light dimming, the milling crowd becoming a crowd of shadows, their excited voices dropping to a low murmur. Yet Sheryl stood out, clear and shining. A beacon.

Sheryl stared at Cayce, and there was kindness in her eyes. Giving Cayce a small smile, she held out her hands, and Cayce moved toward her. This all started to take on an aspect of reality, as if Cayce had risen up out of his body and returned to the crime scene. He could feel the heavy heat and humidity outside pressing in, hear the whisper of the leaves as the wind rustled through them, high up. In spite of the peculiar sense that he and Sheryl were somehow brighter, more *real* than everyone else, this had all the earmarks of reality. When he placed his hands in Sheryl's, the girl's palms felt warm and alive as she tugged him along.

And then they were moving with alarming speed, feet barely touching the ground, heading down the two-lane road in front of the trailer, then stopping suddenly by a dirt road after going only what seemed like a mile or two. Cayce yanked back at Sheryl's hands, wanting to run. He didn't want to see what was around the curve in the road.

But suddenly, they were there. He saw the old woman and the old man, their heads bashed in, their blood soaking into the dirt road like chocolate syrup, eyes staring up at the relentless morning sun.

"No!" Cayce screamed, "No," and he turned in his bed, sobbing and clutching at his sheets and pillow.

Dave hurried into the room, sat on the side of the bed, and gathered Cayce up in his arms, holding him close. "Shhh," he whispered, stroking Cayce's hair. "Shhh. You just had a bad dream."

Cayce forced his face close to Dave's to make sure he understood. "*Not* a dream. We have to call the police." He sat up and reached for his cell. "We have to get hold of JT Simmons. *Now*."

Chapter Thirty-One

Ian was getting sleepy. Myra wasn't surprised. When had he last slept? One night ago? Two? He was having trouble keeping his head from nodding. Myra knew the right thing to do would be to take over, but she wasn't up to the task. Here in the backseat with Luke, she couldn't stop crying.

His head drooped again, and Myra screamed when she realized he was headed straight for a big walnut tree on the side of the road. Her scream jolted him awake, and Ian threw himself back against the seat for leverage, grinding the brakes down almost through the floorboards. They stopped with a jolt that sent Myra flying halfway into the front seat and Ian hard into the steering wheel. She was surprised the tree was still in front of them and the car hadn't connected with its unyielding wood.

They were stopped horizontally across the road, blocking both lanes. A white pickup came barreling down on them, horn blaring. At the last minute, the truck swerved and went up onto the shoulder of the road, sending up a spray of dust and gravel into the heavy air. It continued on, the driver laying on its horn, extending his hand out the window, middle finger pointed toward the sky.

Ian was shaking as he put the car in reverse and righted it, returning to the proper lane.

Myra composed herself, crawling over the seat to put the rest of her body into the front, settling into the bucket seat next to Ian. She turned to him. "You need to get some rest. We all do."

She could see he was tempted to argue and knew him well enough to determine what he was going to say—that they needed to put as much distance between themselves and Fawcettville in as little time as possible. He would probably add something like, if she was brighter, she could have figured that out for herself. But he didn't say anything, and his handsome face was dulled with exhaustion.

"Ian, are you listening to me? I know we need to get out of here, but we can't do it when you're falling asleep at the wheel."

"Shut up, Myra. I know."

Ian felt in his pocket, where she had earlier watched him put the old man's wallet. She had seen him look at the array of credit cards inside, so she knew they had the means to stop for rest and hoped he was thinking the same thing. They could find a quiet motel off the beaten path and settle down for just a few hours. Wouldn't just a few hours' sleep be lovely?

Ian got the car moving. He looked over to Myra. "Poke me if I start nodding off again, okay? I think I'll be all right. Meanwhile, let's keep our eyes peeled for a motel."

The sky was now completely light. They would be safe in this car; no one would find the bodies of the old couple for hours, at least. It hadn't looked like anyone had been down that particular dirt road in days—quite likely weeks. They themselves had lain in wait for what seemed like hours, hoping for someone to come by.

Ian looked over to Myra and touched her thigh. At least she had managed to stop crying. She smiled at him when he touched her. This was how it always went; she was hungry for his touch, for a kind word from him. Only him.

"We're going to be okay, sweetheart. We'll use their credit cards to buy us a few hours of rest, and then we'll use them one last time to buy us some plane tickets. We'll get as far away as we can. By the time they're onto us, we'll have found a way out of this lousy country."

He didn't say anything about the boy, and that frightened Myra. But she didn't want to start that argument with him once more.

Myra sat up straighter and pointed. "Over there." She figured Ian had missed the one-story cinder block motel, it was so unassuming. The neon had gone dark, but the dull sign continued to illuminate the words "The Blue Horizon Motel."

Myra thought the place didn't look like much, just a concrete box with eight doors in a line. All the doors were metal, painted white, with some of them rusting. But inside, there would be a bed and welcome darkness. The thoughts of getting Ian in there, watching him fall asleep, were the most glorious thoughts she had ever had. As Ian signaled to turn into the little parking lot, she closed her eyes and smiled, imagining him stretched out on the bed and snoring.

"It isn't the Ritz, is it?" Ian said, situating himself between two yellow lines and looking through the grimy window of the office. "But it will have to do. I can't drive anymore...and I know you aren't going to do it." He looked over at Myra, lips pursed.

She knew she had been insulted, but she gave him a small smile, as if she hadn't caught on. "I'm really beat too. We'll be a lot better off, a lot more alert, if we catch a few hours of sleep." She glanced into the backseat, where Luke was backed up against the upholstery, eyes wide. She winked at him and wished she could tell him not to worry, that everything would be okay soon.

Myra had a thought. "We can't be seen going into the room with the boy like that."

"What are you talking about?"

"What if someone looks out of the office and sees one of us carrying a child all bound up in bungee cords with duct tape across his mouth? Don't you think it would set off some alarms?" Myra tried to keep the sarcasm out of her voice, suddenly afraid she had insulted Ian. "I mean, it's up to you, but..."

Ian scratched his chin. "I guess you're right."

"I know you knew what's best." Myra was getting better at playing the part of the stupid woman and helpmate. "I can just carry him in." She looked over the seat at Luke and smiled, nodding to him. "You'll behave, won't you, Luke?" She winked again, hoping the little boy wasn't too terrified to understand, hoping he was clever enough to realize she wanted to help.

Luke nodded once, twice.

Myra turned back to Ian. "See? Why don't you go ahead and get us a room?" Myra looked around the parking lot, empty save for a rusting old pickup truck, its color gone beyond any definition other than blah. "I'll take care of Luke."

Ian hesitated, and she was afraid for a moment he would make her go instead. She wanted the time to whisper quickly to Luke, to tell him of her plan, to calm him. Ian looked toward the office, then back at her, turning around finally to peer at Luke. "I guess it will be all right. But you make sure the kid isn't out of your sight for a minute. Not one minute. You hear?"

"You have nothing to worry about, darling. The Beast protects, remember?"

Shakily, Ian responded, "Right." He exited the car, and Myra watched as he walked to the office. She got to her knees on the seat and reached over to begin unbinding Luke. The cords were off in short order. She paused. "There's no other way to do this, honey. It's gonna hurt, but only for a second." Quickly, she reached up and ripped the duct tape from across the boy's mouth. He let out a little cry, and his eyes teared up. Myra immediately felt bad as she saw the red rise up on his soft little face, in the exact shape as the rectangle of tape. "I'm sorry." She got out of the car and hurried to sit in the backseat beside Luke.

"We have to make this fast. Do you understand?" Myra kept glancing toward the office window, where she could see Ian conversing with a rail-thin woman with dyed red hair. She hoped the police weren't already onto them and the red-haired woman wasn't pressing some silent alarm button under the desk. She put her arm around Luke. "Listen, I'm on your side. I want to get us both away from him. But it ain't gonna happen if you don't behave. Understand?"

The boy spoke at last. His voice was tiny, and Myra's heart lurched. Somberly, he said, "Uh-huh."

"What we're gonna do is go along with whatever Ian wants, okay? Even if it scares you, just go along. Got it?"

Luke nodded.

"Once Ian's asleep, you and me, we sneak out. The office is right there. I'm going to take you over there and leave you outside the door. I can't come in with you, honey. You just tell the lady to call the police. They'll find your daddy for you." Myra paused, hoping she would have time to do all this before Ian awoke. She prayed she could get away in the car before Ian's eyelids began to flutter and he noticed what happened.

And there were a million hopes after that one: that she could get beyond the Pennsylvania state border, that she could find a flight to somewhere far away, that she could start a new life for herself with some other name, a third name...

Ian was coming back out of the office. He had some papers in his hand. He was smiling; Myra knew everything must have gone okay. She reached down and gave Luke's chubby thigh a gentle pinch. "Remember what I said. Now, I'm going to carry you inside."

Ian opened the car door. His handsome face was marred by fatigue; his eyelids drooped and his jowls sagged. He had aged ten years, Myra thought.

"Come on, let's get some sleep. You talk to the kid? He knows the score?"

Myra nodded. "Oh, I talked to him all right. We won't be having any trouble from him." She looked deep into Luke's eyes. "Will we, Luke?"

Luke shook his head.

Myra slid from the seat and bent to gather Luke up in her arms. "Good boy," she whispered. And Luke slid his arms around her neck.

Myra began to see light, freedom, escape. It was so close she could almost touch it.

The three of them made their way to the door of room number seven. Myra hoped it was lucky.

After the morning's glare, the darkness of the room made it almost impossible to see. Myra groped her way to a bureau and found a lamp. She pressed the button at its base, and a harsh yellow light filled the room. The lamp looked like one her mother used to have, made of metal, three stacked diamond shapes, gray on top, tan underneath, topped with a tall thin shade. Myra wondered if the rest of the room was done up in 1960s décor. She looked around and took in the painting over the bed: big mountains against a luridly blue, purple, and orange sunset, a threadbare floral-print comforter, a desk and chair in one corner. The carpeting was worn, a burnt-orange shag with several bald patches and burns. The room smelled like smoke.

"I hope I don't have to tell you to keep the curtains shut." Ian looked pointedly at her. Even when he was completely exhausted, he could still manage a withering stare. "I'll be right back."

Myra wondered what he was doing. Getting their luggage, perhaps? Just like a real family vacation...

Ian came back before she had time to imagine more scenarios that didn't involve reality. In a way, he did have some luggage: a heavy black bag in one hand, the bungee cords and roll of duct tape in the other.

He shoved the cords and tape at her. "Tie him up."

"Oh, Ian, do you really think we have to? We can put him right between us on the bed." Myra let loose a high-pitched little laugh. "What could go wrong?"

Ian glared at her. "What could go wrong?" He laughed. "Shall I start making a list, Myra? Besides, I don't want it on the bed with us. It can sleep on the floor."

Myra knelt before Luke, trying to communicate warmth with her eyes. She began wrapping the cord around him, wanting to tell him everything was going to be okay. She wanted to ask him if the cords were too tight, but there was, in the end, nothing she could say to comfort him. If Ian suspected her even in the smallest way, she feared his fatigue would vanish.

She got Luke bound—he stood and let her do it without complaint. Then she took the scarf she had used earlier as a blindfold and tied it around his face, covering his mouth, hoping Ian wouldn't notice she wasn't using duct tape. Myra could still see red marks where the tape had been. Some were even scabbing over, and she knew she had really hurt the boy when she ripped the tape from his face.

She grabbed a pillow and blanket from the bed and made a place for him on the floor in the corner and within view of the bed. "Now, you just go to sleep," Myra said, trying to make herself sound stern. "No funny business. Understand?" Again, Myra winked at Luke, who nodded and let her help him lie down on his back.

When she turned around again, Ian had removed the lamp and the water pitcher and plastic glasses from the bureau and put them on the floor. The lamp was still on. Placed so low, it gave a weird and unearthly glow to the room, making Ian's face look demonic. *Not far from the truth.*

Myra asked, "What are you doing?"

Ian smiled and said nothing. He squatted and began rummaging around in the black bag he had brought in from the car. Ian pulled out several black candles in holders. He placed them on the bureau, almost in ceremonial fashion. At the end, he brought out (almost with a flourish, Myra thought) the big chef's knife from the kitchen.

Myra began to tremble. "Oh, Ian, I thought we agreed to make Luke our own." She lowered her voice to a whisper. "We can't have another death on our hands." She hoped Luke wasn't able to see what was going on. Myra wrung her hands.

Ian just smiled at her. "Your idea, dear one, was stupid. The Beast says we can't leave any witnesses." He gestured toward the bureau. "Like my altar? This is where we'll do the sacrifice, before we leave." Ian giggled. "Won't the cleaning lady be surprised?"

Myra shuddered.

Ian rubbed his hands together, then twisted one in his eyes. "But right now, I'm totally exhausted. I need to get some sleep. Join me?"

Myra took his hand and let him lead her to the bed. She didn't want to get into bed with him, but if this was part of her route to freedom, she would play the part, even if he wasn't *too* exhausted.

Fortunately, Ian wanted nothing more than sleep, and as Myra lay stiffly beside him, regarding the cracked ceiling with cobwebs in its corners, she heard his breathing quickly deepen. She turned softly on her side. Ian's mouth was open, and a little line of drool dripped down his chin.

She wanted to jump up immediately from the bed but knew she should give Ian some time to sink more deeply into sleep. She turned back over, placing her hands across her chest, and waited. She could turn her head and see the little digital clock on the nightstand. She would imagine an hour had passed, would check, and see that it was only five minutes.

At last, Ian began to snore.

It's time, Myra. Get your courage up. You won't have another chance. And yet she remained frozen, unable to move, terror constricting her. Was she capable of betraying Ian this way? *What's wrong with you? He's going to kill that little boy. And it will be ten times worse than with the girls. At least you were jealous of the girls...*

Myra lay there for several more minutes, listening to Ian snore and thinking how worthless she was. *How could I have let it happen? Again and again? Did I ever even love him?* Myra glanced at Ian's face—so handsome and chiseled—and thought how even the most beautiful things can be hideous and rotting underneath.

Get going, girl. You don't have all day. Myra thought of the knife lying on the bureau. It wasn't just about continuing with a cockamamie plan to flee from justice; it was about saving someone's life, someone who had barely begun living his life. She couldn't let anything happen to Luke.

Myra wondered why she cared so much, why she was so desperate to save the boy when she had done nothing but watch the three girls as Ian stole their lives away. How could she have stood by so emotionlessly, actually videotaping two of the girls as they drew their last breaths in misery and pain? Now sympathetic emotions seemed to be returning, like she was an accident or stroke victim learning to walk again.

Maybe her sympathy had something to do with what had happened when she was thirteen. Her parents had taken her to Youngstown, to a girl's home run by the Catholics. It was a hard six months, there with other girls like herself and then again, not. Some of them were so tough, so mean. They made fun of her, asked who would want to fuck a fat thing like her.

The baby had been a boy. They let Myra hold him for just a minute or two after he was born and they had him cleaned up. Soft pink skin, crinkly, and little slits for eyes. But, oh! He had a thick crop of dark hair on his tiny head, and his little fist, even in the delivery room, reached out and gripped her finger.

And then they whisked him away.

Myra had never seen him again. She wondered what he was doing now, if he looked like Luke; they would be about the same age.

Don't get all stupid and sentimental. Tick. Tock.

Myra slowly sat up in bed, silently moving her feet to rest on the floor. She didn't make a sound. She didn't even breathe, looking across the room to where Luke lay staring wide-eyed at her. Her heart thudded so hard in her chest she worried about it waking Ian. Slowly, she turned her head and looked over at him. He was out completely, one arm thrown across his face, his breath alternating between snores, snorts, and deep heavy breathing. She thought she could see his eyes moving back and forth beneath the lids and wondered what horrors he dreamed of.

Very cautiously, being sure not to make the bed move at all, Myra stood. She stayed in one place, taking deep breaths, trying to slow her pulse, the blood thrumming in her ears. Finally, she moved, tiptoeing across the room, grateful for the old shag carpet under her feet. She squatted beside Luke, wincing a little when her knees cracked, and began to untie him. She couldn't say anything, couldn't warn him not to speak or make any noise at all; she could only hope he was smart enough to know that absolute quict was imperative. She prayed he understood.

His life depended on it.

Ian continued to snore as she helped Luke to a standing position. She put one finger over her lips and moved her eyes toward Ian on the bed. Luke nodded. She took his hand, and they began slowly moving toward the door, placing their feet surely and softly.

The door open, Myra was nearly blinded by the bright sunlight. She squinted and paused. There was the office, just across the asphalt. And there was the car, waiting.

Myra closed her eyes. She almost let out a strangled wail of despair. *I don't have the keys! What good is a car without keys?* And with the thought came memory, a clear mental picture of Ian getting out of the car and casually stuffing the ring of keys into his pocket. *The keys are still in his pocket. Shit.*

Myra bit her lip, thinking hard, thinking fast. She looked across the road and saw woods. And the road itself? Well, she had hitchhiked before and could do it again. *But they're probably already out looking for someone who looks like you. There are most likely bulletins on the radio.*

Her reverie and her inability to come to a decision were interrupted by a voice behind her. "Going somewhere?"

Before she had a chance to respond to Ian's question, he had taken hold of her hair and yanked her back inside. She screeched, looking up into his rage-filled face, eyes blazing, truly a demon. She let go of Luke's hand and screamed, "Run, Luke! Run!" She didn't get to see if the little boy did as she told him, if he was running toward the office and safety. Ian pulled her back into the room by her hair and hurled her against the wall. She slipped and went backward, her head connecting hard with a corner of the bureau. She gasped and shut her eyes, seeing stars. The pain was immediate, intense, and throbbing. There was a trickle of warm wetness at her neck.

But there wasn't time for pain or wondering if she would be all right. Ian was headed out the door. She knew he could take just a few strides and catch up with the boy, swooping him up and bringing him back, where he would not hesitate to plunge the chef's knife right into his heart.

Vision blurry, Myra scrambled to a sitting position and without thinking picked up the lamp on the floor beside her. She yanked its cord from the wall socket and got up on shaky legs. Her stomach heaved; she was afraid she was going to vomit. A voice inside screamed, "No time! No time!"

Myra staggered into the blinding sun and gained on Ian. He was reaching out toward Luke, who was only a foot or two out of his grasp. She raised the heavy lamp high and, using all the strength she had, brought it down hard on the back of Ian's head.

He groaned, staggered, and fell, his face slamming into the concrete.

All of this took only seconds. Luke stopped to look back, his little head cocked in wonder.

Myra shooed him away. "Go! The office!"

He turned and started toward the glassed-in room, where already the redhead was emerging, eyebrows drawn together in alarm. She held a cordless phone in her hand. "What's going on here?"

Myra didn't answer. She scrambled over to where Ian lay, blood pooling from both his face and the back of his head, and retrieved the keys from his pocket on the very first try.

Bleary-eyed, head pounding, Myra rushed to the car, unlocked it, and slid inside, all the while listening to the woman yell, "Listen here, you! What's going on? Don't you go runnin' off!"

With shaking hands, Myra got the key into the ignition, made the engine roar when she pressed down on the gas too hard, threw the car into reverse, then drive, and finally peeled out of the parking lot, glancing into the rearview mirror.

Luke stood next to the red-haired woman, both of them looking bewildered. Ian lay on the concrete, inert and bleeding. She hiccupped out a short sob and brought her hand to her mouth.

Gunning the car, Myra grinned as it picked up speed. Before her, the open road stretched out to endless possibilities.

She gasped when she looked in the rearview mirror and saw the whirling red-and-blue lights.

How did they get here so fast?

The siren whooped, and Myra debated for only a moment whether to try to make a break for it, see if she could outpace the police car. There was no way. No way. She guided the car to the side of the road. Gravel crunched. She placed her head on the steering wheel and, at last, wept.

Chapter Thirty-Two

Cayce awakened. He hadn't realized when he had fallen asleep but figured the weariness and the stress must have contributed to such exhaustion that, finally, there was nothing left. Sleep must have come to him like passing out.

He had wanted, he remembered, to go right to the police, but Dave made him stay in the bed after they called Simmons. Cayce believed he'd never sleep again.

Yet here he lay in his dim bedroom, sunlight peeking through the slats of the vinyl blinds. Downstairs, he heard Dave moving about, voices on the radio. Or was it the television? He turned on his side and caught his breath.

Something was different.

The panic was gone. There was no reason for it to be, but he felt a delicious sense of calm. A voice inside—he wasn't sure it was his own—whispered, "Everything is all right."

He didn't know how he knew or why, but the peace at his center told him something had changed. He shot up in bed and cried out, joy infusing his voice, "Luke is okay! He's okay!"

He heard the thunder of Dave's footsteps running up the stairs. Dave paused in the doorway, smiling. "How did you know?"

Cayce shook his head, grateful for the intuition and the certainty. Cayce swallowed, nearly shaking with relief and euphoria. "I don't know. Or… I do. I just don't know why. It's over, isn't it?"

Dave nodded and let out a short laugh. He crossed the room and sat down next to him, pulling Cayce to him to hold him close, to kiss his neck, his hair, moving out to cover his face and eyes with kisses. Finally, there was one long, lingering kiss. He pulled away. "Yes. Yes. They've caught them. And Luke is okay. JT Simmons just called. It's all over the news." Dave pulled Cayce close again, surrounding him in a tight embrace.

Cayce squeezed back, reveling in the comfort of Dave's solid form. He buried his face in Dave's chest. Dave stroked his hair. "Do you want to hear how it all came about? It's not all pleasant."

Cayce moved away. "Not now. I know what's important." He closed his eyes for a moment, and an image, almost from nowhere, assailed him: a young blonde woman behind a video camera. He looked into Dave's eyes. "I need to talk to her."

"Who? JT?" Dave looked bewildered.

"No. The one who took Luke."

"I believe she's in hospital, under heavy guard."

Cayce stood suddenly, looking around the room for his jeans, struggled into them, and pulled a clean T-shirt over his head. "Come on. We need to go get my son…and then I need to talk to her." He tugged at Dave's hand, impatient. "I have to see her face."

He pulled Dave down the stairs and through the kitchen. He opened the kitchen door. Cayce stepped out and tripped over something lying on the welcome mat. He looked down and gasped and then laughed. "Oh my God!"

It was Oreo. He was getting up on his forepaws, brown eyes staring, affronted at what he felt was a kick from his master. Cayce dropped down to hug the dog. "Oreo! You came back! You came back!" The dog was licking Cayce's face, and Cayce found himself crying—yes, again—but this time for joy.

He stood, willing himself to let go of the prodigal mutt. He said to Oreo, "I'd love to bring you with us, buddy. But a bigger reunion is in store. I promise. C'mon." Cayce led Oreo into the kitchen. He filled his food and water bowls. "You just wait here. Wanna see Luke?" Cayce asked. Oreo wagged his tail and panted. It looked as though he was smiling.

*

Myra lay in a bed at City Hospital. The back of her head throbbed, and the thick wad of bandage there made the pain even more acute. Outside, two uniformed policemen stood guard. They were keeping the press away, but she could hear one or two of them manage to get close and beg for entry.

She had nothing to say to them. She closed her eyes and wished Ian had killed her.

And where *was* Ian?

No one would tell her anything.

A nurse came into the room. She had dark brown hair and the palest of blue eyes. She was pretty and young, like Myra, yet Myra didn't like the distaste she saw on the nurse's face.

"I'm not supposed to do this," the nurse announced, voice quavering. "But I think it's the right thing to do...and I'll take the consequences."

She disappeared, closing the door behind her.

The door reopened a moment later, and there he was. Luke's father. Myra was surprised at how depleted the young man was. She remembered him looking stronger in the restaurant, a bundle of energy, hurrying between his tables. Now his dark hair hung limp and dirty, and his eyes simply stared.

Myra bit her lip, trying to force some saliva into her mouth, trying to get her tongue to form around the words "I'm sorry," but she couldn't say anything.

Cayce watched her and, for several minutes, didn't approach the bed.

Myra wondered if he had a weapon concealed somewhere, if this was a setup, and they were going to allow Cayce to kill her.

It would be a relief.

Finally, Cayce moved toward her. Myra whispered, "I have a baby too" and started to cry.

Cayce sat down next to her on the bed, smoothed some hair away from Myra's forehead, and looked straight into her eyes.

"Thank you," he whispered. "Thank you."

Epilogue

The Ohio River was almost soundless as it flowed nearby, its water a greenish brown in the sun. The light glinted off the water in flashes. Cayce leaned back on his elbows on the old blanket he had dragged out from the linen closet and watched them, down near the muddy, pebble-strewn shore.

Luke. Dave. Oreo. Dimly, Cayce heard Dave explaining how the river began its course in Pittsburgh, where two rivers joined—the Monongahela and the Allegheny—to form the mighty Ohio. It flowed and flowed and did not end until it reached the Mississippi.

Luke wasn't paying much attention to the geography lesson. He was too busy throwing a stick he had found into the water's shallows and laughing with glee as Oreo went after it, secured it in his teeth, and bounded back to lay it at Luke's feet. Oreo would wait impatiently, tail a blur, for Luke to toss it again.

Cayce turned to grab a beer from the cooler, his hand brushing over the ginger ale that was for Dave. He brought the cold Iron City to his lips and thought about starting up the little Weber they had brought along, so the hamburgers and hot dogs would be ready before the sun set. But now, he thought, setting his beer back in the melting ice of the cooler, he'd just allow himself to lie back for a bit. The heat of the sun on his face felt good. So did the contentment at being here, like a family, with two of the males he cared most about in the world.

He thought sleep would come, but no. Red, like blood, swirled across his inner lids, and his breath caught. His heart picked up its pace.

In his mind's eye, he saw it: a red mitten in the snow.

Cayce sat up and mumbled, "No," forcing the image from his brain.

"Come on, Dad! Don't just sit there on your lazy ass!" Luke cried, beckoning.

And Cayce stood on shaky legs, forcing himself to smile. "What matters is right in front of you," he said softly to himself. He called out, "You watch your mouth, son!"

And he started toward them, his boy and the man he was coming to love.

About the Author

Real Men. True Love.

Rick R. Reed draws inspiration from the lives of gay men to craft stories that quicken the heartbeat, engage emotions, and keep the pages turning. Although he dabbles in horror, dark suspense, and comedy, his attention always returns to the power of love. He's the award-winning and bestselling author of more than fifty works of published fiction and is forever at work on yet another book. Lambda Literary has called him: "A writer that doesn't disappoint…" You can find him at www.rickrreedreality.blogspot.com. Rick lives in Palm Springs, CA, with his beloved husband, Bruce, and their fierce Chihuahua/Shiba Inu mix, Kodi.

Email: rickrreedbooks@gmail.com

Facebook: www.facebook.com/rickrreedbooks

Twitter: @rickrreed

Website: www.rickrreedreality.blogspot.com

Other NineStar books by this author

Unraveling

Sky Full of Mysteries

The Perils of Intimacy

IM

Chaser

Raining Men

Blue Umbrella Sky

Coming Soon from Rick R. Reed

Legally Wed

Same-sex marriage had just become legal in Washington State and Duncan Taylor didn't plan on wasting any time. He had been dating Tucker McBride for more than three years and, ever since the possibility of marriage had become more than just a pipe dream, it was all Duncan could think of. He thought of it as he gazed out the windows of his houseboat on Lake Union, on days both sunny and gray (since it was late autumn, there were a lot more of the latter); he thought of it as he stood before his classroom of fourth graders at Cascade Elementary School. He thought of it when he woke up in the morning and before he fell asleep at night.

For Duncan, marriage was the peak, the happy ending, the icing on the cake, the culmination of one's heart's desire, a commitment of a lifetime, the joining of two souls. For Duncan, it was landing among the stars.

And for Duncan, who would turn thirty-eight on his next birthday, it was also something he had never dared dream would be possible for him.

Now, too excited to sleep, he was thinking about it—hard—once again. It was just past midnight on December 6, 2012, and the local TV news had preempted its regular programming to take viewers live to Seattle City Hall, where couples were forming a serpentine line to be among the first in the state to be issued their marriage licenses—couples who had also for far too long believed this right would be one they would never be afforded. Many clung close together to ward off the chill, but Duncan knew their reasons for canoodling went far deeper than that.

The mood, in spite of the darkness pressing in all around, was festive. There was a group serenading the couples in line, singing "Going to the Chapel." Champagne corks popped in the background. Laughter.

Duncan couldn't keep the smile off his face as he watched all the male-male and female-female couples in the line, their moods of jubilation, of love, of triumph, traveling through to him even here on his houseboat only a couple of miles north of downtown. Duncan wiped tears from his eyes as he saw not only the couples but also all the supporters, city workers, and volunteers who had crowded together outside City Hall to wish the new couples well, to share in the happiness of the historic moment.

And then Duncan couldn't help it; he fell into all-out blubbering as the first couple to get their license emerged from City Hall. Eighty-five-year-old Pete-e Petersen and her partner and soon-to-be-wife, Jane Abbott Lighty, were all smiles when a reporter asked them how they felt.

"We waited a long time. We've been together thirty-five years, never thinking we'd get a legal marriage. Now I feel so joyous I can't hardly stand it," Pete-e said.

It was such a special moment and it was all Duncan could do not to pick up the phone and call Tucker and casually say something like, "Hey honey, you want to get married?"

But he knew he had to wait, even if patience was a virtue Duncan had in short supply. On Sunday, when the first marriages would take place, he planned on bringing Tucker to their favorite restaurant, an unpretentious little joint on Capitol Hill called Olympia Pizza. There, amid the darkened and—for them—romantic interior, with the smells of garlic, basil, and tomato sauce surrounding them, Duncan would propose, saying something clever like:

"I'm thinking about changing my Facebook relationship status to 'engaged.' Would you mind?"

In his mind, Tucker would chuckle and then rub at the tuft of blond hair that grew from his chin, regarding Duncan with his dark blue eyes. Duncan could see the flicker of the candle lighting up his man's features as he held the silence for a few moments, building the suspense. Then he would say something like, "I think I'll change mine too."

That would be one way it could play out—very twenty-first century.

Duncan would then imagine all his friends and family congratulating the newly minted fiancés with "Likes" and words of encouragement and shared happiness. Maybe he could get their waiter to take a picture of them, holding hands over a sausage and mushroom pie, right after the moment when they went from two guys dating to two guys anticipating...marriage.

Duncan found himself wiping yet another tear from his eye. Sunday was going to be perfect.

*

Because Tucker spent Saturday night on Duncan's houseboat, they rode over to the Hill together and parked on 15th, just a few steps away from the pizza restaurant where they had been regulars ever since their first date here three years before.

Even though it was only 5:30 or so in the afternoon, the day had grown dark, and there was a damp chill in the air.

Duncan locked his Ford Escort and hurried down the street, eager to get inside, eager to set in motion, well, the rest of his life. His heart beat a little faster, and his breath came a bit more quickly. Inside, he felt filled with brilliant light.

Tucker called from behind him, laughing. "What's gotten into you tonight?"

Duncan slowed to turn and cast a glance back at Tucker, who looked very fetching in a pair of worn Levi's 501s, a form-fitting black T-shirt, and a black leather jacket that contrasted wonderfully with his almost white-blond hair.

"What do you mean?" Duncan asked.

"Well, there's a real *spring* to your step is the only way I know how to put it. This is different from the usual swish in it." He laughed and caught up to Duncan, squeezing his bicep to show he was only kidding with that last remark.

"Just hungry," Duncan replied. But hunger was actually the last thing on his mind at the moment, as his hand worried the velvet box in the pocket of his cargo pants. He hadn't planned it, but on Saturday he was downtown and he couldn't resist wandering into Ben Bridge, just to see what they had in the way of wedding bands.

He saw it right away. He knew that the fact his eye fell upon it first thing was fate talking to him. Before he had even spoken to a salesperson or glanced at another item, he saw the simple white gold, diamond-studded band in the display case. "That's for Tucker," he whispered to himself. He hadn't planned to buy an engagement ring, and he certainly couldn't afford its exorbitant price tag, but the thought of the light that would come into Tucker's eyes when he opened the box was so thrilling and romantic, he couldn't resist.

The clerk, a young woman whose dark hair, olive skin, and green eyes mirrored Duncan's own, came up to him. "Can I show you something?"

Duncan recalled being at a loss for words. This little side trip into the jewelry store had really been intended as only a fantasy, a sort of appetizer for the better things to come.

"I just love that simple band with the diamonds right there." Duncan had pointed down to the ring.

"Oh, it's a beauty. Would you like to try it on?" She was already stooping down to take the ring out of the display case.

"Oh, it's not for me." And suddenly, Duncan had stopped. He was so filled with love for Tucker, he was unable to speak. He gnawed for a moment at his lower lip, looking away from the smiling and expectant face of the clerk, and drawing in a deep breath to compose himself. What did he have to lose, anyway? He smiled and looked down to see his hands trembling. "It's for my, my..." His voice had trailed off. What to call Tucker? He was his boyfriend, he supposed, yet he seemed like so much more. But partner was so presumptuous, because they didn't live together for one and had never registered as domestic partners in the state for another. "It's for the guy I hope will be my fiancé," he had finally blurted out, hoping the clerk didn't notice the tear he could feel standing in the corner of one eye.

He wondered what she would do. Would she regard him with disdain? Would her attitude change? Would she laugh?

But her face had immediately brightened, and her smile was as wide as his own. "That's fabulous!" she exclaimed. "I'm so happy for you." She had pushed the ring across the counter. "He's a lucky guy. And I'm not just saying that because he'd be getting this gorgeous ring, but mostly because he'd be getting you." She winked. "You're a catch."

Duncan had picked up the ring with one hand and reached for his wallet with the other.

Now, in the restaurant, he was just about to burst with what he wanted to ask Tucker. With anticipation. With excitement. With the promise of a seismic shift in his and his boyfriend's lives.

Wait. Wait, he told himself, over and over, as they followed the hostess to a table near the back. Wait, he told himself again as they perused the menu, both ordering a Stella Artois.

When the pizza arrived, so would Duncan's proposal.

Duncan forced himself to make small talk as they sipped beer. He let his gaze wander over to the table next to them, where an older couple sat, indicating with his eyes that Tucker should look as well. Tucker looked at the man and woman, who both appeared to be in their seventies, with gray hair and clothes that kind of matched, baggy jeans, cardigan sweaters. She wore a brightly colored scarf around her neck and his glasses were square, blocky and, whether he knew it or not, kind of cool in a retro sort of way.

"How long do you think they've been together?" Duncan asked, leaning forward and placing a hand atop Tucker's.

Tucker leaned back, putting his own hands in his lap, and screwing up his gaze in what Duncan would surmise was deep thought. "Gee. It's hard to say. Probably a long time. I'd guess Gramps and Granny there are in their seventies and I bet they're each other's first, so maybe fifty years or more."

"That's what I was thinking too. Notice how quiet they are together?" Duncan admired the way they stared into each other's eyes and how the woman held her fork aloft with a piece of fried calamari on it for her husband to try.

Tucker snorted. "They're probably all talked out. After half a century, they probably can't think of a single new thing to say to the other." He laughed. "He's probably thinking he can't wait to get home so he can plop down in front of the TV and crack open a beer, and she probably just wants to bury her nose in a Harlequin romance, so she can get a glimpse of what she doesn't have anymore."

Duncan felt the statement cut through him and tried to convince himself that Tucker was merely going for the obvious interpretation, the one most people would make. "Oh, don't be such a cynic!" he cried. "I think they've just been together so long they're really contented around each other. They probably don't feel the need to fill the silence up with idle chatter." *As you're doing right now,* Duncan chided himself.

"Maybe." Tucker scanned the restaurant. "I hope that pizza gets here soon. I'm starving."

"Me too." Duncan rubbed the dark stubble on his chin. "I'm sure it'll be worth waiting for." Making sure

Tucker wasn't looking, he moved the boxed ring from his pocket next to him on the booth bench, so it would be ready when the moment arrived.

The waiter, and the moment of truth, showed up just then. The waiter was a lanky kid with a neck tattoo and a shock of auburn hair that fell over one eye. "Here you go, guys. Careful, that pan is hot."

"And so are you," Tucker quipped.

The waiter grinned, his gaze cutting to Duncan, who did not grin back. Duncan swallowed, suddenly feeling a distinct lack of spit in his mouth. His heart beat just a little harder.

The waiter wandered away.

"God, that smells terrific."

The aroma of the pizza wafted up, embedded in the steam rising off the hot, cheesy pie. Even though the smell of tomatoes, garlic, Italian sausage, and basil were the sweetest perfumes to him, Duncan didn't feel hungry.

His proposal was now front and center in his mind, and he swore he could not entertain the thought of taking a bite until he got his special moment underway. Later, the dinner could turn into a real celebration. Hell, the whole night could.

Tucker was about to reach for the spatula to lift a slice onto his plate when Duncan grabbed his wrist. "Wait. Before we get started, I have something I want to ask."

Duncan reached down, feeling for the box at his side. His nervous reach hit the box and knocked it to the floor. "Shit," Duncan whispered. When he quickly ducked to grab for the box among the shadows and grit beneath the table, he whacked his forehead on the edge. He saw stars.

"What the fuck?" Tucker was laughing.

Duncan groped around in the dark, feeling for the box. *This isn't the way things are supposed to go at all. Where is that damn thing, anyway?* Finally, his hand lit on the velvet box. In the fall, it had opened. He reached inside and found, to his horror, that the ring itself had rolled away. He groped around on the floor some more, until he felt the metal of the ring under his fingertips. He breathed a sigh of relief and grasped both box and ring, righting himself and being careful not to hit the back of his head as he reemerged from beneath the table.

What could he do but laugh? So he did, putting the ring and the box on the table in front of him. "Hey, it'll be a good story to tell our grandchildren, right?" Duncan continued to laugh, rubbing at the knot already forming on his forehead. He thrust the ring toward Tucker. "This is for you." He managed to make himself stop laughing, even though there was something giddy going on inside himself that he didn't quite understand.

Was it joy or the beginning of a heart attack?

Tucker picked up the ring, examining it. He looked with a questioning smile across the table at Duncan.

"It's legal now," Duncan gasped, the carefully chosen words he had imagined and planned on saying deserting him.

"What? Pot?"

"Don't be stupid." Duncan stared across the table, feeling as he once had when he was a teenager on Thanksgiving weekend driving on a slippery highway. It had rained earlier and the temperature had dropped. The roads were slick, but not frozen—until he tried to make it across the overpass. The car did a figure eight and all he could do was wait for the impact, whether it was with a guardrail or another car. He knew the only thing that would stop the desperately fishtailing vehicle was a collision. He could still feel the impact all these years later.

He felt that way now, helpless to do anything but push onward.

His mouth was utterly dry. He took a gulp of beer and licked lips that felt chapped. "Marriage. We can get married now."

Tucker's laugh was high-pitched and nervous.

"You and me?"

Duncan laughed again, but there was no mirth in it. Reality couldn't have been more different from his fantasy. "That. Was. The. Hope." He managed to get out between breaths that verged on panting. He looked desperately into Tucker's blue and now, he could see, uncommitted eyes. He tried to swallow again, but was unsuccessful and finally said, "That's an engagement ring."

The words he had planned on saying, clichés all, now came back to him, and even though he knew he was in a car headed for a collision, he forced himself to say them, "Tucker McBride, would you make me the happiest man in the world and agree to be my husband?"

Just then, the one-eyed waiter waltzed up to them. "Get you guys a couple more brewskis?"

"Get out," Duncan hissed, out of character, but fearing he would scream.

The waiter hurried away.

Tucker didn't meet his gaze. Instead, he stared down at the ring, turning it around and around with his fingertips, as if endlessly fascinated by the shiny object.

Finally, Duncan asked, hope barely there, his voice just above a whisper, "Would you marry me, honey?"

And, at last, Tucker looked up at him, tears standing in his eyes. He put the ring back on the table and then shoved it toward Duncan.

"No," he said.

Duncan stared hard at this man across the table, this man with whom he had spent the last three years, through good times and bad, through hot summer nights and hot winter ones, too, through dinners, movies, bar crawls, and quiet evenings at home, and suddenly felt as though Tucker was a stranger. Duncan blinked back tears. He put a hand to his stomach, which was churning with what felt like acid. Not a single coherent thought formed in his head, so he certainly couldn't think of what to say in response to Tucker's eloquent refusal.

He picked up the ring and stared at it and almost wondered how it had made its way into his hand.

He slid the ring onto the third finger of his right hand and grinned at Tucker. "Guess I bought myself some bling this weekend, then." He held his hand out in front of him, as though to admire the ring, but all he was really feeling was the fear that the smell of the pizza and beer were going to make him throw up.

The two men sat for a while in silence.

Finally, Duncan recovered sufficiently enough to ask, "No?"

Tucker gave him a sad smile, one that Duncan was horrified to see was fashioned mostly from pity and concern. Tucker shook his head and removed his gaze from Duncan's to scan the restaurant. Duncan watched as he made what must have been eye contact with the waiter, and he pointed to their beers and held up two fingers.

"I'm sorry, babe. I thought what we had was kind of an easy thing, you know? No strings? That's why I liked having my place and you having yours." He went silent as their waiter brought two more beers, setting them down before them silently, and then hurrying away. Duncan stared at the sweating bottle before him as though it were a pile of something a dog left behind, a St. Bernard, maybe.

He didn't touch it.

"You're talking in the past tense."

"Huh?"

"You're talking in the past tense—what we had, what you *liked*."

Tucker smiled sheepishly. "I guess I am, huh?" He scratched at his neck. "I didn't realize it, but maybe my mind is getting ahead of me."

Duncan toyed with a paper napkin on the table. He didn't look at Tucker when he asked, "So, you're not only saying no to my proposal, you're breaking up with me as well. Right?" He stared down at the diamond ring on his own finger. How could he have been so stupid?

"I didn't intend to, honey."

"Oh stop with the terms of endearment already." Duncan felt like he was about to cry, and that was the last thing he wanted Tucker, or anyone else in the restaurant, to see.

"Okay, I didn't intend to." He reached across the table to grab one of Duncan's hands, and Duncan snatched his hand away. Tucker grabbed it again and held it.

"I don't know if I can stand your kindness," Duncan whispered. He was pretty sure Tucker hadn't even heard him.

Tucker licked his lips and went on. "I had no intention of breaking up, but now that I see how far apart we are in terms of what we want, maybe we should." He squeezed Duncan's hand.

"That's it? You don't even want to try? I thought you loved me."

"I do. I do. I love being with you. I love having sex with you." Tucker gnawed on his lower lip for a moment and then said the line that had stung lovers' hearts worldwide since the beginning of time: "But I don't think I'm *in* love with you. That spark just isn't there."

Duncan looked up to see Tucker staring sadly, hungrily at him, as though he was looking for something. What? Forgiveness? Absolution? For him to say Tucker was excused?

"You don't need to go on," Duncan said. It was odd. Moments ago, he felt near tears, edging on hysteria, and now he felt nothing. A curious numbness, almost like shock, had crept in, leaving him feeling dead inside.

"But I want you to understand how much you meant to me, what good times I had with you—"

Duncan cut him off with a bitter laugh. "There you go again with the past tense."

"Sorry."

"Why don't you just go?"

Tucker stared at him as though Duncan had reached across the table and slapped him. Finally he said, "Without eating?"

Duncan stood. "Enjoy it." He reached into his back pocket and pulled out his wallet, threw a couple of twenties on the table.

"No, Duncan, don't. Sit down."

But Duncan was already moving rapidly away from the table and out of the restaurant.

Outside, rain had begun to fall. Not the typical Seattle winter rain, which was more like a mist, a fine drizzle that left one feeling damp instead of drenched. This one was a downpour, splattering hard off the sidewalk and cars, blinding. Lightning lit up the sky and thunder rumbled, also rare for Seattle.

But did Duncan hurry through the sheets of water pouring down from an angry sky?

No.

He wandered, almost leisurely, back to his car, letting the rain soak through his clothes, run in icy rivulets off his head, down his neck, to trickle down his spine, chilling him to his very core.

He didn't care.

The rain matched his mood.

Once he got to his car, he sat with his head on the steering wheel, shivering. He thought about how City Hall today was an assembly line of weddings. How, all over the city, gay couples were celebrating being, for the first time in his state's history, legally wed. He pictured the scores of couples right now at the Paramount Theatre downtown, where the city was throwing "A Wedding Reception for All." He thought of the smiling faces, the linked hands, the hugging, the kissing, the shared dreams and hopes for the future, the joy of the witnesses, the popping of champagne corks, and the slicing of wedding cakes topped with two brides or two grooms.

He had never felt more alone.

Drawing a big breath, he wiped the tears and rain away from his face, turned the key in the ignition, threw on the windshield wipers, and pulled out of his parking space to start home.

He turned on the radio and tuned to the "adult contemporary" station he preferred to listen to while driving.

Karen Carpenter's plaintive voice emerged from the radio speakers. "We've only just begun," she sang.

"Oh shut up, Karen. Have a hamburger." Duncan snapped the radio off.

Also Available from NineStar Press

Connect with NineStar Press

www.ninestarpress.com

www.facebook.com/ninestarpress

www.facebook.com/groups/NineStarNiche

www.twitter.com/ninestarpress

www.tumblr.com/blog/ninestarpress